THE GUARDIANS OF THE ASPIS

SARAH L. ROSE

Cover, interior, map art and design by Sarah L. Rose. www.sarahlrosebooks.com

If you think you find similarities to any people or places, dead or alive, you're seeing things. This is all made up in my head.

Edited by Sam Helmer at Wise Cat Editing. Visit https://wisecatediting.com.

Edited by Kelsey Holts at Little Red Herring Proofreads. Visit https://www. littleredherringproofreads.ca

ISBN: 978-1-7388454-0-8

ASIN: B0C4XJBGBV

This one is for past me. Dreams do come true, you hard working son of a bitch. Future me: you better not disappoint.

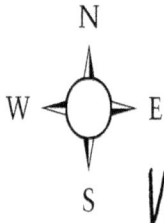

Nuo's
Map of
ARDE

★ Towns
● Cave
🌿 Crystal Cave
▲ Treasure
◇ Nuo's Faves
✕ Weapons

Aethar
Wastelands

ONE

E yes down. Don't react. Blend in.

My methods of staying alive had worked for twenty-five years. It ended one blistering cold morning when the Keepers of the Law knocked on the wooden door of my run-down shack. Their shouts had been my only warning.

"Olivia Dacla!"

Someone had sold me out, and the betrayal would lead me to my eventual death. I abandoned everything and ran.

I'd been fleeing the Keepers for what felt like hours, swallowing my pain. But to what end? I knew what I would find when my feet stopped: death or prison. Although, I may have lost that second option.

My feet slid on the soft needles of the forest floor. My lungs were as much on fire as my throat. I was too thin and too weak to make it.

The snow didn't reach the ground thanks to the tall cedars, making it harder to follow my tracks. But the men *were* following me.

"Shit." I ran under a low-hanging branch. It caught my wool hat and tore it from my head. My dark blonde hair tangled around me, catching in my mouth, and I struggled to spit it out.

That's when I lost sight of the path. My foot caught on a root, and my leg twisted, sending me face-first to the cedar-covered ground.

My warm breath swirled around me as the colours of the forest grew bright. I brought a hand to my lips. Blood stained the tips of my finger.

I listened for the number of Keepers still tracking me or how close they might be. Holding my breath, I concentrated on the sounds of the forest, trying to silence the racket in my chest.

A minute passed before I picked up a distant hissing—a rushing river. I made another reckless plan. I would cross the river, hopefully losing the trackers in the process.

"What were you thinking?" I scolded myself. I pressed my frozen fingers to my temples.

I hadn't been thinking. God, I had nowhere to go. The only comfort I would find after fleeing the Keepers was that my last breath would be where I chose it. I'd finally meet the god of death. The tall, dark figure my mother told tales of.

As I went to stand, a fierce pain leapt up my leg. I sat back, landing hard against a tree, my good foot sliding on the needles and snow.

"No, no, no." The back of my head thudded against the hard bark of the tree. My right ankle was probably broken.

If I could go back to just a few weeks ago, tucked in the warm sheets in Stephen's cottage, candles lit and the fire crackling ...

He was the most handsome man in our village, with beautiful golden hair. Every young woman wanted the Keepers to select them to be his bride. I had been his secret—everything we did had to be a secret.

But at this moment, with my muscles tensing from the pain, I could not remember the warmth of his hands or how his mouth travelled my body.

Lips I would never feel again.

Distant shouts rang through the cedar trees, but I couldn't make out how far the group was. I needed to move. The chilly air cooled the sweat sticking to me, my threadbare pants unable to keep out the cold. My boots were the only thing I owned in good condition.

I tried my ankle. "Ow."

I wrapped a hand around my calf where the pain intensified. There was no use sitting there, reminiscing. I had to force myself to move forward. Surviving would depend on how far I could get.

I limped toward the river, crying out at every step. Only the adrenaline pushed me on.

I was becoming numb. It wasn't the cold or the endless running—it was the betrayal seeping through my veins. All emotions, all sense of self-preservation ... gone. Just the feeling of something missing that was once there.

I would've laughed if it didn't hurt to do so. I'd been running from one death to another as if I was a hero. I was no hero. Had the Keepers known of the extent of my transgressions, they would have come for me long ago. Stephen wasn't my only secret.

The Keepers of Law were a farce. They fought to convince the public we were all unified. Like we were one of them. But we were controlled and used. Their laws were antiquated, suffocating and binding, with no room for error.

Thank the skies above me none of them could guess what went through my head.

A faint echo floated toward me. "Tracks," a man's voice was yelling. There was a series of shouts and a heartbeat later, silence.

I knew too well their hunting calls. I would hear them when I was alone in my suffocatingly small shack.

"Dammit," I cried, reaching for a tree to brace myself. The pain intensified, and the adrenaline was no longer strong enough to battle it.

I had travelled this far from my small village only once—south to the edge of my world. This time I went north. I wasn't sure what I would find when I reached the river. I only hoped I could cross it and hide my trail.

I came to a soul-crushing stop—I had found the river. Only I couldn't cross it. I stood on a ledge beside a dark and menacing waterfall about halfway up the side of a hill.

I ran my hands through my hair, pulling the strands as I turned in circles. I was running out of options.

I hobbled to the edge and leaned over. I may be able to descend slowly and cross the river below. Above me was a steep incline with icy rocks. I would never make it to the top.

Bottom it was.

My boots proved their worth as I navigated the slippery decline. The mist above the water blended with my breath as it hit the winter air around me. But as I neared the bottom, hope failed me. The rapids, raging over hidden rocks beneath, were not something I had the skill to navigate. Especially with my ankle.

"No." I slumped down near the base of a frozen tree.

I sat staring into the rushing waters without seeing anything at all.

Sobs formed in my chest as my hope faded, like a candle that had run out of wick. This was it—my end would be here along this river. I had no more strength, a hurt ankle, no food, and I was growing colder by the second.

"Stop it, Liv. You're not going to cry for your death."

My mother told my sister and I not to give up hope. She was convinced the world had been good once and could be again. Stupidly, I had believed her. My sister, with her cold and hopeless heart, did not. Rebeka was nothing like me and nothing like the woman my mother tried to teach her to be.

My sister had been there today when I ran from the Keepers. She saw them approach my shack. Her eyes had swum with tears and my heart had filled with more pain than I had thought possible. I would never see her again. I could still hear her screams as they aimed their weapons at me when I escaped around trees and ran up the animal paths behind my home.

I wrapped my arms around myself and leaned back against the tree while I waited for night to fall and for someone to find me. I prayed it was Death and not the men hunting me.

The grey skies turned everything to blue, then finally to black. I never feared the night, but I sensed this one would be the worst I had lived. The forest became layered shadows beside that river and all I heard was the rushing waters as I tried to make out one tree from the next.

I had never hurt anyone or done anything truly bad. I was here, slowly freezing, because I had just wanted a taste of life.

In this small world, it wasn't permitted for Stephen and me to spend time together. I was not marriageable. I had no profitable skills, and I was difficult. So I lived alone in a small shack that no one else wanted, that no one visited, left to fend for myself.

Stephen had not yet had a wife arranged, though he would in time. He had a reputable business repairing items like shoes or farming tools. Often, as poor as the villagers were, they would pay in goods—illegal alcohol, books or whatever valuable items they hid under floorboards. The Law Keepers never looked twice at Stephen—and sometimes even they paid him with goods they shouldn't have in their possession.

We all know the people who make up the Keepers—those who blindly follow the rules and love their masters. The citizens joined in, thinking this life was a choice of their own free will.

I hated the villagers as much as the Keepers.

It was only a week ago I was walking in the village. The mud had collected on my boots and my ratted brown pants. My steps were heavy as I stole glances at the townspeople working on the work-down street.

Blending in was vital.

I pretended I didn't see the Keepers beating an elderly woman. She had stopped her assigned chores to watch them walk by. I had nearly run into one of the Keepers myself, forgetting to keep my eyes lowered. The man then warned me they were waiting for me to make a mistake.

I'd been visiting my sister Rebeka, which went about as well as it usually did. I don't know why I felt hopeful before the visit. Sharing the same blood couldn't force companionship. Though her features were warm—rich brown hair and hazel eyes—my sister was as cold and colourless on the inside as my skin and eyes were out.

My skin was unusually pale and unmarked—the people in my village aged fast. You had to work hard to survive, which took a toll on your body and mind. Considering how life hadn't been easy, I didn't have scars to show it. My scars were hidden under the skin. Buried deep and held there.

Rebeka lived in the same house our mother raised us in. My mother, strong and as bright as the sun, took all the light from my world when she died. I was thirteen. Rebeka was left to raise me, and she did so until she married. I was eighteen then. She was only twenty. Those years all seemed grey next to the colourful childhood I had. She was perfectly happy with her place in the world. Rebeka followed the rules, said the right words, and played the right part. She's expecting her second child now.

She held onto her round belly when the Keepers were waiting outside my shack today. It wasn't like I could hide from them. With gaps between the rotting wood planks, you could see into my single-room hut. Perhaps I should feel lucky I'd made it to twenty-five. Not everyone in my small village did.

CHAPTER

TWO

G lorifying dying seems morbid, but it became a soothing balm while I held myself on that forest floor. There was a sliver of starry sky visible between the trees as I watched my breath send spirals into the air. Would the afterlife take me to the stars? I was taught it was a final end when our body goes to the ground. I can't imagine we are all so wicked to deserve that.

My mother always said the world was a better place thousands of years ago. Gradually, greed, mistrust and lust for power overcame humanity. Our technological society spiralled into chaos and war. The land was so severely damaged and the population so heavily diminished that the first Keepers took it upon themselves to steer the survivors away from our past mistakes. They instituted strict control over all behaviour in hopes that it would prevent further corruption.

I couldn't believe it was always this way. I dreamed of a place where I could roam free, I could read books, could choose a man I wanted for myself, and I could live in any way I wished.

But I would never see such a place.

On this small continent remained what was left of whatever

truth once existed. We stayed close and worked together for a life that was barely worth living.

The forest surrounded my village, and the village past that. And the one past that. I had never met anyone who had been outside the forest, the exception being myself when I had found the edge of the world.

Our home, the Endless Forest—a silly name because it does indeed end— was surrounded by violent seas. The coast was forbidden to visit. Beyond that, if any lands are still above water, only wastelands would be found.

"*Never lose your imagination.*" I could hear my mother say, even now. "*Magic is real, Liv, my love. Don't forget the stories I've told you.*" Her thick brown hair was a halo around her loving smile.

She expected me to believe her stories of old kings and forgotten gods—that our legends were only lost over time, told secretly by very few from one generation to the next. My mother's heart was wild, and it was that heart she passed on to me.

"*I want to live in one of those stories,*" I had said, hating my grey world.

But I was always eager to learn more. I could close my eyes, and before falling asleep, I'd escape to a better place. There, I didn't have to hide that my mind and heart did not belong with my people. I tried to do that now, waiting by the river.

My arms were frozen around myself. I searched the collection of stars I claimed as my own as I shook from the cold—five bright stars travelled over the horizon just before the sun rose. No other time of night would you see them.

I first saw them after my mother's death, when I fled to the coast to escape the pain. The trip was strictly against the rules. I stayed for three days, looking past the high cliffs to see miles of ferocious waves until the sea met the sky. Eventually, the hunger got to me, and I returned to Rebeka, saying goodbye to my secret constellation.

It was rare to see the stars and the sun even more so. My world had no colour. Tonight was no different. My stars were hidden from me in the dark.

My limbs had gone numb. My stomach was eating away at me. My lips were cracked. Were they bleeding again? I didn't know. I couldn't feel them.

Why had the hunting team not found me? Maybe they assumed I had fallen into the river.

I had given up, yet Death still didn't come. He had forgotten me just as everyone else had.

Betrayed—that word held more meaning than any other. It defined me now.

In and out, my mind faded. My breathing turned laboured as my body convulsed, trying to fight to live when my mind had given up.

The dark river ran, washing away any semblance of sanity I had with it. My eyelashes eventually froze my eyes shut ...

I could hardly move—I struggled to get air into my lungs. My arms were frozen around my middle.

I was dying, slowly, painfully. The frigid night grew quiet as the living went to sleep, and in the cold silence of night, Death still did not come.

The quiet transformed, becoming its own presence.

I forced my eyes open, cracking the ice that had formed on my lashes.

The silence was absolute—but the night should be full of noise.

The sound of the rushing rapids had disappeared. The wind died in the trees, absent. All was eerily and wholly silent. My shallow breathing and blood pumping through my ears sounded as if I was trapped in a small box.

Had I passed, finally, into another place?

Something was wrong. I hadn't left my spot against the tree, but the river before me was not the same. The water had *stopped moving*. The trees were fixed in place. Not a branch moved or danced in the night air.

My mind stumbled over what I saw.

The water on the falls was static, and the rapids were unmoving over the rocks. Time had ceased, as if some great power had paused the world. Droplets of water hung, suspended in mid-air above rock and waves.

Out of the corner of my eye, I caught movement.

I struggled to see what drew my attention. Across the river, behind the trees, a light flickered, casting shadows in and around the roots. It disappeared behind tree trunks, reappearing again as it crept along the river's edge.

Then, the light stopped across the river from me. It raised from the ground as if taking in its surroundings before gliding again toward me—overtop the unmoving waters.

It's not possible.

Not a lamp of some kind—the light wasn't being held. The light was moving *on its own*.

If I could move, I would have run. Fear became hot and cold, rushing in and out of me like two gales of wind colliding.

I had tried to convince myself that I would rather die than be imprisoned by the Keepers. But I lied—I was still afraid of dying.

My frozen body failed me as the light crawled across the still waters. The air changed. Something like a bell, or high-pitched static had exploded in my ears, leaving an intrusive ringing.

The light intensified as it neared me, forcing me to shut my eyes against it.

Then everything changed.

My heart raced. Fear dissolved into elation, soaring high with the hope that I would be taken from this slow, miserable way to die. I could sense something *other* coming for me, something incorporeal.

Sobs tried to escape my chest. He was finally here, the god of Death, to reunite me with those I had lost.

Light enveloped me, the deadly cold changed, and a warmth crept along the icy floor. Brighter and brighter, the light grew.

I sighed in relief. *I'm ready.*

A voice enveloped me, stripping me of the light's warmth and plunging me back into my body's frozen state.

"Your body is failing. I will take you from this place." It was several voices and yet one, made of static and bells.

Yes. I screamed, but it was only in my head. *Please, I can't go back.*

"This is not the end. This is not death." The voice grew louder.

Wait. My adrenaline kicked back in. *Where are you taking me? I don't want to feel this anymore.*

"This pain will fade. You are not meant for this place." The layered voice seemed like it was trying to comfort me.

The light grew brighter, and the warmth returned with a hunger, thawing my frozen skin. My eyes cracked open. The trees were barely visible from the white-hot light taking over.

The warmth slithered through my skin and crawled into my blood with pointed claws.

Too warm.

Way, way too warm!

It was scorching me, like an iron in burning embers, setting fire to my veins.

I was defenceless to it. I tried to move and thrash about but couldn't. I couldn't tell where my body was—here and yet not. I was fire floating, stretched from all sides by invisible strings, yet collapsing into nothing. I was on the ground yet sailing into the sky, stars glowing brightly all around me.

There was a whooshing so loud my eardrums threatened to burst.

The light overtook everything, and everything became nothingness.

I tried to scream, but I had no voice. I was nothing.

Was this death? If it was, I wanted to return to the dying world and the pain. Nothing was as bad as this.

As soon as the thought passed through my mind, it all stopped.

The bubble popped, and nothingness became something.

"Wake the Aspis," the many voices said.

And everything went black.

THREE

D*rip, drip, drip.*

I tried to block out my situation.

Was I in the afterlife? I always wondered if the beyond was pits of fire and unending pain. But this place, this could be much worse. It was pitch black, damp, and so very, very quiet. I might have gone insane.

Drip, Drip.

Although it sounded like water, something told me I was no longer by the falls. The air around me was damp. The smell of water on rock and soil didn't fit my frozen forest.

Something smelled like death—like the critters I would come across in the forest days after they met their end.

I sniffed again. Was it me? I wouldn't be surprised if some parts of me were frostbitten and decaying.

The last thing I remember was the bright light vanishing, plunging everything into blackness, and an echo of the voice inside me—*Wake the Aspis.*

What did that mean? I'd never heard the word.

If this was death, then the powers of the universe had a very evil imagination.

Was that water dripping in the distance?

Feeling was coming back to my body in tidal waves—a horrible ache that began as a tingling and became a roar. Even my scalp hurt.

I couldn't move.

I tried speaking, but not a sound came out. My throat was dry, like a desert with no wind, just miles of scarred earth.

I couldn't be making up that goddamned dripping sound! I wanted to scream. The drip, drip, drip began to sound like marching footsteps ...

Voices echoed.

Another glow appeared before my closed eyes.

No. Not again.

The glow intensified and landed on me. But the temperature didn't change, and the glow was not blinding. I was grounded and made of painful flesh and blood.

"Dear gods," a voice gasped—male.

"Damn, Brekt. You were right," a woman said, sounding confused.

More footsteps, coming closer. Terror seeped into my bones. My mind begged for me to get up and run, but I could hardly lift my eyelids. Were these the men who had come to my shack? A woman hadn't been part of their group.

The bright light shone directly in my eyes. I shut them, bursts of light sparkling behind my eyelids.

"Nuo, bring your light over here too. We found ... something."

More footsteps came closer before there was an inhale of alarm. Something scared them.

It was me.

"Fuck me, what is that? Is that pile of bones what I smell?"

"She's moving," a deep voice said, "And looks like her fingers are ... frostbitten?" Confusion laced his words.

"Well, that doesn't make sense. She's in a damp cave."

"Is this what you were looking for, Brekt? Why you dragged us this far into the cave?" asked the woman.

A cave, it made sense now ... while also making no sense at all. I wanted to ask them how I got here, but I was too weak to make a sound.

And how could I understand what they were saying? The words they were using were not my native language. Somehow when they spoke, I recognized every word and its meaning.

Had I hit my head? Maybe this was a bad dream.

"We need to move her. She looks close to death," the woman said. "Think she's an Aethar?"

That word held no meaning, just like *Aspis*. Were these people connected to the strange light? Did they bring me to this cave? No, they wouldn't be so confused.

Warm fingers touched my cheek as they brushed the hair out of my face. There was another inhale. This time quieter—more surprise than shock. I thought the person had recognized me but quickly discarded that thought. Not many knew my face.

"No," the deep voice said, "She's not an Aethar."

I didn't recognize his voice. He was not a Keeper. The men who had come to take me away did not speak this strange language.

It occurred to me—that light used the same language as these people. I hadn't questioned it at the time, only now realizing it was all wrong.

"I can't understand how she's alive. Should we not put her out of her misery?" Another voice said quietly as if I wouldn't be able to hear him. If he was taking pity on me, it must be much worse than I thought. I must look like death.

"We take her." My panic intensified at what the deep voice said. "Nuo, you and Bas take the crystals we found and run ahead to the cart. Get it ready."

Hands reached for me, grabbing me under my arms and collected me behind my knees.

"She's freezing. I don't think there's any fat or muscle left on her," the deep voice whispered beside me. The warmth from his hands burned. He should not be touching me like this. He should know the rules.

I braved opening my eyes—blackness in the shape of a man looked back. His form was cut by the light behind him.

My shallow gasp echoed in the dark—his eyes shone when the light reflected off them, like the eyes of the animals in the forest at night. I feared those iridescent eyes that appeared near my shack back home. But how could a man's eyes shine like a wolf's?

Wake up, Liv, you're dreaming again. People's eyes don't do that.

"Hold on a little longer," he said to me. "We need you out of this place to treat you."

With everything I had, I opened my mouth to try and speak. Why was I in a cave? Why could I understand a language I'd never learned?

In the end, I tried to convey, *"Let me die here,"* but nothing came. The time it would take for me to heal from this state—it was agony to even consider.

In the way he hesitated, I knew he understood, though he didn't listen.

I was lifted up, the pain forcing a cry from me. Every movement hurt as he began walking. How did they think they could save me? I was a skeleton in his arms. Food was scarce at home, and I knew I had been getting too thin over the last several months.

"You'll be okay soon. Just a little longer," his words were meant to calm me, but they were a knife in my chest. I tried again to mouth the words to him, and he silenced me with a soft, "Don't bother trying to talk."

"She should be dead. Something cruel has kept this one alive," the woman pondered, "You're going to have to explain some things when we get out of here, Brekt."

There was no reply.

I slipped in and out of awareness.

After a time, light gathered ahead of us at the mouth of the cave.

Then, the air changed. It didn't smell like it belonged to a suffocating forest or a salty ocean. Wild, clean air that was warm and alive crawled into my lungs.

I wasn't anywhere close to my old cedar forest. I knew I was far from home.

Blackness started creeping in and around the edges of my vision, and my body ultimately gave out.

I woke to a terrible screaming—painful cries that rattled my soul. My lungs burned while my ears were assaulted like hammers to my head.

"Kaz, keep her quiet." A body held me down. A piece of cloth was shoved into my mouth, and the screaming stopped.

Was the noise me?

My eyes flew open. The blinding light from the sun hit me. I could make out a figure above me with a hand over my mouth. Her skin was pitch black, yet some parts were stark white. My mind demanded I escape her touch, but my body denied me in my weakened state.

What was this woman? She held me in place as her eyes met mine.

"I gave you something to keep you alive until we get back to town. It's probably making your ailments feel that much more obvious. If you've lived this long, then you can manage another few hours ... or so."

Her tone was sure, no bullshit. I had not met many women like that in my life, save for my mother.

She wasn't anyone I had crossed paths with before. Her hair was knotted into long dark strands and she had metal bits in her ears and face. The little I could see of her body while she held me down was dressed in dark leather clothing.

Keep it together. Think. Yet all the thinking in the world could not make any sense of this situation.

I could tell we were in a cart, moving over an uneven road. A strange animal smell hung in the air.

How did I get here?

The sky was nothing like I'd ever seen— it was clear and blue, and it reminded me of Stephen's eyes. I shut the thought down.

I studied the woman atop me, hoping to determine where she came from. Her arms were entirely black, but the hand over my mouth was paler than my own skin, with scale-like markings along the tops. Black lines moved from her collarbone up her neck to her jawline like she'd painted herself. Her face was as black as her arms, but a streak across her eyes from temple to temple was white. Her eyes were so dark they were black themselves. More dark lines travelled up her chin and over her lips.

"Stop looking at me like that. They're just tattoos."

Tattoo? I had never seen such a thing, yet this woman had pitch-black lines in very deliberate and intimidating patterns. The metal I saw earlier were piercings in her ears and nose.

What did these people want from me? I could move my head just enough to see the wood panelling of a cart and leather sacks spread around me. Beside my head was a glass jar, but I couldn't turn to see what was in it.

Something hard pushed against my legs. This woman wore weapons around her middle. I trembled under the weight of her body.

If I wasn't terrified before, I was now. Weapons were forbidden, especially for women. Some men in the Keepers wore weapons if they worked their way up to higher ranks, but the women were never allowed to be in those ranks. These people must be outlaws. How far had I run from home? I was certain the other towns had the same rules as we did.

My breathing came in quick and small gasps. The physical state I was in, the woman pinning me down, the sun shining (which I would have basked in had I been able to stand on my own two feet) ... and the realization I had lost all control over the outcome of my life— I was overcome.

"Pick up the pace, Bas," the woman said, sensing my state. She met my stare. What flashed across her face made me flush hot.

Pity. I didn't want her pity.

"My name is Kazhi." It was a name I had never heard in my life, which perfectly matched the look of a woman I had never seen. "If it helps to know, I am trying to heal you, not hurt you. The liquid before was the medicine," She paused, considering. "We can't let anything out here hear you. If I take out the cloth to give you more medicine, will you scream?"

I didn't have an answer for her. I didn't trust anything right now, not the situation or how I would react, so I managed a shrug.

"Then I will wait to give you more of the drink, sorry."

I wasn't sorry. Part of me didn't want to be healed. Blue skies or not, I wasn't ready to face living again, not after everything that happened. Especially not if I was somewhere I didn't know. I would never be able to stay hidden here.

CHAPTER
FOUR

Mercifully, I faded in and out on the journey in the cart. I was eventually awoken by someone moving me.

"Stay silent until we say otherwise," the deep voice rumbled. He lifted me as if I weighed nothing. It was the same man who carried me from the cave.

A whimper left me as he shifted me in his arms. My body hurt everywhere. My bones pushed against the hard ridges of his broad chest.

He left the cart behind, and I became vaguely aware of sounds around me—people talking, many people. We were in a crowded area.

My spirit, which had all but diminished, perked up at the onslaught of scents that hit me. I could smell the most delicious foods. My parched mouth began watering.

They were not familiar aromas to me. They were foreign and rich, unlike the foods from home—the simple livestock and vegetables from a rotted garden.

I couldn't grow much in the small patch I had, where little light reached through the trees surrounding my shack. I kept several goats over the years, but their poor diet made them too skinny. They didn't provide much in the way of milk or meat.

The man carrying me walked slowly, perhaps to avoid jostling me around too much. A short time later, I heard a door opening. The man walked through, and when the door clicked shut, the sounds from before grew muffled, and the scent of food faded.

He ascended a staircase. God above, if I was uncomfortable before, it was nothing like walking up the stairs bouncing in his arms.

Up several staircases and down a hallway, he finally turned into a room.

"Kaz, I'm going to set her down in the bathing room," his chest rumbled against me as he spoke. "Nuo shut those window curtains and put blankets under the door. Bastane, bring in the bags of the magycris."

Why were they shutting the curtains and putting towels under a door? I added another word to the list that made no sense— *Magycris? Aspis? Aethars?* Where in the endless forest was I?

I tried to squirm away, but his grip was unrelenting.

"No way, man. We've already used some on her. We need that to get—"

"We'll get more, Bas. This is necessary."

"Well, I wouldn't know, would I? You haven't explained anything, just that we needed to bring her back. We don't have time to save every poor soul we come across," the other man—Bas —replied. I heard him rummaging through a pack while he spoke.

"Pffft, you're leading Bas?" a third male voice chimed in. How many were there? "We all know whose brain runs this operation."

Bas scoffed. "Nuo, you can't convince people you're smart by repeating it endlessly."

I was lowered, landing in a large bowl—a bathtub. My fingertips hit the cool material beneath me. It was made of smooth rock, maybe clay.

The tub from my mother's home was a metal basin, which had been previously used as a water trough for the animals. There wasn't enough room for a tub in my shack, so I used a small pot and boiled water.

"You'll have to take it from here, Kazhi," the deep voice said. "She may feel better healing next to another female."

Heavy steps left the room, and silence took over, leaving me alone with the terrifying woman.

She was peeling off my clothing for me, unhindered by my weak protests.

I focused on my own skin rather than the tattooed woman as layers came off. If I had food in me, I would have been sick. My skin was many shades of pink and red, pale and cracking, clinging to bones. Once Kazhi had taken off my boots and thin socks, the tips of my toes were revealed as a nasty shade of purple.

No wonder they gasped when they saw me—I hardly looked human.

CHAPTER
FIVE

"This is going to hurt," Kazhi said, matter-of-factly, "I've never seen someone healed from this kind of condition. I'm going to make you drink, don't waste a drop of it. It's a lot of effort to get ahold of such remedies.

"Try to keep your cries to a minimum. We don't want the entire town to think we are murdering someone in here."

Her black eyes never blinked while telling me she was about to cause me great pain.

I had a feeling she wouldn't scream if it were her.

She grabbed my head and held it at an angle for me to drink.

"Small sips at first." She held the drink to my mouth.

The liquid hit my tongue, nearly choking me. It was an effort to force it down my dry throat, but I remembered her warning and kept it in. I didn't want to know what would happen if I spilled a drop.

After the first few sips, my muscles began to seize.

"All of it now, quick." She poured the rest into my mouth, and I miraculously swallowed it whole.

I gave it a second, the liquid sliding down and settling in my empty, aching stomach, and waited for it to get worse. I turned a searching eye toward her, and then the burn hit me.

SARAH L. ROSE

My back bowed out of the empty tub. My head hit the side with a painful crack. I grabbed onto the tub beneath me as my jaw clamped shut. If they worried about me screaming, it was a wasted thought. My mouth had glued itself shut. I couldn't breathe from the pain. It was consuming.

My blood boiled, my insides burned, my skin charred.

When my body started spasming from lack of breath, my mouth and lungs opened. I inhaled, and that's when the scream tore from my lips. Soon enough, Kazhi's hands were on my mouth, silencing me.

I thought she was speaking, but I couldn't hear from the pounding in my head. The metallic and hollow pounding reverberated in my skull, or was that my fists pounding on the tub?

Time was endless—one spasm led to the next as my body stitched itself back together. There was so much damage from the weeks of hunger, the long run into the forest, the twisted ankle, the freezing temperatures ... The medicine had a lot of work to do.

What was this liquid that had such power? She mentioned healing, but this? This was tearing my mind apart.

It was an eternity of writhing in my own personal Hell. The pain shifted from inside to out, becoming sharper, like needles. But they weren't puncturing me. They were scratching me, making me unbearably itchy. I clawed at my skin.

"Make it stop!" My yells were muffled from under her hand.

When she realized what I was doing, she let go of my mouth and grabbed my wrists. "Hold on a little longer. You are a lot stronger already."

We battled. She held me down to keep my hands from scratching my skin. I rolled back and forth and up and down, trying to get any friction I could to relieve the unbearable itch.

When I didn't think I could take any more, it receded. The itch became a tingle, then a whisper of pain, a pulled muscle, a healing scab.

Then the ache was like waking up from a bad dream—in the back of my mind but not in my body.

26

I was awake, whole.

I opened my eyes. When had I closed them? Kazhi held my wrists, her eyes roaming curiously over my body. Her eyebrows pinched, forming questions though she didn't voice them. I suddenly remembered how naked I was.

I inspected myself. Why was she confused? My legs—they were full. My feet were free of frostbite, my stomach flat but not angled over bones. I sat up … I sat up! The movement surprised me, the rush sending a pounding to my head. I cradled it, squeezing my eyes shut and waiting for it to subside.

"Give yourself a moment to adjust. When was the last time you were standing?"

"I don't know, a few days?" The last time I stood, it was not without difficulty. Dropping my hands, I wiggled my ankle. Healed.

"You should be okay in a minute. Before we healed you, did your skin not bear any tattoos or markings?" she asked.

I covered myself, wary of her intrusive gaze.

"What kind of question is that?" I played the obedient citizen as always. "Why would I have tattoos?"

"Many do, or other markings."

I paused, taking in her tattooed face once more. The black and white strips of skin along her jaw and across her eyes were almost dizzying.

"Not where I am from."

I worried where these questions were leading. She was asking everything backwards. Where was she from that most people had tattoos or markings? Shouldn't she be hiding the fact that she bore them herself?

She grabbed my jaw and tilted my head to examine my neck. She then leaned it the other way. I pulled my head back, uncomfortable with her being so familiar.

"I don't see any signs of your legacy either. Hmm. You must come from a sheltered place." Her eyes narrowed in suspicion. "Where are you from?"

Legacy? I didn't answer. Surely my town name would be recognizable. We couldn't be too far from it. I didn't want them to know where I was from and lead me back to the men trying to round me up.

"Fine," she said, "but you will tell me soon enough. As long as you aren't one of the Aethar, you know we won't hurt you. So it would be easier if you told me now to save yourself the trouble."

"I am not … uh, one of those," I replied, not knowing what one of those was.

All of a sudden, she was up and moving.

"Looks like you'll need clothing now, and nothing I have will fit your frame. You're much curvier than I am."

Right. I was going to have to get out of this tub. I wiggled my legs, making sure they worked. I pressed my toes against the end of the tub, amazed they had feeling in them again.

"Why are you helping me?" I surprised myself by asking. It probably wasn't the best idea to question any help I could get, but help was out of character for most.

She paused briefly to stare. "Any Guardian would." Her answer confused me even more. Then she was gone from the room.

My list of strange words was growing by the minute.

I grabbed the side of the tub and scrambled to get up, falling to the ground and banging my knees. Unfortunately, the medicine hadn't made me coordinated. I stood on wobbling legs, putting my hands out to steady myself.

But I was on my feet. I couldn't explain my amazement at being alive and whole after my time by the freezing river.

Taking in the room, I connected with grey eyes—my eyes—in a stand-up mirror against a red stone wall opposite the tub.

I had not looked this good in … well, ever. Pink blushed the tops of my cheekbones that had a healthy roundness. My lips were rosy and full, not cracked and colourless like they usually were in the harsher weather. My hair—still dark blonde and dull, in my opinion—fell to my shoulders in soft waves.

My chest, which had always been a generous size, was full

once more. My waist was trim, and my hips curved out, embodying a healthy figure I'd never had. When I twisted to the side, I found my backside filled out. I was plump and healthy, which I never could achieve on the sparse diet I was accustomed to.

Kazhi returned, holding an oversized shirt for me. The door remained ajar to the adjoining room behind her. My attention went past the threshold.

My eyes connected with those belonging to a large, dark figure leaning against the wall.

He was over six feet, with broad shoulders. His arms, which were packed with muscle, sported countless tattoos against his tanned skin. He wore a black top with the sleeves rolled up and black pants. The dim room cast his eyes black, and his long dark hair was pulled back behind his head in a knot, the sides shaved with tattooed designs running over and behind his ears.

His gaze travelled down, and flashed back up when he realized he was taking in an entirely nude stranger. His form darkened like a shadow had crossed over him, blending him in with the room's darkness. He blinked once, pulled away from the wall and disappeared from sight.

"It's one of the boys, so it's going to be a little big." Kazhi held up the shirt, startling me. I had forgotten she was there.

I blew out a frustrated breath at the stupid mistake—I hadn't bothered to cover myself up. That one would surely cost me if the wrong people found out.

I checked the mirror once more. I didn't want the strangers to see me as the townspeople had—different from them. I'd always had a wild heart and a clumsy mouth. It was an easy prison sentence being naked in front of that man.

But what troubled me more was the flash of colour I had seen in his eyes as he looked away, like shining an oil lamp in an animal's eyes at night. They glowed with iridescent blue-green.

I would have blamed the medicine had I not seen it before in the cave. Something was ... wrong.

The strange words, the tattoos, the animal-like eyes. What was happening to me?

"You'll have to cover yourself with this for now if you can stop staring at your own ass."

I spun in Kazhi's direction, confused at the language. She stared at me with her black-as-night eyes. I peeked around the door to see if anyone was listening.

"What was in that drink you gave me? And what is a Guardian?"

Shock seized me—I'd spoken their language without hesitation. The words formed on my tongue and flowed freely from my mouth. I touched my lips as if expecting them to be different, having let the strange words escape.

I had spoken before, and it hadn't dawned on me that it should not have come so naturally.

"You don't know what a Guardian is?" She was assessing me, clearly thinking I was crazed.

I shook my head, waiting.

"The liquid is magycris—liquid made from the magics extracted from crystals." She kept her eyes on me, watching my reaction, waiting for something. Recognition? Understanding?

Nope, not here.

"Never heard of it," I replied honestly. It sounded like it should be something forbidden. If I hadn't heard of it, most likely, it wasn't an approved medicine by the Keepers.

Did this woman actually believe magic could be inside a crystal? I reminded myself what she looked like. She could believe in anything.

"I have a feeling you're either a really good liar or your home is very, very far away," she said, passing me the shirt. "Like a world away."

What?

"What the heck does that mean?" I asked.

"I meant what it sounds like. Something is ... off about you. But I'm not answering any more questions until the boys are present."

I slipped the top over my head and drowned in the large fabric. It was soft and smelled like leather and pine—an inviting, masculine smell. The hole in the neck was so large that it fell loose around my shoulders.

"You're going to have to answer a lot of questions. Nuo's going to zero in on the fact that you've never heard of a Guardian. You're sure you aren't an Aethar?" she asked while stepping forward. I flinched back as she wrapped her arms around my sides, tying something around my waist. She was securing the shirt, making it look more like a very short and *very* revealing black dress.

"I told you, I'm not."

"You'd better hope not. Otherwise, we wasted the magycris on you. Nuo would see to that."

Meaning he would kill me.

She watched me as I swallowed, noting my fear.

As she finished tying the belt, I examined her leather top. It was black, covering only her top half. Her stomach was exposed and tattooed with scale-like designs resembling a snake's belly. She wore a skirt over black shorts and leather straps crisscrossed down to the tops of her thighs. On her feet were thick leather boots with fur linings. Both of her legs were on display and tattooed a solid black. It was hard to distinguish if the natural colour of her skin was black, stark white, or hidden completely.

Kazhi was shorter than me and much leaner. Her chest was small, but the rest of her was built with muscle. She was feminine with a trim waistline packed with abs. I would have to ensure I didn't anger her or get on her bad side.

"All right, Bones, you're covered."

"I can't go out there wearing this," I whispered to her, pointing at myself.

"Why?" Her head angled. Black eyes, surrounded by a strip of white skin, followed my every move. With the stripe patterns on her face combined with the way she moved, she reminded me of something reptilian, like the summer snakes I used to see hiding behind my small home. They would watch me as I moved past, seeming to know much more than a small animal should.

"I'm barely covered," I answered as if it were not obvious.

I stopped myself, needing to be watchful of my tone.

Kazhi laughed and just walked out of the room. That wasn't a reaction I expected.

CHAPTER
SIX

My heart thundered as I peeked out of the bathing room. I grabbed onto the edge of the door, partly to use as a shield and partly to stop my fingers from shaking.

Luggage was strewn about in heaps—this was not where these people lived. A borrowed room, perhaps.

There were two large beds against the far wall with brown coverings, and the carpets underneath were a mix of reds and browns. Candles lined the room, their flames bathing the room with a soft glow. To my left, where the strange-eyed man was standing only a moment ago, were two curtained doorways. I threw up my hands, shielding my eyes from the afternoon light as someone threw the curtains wide.

My breath hitched—a man stood bathed in the light, and recognition ignited new fears as he turned.

How was it possible ... How was Stephen standing before me?

Had he set this up as an elaborate method of trapping me, to hand me over to the Keepers?

No, it wasn't him, though this man could certainly be his brother.

It was difficult to find the differences. He was still quite tall. Light blond hair fell around his face, grazing a jawline dusted with a day or two worth of beard. His skin was much darker than Stephen's, almost golden. His eyes were bright blue against the tan of his skin. If there were such a thing as a traditionally handsome man, this would be it. Daylight shone through the room, lighting up his regal features.

I stepped closer, leaving behind the door that was shielding me.

His eyes were shameless as they travelled up my bare legs and over the curves of my body.

I could feel it coming now—the comments, the judgment and the accusations about my scandalous appearance. He would be getting ready to accuse me of all manner of things and then call the Law Keepers.

But he said nothing.

Another man brushed past and sat down on a bed before me. I let out a small gasp at the close proximity.

Roughly two feet separated us. The second man was facing me, brows knitting in confusion. I backed up and slammed into the wall. He exchanged a look with the blonde man by the window.

"No need to be so afraid, Bones." The bed shifted as the man leaned forward. "Not going to hurt you after wasting the last of our magycris bringing you back to health." His tone made it sound like he was making a logical observation. As if I shouldn't be scared of them.

I waited for one of these two men to explain something, *anything*. I was afraid to open my mouth and ask the wrong questions.

"Don't react," my sister's voice echoed through my head. *"Your face always gives away what you're thinking,"* she would hiss at me when we walked through town together.

The man on the bed had brown hair brushed back from his face. It matched his honey-brown eyes. Where the other two men looked like they came from warmer climates, his skin was paler and yet carried a pleasant warmth from days in the sun. His face was serious—clean-shaven with boyish features.

He picked up a pair of round glasses and stuck them on his face. He wore dark clothes like the others and had an open vest with endless pockets with a black shirt underneath. There was a belt across his chest holding tools—binoculars, pens and papers.

"I think an introduction might help." He lowered his attention to his lap, where he held a book. He began scribbling as if he could care less about what might help. "My name is Nuo. The one that walks around like a prince back there is Bastane. I'm guessing you are quite close with Kazhi now, and the brooding one that's taken off is Brekt."

He sounded bored as he listed off their strange names. I searched for the brooding and dark-haired Brekt—sure enough, he was nowhere in sight.

Nuo didn't appear to have tattoos but was well-built like the rest. His body was large, and his shoulders broad. All three men looked like they might be in their late twenties. Kazhi's age was a mystery under all those tattoos.

I pressed myself further against the wall, wishing I could cover myself up, worried about the customs here. These people were acting all wrong.

"Wh—Who are you people?" I stuttered.

"Guardians," the man called Nuo said. "Obviously."

"I already told Ka—Kazhi," I tripped over the strange name, "I don't know what that is. Are you Law Keepers?"

Nuo raised his eyes, peering over his glasses at me.

The prince in the back walked toward a cushioned seat in the far corner of the room.

"Where are you from?" he said, in a voice so different from Stephens. I relaxed a little, comforted by that fact.

Women adored Stephen, and I knew this man drew the same kind of attention. The way he moved, so very sure of himself, told me he knew it too.

He wore a light grey shirt covered with a black leather vest and a fur-collared black cloak that hung behind him. There was a bow strapped to his back that he removed before sitting. A belt around his waist sported several knives.

If I weren't already stunned into stillness, I would be now. The number of weapons this man held was trouble. He had black tattoos like smoke winding up his wrists and disappearing under his rolled-up sleeves. He bore no markings on his neck and face like Kazhi, but there were metal rings in his right eyebrow, both ears and even in the left side of his nose! I had never seen anything like him. I wished I had stayed holding onto the door.

"She won't say where she's from." Kazhi came into view. She held out a small piece of bread, passing it to me. I took it without thinking. She turned and headed for the bed opposite Nuo, flopping down on her back and chewing on the piece of bread she had saved for herself. "Also, can't tell her legacy."

Legacy? Guardian, magycris, Aspis, Aethar ... the list was growing longer.

Nuo looked up from his book to study me.

"Well, I don't think she's anyone we have to worry about at the moment. No weapons. Scared out of her skin—we will wait for Brekt to return and tell us what he plans to do with her."

Like my fate was for them to decide.

Where was the woman who ran from the Law Keepers? The one whose spirit my sister tried to tame?

The bread I held crumbled as my fingers tightened around it. I had escaped my home and chose death to prevent myself from imprisonment—*I* was going to decide my own fate. Nuo didn't know if I was a threat. Not that I was. But I resented that he took one look at me and summed me up.

However, I couldn't start running my mouth. I had to school my features. I had practiced for years to be a detached, rule-abiding citizen. *Don't react. Blend in.*

Be nobody, yet don't let them win—I was at war with my own mind.

"You don't know anything about me," I whispered.

Clumsy, foolish and amateur—I was off to a great start. No wonder Rebeka always gave me warnings.

Nuo forgot his writing. I swallowed, digging my fingernails into the stone wall, willing myself to come up with anything to say to blend back in.

But what was I blending into? Not like these three resembled anyone I was used to hiding from. They didn't look like model citizens.

"Where am I?" My tone was too meek to be called demanding.

"The Last City." Nuo returned to his notes, losing interest in me again.

"And where exactly is that?"

Nuo let out a frustrated breath, put his things to his side and rested his hands on his knees. "Listen, I'm not interested in going over the geography of western Arde, just tell me where you're from, and I will tell you how far you are from home." He grinned like it was hard for him to be polite.

"Not from Arde," I replied dryly.

The room stayed quiet.

Behind Nuo, Kazhi and Bastane exchanged looks.

Nuo snorted. "Everyone is from Arde."

"Well, I'm not."

"The entire planet is Arde, girl." His hands went into the air, exasperated.

"No, it's called ..." I paused. What was it called? We just called it home. "What part of the Endless Forest are we in?"

He reassessed me, obviously considering me slow. He glanced over his shoulder at Kazhi, who was sitting up now, watching me. Once again, she reminded me of a snake.

"Told you, Bones." She chewed on her bread. "A world away. We are not in an endless forest. You are in Arde. Specifically, in the Last City that rests north in the lands of Veydes."

I stood staring, her earlier statement returning to me—*a world away*. Was this not home? Not my lands? My forest? That would explain the language but absolutely nothing else. She said it so casually, as if it meant nothing to her to suggest such a thing. I studied one face to the next, waiting for them to make sense.

Their clothing, tattoos, and weapons—all so unlike any material I had seen before. I thought of the weird shine in the other man's eyes. My heart picked up. I searched the room, frantic. The doors on my left were open to a balcony.

Before I could even think, my feet took me past the curtains and out into the bright sunlight. I raised my hand to shield my eyes. And I took in the streets below.

All the questions in my head turned silent. I had no words, explanation, or meaning behind anything I saw.

CHAPTER

SEVEN

G aping from a stone balcony, I peered over a metal railing
that was several stories high.

No buildings this tall existed.

The balcony faced a large square with a fountain. The paved
square was surrounded by pink and red stone buildings, all
sporting similar balconies. The bottoms of the buildings were
shops and markets full of foods, goods and people shopping.

All that could be expected, something that *could* exist, though I
had never seen it myself.

There was colour everywhere, people mingling and laughing.
Women walked with men wearing clothing ranging from fully
covered to barely anything. People of all colour with tattoos
marking their bodies—still, none as much as Kazhi's—walked side
by side, socializing.

That was not normal at all.

There were women wearing weapons. A couple was sitting by
the fountain, leaning into each other, kissing and touching in
public. The atmosphere was alive in a way I had never felt.

This couldn't be part of my forest. I would never have
considered such a thing possible, to travel between worlds, unless
I saw this with my own eyes.

On their shops were signs—somehow, I could read them too. Somehow this information was just in my head.

That Light—it had done this. I could feel it in my bones. *"I will take you from this place,"* it had said. But how?

"Still not willing to say where you're from?" Kazhi appeared at my side, making me jump out of my skin.

"I told you, not from here," I replied with a hollow voice.

There was no discernible expression on her face.

"This makes sense to you?" I questioned. "Have you met other people from different worlds?"

"Oh no, never. But you don't make any sense otherwise. I'm used to strange, however. We all are. Your skin alone says you're not from here." She was staring out at the sky, unbothered.

"What's wrong with my skin?"

"It would display your legacy somehow. You have no markings."

"What's a legacy? You mentioned it before."

She studied me for a moment. "Wonder if Brekt knew what he was going to come across in that cave?"

That was a question I would really like answered, along with a million others.

My attention was drawn back down to the streets as a familiar man came around the corner of a building, walking toward ours. It was the same man that had been leaning against the wall earlier, eyes roaming over my naked body before they flashed with an iridescence.

Brekt.

As soon as his name entered my thoughts, he looked up at the balcony and stopped walking. The openness in which he regarded me made me flush.

His attention was commanding. I couldn't look away. He was eying me curiously—eyebrows pinched as if expecting something. Did he wonder about my skin as well? Too much of it was on display for my comfort.

His dark shirt was buttoned in the front, the top few left open, and the sleeves were rolled back to his biceps showing off muscular arms. He wasn't wearing weapons like the others.

When I didn't make a move, he pushed forward again, continuing toward the building, and was out of sight. Only once I was released from his stare did I relax.

What kind of reaction was that?

I turned back to the room to find the two other men staring out the doors at me. Nuo was leaning against the door frame while Bastane, the blonde one, now held something at his side.

A long knife.

I clutched my chest as I stepped back against the railing.

What did I expect? I escaped one bad reality for a new one— one where I was an unknown stranger and a possible threat. I turned to Nuo, pleading.

Nuo quickly realized what Bastane held. He sighed and grabbed the knife from Bastane's hands with surprising speed.

"Again," Nuo kept the knife in his hands instead, not at all making me feel better, "We don't have to worry about her, even if she's lying."

"I would say we have a lot to worry about when it comes to strangers." Bastane gave Nuo a look.

"I believe her." Kazhi casually walked back into the room. "I've always believed in other worlds or different dimensions. That's where they say Erabas is."

They knew someone who had gone to a different world?

"Erabas is long dead." Bastane scoffed. "How could you think the gods have something to do with this?"

Kazhi simply shrugged.

Bastane was eyeing me still. "Well, which is it? Are you from a different world or dimension?"

"How the heck should I know?" I practically shouted back. "I didn't think things like that existed. Where I'm from, even talking about those things is most likely outlawed."

And to talk about the Keepers in that tone was definitely

outlawed. If this was a big joke, I should not speak badly about how things are.

Kazhi was hopping back on a bed. "They would outlaw you talking about different worlds? That sounds incredibly barbaric."

Ya, no kidding, and she didn't even experience it. Most conversations were taboo. I spoke openly to very few people.

"What do you mean by the gods?"

Nuo's eyes widened a fraction as I toed my way back into the room. Bastane returned to his chair, and Nuo lifted an arm, bending at the hip, motioning for me to use the bed. I wasn't that brave, so I returned to the wall, putting it behind me.

Nuo nodded and reclaimed his spot on the bed. "So you don't know of our gods or the Guardians, you don't know what your legacy is, and you have no idea where you are?"

That summed it up nicely.

"So how did you get to the cave, the one we found you in? You were near death."

The strange light and running from the armed men—where did I start?

"I ... don't know. I hadn't been in a cave. I had been freezing beside a river."

Nuo's features tightened with irritation. "What else do you remember?"

"I was running, then I saw a light, and I heard a voice. It was so bright, almost painful, and I felt myself moving."

"So you remember us finding you—that was our torch, and we spoke in the cave." I didn't miss the look he gave Kazhi.

I opened my mouth to argue that his torch was not the light I meant, nor was it their voices I heard.

"She wasn't in great condition. We all saw that. Her mind must not have been in any better shape," Kazhi mentioned.

"I know what I saw." It was true, I was in horrible shape and fading in and out for days, but I remembered the light. I remembered the voice and how it sounded, ringing in my ears. I did *not* imagine it ... right?

"You saw a light," Nuo repeated.

"Yes, it was bobbing up and down."

"Like someone was carrying it?"

"No. Yes. Maybe. I didn't think so." My mind wandered back to the forest, my eyes unfocused on the room around me. "It was low to the ground, weaving in and out—" *of trees*, I was going to say, but he was staring at me like I was nuts.

"So the person could have been short?"

"I— You think I was kidnapped? That someone brought me here?" Maybe I was still close to home after all.

"Could be, and you heard a voice."

"Yes, but it was strange, like many voices layered."

"Perhaps your state of mind confused many as one."

"Why would they bring me here? Why not straight to the prison?" I wondered aloud.

"Prison?" Bastane asked.

Oops.

"I mean—" Why did I say that? "I mean to say, back home, there were bad people. They would lock up anyone not following the rules. But I didn't do anything wrong."

"Sounds like Aethar logic to me." His tone was low, and I didn't mistake the edge in it.

But it was Nuo I watched. Kazhi had warned me that he would be the one to fear if they thought I was this Aethar.

The stillness in which he sat told me I should worry.

"Look at her." Kazhi lifted a hand. "She doesn't fit the profile."

I held onto Nuo's stare, silently pleading.

"If someone was after her," Bastane added, "They may come back searching for her."

Nuo's shoulders relaxed. "And they may have motives with her that we don't agree with—unless you *are* an Aethar. But I will tell you now, if I find out that you are, I have a very special method in which I deal with them."

I shook my head slowly, hoping, praying.

"Good. Cause you'd wish you were left in that cave."

Nuo waited a moment, watching for some incriminating evidence but seemed to accept my answer.

"I see only a few options while we figure this all out." Nuo continued. He must be the one to lead the group. "You don't know how you got here or how to get home—"

"I don't want to go home," I cut him off. "I mean, I also don't know how I got here, so I can't go back."

"Okay, and what will you do if you don't go home?"

"I—I—" What would I do here?

"Wake the Aspis," the voice echoed in my mind.

Get yourself together, Liv. You're going to sound as crazy as they think you are.

I stood up straight. "I don't know anything about your world. I don't even understand how I know your language. It's not my own." Nuo seemed as if he were about to suggest something, so I added, "And I also don't want to go back home. There's nothing for me there." If they thought they'd help me find a way back or put me back in that dark cave, I would make them understand I wasn't going.

"What happened back home?" a deep voice said from my side.

The door was held open by a very dangerous-looking man focused solely on me.

Brekt had just come in from the hall.

I craned my neck to gape at him, and I was five foot six. He was massive and possibly the most intimidating man I'd ever seen. I was used to softer men like Stephen, who worked hard but was not well nourished nor sculpted to be a soldier. Though Brekt may not be a soldier, he was a fighter. Any man or woman would consider him a threat.

Now that he stood closer, I noticed his eyes were obsidian, with just a hint of warmth. He had a scar running down the right side of his face, starting above his eye, down the temple and to the jaw. His jaw was sharp and sported the dark shadow of a beard only recently shaved.

Snakes were tattooed on each side of his head, similar to the scales on Kazhi's hands. The same smokey design that was on Bastane's arms went from Brekt's neck and disappeared over his shoulder.

But it was his probing gaze that held my attention. It gave me the strangest feeling. It wasn't common to be looked at with such intensity. My heart picked up—fear mixed with intrigue.

"She hasn't told us much." Nuo spoke up for me. "And what she has told us sounds like a fevered dream."

"And your name?" Brekt's tone was demanding, and I became an animal caught in a predator's trap.

But he was the first one who had asked for my name.

"Olivia," I breathed.

How embarrassing. For once, I was speechless and not from a lack of acceptable things to say.

Brekt's face changed at hearing my name. Was it because it was so foreign? Did he think I was one of those ... Aethars?

No, it seemed like it unnerved him.

"I like Bones better," Nuo said, breaking my focus. Brekt cut a look to Nuo and entered the room, closing the door behind him. He passed in front of me, leaving me to stand alone against the wall.

"We were hoping you could clear a few things up." Kazhi said to Brekt. "As in, what we are doing with the girl and how you knew where to find her."

My gaze followed Brekt around the room, also curious how he knew. He went to the side of a bed and leaned down, grabbing a leather bag and a belt. He tied the belt around his waist and began strapping on the weapons he had left behind.

"Thought I heard something. Went to check it out. Found a girl," he shrugged. Another belt, sporting small knives, was added across his chest. The man could probably kill with his bare hands yet was armed to the teeth with weapons.

"I didn't make a sound, " I said.

Brekt froze, half bent over as he strapped even more knives to his boots. He stared up at me through his lashes.

"Yes, you did."

My eyes narrowed.

He returned the look, daring me to continue. And, being afraid of everything and everyone all of the time, I crossed my arms, and turned my face away.

Who was this man? And who did he think he was ordering me around?

He was large and armed with a lot of sharp metal. That's who he was.

"What's your legacy, Olivia?" Brekt asked.

"I don't know what that means." I was getting irritated.

All four sets of eyes were on me now. Black, obsidian, brown and blue, all curious and waiting.

"You don't know what that is?" Brekt then turned to Nuo, who shrugged.

"She was telling us a story, how she's not from here and came to us from a place she refers to as Home. She's never heard of the Guardians, Aethars, Veydes or Arde either."

He made me sound like I was simple-minded.

Nuo studied me. "A child of Arde is born with the blood of one of our four gods. Each god has left certain gifts to their legacy. Each child belongs to a certain god."

Nuo pulled at his shirt, exposing his neck and tilted his head.

My hand flew to my mouth. Three thin slices went horizontally along the side of his neck, like the gills of a fish. But unlike a fish, they stayed closed and unmoving as I stared.

He sat upright again and pointed to himself. "Sea legacy. A child of Mayra, goddess of the Sea."

I eyed the others, trying to find gills on their necks, but I only found smooth skin.

"I have a second set of lungs." Nuo grabbed my attention again. "I can breathe underwater. I am not a pure blood—not that there are any pureblooded Sea-legs left—so I can't stay underwater for very long without wrinkling, and I can't go very deep."

I nodded my head as if I understood.

I waited for the others to offer more information, but they were all bored and disinterested in Nuo's shocking revelation.

So I asked, "You all have something w—" *weird*, no, that wasn't a good word, "something different about you?"

Nuo nodded. "You'll learn if you're staying here. Everyone is a child of the gods of Sea, Mountain, Night and Day. The gods are Mayra, Ouras, Erabas, and Rem."

There was that name Kazhi had mentioned, *Erabas.* She said she thought he had gone to a different world. Had a god left their world?

"The fact that you are not part of a legacy will be your first giveaway that you are an anomaly. I wouldn't let others know that if I were you. And we are all speaking the common tongue of the gods. You will run into small villages that speak different languages. I would advise not acting shocked when you hear them."

The others now moved in unison. They grabbed weapons and packs, getting ready to leave. Nuo stood and joined them.

"Wh—where are you all going?" Were they going to leave me here alone in a strange world I knew nothing about? The idea of taking off on my own was unfathomable. I would surely die left to my own devices, especially if I was so obviously not from here.

"We came to this town with a purpose," Bastane explained while on the move around the room. I stepped out of the way as Kazhi reached around me for another bag. "We were in that cave hunting crystals to sell. We were also supposed to hunt for food before we found you and sell some supplies for coin. We'll finish what we started and come back for you when we're done."

"What am I supposed to do while you're gone?" What if they were gone more than a day? Two days? I couldn't leave this room. I didn't know what awaited me out on those streets.

Brekt paused what he was doing and walked across the room toward me. I pressed further into the wall as he took in the shirt I was wearing.

"Don't ruin that while I'm gone. That's one of my better shirts." His eyes raised to meet mine in warning.

I blushed, realizing the scent of the shirt I had enjoyed earlier was his. His eyes changed a fraction as he continued. "You should sleep while we are gone. From what I saw, you've been through a lot and may have quite a story to tell when we get the chance. There's food on the table over there." He pointed to a table between the beds. "And a water bucket for drinking as well. Don't leave the room. The city is safe enough, but you don't know what you're doing here."

"How long should I expect you all to be gone?" I looked away to the others, who were nearly ready to leave. I had a hard time keeping eye contact with this man.

I may have also checked his neck once more to ensure he didn't have gills.

"If we don't come across any more dying women, then we should be back after dark or early tomorrow." Brekt headed for the door. The others fell in line behind him. Kazhi stared at me with her near-black eyes as she passed. Again, her face was unreadable. Nuo clapped me on the shoulder, making me jump, and Bastane just walked past without even glancing my way.

The hair on my arms raised as the door clicked shut, and a thought hit me that I never thought I would have—I no longer knew how long a day was.

CHAPTER
EIGHT

"**Y**ou should sleep while we are gone," Brekt had advised. I let out a crazed laugh at the thought.

I picked up pillows and lifted blankets, searching for something to use as a defence as I thought back to those moments when I was called outside my little shack in the woods.

"*Come out now. We have been warned of your wild behaviours.*" I could still hear the Law Keepers chasing me, looking for my footprints amongst the bed of needles under the trees.

My last moments in my single-room dwelling were snippets. I'd taken shelter in that shack for seven years, alone since I was eighteen.

"Yes!" I said aloud. I had torn apart the rented room in the new world. I lifted a knife between two fingers, left under a pillow by one of the Guardians. I had no idea how to use it properly, but I was relieved to hold something sharp in case someone came snooping while they were gone. I weighed it in my shaking hands, nervous to both be carrying a weapon and that the wrong person might see.

A warm breeze blew in from outside, shifting the dark red curtains. The fabric floated up, twisted and settled back again. My shoulders relaxed, knowing I was away from the harsh winter winds. The change in weather was another sign—maybe I had travelled further than I wanted to believe. That meant, for now, I was safe from freezing to death and from those who would condemn me for holding a weapon.

I paced from the window and back again—was I safe? I knew nothing of this world. I gripped the knife as I reached the balcony door.

They were children of *gods*. I didn't know where to start unpacking that. They had extra lungs and shiny eyes. That, more than anything else, showed me that I was no longer home.

They spoke of crystals and that healing liquid *magycris*. They asked if I was an *Aethar*. I had some answers for the crystals now—they sold them.

They were hunters, which explained a lot of the weapons but was that the only reason they carried so many? What else did they use those weapons for? They sold goods for money—or *coin*—as Bastane had said, but was that the whole story? What was a *Guardian*? What was it they guarded?

"Ugh, this is so frustrating." I tried to swipe the hair from my face, flinching when I remembered I was holding a knife.

I gently set the knife down on the bed.

I explored the room for differences from home, but all I found were items I was familiar with. It was similar to my world, yet, it had so much more to it.

I ran my hand along blankets as soft as flowers that bloomed in the springtime. The only fabrics I could afford, or given as charity, had been itchy and uncomfortable. The chair, the curtains, the pillows—I wanted to touch everything, to feel the things that were so new to me.

I ran my hand along the smooth wood table. Back in the bathroom, I felt the tub with a new appreciation and found my clothing in a pile beneath it. I held my old pants up in front of me, which were stained, ratted and now a bit too small.

I eyed my bare legs, wiggling my toes that were getting cold from the stone floor, wondering what Rebeka would say about me now. I was half-naked in a room that had been full of strange men only an hour ago.

I was exposed, vulnerable and unprepared for what would come next. How would I react to a world of strange people and landscapes when I went outside?

I bit down on the panic that began to bubble and walked back to the main room. My feet padded softly as I strode to the balcony and noticed this time around that there was a small sitting area.

Instead of sitting, I raised my face toward the sun. The warmth was a welcome feeling as it was so rare to feel back home. I closed my eyes, energized, and enjoyed a sensation I was robbed of in my old world.

"The wastelands were once rich, lush lands that our people could roam," my mother had once told me. *"There were mountains, deserts and forests that never got cold."* Fairy tales.

Her mother, and her mother before that, guarded the stories so that one day, a daughter brave enough might find their way back.

"I want to be that daughter," I had told her, making her smile. But the edge of our lands was forbidden to visit. We were not allowed to risk anyone sailing the ocean, so I never tried. I only travelled to its edge, dreaming that something more was out there.

Maybe, one day, I would have gone. Instead, I was brought to a new world.

I took a seat on the balcony, studying the surrounding area, the people below.

People walked below, shopping and conversing. The differences were staggering, the biggest being the freedom in which they walked and lived as they wished. I couldn't see from this height who had gills, strange eyes, or any other tells that they were blessed by gods. Everything tilted around me, and I was losing balance on a tightrope. I should have avoided glancing down.

There was a strangely shaped contraption sitting near a shop. It had a seat indicating it was for riding, with a bar in front to hold. It was smaller than our horses, sitting as high as my shoulders.

There were grooves and pits designed along its side. Some pits were bright colours and some black. The material was a stone rather than metal and shone when the sun hit it.

"Something is familiar about you," I whispered to the thing. Several objects were piled near and around it, like no one had touched it in a while.

Learning nothing new from the outside, I headed back into the room. The sun was setting behind the buildings, casting shadows through the room. I headed to the bathing room to relieve myself on their version of a toilet, also made of stone.

In the main room, I grabbed more bread and sunk into the pillows on one of the beds. I stared at the ceiling, which had a faded painting of figures and monsters.

"Mmmm." I took another bite and closed my eyes to embrace the flavour on my tongue. The bread I managed to bake at home was always so tasteless. This was buttery with a hint of sweetness, and I grabbed another piece before leaning back to study more of the ceiling.

I crossed my ankles, chewing as I took in warriors and battles.

The warriors were clad in black armour, holding swords and bows above their heads. Their screaming faces were painted so well that I felt their anger. It was violent and chaotic. Blood pooled beneath their feet. There was a black monster the warriors fought beside—though the top of the painting had cracked and chipped away—and smoke danced all around the beast. The smoke was just like the tattoos on Bastane's arm and Brekt's shoulder. Perhaps one of their gods.

The warriors and the black beast fought against greyish, not-quite-human figures. Their skin was formed strangely, and their eyes glowed red. I hoped that those things didn't exist.

My mother would recite to me stories of monsters. These grey beings on the ceiling reminded me of some of those monsters. Those stories always gave me terrible dreams.

Thinking of stories made me think of books, and books made

me think of Stephen. What was he doing now? Was he already over me and moved on? Was my sister?

I huffed the hair out of my face. *Don't think of them. You needed to survive.*

This place, *The Last City*—was it the last of its kind? Was their world torn like my own? Where would tomorrow take me?

A small part of me might have, for just a moment, felt excited that I might see something more in this life. After accepting I was going to die by the icy river, it was a strange feeling.

I polished off the bread and let myself bask in the comfort of being full for the first time in years.

With thoughts that held traces of hope and a sharp knife I tucked under my pillow, I drifted off and finally fell asleep.

I woke, alert, from a violent dream that left me disoriented. Moonlight came into the dark room through two open doors.

I rolled onto my side, a warm breeze sweeping across my bare legs. I shot up, eyes flying open.

A figure was sitting at the edge of the other bed, back to me, head bowed.

Slowly turning, Brekt glanced over his shoulder and just like before, there was a flash of iridescence in his eyes. I backed up against the headboard—memories of the forest, the cave and the traumatic healing came crashing down.

Scanning the room, I noticed he was the only one that had returned. Meaning I was alone with a tattooed, large, very deadly-looking man. I once more felt like prey caught in a trap.

This situation would get us in considerable trouble with the Keepers.

But that was back home, and I wasn't there anymore. This wasn't illegal, as far as I knew, but the uncertainty remained. I had been alone with only one man before.

My fingers dug into the blanket beneath me as I failed to think of something to say.

His attention wandered down past my waist, and when another breeze crossed the room, I realized my shirt was hitched up, both of my legs bare.

I tugged the shirt down as fast as I could, causing it to pull off my shoulder, revealing the tops of my cleavage.

This wasn't going well.

The room was dark, but the glow of the moon was bright. He must have seen much more while I was sleeping.He smirked as if he knew what I was thinking.

"Sleep well?" his deep voice rumbled as he slowly stood and turned. He folded his arms, waiting for my answer.

I nodded. "Where is everyone else?"

"Dealing with a few things before they come back to get some sleep. I came back ahead to see that you were still here. Now that that is answered, I was hoping you could answer a few more questions while we are alone."

"Okay." I sat up straighter.

He watched me for a moment, not asking anything at all.

"Olivia," he quietly tested my name. The way he said it emphasized the O. *Oh-livia*. His low timbre sent a chill down my body. "Do you know who I am?"

Dark eyes held mine. Could they read every thought on my face?

"No," I answered, confused. "I was telling the truth. I am not from here. Are you well-known or something? Don't be insulted. I'm sure I would know you … if I was from here." I was rambling, my hands flying up as I spoke.

He followed my hands as they flew through the air, and then his eyes landed back on mine. I wanted to bury myself under the blanket and hide from embarrassment.

"Some know of me." He shifted on his feet.

I nodded like I understood this conversation, but also to stop myself from saying anything more.

THE GUARDIANS OF THE ASPIS

I tucked my hair behind my ear, wishing something could hide me from his intense stare. Sitting here in only his shirt, I might as well be completely naked again. I grabbed a pillow and pulled it in front of me.

"So you don't recognize me?"

"No. Should I?"

What a strange question. Maybe he didn't believe me. Maybe he thought we had met before.

"Never mind then. You will come with us when we leave tomorrow. I don't know how far we will take you, but we won't leave you to fend for yourself in case people are looking to hurt you. Once we find a spot you'd be more comfortable with, we will get you settled."

"Why is this city not comfortable?" I leaned forward. "And why is it called the *Last* City?"

I sat back again, worried I was asking too many questions.

Brekt kept his arms crossed, staring down, but now he was back to roaming. He was taking in my hair, resting against my shoulders, and I resisted the urge to let it fall forward to hide my face. He scanned my eyes, my nose. Then he landed on my mouth.

Without consciously willing it, my tongue went to my lower lip. His eyes shot back up to mine.

No wonder I was going to be put away back home. I couldn't hide anything. Did I have no control? I didn't know this man. What I did know was that he could likely break bones with his bare hands.

I tried to think of something to say and was relieved when he beat me to it. "The blade under your pillow—I expect it back when we leave the city."

The room was heavily shadowed, but I knew he could see everything written on my face—the fear, the nervousness—he didn't miss how I was staring. He was probably used to that reaction from women.

Unable to sit there any longer, I got up from the bed and walked around past him to the balcony. I needed fresh air. His head moved with me—eventually, he had to turn as I left the room.

I took a seat on one of the balcony chairs. "Well? You never answered why this place is called the Last City. And why would you help me anyways?"

I heard him huff a laugh before he came out and leaned against the door frame.

A cool breeze brushed across my neck and sent strands of my hair floating around me, exposing my skin to the night air. It was an unusual sensation to be hot and cold all at once.

"This city is secluded and doesn't have a lot of outsiders. Though not much happens here, they aren't as open-minded. It's called the Last City because it's the last stop before you head north into nothing. Aside from the Guardian camp, several days away."

"Guardian camp?"

"The camp run by the Guardians of the Aspis."

My body froze, and my mind stilled.

"Aspis?" I asked casually as if it didn't have meaning to me.

Brekt regarded me with suspicion. "You really aren't from here, are you?" He studied me, perhaps looking for features like theirs, only to come across bare skin.

I shook my head.

"I didn't think you were real." His voice was so low that I barely heard, like he was talking to himself about something secret.

"What do you mean?"

He shifted away from me, uncomfortable. I opened my mouth to question him more when the door to the room crashed open, and three sets of footsteps came in. Lights were turned on, and someone laughed as bags were thrown to the floor.

"We will talk another time." He pushed off the wall to head back inside. "The reason we are helping you, Olivia, is because that is what Guardians do."

He left me on that balcony with so many questions.

CHAPTER
NINE

T wished more than ever I could be made invisible right now. I walked back into the room, sticking close to the wall, just as I had earlier. Nuo, Bastane and Kazhi removed their weapons and layers of clothing, preparing to settle in for the night.

Once dressed down to simple pants and tops, they relaxed on the two beds and chairs in the room. The blonde, Bastane, had pulled out two bottles from one of his bags and passed them around. Brekt grabbed the second one and brought it to his mouth as he fell into one of the chairs.

He leaned back in the seat, legs spread and gulped down whatever was in the bottle. He glowered at me over the rim as he tipped it up, then looked away as if wishing I wasn't there.

What a contradiction to have people be so helpful, without judgment, yet quickly turn cold toward me. I was clearly not wanted here, but they showed more kindness to me than anyone would have back home.

Nuo—the man with the gills—noticed Brekt tipping the bottle back and gave me a sideways glance as if I was to blame for the sour turn of his mood.

"Slow down, brother." Nuo reached to take the bottle.

Brekt swatted him away and put the bottle in his lap. "I am in need of relaxing tonight."

"Don't go dark on us now," Kazhi mumbled.

Nuo seemed to consider if it was worth a fight, and I could tell when he decided it was not.

"Right. Well, who's up for a game?" he asked, holding up a deck of cards.

My mother had taught Rebeka and I a few games when we were children, but I was never much of a fan.

Bastane and Kazhi were eager to play, but Brekt continued to drink from his bottle, watching his friends as they spread cards and tossed coins in between themselves.

"Do you want to play Olivia?" Nuo turned to me. "We are going to be throwing in some bets."

I shook my head—betting was absolutely off-limits.

I swallowed and headed for the bathing room, needing an escape. I shut the door behind me, muffling the sounds of their laughter and coins jingling between them as they passed cards around.

I moved around the room. What was I going to do now? Was I going to hide in here? For the whole night?

There was no way I could go back out there and sleep while four strangers gambled around me.

I sat against the wall opposite the door and wrapped my arms around my legs, hugging them to myself.

I should be more upset that I was taken from the world I knew and understood. A normal person would be trying to escape to make their way home. I was scared out of my wits, but more than that, I felt relief.

I did it. I got away.

My mother would be proud that I had escaped.

But what would I do tomorrow? And the next day? They were going to take me somewhere safer, and anything would be better than what I had left behind.

The Aspis, the same word that light had used. I could laugh at the idea that I was brought here for any reason. Why me? The Light must have given the wrong message to the wrong person.

But using logic couldn't explain what happened. There was a man with *gills* outside this room. I needed to find out what this Aspis was—it had to explain something.

I stared at the closed door while listening to them play on the other side. The only one I didn't hear was Brekt's deep timbre. Why the sudden change in his mood? He didn't seem so sour before the others had arrived back.

"It feels good to be away from North Aspis." Nuo's voice was muffled by the closed door. "The cold was making me dry out. I need a good ocean to jump into."

Kazhi spoke next. "I thought I was going to murder someone to find a way to make it through the boredom. I don't care if you three thought the training was worth it. That place is a barren pit of Hell. I will never go back there."

"You get used to it, Kaz," Nuo replied. "If Brekt and I made it for as long as we did, I would expect someone of your capability to make it longer than that."

"I need a little more action than banging swords all day—for months straight."

"I, too, did not enjoy it there," Bastane added.

"No throne for you to sit on, prince?" Nuo replied.

Seconds later, something crashed against a wall, followed by Nuo's laughter.

As they bantered back and forth, I considered how foolish I was hiding here like this. I had too many questions. Past this door, there was a new world to explore. A curiosity and a new thirst for life had been ignited in me.

I wanted to run out into their world, head first, into the unknown and become part of it. That meant facing the risk, going back out there and joining them, taking a chance tonight and sleeping next to strangers.

I stood and walked past the mirror, nodding to the woman reflected there, encouraging her to be bold and to allow herself to live.

I always believed people deserved a chance. I believed *I* deserved a chance.

Get to know them. Be brave. You can do this.

"Who ate all the bread?" Nuo demanded from the other side of the door.

My reflection quickly changed, and my face fell.

That fish boy is going to kill me.

I watched the door, rooted in place. Muffled cursing followed the bed shifting, as someone stood.

"Leave her alone," Brekt muttered.

"How is it that you have become the soft one?"

I opened the door, stopping Nuo short before he could confront me, knowing I had eaten all his food.

He folded his arms and stared me down. I stayed where I was, unmoving. Eyes the rich colour of honey held mine.

"Did you eat all the bread?"

I hesitated before lowering my head slowly in a single nod.

Nuo squinted, but he made no move to say anything further.

Kazhi leaned forward on the bed, a hint of humour in her eyes, though her face showed no sign of a smile. "Nuo is sensitive about people eating his food. He is not one for sharing."

"I'm sorry. I was hungry."

The room was quiet, and all four sets of eyes were on me.

Kazhi and the prince were still on the bed, covered in coins and cards, and Brekt was still in the chair.

His expression didn't give any indication of what he was feeling. But the way he slumped in that chair reminded me of the villagers back home—tired. They had seen too much and had too many hardships to carry on their shoulders.

I wondered what bothered him.

"Well, I'll forgive you this time and only because it looked like you were moments away from starving to death when we found you."

"I need some water." I eyed the jug that was between the two beds. I would never admit this to Nuo, but I was thirsty from all the bread I had eaten.

"I thought you would end up sleeping in the bathing room, Bones." Nuo moved to grab me a glass of water. He returned to me and raised an eyebrow as he passed it over. "Must be the full belly if you thought you could fall asleep on the hard stone."

I glanced up at him. He was mocking a stern look, but there was humour in his eyes. I relaxed, grateful that I wasn't in danger at the moment.

"Olivia can take a bed tonight. I will sleep on the chair," Brekt said.

Nuo's brows drew together as he glanced at Brekt over his shoulder.

"I'm already content here anyway." Brekt patted the arm of the chair, leaned his head against the backrest and closed his eyes.

Kindness wasn't something that was offered so freely back home. The gesture was unfamiliar, and I didn't know how to respond.

"Thank you." I don't think he understood how much I meant those two words.

One eye popped open, and Brekt nodded before closing it again and settling further into the chair.

"You're being weird," Kazhi said as she collected the coins in front of her and shoved them in her pockets. "Bones, you can sleep next to me, but that knife under the pillow stays out of your hands. It would be bad if I woke to the new girl holding a knife beside me. I wake up ready to fight, and you don't want to see how fast my reflexes are, even in my sleep."

I fought not to choke on the water mid sip. How did she know about the knife?

"You seem nervous, Bones. Any reasons why?" Nuo stood before me, still giving me a sour look.

"Because you're—you all—you're ... like mythical creatures from a story," I said quietly, admitting the true reason I felt so afraid. As soon as I said it, I realized how I may not have phrased it in the most polite way.

"I mean—not creatures, but you're not like real people. That's not what I meant either."

Nuo raised a pointed finger to my face.

"The creature would be you. We are not the strange ones here."

Standing out was terrible back home and the last thing I wanted here in their world. "That's not good."

"It's only bad if you let it be."

I blinked.

That sounded an awful lot like something my mother would say.

Nuo moved to get me a second glass of water. Brekt had given up his spot on a bed, and Kazhi was making room for me by putting her things away. They were helping. Granted, Bastane was ignoring me, but there was no harm in that. These people were not like those I had learned to fear back home.

Though they might look like something conjured in a daydream, I hadn't been given reason to fear them. I was taught to be scared, and that made me angry.

"So this *is* another world then," I mainly stated to myself, trying to accept my situation. I'd considered I may have died by that river, or maybe this was all a bad dream.

But it wasn't a dream.

"Before you go around accusing any more people of being creatures, let's find out how you got here, shall we? You don't seem so different from us. I certainly would not have referred to you as something inhuman. Perhaps our gods are not so different from yours."

"There are no gods where I am from. I don't know how similar we are, but no one blessed my people at birth."

Nuo studied me. He took the jug back to the table and sat on the edge of the bed, then began laying out cards in front of the others. "Wanna learn how to play?"

"I'm not allowed to play games like that."

"You are now. Sit"

CHAPTER

TEN

I had a handful of cards, no pairs, and some coins in front of
me that Nuo let me *borrow*. He was using me to earn himself
more money.

I didn't have much choice in gambling, and my heart wouldn't
slow to let me enjoy the game. I stopped myself from inspecting
the door every minute, waiting for the Law Keepers to find me.

But they wouldn't. I was in Arde, playing a card game with
Guardians.

The Guardians of the Aspis.

Would they understand why the Light said I needed to wake
an Aspis? If there was a camp north of here, full of people like these
four, I didn't want to go anywhere near it.

And it's not like I had to listen to the Light.

"What's an Aspis?" I asked.

It was Bastane that spoke up. The low light from the candles
cast the room in a golden glow, glinting off the metal in his nose
and eyebrow. "I'm going to warn you not to ask questions like that
when other people are around. People will start to question where
you're from."

"Down, little prince." Kazhi kicked Bastane in the leg. He gave
her an irritated look before giving her a playful kick back.

"The Aspis is a long story, Bones. It's integral to our lives, this world, and this journey we four are on." Kazhi kept her black eyes on her cards. "I would have to tell you our entire history for you to understand the scale of it. But what I will tell you now is that we are on the hunt for it, and it is a very real being of legend. If you admit you aren't aware of its legends, people will quickly assume you are from enemy lands. They will think you are *our* enemy, an Aethar, even if they also know our legends a continent away."

They were searching for the Aspis? Not only was it a coincidence they had found me, but they were looking for the thing I was told to *wake*.

"We are also hunting for stray Aethars that come across the borders into the lands of Veydes. And with it, we hunt for an evil creature that is the Aspis' enemy. We wish to eliminate all threats to our continent. The Guardian lands within Veydes are territories of peace, threatened by outside sources. The Guardians are those who protect that peace, and we protect the other territories within Veydes as much as our own."

"So you four are all Guardians? The Guardians of the Aspis?" I asked. Kazhi nodded, moving her cards in her hand.

Should I mention the Light again and ask what it meant? Could I trust these people?

I considered what she said, understanding that these four were involved in much more than simply hunting for game and crystals —they were chasing a legend. Why was I getting tangled up in something like that?

"Is the Aspis a large black beast?" I asked.

Bastane looked up from his cards with suspicion. "What do you know of it? I thought you knew nothing of our world."

I pointed to the ceiling above us, with a crumbling painting of a giant black beast fighting alongside figures dressed in black.

"Lucky guess."

Kazhi punched Bastane in the arm. "Maybe you aren't so slow after all, girl."

"Thanks." I studied my hands to stop my eyes from rolling.

"That's the beast," Nuo confirmed while picking up more cards, folding them in his deck, and smiling to himself.

Bastane eyed Nuo before checking his own cards. He worried his lip before moving some around in his hand.

"We just left the Guardian camp in the north." Nuo dropped a card on the bed. "Where we have been training for months. All Guardians are training hard right now, preparing for the return of the Aspis."

"It's gone somewhere?" I picked up a few more cards and shuffled them around. I didn't miss how Bastane was watching my movements.

"The beast you see painted is the Aspis." Kazhi picked up some cards of her own. "The legendary saviour to our people. Currently, it sleeps. Once every era, when the Ikhor—the great evil and the enemy of the Aspis—returns to *purify* our world," she mocked, "the Aspis will rise to fight for the people, to destroy the Ikhor and bring peace for the next era. When one rises, so does the other, and the battle decides how the people will live for the next thousand years. If the Ikhor were to win, it would be a dark future for us all."

I lifted my head to the ceiling, to the figures with the red eyes that the Guardians fought against.

"So this Aspis is a good guy? And what is an Ikhor?"

"The Ikhor is an evil creature that controls the power of the elements. It's not painted above you. It evokes too much fear to paint so casually in public places. The Ikhor will destroy families, burn the earth and cause nothing but destruction until it is taken down. We plan to find it and destroy it."

"Enough, Kazhi," Brekt said from his seat. His attention flickered briefly toward me, "We don't know who she is yet. Let's keep some things to ourselves?"

"I agree with Brekt," Nuo added before turning to me. "Sorry, Bones. But we Guardians have a lot to protect. The people of these lands rely on the Guardians to keep them safe. Though we help those in need, you are still too much of a mystery to spill our secrets to."

Brekt sat up and took a drink from his bottle. He opened his mouth but paused, brow furrowing. He seemed to be debating something. "Tell us more about yourself, Olivia. Clear up some of this mystery for us. You said you were running before we found you. Who was chasing you?"

Could I make these strangers into allies? Although Bastane glared at me like I would never be seen as his ally, perhaps it would be best if I had these strange Guardians on my side.

"You have never heard of the Law Keepers?" I focused on Brekt, even if it was hard to do.

He shook his head, and I had to believe him. None of them shifted uncomfortably or checked the door, fearing we were being overheard.

"Where I come from, we are the last survivors on a dying world," I began.

I had their attention now.

"We were secluded on a forested island, divided into only a handful of villages and controlled by the men called the Keepers of Law. They run the towns and make sure everyone sticks to the rules."

Brekt's rapt attention told me he was curious, but he stayed silent while I continued.

"The rules are endless, as are the demands on the people to help our society continue. Weapons are not allowed unless you're a member of the Keepers."

It all came spilling out. A part of me needed to explain myself. To let someone else take the blame for my weaknesses and failings. I had fought for my life. I had done nothing wrong. It had been *them,* the Keepers, that took my freedom away from me.

"They destroyed anything they deemed a weapon, leaving a few in the hands of their men. There were no books for reading, though my mother believed there once were many. There were only pages about the history of the Keepers or lists of rules and duties. There are no gods—only stories and myths, which were talked of in secret.

"The Keepers decided your life—where you lived, who you married and what you did to earn a living. If they decided you didn't deserve those things, you got nothing.

"To speak out against them would send you straight to the camps, a fancy word for a prison. To seek out a living, a partner or enjoy activities they deemed a distraction from your obligations would send you to prison. You had to learn to hide it all if you had any interests or opinions that did not align."

I was focused on my hand, moving cards around in a trance as I spoke.

"Worst of all, they turned the citizens on each other— promised money or freedoms to those who reported unlawful members of society."

The room was quiet. I chanced a peek at Brekt to see his reaction. I imagined I would see pity on his features. It was a miserable life, for sure.

But he was unmoving. He had stopped drinking, and the others had stopped playing. I fidgeted with the hem of my borrowed shirt, uncomfortable with the attention.

"You were forced to live like this?" Brekt asked.

"We all were."

I was a little shaken, having revealed so much, knowing my tone suggested I did disagree and I did have my own opinions. I forced myself to remember that he was not part of that society. "Someone told them to come to my house, that I wasn't following the rules. Someone—"

I stopped.

Some things were too much to talk about. I wasn't ready. Even though this was a different world, my mind could not wrap around it—old habits and all.

So instead I said, "That's why I was running. To avoid going to their camps."

"And I thought our world had problems," Kazhi mumbled.

"When I was beside the river—"

Another moment. Another chance to find allies. "The light I saw and the voices I heard—they spoke of the Aspis."

It was subtle how they all shifted as one. Cards were lowered, and the bottle set down. The pause felt like it was not only these Guardians but the entire world that waited to hear what came next.

"What did they say?" Kazhi asked.

"I don't remember much, but I remember the last thing I heard was something about waking the Aspis."

I couldn't track who looked at who, but I knew—this would either get me killed or in big trouble. Their faces told me it wasn't good.

"You heard someone say to wake the Aspis?" Nuo didn't blink. "They said this to *you*?"

"I believe so, though I can't imagine why."

"Interesting that it just so happens Guardians fight alongside the Aspis. And that you were delivered to our feet," Kazhi mused, "Perhaps workings of the gods after all."

Nuo made a noise suggesting he disagreed. "Why would the gods send a woman barely alive to help the Guardians? Our job is to fight against the Aethars. That's what we do. What help could Olivia offer?"

"If this is the workings of the gods," Bastane said, "We should not question it."

"No. I find this information more reason to leave her behind."

I couldn't deny the sting I felt at Nuo's words. He was right, but I hated how useless I was.

"How is that more reason? Perhaps we should deliver her to the Guards." Kazhi flipped her cards around, losing interest in me.

"Who are the Guards?" I interjected. Did I walk from one prison sentence to another? Trusting them had been a bad idea.

"The *Guards* of the Aspis fight *with* the beast against the Ikhor. At its side—as its personal Guardians. They are the elite." Kazhi looked to Brekt now. "Perhaps we should deliver Olivia to the

Guardian City to meet the Guards. It's their goal to wake the Aspis, and it seems she is a part of that goal."

My head swam, trying to keep up with all they were saying.

"We don't know that she is part of anything." Brekt gave her a warning glance.

Nuo folded his arms. "The Guards are too busy to be bothered with a stray woman claiming some voice spoke to her of the Aspis. They are trained. She is not." There was no apology on his face when he suggested I should be left behind.

"I don't think the Guardian City is a place for her. The road there is too dangerous," Brekt grumbled in agreement.

"Nevertheless," Kazhi argued, "It seems we were meant to cross paths with Olivia. We should at least take her to Bellum. Perhaps the Guards will meet her there."

"And what about what I want? Maybe I don't want anything to do with this Aspis or your Guards." I gripped the cards in my hand.

Could one of these elite Guards have the answers to why I was here? Maybe they knew how to travel worlds as well as fight alongside legendary beasts. Either way, it would be *my* decision to meet them or not.

"We decide if you come with us," Nuo said, "The Guards hardly need help."

"I say we take her as far as Bellum and decide along the way." Bastane twisted toward Brekt. "In case she has a role to play. I do not wish to anger any of the gods."

Before I could say thank you, he added, "We can also keep an eye on her in case she's lying."

I gripped my cards tighter.

Fine. They didn't trust me. But the bright side to this situation was that I was out of the cold, away from the Keepers and being fed by these people. I could go with them to this new city and learn more about this world, and maybe along the way, I would find the answer to why I was here.

Brekt took another drink. Nuo made to say something more, but stopped when Brekt was staring hard at him.

So Nuo was the voice that ran this group, and Bastane was the suspicious one, but Brekt made the final calls. Kazhi was yet a wild card.

I was thankful when the wild card changed the subject. She was the first to lay her cards down on the bed, claiming she was folding. "To Bellum then. Olivia can stay there if she offers no use to the Guards. And we can go on our way, doing what Guardians do."

"What're they like? The Guards?" Would she give me more information?

"Private." Bastane slapped his cards down on the bed and smiled. "They are the elite and won't appreciate lowly Guardians talking about them to strangers in their territory. Let's remember whose side we are on."

"Perhaps I'll send word to them tomorrow and ask what they think," Nuo mocked. "Maybe they'll tell us Olivia is the next member they didn't know they needed."

"I doubt they'd appreciate your humour, Nuo."

"I swear, Bas, you are the stuffiest Guardian I know."

"The best ones are. The worst ones act like everything's a joke."

Nuo pointed to himself. "Me?"

With a grin in my direction, Nuo put down a strong hand.

I counted his and bit my lip to stop my smile. "Two pairs," I said, silencing them all.

"Nice, Bones," Nuo beamed, "That's more for me."

I forgot I wasn't playing for myself.

He scooped all the coins that lay between us but set one in front of me.

Though I felt no kinship toward the man, I said, "Keep it. For the bread."

"Deal." He smirked over at Bastane.

"Ugh." The blonde prince glared as Nuo took all his money.

"Great," Kazhi sighed.

When I turned to Brekt, he stayed silent. He was still staring, eyes roaming over me with sharp interest.

CHAPTER

ELEVEN

I was still awake. My mind had wandered down dark paths and nearly fell into dreams full of things I didn't wish to face. I was exhausted, but instinct told me I was in danger and to stay alert.

"Not sleeping either?" I heard Nuo whisper to Brekt from across the room.

Kazhi was breathing deeply beside me. Nuo had woken up ten minutes ago for water and didn't go back to sleep. Now he was leaning against the framed door to the balcony.

The moonlight reflected off his brown hair—earlier brushed back. It now fell, a mess around his face. His pants hung low on his hips, but otherwise, he wore nothing at all. I was wrong, thinking he didn't have any tattoos. He had more than the other men. Lines of script ran down the full length of his muscular back, accenting his deadly figure.

In this light, it was impossible to see the signs that he was different—blessed by a god.

Brekt was outside, covered by the curtains. He had left his chair an hour ago.

"What's keeping you awake?" Nuo whispered.

"Bad dreams."

"Same ones?" Nuo broke away from the door and went to sit on the other chair. The legs scraped along the stone before he sat.

"Yes, and others. More vivid tonight."

Did he have dreams of his past? Mine followed me everywhere, like walking through a spiderweb, always sticking to me and impossible to untangle. Did his keep him awake, afraid to sleep?

Nuo laughed and said something else. I strained to hear more, but their whispering grew fainter.

I pulled the blankets up to my chin. The knife Brekt had let me keep was under the pillow. I was aware of that knife all night, nervous I would still find a way to cut myself, even with the pillow covering it.

Nuo and Bastane had shared the other bed, and Brekt had stayed in the chair, falling asleep in an uncomfortable-looking position.

My heart raced that first hour. Sleeping in the same room with three men resurfaced fears branded into me over the years. Fears that had left marks I couldn't simply wipe away.

I wasn't afraid of the men doing something—though I knew they could rip me to shreds—it was the fear of repercussion, of doing something I was told was against the rules.

But if someone wasn't getting hurt, what was the purpose of those rules? Drinking, sex before marriage, talking of gods and monsters—why were those things bad? I enjoyed them and thought of doing them often.

When the fear of punishment is dangled in your face, you start to believe that fear is real. You become guarded, then fearful, then controllable. For those who weren't able to hold onto some spark inside—you become broken. I'd seen it.

Only in recent months had things changed for me because of Stephen. It was short-lived and most likely one of the reasons I was caught.

I didn't believe Stephen would have snitched on me, as he would have gotten in trouble as well. Whatever I had done, I hadn't given him away in the end.

My thoughts wandered to Stephen and his cottage before sleep took me. He was handsome and so sure of himself but vastly different from the men in this room.

My only good memories from the past several years had been tainted after I had run up to Stephen's cottage during my escape, looking for help. Thoughts of those last moments haunted me as I drifted off to sleep.

The next morning, the four began to pack up. They all moved efficiently around each other, gathering weapons and filling their bags.

The sun had only just started to rise, basking the room in a golden glow. Shadows passed over my bed when one of the Guardians walked by.

Nuo had the most bags of all. He lined them up along the end of the bed where I sat, paying me no attention as he checked the pockets and moved papers from one spot to the next.

He picked up one bag, set it down, did this again two more times and then nodded. He threw two bags in my direction.

I jumped, trying to dodge the one thrown near my feet.

"If I'm supposed to include you in budgeting for food and accommodations, then you get to make yourself useful." He pulled the glasses from his face and folded them into one of his front pockets. "Those two aren't as heavy—you are now upgraded."

"Upgraded? From what?" I lifted one of the bags to test its weight. It was heavy.

"From Bones to Bag Boy."

Bastane snorted from the chair he was waiting in. He was playing with a knife, having finished packing already. His blonde hair fell around his perfect face as he flipped his blade in front of him.

Seeing him play with the blade … I controlled a shiver. And

with his fur collar, he did look quite princely. I couldn't believe I mistook him for Stephen.

Kazhi was outside, leaning against the railing, staring at the sky again. Brekt was still in the bathing room.

"Bag Boy?" I was cranky from lack of sleep, and my tone implied that.

"Yeah. I used to be Bag Boy, carrying all the important stuff these guys aren't trusted to carry. Now I'm upgrading you to Bag Boy."

Strange that he trusted me to carry them.

"What are you upgraded to?"

His hands went to his hips as if he were pondering the question.

"I'm Bag Leader—you're under my tutelage now, Bag Boy."

He threw a bag over his shoulder, smiling at me. "I've changed my mind. I didn't want you to come with us. But I realize the others are right. We will take you as far as Bellum and then decide what to do from there. And you can help me take some more of their money along the way."

One side of his mouth curved up, forming dimples. He was handsome, with an air about him that lightened the space. He was a different man than what I saw after eating his food last night.

I smiled shyly then, nodding as I accepted my new role.

"Come now, Bag Boy, don't you start giving me smiles like that. Our training program has to stay professional," he mocked with a stern expression.

Bastane barked another laugh. "Nuo has a way of tricking women into thinking they like him. My advice, Bones? Realize now that he's just a bragging, overcompensating, too-smart-for-his-own-good, asshole."

Nuo gaped at Bastane as if wounded.

My smile grew, and, against Bastane's warning, I might have started to like Nuo. But that thought left me as the bathing room door opened and Brekt walked out. Without a shirt. Wet from his bath.

I couldn't help staring. Bastane had cautioned me from the wrong man.

Men did not exist like him, not back home anyways. I couldn't pinpoint the draw, as the other two men were handsome. Stephen was handsome too, but Brekt—he was temptation.

His thick, dark hair hung past his shoulders. His chest was broad, cut with more muscle than I thought one person could have. The smokey tattoo on his neck travelled down to his left shoulder and ran down behind his back, appearing again along his right hip and following the deep cut lines that ran below the top of his black pants.

All of them had been tattooed with features of reptiles and smoke. Brekt's tattoo was a black serpent, with writings etched around the edges and through its scales. Smoke travelled the edges of the snake as if it were floating through a black cloud.

What had he dreamt about last night that kept him awake? *"I didn't think you were real."* I wanted to know what he meant.

He lifted a shirt above his head, the muscles along his chest shifting. That small action caused my gaze to wander to other parts of him and suggest thoughts I shouldn't be having about a stranger, just from being topless.

"Eyes up here," Nuo snapped, catching my attention once again. He laughed at what must have been advertised on my face. This time, when I blushed, it was from embarrassment.

He shrugged, "Guess I've already lost. Makes it easier for us to have a proper student-teacher relationship." And the way he said it didn't sound proper at all.

I *would* like Nuo. The freedom with which he spoke was something I envied.

When I looked back, Brekt had his shirt on and was adding the straps of his weapons. Kazhi had returned from the balcony, sticking her bag over her shoulder and heading toward the door.

"Up you get," Nuo commanded.

"But wait. I can't go out like *this*. In just a shirt?"

Kazhi stopped and scanned me up and down, confused. "I put

a belt around you, so it's like a dress, covers all your bits from wandering eyes." She glared at Nuo, who shrugged as if saying he was already guilty of his eyes wandering.

"I don't even have shoes."

"Your old shoes are at the end of the bed. They're weird, but I figured they didn't have holes in them, so I didn't throw them away. Don't you look around?"

I jumped down and walked to the foot of the bed. Kazhi was already out the door, and Nuo was right behind her. I scrambled to get my boots on.

Stephen had returned the boots to me just weeks ago, repaired and in better condition than ever, asking that payment be I come to have dinner with him, secretly, of course.

As I tied the laces, I tried to avoid thinking of how dinner had led to kissing. Which had led to other things.

I stood, shaking myself, as Bastane passed by, holding out another bag for me. I took it without thinking.

He kept walking and was out the door.

I stood staring, wondering how he thought I could carry all this. I dropped the bag on the bed with the others. Did he always walk around like he owned the place?

Prince indeed.

I put one bag on my back and the other over my shoulder. I was staring at the last bag when a large hand reached down on the bed and grabbed it from me.

I tilted my head up, my breath catching.

Brekt was next to me. My shoulder pushed against his chest as he grabbed ahold of Bastane's bag. His hair was tied up again, and the tattoos above his ears were visible once more. The smell of soap mixed in with his pine and leather hung around me.

His warm breath brushed my shoulder. He paused, locking eyes with me, and a shocking current of heat caught me off guard. They were richer than I had noticed before—obsidian but with more warmth when you stood this close. None of the iridescence showed, making it seem like I had imagined it before.

My mind emptied of thought.

He straightened, putting the bag over his shoulder. He went to the pillow to grab his hidden blade and tucked it into his belt before leaving the room. Pausing at the doorway, he raised an eyebrow as if to say, *Hurry up*.

I gathered enough self-control to move my feet and followed the four out of the room.

I was off to see the new world.

CHAPTER
TWELVE

"What on earth is that?"

What stood before me was the strangest creature I'd ever seen—larger than a horse yet wearing straps and reins like one.

It had leathery skin with brown and sand-coloured stripes along its body. The front of its long horse-like face had a horn near the end of its nose. Its feet were wide and had funny little cloven hooves, more like the feet of a deer. The smell was the worst part.

"That's our driver." Kazhi hopped into a cart strapped behind the creature.

Nuo came around from behind the cart to climb in next to Brekt, who was seated with the reins in his hands.

"We will rely on Bert here—although he is extremely slow, in my opinion—until we get more crystals."

If he assumed his explanation would make sense to me, it didn't.

"What will you use once you get more crystals?" I asked.

"A crystal-powered airship. And before you ask, yes, you'll see one at some point."

My question would not have been if I saw one but rather what an airship was.

I wasn't sure where I was supposed to sit. The four had already settled in—Bastane in the back with Kazhi and the other two up front and ready to go.

Nuo unrolled a paper with markings like a map and slid his glasses back on. The four expected me to fall in line with little to no explanation, so I headed to the back of the cart. I threw my bags up, finding a seat next to Kazhi.

The cart began rolling, and I reached out to steady myself. I knew this was the cart they had carried me in after the cave. I checked behind me, curious to see the Last City from the outside.

The day was bright, and I appreciated the clear sky as much as I had yesterday. We were on a dirt road, having just left a stable.

The stable was large and able to house many of these *Bert*-like creatures that travellers left behind before heading into the city itself.

The Last City was various shades of stone, none of the flat-topped buildings going higher than four or five stories. The bottom floors were made up of shops filled with customers.

I had watched the men and women as we left the inn and walked the streets—none of them balked at my bare legs on display, surprising me. What also surprised me was seeing how genuinely different these people were from me.

Several people had near-invisible lines along their necks—gills like Nuo. Some had markings on their skin similar to the spots and stripes of an animal. One woman even had large, pointed ears. No two people were alike, yet they all wore dark clothing and had tattooed skin and piercings, making me truly stand out. More than once, I moved to hide my unmarked skin behind my travel companions.

The crowd had sure noticed the Guardians as they travelled toward the stables with sure steps. Brekt had asked if I recognized him, and from the number of looks they got, I wondered how many people were aware of who he was.

Kazhi sat next to me in the rolling cart, staring at an empty blue sky.

"What are you looking at?" I asked.

"Wondering if there really are other worlds with people on them."

"Oh."

So I searched, too, though nothing was visible in the bright sky

"What's your purpose here?" she mused. We turned at the same time to inspect the other. It felt strange to hear someone repeating my thoughts.

I had been useless back home, so why would the Light decide to send me here? It had to be a mistake.

"You think a god had something to do with it?" I asked her.

"They are powerful enough."

"What do they look like?"

Bastane, who had been listening, was the one who answered. "The gods are not often seen. They choose who they grant an audience to. They are also not to be questioned."

He threw his arm over the cart's edge and faced the road ahead.

"That painting on the ceiling," I asked Kazlii, ignoring Bastane, "of people fighting beside a large black beast, the Aspis—they fought against people that were strange, creepy almost. They had red eyes."

But Bastane laughed and interrupted once more, "The Aethars are creepy, pray that you don't have to meet many."

So those deformed figures the beast was fighting against were the Aethars? That was what they had accused *me* of being. How could they compare me to those people?

The cart rolled past trees that rose high in the sky, their giant green leaves giving us shade to travel under. The Last City was nestled between large hills and cliffs, and the edge of a forest lay ahead.

The trees were different from those back home—the leaves were more prominent, and the trees stood taller. The forest was lush, and the sun came through the cracks in the treetops— beams of light hit the mossy ground sprinkled with tiny purple flowers.

Nuo twisted in his seat, lowering the glasses on his face.

"Soon, we will leave the lands run by the Guardian camp in the north. Though not having official borders, most know that to reach the Last City, you've crossed into lands where you will only find those allied or training as Guardians."

"Who will we meet once outside the borders?" I asked, nervous about his answer.

"Tradesmen, merchants, and the occasional Aethar." He smirked. "There are two other camps in Veydes, so most citizens are allied with the Guardians. Some places, however, don't turn away business from those crossing the desert or seas, even if they aren't welcome."

"Desert and seas?"

"The only connection from our lands to the dead continent of the Aethars is a vast desert in the far south. It takes weeks to cross and would kill most who tried."

"But the Aethars make it across?"

"They enjoy torment and pain."

I shivered, thinking of the drawings. Was that why they looked so horrid?

"What does it mean to train as a Guardian? Do you choose to be one?" I asked.

"For some, it is a choice. Guardians are followers of the Aspis and protectors of the people. Our people train at three camps: North Aspis is our most secluded and the harshest for training, and the Guardian City, our oldest training centre. And lastly, there is South Aspis, where the veterans train and act as sentries at the edge of the desert. They are the first line of defence against Aethars trying to come across to Guardian land.

"Every thirty to fifty years, a new group of Guardians are picked to be the Guards of the Aspis—the strongest of anyone training so that if the Aspis returns, there will be Guards assigned and ready to help it."

He glanced over at Brekt, who was glaring at him. Nuo smirked, then winked at me. He whispered, "It's not really a secret.

I don't get why we are getting the evil eye from the Big-Bad-Brekt over here." He turned back around and faced forward again. "Between you and I, Bag Boy," he said over his shoulder, "the more you know, the fewer questions you'll have to ask a stranger." He leaned toward Brekt.

I couldn't tell from his back, but I felt as if Brekt rolled his eyes.

So they needed the Aspis to save the world from the Ikhor, an evil being. That's the very little I understood from everything they'd explained so far.

"Are Guardians a ... type of legacy? Like you are blessed by the god of the Sea?"

"No. Your legacy, simply put, is what bloodline you're blessed with at birth by one of our four gods. Your legacy is often visible—for instance, I have gills as I am blessed by Mayra, the goddess of the Sea. Your legacy is what you are born as but not who you become. Aethars are blessed by the gods as well—they have four legacies, just as the Guardians do. All people on Arde are children of the gods."

I considered what he meant and decided a legacy must be a race of people, and a Guardian was what you choose to do as a living. I wondered if there was any division between the legacies.

Back home, there was a huge divide between men and women and the colour of their skin. It was all so stupid. Each individual had their own set of strengths and weaknesses.

In the end, that didn't even matter—the Keepers decided for you if you had any value, just like they had decided I had none.

"So, what are the rest of you?"

Bastane glared at me but answered, "I was blessed by Rem, the god of Day."

"What does it mean to be blessed by Rem?"

"All have the signature golden eyes. Some have golden hair. The pure bloodlines have both and also skin of gold. We are tough people, able to withstand harsh climates."

"Your eyes are blue?"

"I am not from a pure-blooded line. Over time some lines are watered down unless a new child is born and given favour by their god—they are then considered a first child. My eyes are not entirely blue, and that is because my family's blood still carries a strong blessing from Rem."

He looked away when I searched to find the gold.

I eyed Kazhi, hoping she would be more forthcoming. But she didn't bother to give up any information—she was staring at Bastane with a strange expression on her face.

"None of us know what Kazhi is." Nuo put his arms behind his head. "So don't try. You'll find some legacies keep their god hidden as protection. Feuds and such. And our friend here is a son of Night." Nuo patted Brekt on the shoulder. A low grumble came from the driver's seat.

Nuo grinned back at me. "You won't see many legacies of Night. The histories and the Temple of Erabas have disappeared over the ages, along with the bloodlines. Brekt here is possibly one of the last." Nuo shoved a thumb in Brekt's direction.

"What features do the legacies of Night have?" I could already guess.

"Acute senses, eyes that can see in almost pure darkness, and possibly other features lost over time," Nuo answered.

Brekt's animal-like eyes made sense now. Knowing he could see well in the dark had me questioning how much he witnessed in the room last night during our conversation.

"There's another legacy, right? You said four?"

"The God of Mountain, Ouras. His legacy is blessed with features that help them blend into their landscape—the skin of a mountain cat, scales of a cave lizard, and pure bloodlines can even change their features to hide."

Did Kazhi's striped tattoos mean she was a child of Ouras?

"I'm never going to remember all this," I sighed. "What kind of animal is Bert called?"

Since Nuo was up for talking, I wanted to know more.

"An angula. You don't have those?"

"No."

I wasn't accustomed to talking this much. The feel of it was refreshing, if not a little unnerving.

"We have an animal we call a horse. They pull our wagons, and people also ride on their backs."

"A horse? What do they look like?"

So I explained a riding horse as best as I could, saying there were even different breeds. Kazhi coughed, Bastane snorted, and when I glanced between the two, they were pretending as if they hadn't been just laughing.

"Sounds weird and foreign to me," Nuo said, turning back around.

The cart rolled out of the forest, hitting the blinding rays of the sun. I sat up straighter to peek over their heads to see the road ahead, and I was blown away by the sight.

Rolling hills of greens and rich browns went as far as I could see. Small groupings of trees poked up out of the earth here and there, but the rest was so open and wild. I'd never seen so much land in all my life. I felt so small, yet infinite at the same time. The few clouds in the sky sent shadows rolling over the hills in the distance, and I sighed at the beauty.

"Don't get out much?" Kazhi had her head back against the side of the cart, facing the sun.

"No. There were not many places I was allowed to go." I was dazed, my wonder roaming over the hills.

The breeze was warm, but I was starting to feel a little chilled. Eventually, I had to curl my legs closer to keep myself warm.

Thank goodness Kazhi had found me some undergarments. Bastane would be getting an eyeful, not that he paid me much attention.

"Allowed?" Kazhi asked.

My spine stiffened.

"Was it your man?" Bastane joined the conversation, asking with genuine curiosity. Almost with concern.

Strange.

"No, nothing like that. It was the Law Keepers and their rules.

85

Travelling wasn't permitted for someone—" I was going to say someone unmarried. "For myself."

"What's wrong with you that they wouldn't let you travel?" Kazhi turned her head, which was still resting on the cart.

"Nothing is wrong with me," I replied, offended. "I didn't make the stupid rules." I blushed and clapped a hand over my mouth as if to prevent more from spilling out.

I hated to admit what I was forced to do by the Keepers or the person I was forced to be. Sitting next to Kazhi, a woman I assumed had complete control over herself and her life—I felt small.

If I was being honest with myself, I felt weak.

"A little jumpy, Bones?" Kazhi raised a brow in question.

I let out a breath. *You're not back home.* I was gone. Rules here were different. How long would it be until I fully understood? I was free.

Nuo tapped his fingers on the backrest. "So, BB, does that mean you didn't have a man?" He smiled down at me.

Brekt, ignoring us so far, turned his head slightly as if waiting to hear what I had to say. What did I have to say? I had been seeing a man secretly, which might have led to me fleeing for my life. But he wasn't my man, though he was my first. I had always thought that would mean something. But in the end, it was just a passing indulgence.

"I think you asked the wrong question, Nuo," Bastane smirked, "I would say the answer was yes."

Creases formed in the corners of Bastane's eyes. Finally, I could see the sign of his legacy—around the black pupil was a ring of gold that faded into blue.

"No," The irritation was thick in my voice. "I mean—I didn't say either way."

"That's the look of someone pining," Kazhi said.

"I'm not pining."

But I was getting flustered. I didn't want to think about

Stephen. I didn't want to pine. That was over. It was all over. Everything I'd ever known was over.

"I'm not going back, so it doesn't matter." I folded my arms and focused on the road we had left behind.

"Something happened." Nuo was no longer smiling.

"Many things happened. Things I would rather not talk about. I didn't have a man. One existed, and then he didn't."

"I'm free if you want someone to hold you while you cry."

It took me a moment to register that he was trying to make light of the situation. And I couldn't help it—I laughed. The bold statement caught me off guard.

"You have a lovely laugh, BB," he crooned, sarcasm in his tone.

"Did you already forget, Bag Leader? We keep it professional," I mocked with a serious face.

He laid a hand on his chest. "Cursed Night, how I must suffer." With that, he turned around, facing forward again.

We travelled for miles, and I realized this place was not so different from home. It wasn't as shocking as it could be.

I found myself relaxing. After the events back home, I decided to lock away those bad feelings for another day. I was excited to see what came next, even if I didn't understand it.

I had readily accepted my only choice was death. Yet here I was, no broken bones and watching sunbeams light up the mossy ground under a blue sky. I was in a dream, but the shock in my system reminded me that although my surroundings had changed, what had happened had been very real.

Then there was Brekt holding the reins. He sent a different kind of shock through my system. I peeked over at him every now and then, but he hadn't joined any conversation. He appeared exhausted. A sense of sadness lingered behind his eyes, pulling at his features.

Rays of sunlight swam over his head as the cart moved between trees. His black hair had warm tones when the light reflected off it.

Gold touched Nuo's hair, being a lighter shade of dark brown.

The sun rays glinted off the rings in Bastane's eyebrow and lit up all of the weapons throughout the cart—metal sparkled and shined all around me.

There was a lot of colour in this new world. My memories here, would they be tinted warm like those with my mother? Or stained grey, as they were after her death?

THIRTEEN

After a couple of hours of watching the landscape, just as I was dozing in the sun, Brekt snapped his arms back with a jolt, pulling the reins to his chest.

"Weapons!"

I was thrown down to the cart floor. My head smashed against the wood where Kazhi was not a second before. By the time I looked up, both her and Bastane were gone.

"Stay down, Olivia," Brekt yelled from somewhere past the cart. Fear coursed through my veins as I stayed low.

I hadn't seen a thing, but with one word from Brekt, they had flown out of the cart. I inspected the wagon—their weapons were gone with them.

A loud clang sounded. Metal against metal. It started with one —then many. We were being attacked from all sides.

My heart was trying to escape my chest.

Nuo said we were leaving the Guardian territory. Was this world so dangerous that we were attacked already? I dared a peek between the slats of the cart. Several bodies moved past, wearing shades of tans and browns, some in green. The Guardians in black were easy to pick out. My four new friends were heavily outnumbered.

I lifted my head to look for faces when a pair of hands wrapped around my ankles and pulled. I was yanked down the length of the cart and off into the open air. A moment later, I landed flat on the dirt road. Bits of rock scattered and dug into my back as the air left my lungs.

Standing above me was an absolutely horrific person.

I've never screamed in fear, even running from the Keepers into the cedar forest.

But I screamed now.

The figure was wearing tan-coloured wool robes loose around his body. But his skin ...

I'd seen scars from a fire. This was something else. This—*man*—was melting over every part of his body. He had no hair and had strange red markings over his severely scarred skin. They were cut into his flesh, red and raised.

He reached down and grabbed the front of my shirt, lifting me off the ground.

"No fight in you?" he asked in a slimy voice. "Maybe while we take care of the others, I can find something else to do with you." He scanned the exposed skin along my body.

Nausea overtook me.

Fight, Liv.

Swallowing back my disgust, I lifted my foot, kicking him square in the chest, using everything I had. He stumbled back just enough for me to get away.

I ran from the road, the cart, and the only people who could protect me. I wasn't sure where I should run. Ahead, there was a small hill with rocks tall enough to climb or hide behind. I almost reached a spot to hide when someone pulled the back of my shirt. I lost my footing. I went down, pulling my attacker with me.

I grunted as I hit the ground, scraping my knees and landing hard on my hands. The man from before landed on top of me, laughing, "Not fast enough, girl. Look at all the clean skin on you. What I would love to carve into it. We could write a little message to all the Guardians who plague these lands."

A hand dragged up the length of my thigh.

"Oh, fuck," I cried. It was the first time I had cursed aloud in front of another person in years. I spun to push him off me. I was not letting him scar up any part of my skin.

I faced him, still on my knees.

I barely had time to take in that misshapen smile because he was suddenly airborne and tossed to the side.

In his place now stood Bastane.

He scanned my scraped knees and must have decided I was okay, because he nodded his head toward the rocks, indicating I should hide now.

"Thank you," I said as I clambered up toward the rocks. I crouched behind one, peering over the top.

There must have been about ten men, possibly some women, with strange clothing fighting against the four. Bodies were on the ground already, but the four Guardians still stood.

The scarred figures all had weapons. But the most impressive and terrifying sight was the four warriors, for that's what they really were. They fought with such ease and precision that I knew that they had trained together for years. They moved like fluid around each other—like they were attached to the same mind and acted on the same thought.

Brekt would raise a sword, and there was Bastane underneath with an arrow. Nuo threw a low kick, and Kazhi threw a knife into a throat.

They said they hunted game and looked for crystals to sell. I think they held back a few details.

The attackers were going down fast. Just when I thought the Guardians were winning, another group of scarred strangers came screaming from around a bend.

There were too many.

Blood pooled around bodies and coated the discarded weapons. I would have been sick if I wasn't so focused on the battle.

The swarm coming up the road split into two and circled the Guardians but still, the four did not stop.

What would happen to me if the Guardians lost? How much would I suffer if the scarred people got their hands on me?

This world was so very different from the ruined one I came from.

Don't react, and they won't see you.

Over the years, we learned that inaction kept you alive.

Don't react. Blend in.

Action is what killed my mother.

Hiding from the fight is what I was taught to do, but it was not the person I wanted to be. I wanted to be strong. I wanted to be a hero. I wanted people to see someone that was more than just a product of a simple-minded and highly controlled society.

But how could I prove that when I was scared to let people see me?

A laboured wheezing came from somewhere that I couldn't place. But the bodies closest to me were still as death.

Too late, I spun to find my attacker. He was standing behind me, smiling, bloody and now carrying a sword in his hand. Bastane hadn't killed him.

I had a moment to decide what part of me would take over.

Was I afraid to die? *No.* Would reacting send me to prison? *No.* So did it matter what I did right now? *Absolutely not.*

Don't react? *Not this time.*

"*Shift your feet,*" my mother's memory echoed, a woman stronger than any I had known.

The wheezer stopped smiling. Was he wondering what I could be planning in only boots, a weird shirt and clearly no weapons?

Unlike my attire, there were many layers to me. I let a few of those fall off as I planted my feet further apart.

"*Balance your weight,*" my mother's lessons demanded. I lifted my hands before me.

The wheezer cocked his head to the side. His smile grew, knowing this just got more interesting.

He raised the sword above his head.

"An opening," she would've commanded.

I lifted my foot and thrust my hips forward. He shot back against a boulder behind him with a shocking amount of force. The sharp angles of the boulder bent his spine back the wrong way. He fell over the boulder, dropping the sword that was still above his head. It fell to the other side of the rock. Out of reach.

He coughed, stunned long enough that I could grab the sword.

It was heavy in my arms, weighed down further by the realization of what I was preparing to do.

I had never used one before.

His neck was exposed.

Bile rose in my throat. Memories flashed in my mind. A mangled body. Bruised. Broken. Blood everywhere. I had stuffed those images away. They returned to me in my dreams, haunting me, not letting me forget.

That slight hesitation, the voice that told me I wasn't a killer, cost me.

The wheezer stood up, laughing in his strange mousy tone. He eyed the sword I held before me.

"Doesn't look to me like you've been trained well, little Guardian. Are they going soft after so many years without their hero saving them?"

"Don't come any closer or I'll kill you."

"Missed that chance, pretty thing."

He rushed me, grabbed my wrists where I held the sword and pinned me in place while he laughed. He pushed me back, leading me to the rock, where I would be cornered with no escape.

Without thinking, I smashed my head into his nose. Blood poured and ran down his front as he screamed in anger.

"Bitch!" He lost his grip on my wrist.

I didn't hesitate. Grasping the sword with sweaty palms, I pushed it forward.

It sank into his chest with horrible ease.

The man went silent, gaping down at his chest. I didn't let go of the sword.

He raised his eyes. They weren't red like the paintings suggested, but they were filled with malice, all the same. Those eyes showed me a promise of death.

He took a step forward—how he was moving with a sword in his chest, I didn't know. I backed up against the rock, cornered just as he planned.

"Please," I said weakly.

He opened his mouth, but nothing came out. His hands wrapped around the sharp blade to pull it from his body.

These Aethar, these nightmares, how did you kill them?

I was shown how, when a second blade came through his chest, right where his heart was beating.

Over the man's shoulders, Brekt stood, glancing down at the sword in my hands.

I swallowed and tasted fear.

The man fell at my feet the same moment I lost the contents of my stomach.

I had puked all over my attacker's dead body.

When I looked back up, Brekt was gone, returned to the battle behind me. I had frozen. I would have died if Brekt hadn't come when I was trapped against that rock. And with the first attacker's heart bleeding out before me, I nearly passed out.

There was so much red.

Blood pooled around him. Flashbacks of my past life in the village hit me—a battered face, a broken arm, broken fingers—I blocked the images out.

I was sick once again.

CHAPTER

FOURTEEN

I fled from the rocks, leaving the dead body and the contents of my stomach behind. The battle was still going, with only a few Aethar left standing.

Brekt was fighting two scarred people circling him. They were dodging his attacks and moving in on him with small knives.

I drew closer as one of the scarred men came around Brekt's side to his exposed back.

After having just missed an opportunity to be the hero, I was surprised when I stepped forward. Numbly, I raised the sword, still in my hands, and brought it down against the attacker's back. He didn't scream but made a gurgled sound as he crumbled to the ground before me.

Once more, the panic hit, thinking I was caught with a weapon. It had once been enough reason to be punished. I dropped the sword as if I could pretend it wasn't me who had slashed that man's back open.

The sounds of battle died as Brekt took me in. His eyes sparked with interest.

"This is a surprise." Brekt's smile distracted me from the dead man at my feet. The tiredness that hung there earlier was replaced with something new. His appreciation wandered down my body slowly as if he saw me in a new light. I stayed in place, waiting to hear condemnation.

His eyes finally met mine, and my back straightened.

"I don't know why you're surprised," I started without thinking. "I can handle myself. Saved you, didn't I?"

He chuckled his amusement, pushing back hair that had come loose around his face. The action smeared blood across his temple. His deep timbre rocked through me, and I shivered.

"It seems I don't have to worry about you protecting yourself." He reached down and grabbed the sword I had dropped. He lifted it and held it horizontally in front of him. "It's not a light weapon. That's probably why your aim was so sloppy. I'll know not to have you watching my back."

"Excuse me? Is he not dead on the ground?" My hands flew to the body right between us.

He gave me a look, one eyebrow raising.

Brekt nudged the dead man with his foot, rolling him over to show a knife embedded in his throat.

"Where did that come from?" I squeaked. I thought I had saved him, that I had been the hero, and meanwhile, the man was killed by a weapon I hadn't seen.

At that moment, Kazhi knelt down beside us. The black of her arms made it difficult to see all the blood. You might not know it was there if it wasn't for the shine.

She pulled the knife from the man's neck and wiped it on his clothes before pocketing it. When she stood, she looked from me to Brekt—there was no expression on her face—before walking away in search of more of her knives.

Brekt's eyebrow was still raised.

"Fine," I said begrudgingly. "Next time, I'll wait to see what happens and just hope you'll live."

I turned to walk away when he asked, "And the man I killed on rocks over there?" I shuddered, remembering the blood pouring from the wound in his chest. "I wonder if you aimed for his neck and sliced open his stomach instead?"

I spun, ready to fight, but he was walking away from me, his shoulders shaking with laughter.

Who were these people? They just slaughtered ... I don't know how many—and now they were laughing?

Brekt and Kazhi were checking the bodies, taking things from pockets, grabbing their weapons and acquiring new ones from the dead. Bastane and Nuo—where were they? I scanned the area, searching the bodies on the ground. I couldn't find them.

Hooves clopped against rocks. Finding the source of the sound, I was rooted to the ground, and my mouth fell open. Nuo was coming over a small hill returning with the Aethars' mounts and belongings.

"That's a horse!" I pointed. All four figures stopped to face me.

"What?!" Nuo said in mock surprise. Blood splattered across his face, his mess of hair glued to his temples, blood dripping off the ends. "This is a horse? We have them too?"

"That can't be a horse," Kazhi threw over her shoulder, still collecting her knives.

"I would have never thought it true had you not described it earlier," Bastane added dryly as he passed me by to load the belongings onto our wagon. The metal rings in his eyebrow still shone, and his chin-length blonde hair had been untouched, although much of the rest of him was bloody.

I spun toward Brekt, who cocked his head, confused, "You look like you've never seen one before." His smile was devilish as I was left gaping.

They all burst out laughing.

I couldn't believe it. Covered head to toe in blood—my hands still shook from embedding a blade into a man's back—and they were all *laughing*.

I puffed the hair out of my face and walked back to the cart.

I hopped up on the back, shaking from the adrenaline. Bastane returned with a second load of bags—food supplies he'd lifted from the other group—and set them down beside me.

He was taking his time playing with the bags, eyeing me as if he wanted to say something.

"Did that man before—" He paused, holding the bag nervously. "Behind the rocks, did he touch you?" He kept his voice down, so only I heard the question.

Any anger I held for being the centre of their joke left me. "No, he didn't get a chance."

"Good. Anyone tries to get handsy with you, that includes that asshole Nuo, you tell me. They will lose not just their hands but their entire arm."

I blinked. Why would this man, out of all of them, offer such a thing?

"Why?"

He let out a breath. "You remind me of my younger sister. You look like her." He continued to rummage through the bags, pulling out bottles of a strange-coloured liquid and setting them aside. "I know it can be hard for some women in this world. But maybe I don't have to worry that much, eh Bones?" He handed me the glass jar. I opened it and sniffed.

"Ugh." A very potent aroma suffocated my lungs. "I thought you didn't like me."

"Drink that, and you'll know I don't like you." He laughed. I must have made a face because he added, "I don't like new and unconventional. Therefore, I don't like you being around. But I don't tolerate monstrous behaviour toward women."

"Hmm. Well, he only threatened to carve up my skin, so I guess you wouldn't have been that mad anyways. What is this?" I held up the jar.

"A very potent drink that the Aethars make to dull their senses."

Nuo came around the corner and chimed in, "Mostly so they can put up with themselves. Otherwise, living must be insufferable." He dropped the bags he had found.

"So those were the Aethars? The enemies of the Aspis?" I

remembered what Kazhi had told me during the card game. "That's why they were so misshapen on the ceiling mural?"

"Yeah. They're nasty, right? Don't know how any of them ever bed a woman." He grimaced. With his handsome features and charismatic personality, I can't imagine *bedding a woman* was hard for Nuo. Especially if their people were free to do so.

"Why do they look that way?"

"Oh, BB, I don't think you want to know. Especially after what we just saw here. Gruesome stories are going to have to wait. In the meantime." He swiped the drink out of my hands and took a big gulp, "I need to find a bath or a river. Gotta clean up before anyone sees me like this." He winked at me.

I said to Bastane, "Now I understand your warning. He *is* a bragging, overcompensating, too-smart-for-his-own-good, a— ass—." I paused and held my breath.

"Asshole," Bastane finished.

Nuo shrugged.

"You're smarter than you look, Bones. Though don't go getting shy with creative words. You'll stand out in this group more than you already do."

"So those people, the Aethars, are also blessed by the gods?"

Bastane explained, "Everyone on Arde is a child of the gods. But the Aethars chose a different path—a horrid one—when they chose to worship the Ikhor. Most worship their own god and side with the Aspis, for it fights against evil and brings peace to the people. But the Aethar left Guardian lands a long time ago for the barren continent in the east. There, they live like heathens, forming sadistic clans with barbaric practices."

"Why would they worship this Ikhor rather than their gods?"

"You'll find some here in Veydes," Nuo interrupted, "who worship the Aspis more than their god, though none bat an eye when it's the beast. The legends can feel more real sometimes than the gods do."

Bastane glared at him. "Watch yourself, Nuo. Don't go saying something like that around the Council."

"Who's the Council?" I asked.

Nuo gave me a small smile but didn't continue. Did this world have a group like the Keepers who kept an eye on what you did and said?

The cart was filling up fast with food and weapons. They gathered a lot from the fallen Aethars—saddles, straps and even some clothes started to pile up. I was about to jump out of the way when Brekt came to the back where I was sitting.

"Wonder why they were this far north? And so many of them," Bastane pondered.

Brekt faced Nuo, lowering his voice, "Two are still breathing."

Emotion left Nuo's face as fast as lightning. He dropped the bags he was loading into the cart and checked the weapons in the belt across his chest.

"Let's load up the horses. We take them all and sell them at the next town," Nuo's voice was like death. "I'll catch up to you when I'm done."

He pulled two long knives from the belt around his waist, flipped them in the air, then gripped them.

The transformation was unsettling, and I was only able to look away when Brekt laid a hand on my arm, startling me.

"Head to the front of the cart. You'll ride with me."

I nodded, peeking at Nuo one last time. He spun the blades in circles upon his palms as he waited for us to depart.

I rushed to the front of the cart. Two Aethars were kneeling on the side of the road, bloodied, their hands tied behind their backs. They presented themselves as if they hadn't a care in the world, almost pleased they had been captured.

Nuo was walking toward them. He wasn't blinking. His movements were tense, like he was caging raw emotion.

Brekt stopped him. "Find out what they were looking for this far north. Try to contain yourself enough to hear them speak."

Nuo only nodded without taking his eyes off the Aethar waiting for him. Their sneers twisted into a mockery of a smile as he drew near.

Bastane and Kazhi were already atop two horses, leading more behind them, ready to head out.

I stumbled, getting into the cart, and Brekt was soon beside me. His massive form crowded the wooden seat.

"What's wrong with Nuo?" I whispered to Brekt.

Brekt pushed Bert forward to trail after Kazhi and Bastane. We passed the Aethar as Nuo stopped before them, putting his blade beneath the first man's chin and tapping the blade—one, two, three times—against the underside of his jaw.

"He has a particular hatred for Aethar. It festers inside him. More so than the rest of us."

"Do you hate them too?"

"We all hate them. But Nuo's hatred has become a living thing. They have hurt him worse than most. That's why we leave him to do the interrogating. He's more creative with it."

I was about to turn to see what Nuo would do with the Aethars when the world began to spin around me.

"Ughhh." I leaned forward and put my head between my legs.

"What are you doing?" Brekt asked.

I shut my eyes to stop the spinning cart beneath me.

"What does it look like? I'm trying not to pass out."

"Why would you be passing out? Did you lose a lot of blood?"

"You would think that, wouldn't you? That this is from physical harm. No, this is from emotional turmoil."

"What's that?"

I took a deep breath and turned my head to see him peering down at me, trying not to laugh.

"Not everyone can kill ruthlessly and be okay with it. I've never seen so much blood before. I could *hear* you walking through it. And then, thinking of what Nuo is about to do—" I put my head back between my legs.

"Well, if I still had any doubts you might be an Aethar, you've just convinced me. You'd be kicked out of their clans immediately."

I pushed myself up. The world stayed upright, and I leaned against the backrest, taking deep breaths.

"You would have been kicked out of North Aspis, too, for that matter," he added.

"Don't tell the Guards. *If* you plan to lead me to them."

His laugh vibrated through me, bringing warmth that was much needed.

Brekt tied the reins before him and pulled one of the packs from behind us. "Let me see your leg."

"My leg?" I pulled the long shirt up to see that both my knees were torn open from falling.

Brekt was scanning my face. The humour had left him, replaced by that unnerving scrutiny.

How often had this happened in the past two days? Where he gave me that look? Like he was searching for something—some unanswered question.

He angled himself toward me, his leg brushing against my own. He certainly wasn't shy in close proximity.

"Ummm." I wasn't sure what to say.

Should I ask if he was okay? A trail of blood was making its way down the side of his face, next to his scar. He was a mess, but nothing suggested he was in any pain.

He blinked once, and the corner of his mouth started to lift as if he found my discomfort amusing. He searched around in a bag that was initially one of ours and pulled out a small container.

Reaching down, he slid a hand underneath my leg, palming the back of my knee. The contact sent a jolt through me.

"What are you doing?" I attempted to wiggle free.

"Preventing infection." He was eying my knee.

"Oh. Uh, thanks," I said quietly, trying not to squirm too much. His touch was warm, spinning my heart like a tornado laying waste to my chest.

He must have noticed my reaction because he lowered my leg slowly with an apologetic look.

He lifted a jar with cream in it, asking permission. I nodded, and with a light touch, he started dabbing the cream along the cuts. The sting was almost as bad as my erratic emotions.

"Don't pass out now. You're doing so well," he laughed.

A scream tore through the air behind us.

I grabbed onto his arm to keep steady.

"Hmmm, they usually don't scream," he said, unbothered. I removed my hand quickly. He didn't pause his ministrations as he continued, "Who taught you how to fight?"

He worked the medicine into the skin. It took me longer than it should have to realize he was trying to distract me.

"I thought you said I couldn't fight?" I argued, but was grateful for what he was doing.

"Not with a sword, you can't. But you got the sword out of his hands and almost successfully took him down. So you know how to do something. From what I've seen and heard, it sounded like you were sheltered back home. I would never have guessed you would pull that off, let alone try to."

"Not sheltered. Controlled."

"By the Law Keepers?"

"Yes."

"And you let them control you?" He switched legs. His touch sent shivers through me, running up my back and down to my stomach. My breath caught, and all the while, my temper flared.

"I didn't let them. I—"

I didn't know what to say—because that was a lie. Yes, I had let them, but it was impossible to explain.

"Fine. Yes. They were persuasive in their methods to control the people."

"And these Keepers, were there many of them?"

His gaze was intense, questioning. Was this a trick? Could I talk openly without any repercussions? I supposed I could at least try.

Brekt had seen me with a weapon, knew I'd harmed someone, saw me nude and there had been no reaction from him. Perhaps I could trust him.

Perhaps I could free myself of the cage someone else had built.

"If I tell you these things, will you answer some of my questions?" I asked.

"I will try." When I went to argue, he continued, "Some answers might reveal things about others." His head nodded to his friends, "Not just myself. But I will try."

I nodded. That was good enough for me.

"My mother taught me to fight in secret. She taught me many things that were not allowed. She was a strong woman, born into a world made for weak people."

Memories of her were a happy place, a small collection of moments viewed through the eyes of a child. Dreamlike but very real in my heart.

I loved when my mother played music, and I would dance—though my dancing was laughable. The Keepers took that from me. They took her instruments too.

I remember those long ago times in vivid colour, tinted with warm hues from happiness and love.

"I've spent my whole life trying to figure out how she could be everything she was. But I haven't been successful yet."

My more recent memories were brutally desaturated, lifeless, shades of grey and some stained red.

The red memories I buried in a box deep inside. It was carved with the names of those who had wronged me. Those memories cut me up. I didn't know if they were red from anger or an unnamed emotion. Perhaps they were red from blood—stains from the little pieces of my heart cut out.

The shame burned inside my chest for how little I had fought in the end.

"The Keepers don't outnumber the citizens, but their methods are powerful enough that we stayed in line."

Another scream tore through the skies, further away now, behind the hills.

"Your mother ..."

"Is gone." I nodded.

"I am familiar with the feeling—of being trapped. Without control."

That look was back. Like he hadn't slept in a week. I thought about the bottle he had been drinking during the card game and wondered what haunted this man. With the scar running down the side of his face, I could only guess. Who or what had made him feel trapped?

"I want to help you by making one thing clear." He finished off with my knee and closed the lid on the medicine. "You don't live in that world anymore."

"I can't tell if that's a threat or not." I leaned back a bit.

A low laugh came from deep in his chest and found a way to make mine pound harder. "It's an open door. You can let your guard down here. We grew up in very different worlds, but maybe our hardships are not so different. You are not in danger from me, I promise, and neither are you in danger from them." He nodded to his friends again.

The pounding in my chest turned to something else, something warmer. It became hot, sharpening his features until they were branding themselves in my mind.

My attention dipped down to his mouth, noticing how his full lips looked soft and inviting. They contrasted with the tattoos and his strong jaw.

My gaze wandered back up—was he fixed on my mouth too? What was going on with me? I didn't even know this man. Why was I focusing on such things?

His presence was ... demanding. Perhaps I was simply unaccustomed to a man trying to help me. That was no reason to ogle him.

Something knocked against the cart, making us both jump. Kazhi was eyeing me, riding next to us.

"There's a river I remember along this road. Let's clean up and wait for Nuo."

"Lead the way." Brekt replied.

Kazhi picked up the pace and led us down the road toward the river. The world had gone silent behind us, and I wondered how long it would take for Nuo to get his answers.

CHAPTER

FIFTEEN

An hour passed before Nuo caught up with us. He was indifferent as he rode next to the cart at my side, but I noted the new streaks of blood on his arms and face.

"What did you learn?" was all Brekt had said from beside me.

"Nothing worth the length of time I let them live to speak. They were looking for signs of the Aspis."

"This far north?"

They were being careful, knowing I was listening. What it was they were concealing, I couldn't guess.

"They heard the Guards had left the Guardian City. Apparently, groups of Aethars are searching for them. We are not the first group of Guardians they've come across. They thought we'd be easy to take down with our small numbers."

"They should know better by now. The Guardians in the north are of stronger mettle. So they are on the move," Brekt mused, "taking out Guardians, hoping to catch the Guards unawares and looking for the Aspis. They had no clues about where it might be? Nothing of use?"

"None. This group was as unimportant as the dirt beneath our feet."

"Do you not know where the Aspis is?" I asked Brekt.

"The beast sleeps. Its location unknown from friend or foe," he said in a low tone.

"Do the Guards know?"

"The Guards carry more secrets than any of us." His non-answer told me I wouldn't get any more out of him.

When they said they were looking for the Aspis, they meant the location of where it slumbered. How would I help with that? I wasn't even from this world.

We rode on in silence. I studied Nuo when he wasn't watching. His shoulders began to relax, and his demeanour turned from stone to that boyishly handsome man. A transformation. A mask. What was his true face? The cold killer or the easy smiles?

"Did you bury them all?" I asked.

"Bury them? Why would I do such a thing? That sounds like a waste of time to me. I did, however, move them from the road."

I swung toward Brekt, wondering if this was another 'horse' situation.

"Not a joke this time," he laughed.

Nuo's eyes slid over to me. "I've never seen the guy *jovial*, BB. What are you doing to him?"

"Me?" I puffed the hair that was falling in my face. "Like I do anything. And don't change the subject. How could you leave dead bodies lying around? Isn't that morbid?"

"Morbid?" Nuo's brows furrowed. "They're already dead. Why waste our time ridding of the bodies? They will still return to the planet, and animals will make use of their flesh and bones. Anything left will nourish the ground."

"That sounds disrespectful of the lives they lived, even if they were killers." I remembered that they were the ones dead ... making us the killers. "Wouldn't it bother you if they were someone you loved?"

"The person that used the body is gone, BB. They have gone to the halls of Eternal Day. Rem will judge their souls, those worthy will remain in Eternal Day, and those not will face the Endless Night. The bodies—they now belong once more to Arde. We only bury the dead if the need calls for it. No one will come to mourn at their graves, so there is no need."

Huh. None of that felt right to me.

"And you know this is what happens when they die?" I was eager to learn things the Law Keepers never allowed us to discuss.

"Everyone knows it," Nuo shrugged.

Their god of Night, Erabas, hadn't Kazhi mentioned he was gone? So who watched over the Endless Night?

Kazhi was riding ahead. Their horses weren't quite the same as back home. They were slimmer, muscles toned for speed and had three toes. Kazhi moved with the horse as it walked. Her muscular body, still covered in blood, made me look weak in my softness. If I were planning to survive in this new world, I would need to be more like her.

My mother would have thrived in a world like this.

Brekt was once again quiet beside me. He faced the road ahead, not realizing I was watching. His brows were pinched, and the corners of his mouth pulled down as if permanently worried. Perhaps there was someone he had left behind.

"So, Olivia." Nuo was riding behind me, holding the reins of his horse. "Do you have family back home?"

Even with blood staining his face, he was still easy to talk to. He tilted it up to the sun, enjoying its warmth.

I didn't answer for a minute before I said, "I had a sister."

"Did you not want to return to her?"

My hands tightened in my lap. My knuckles turned white before I let them loose. I reminded myself I had trained to hide what I was thinking. So, I calmed and twisted to face Nuo.

"No. I couldn't return to her, even if I knew how to get home."

"Why? Is she dead?"

"No." My voice was hoarse, trying to hide the emotions. "I just can't."

Rebeka and I were not close, even before, and now ... now I might as well be dead to her.

Nuo understood he was asking something too personal. "And

you still don't remember any more details about how you got here?"

"I've told you all I know and understand." I could tell Brekt was listening to every word. He was fine telling them to be quiet when they revealed too much, but apparently, that rule didn't apply to me. "I woke in that dark cave thinking I was dead, and then you found me."

Nuo hadn't believed me when I mentioned the strange light— he thought I was hallucinating in the cave. Did they believe I was brought here to wake the Aspis? What if waking it sent me back to my world?

"You don't seem puzzled at a person being here from another world," I said instead.

"I am puzzled but not ready to say it isn't the truth. We grow up with stories of evil beings rising from the earth, embodying the magic of the gods. Someone coming here from another world is not *too* out of reach for my imagination. Or theirs, I'm assuming." He nodded to his companions covered in blood, tattoos, and weapons. I was in a fantastical world.

He didn't ask me any more questions, so I added, glancing at each of them, "I didn't thank you for saving me back in the cave."

"Your tone at the time suggested you didn't want to be saved, Bones," Kazhi added, having slowed down to join the conversation.

"Kaz, that's a bit tasteless," Brekt scolded before giving me a forced smile. "As you can tell, she doesn't have much social etiquette, even for our standards. Kazhi hasn't spent as much time around people."

"Did you not all grow up together?"

They didn't answer for a moment until Nuo chimed in. "Ugh, all this quiet and secrecy is so uninteresting and let me tell you, BB, this group can be so miserable sometimes—taking everything so seriously. Don't be like them, okay? I need to have at least one pleasant person to be around."

"Shouldn't *you* start taking things more seriously?" Brekt gave Nuo a sideways glance.

"I do take things seriously. I am the one who keeps track of all the supplies and the maps, and I make the schedules. I'm practically the mother of this group. I got stuck with that title because I'm the only one smart enough to do so. But after a while, so much tedium makes one want a little fun, right Olivia?" He tilted his head and winked at me.

He was right. It sounded like a lot was on their shoulders, though I was only just learning what burdens they carried. Yet, Nuo still found ways to make things fun. I envied him—he had the power to control his life, and I wanted to be like that too.

I nodded, hoping he would continue.

"We told you before there are three camps the Guardians train at. That's not a secret," he said to Brekt before grinning back at me, "Brekt and I trained together since we were children at the north camp. We didn't like each other much in the beginning because I was top of all my studies, and he was just the kid with the biggest muscles. Neither of us had friends, so we decided to make an unwanted truce. I taught him to read, and he punched the bullies for me."

"I knew how to read," Brekt growled, throwing a glare at Nuo, who took it smiling. If someone had looked at me like that, I wouldn't be able to smile so quickly. "Nuo didn't have any friends because he was a show-off. He thought people were impressed that he could memorize information so easily, but they just wanted him to shut up. Especially the women."

"You take that back. I had a girlfriend before you ever did. You scared all the women away."

"I sure did," Brekt said with a cocky grin. "I was the biggest and baddest there was at that camp. Once they grew up a little, all that changed, didn't it, little brother? Nuo was sent to the camp young and untrained and was supposed to be the kitchen help. He refused to do kitchen work—and laundry and the stables. So finally, they put him out in the training yard to teach him a lesson. *I* was his lesson," Brekt finished with a wolfish grin.

"Anyways, BB, don't listen to his lies. When we were a bit older, Bastane came along and started training with us. He used to help run his family's large farming business. His older brother took over, and Bastane ran around doing what he pleased. Rich kids, you know. That included an affair with a daughter from a neighbour's farm. As punishment, he was sent to the North to tune him up. Turns out he was meant for the battlefield, not the farms.

"Kazhi, here, is a bit of a mystery yet. She joined only a couple of years ago. But time and near-death experiences had us trusting her quickly, and we stopped bothering about what past she came from. Sometimes the past is too difficult for some to relive, and we learned its best not to ask."

That was something I understood, and I made a note not to dig too deep. Who knew what Kazhi had lived through?

"They stuck the four of us together, seeing how our strengths balanced each other's weaknesses, and we became the force we are today. We've trained all over, ended up back at North Aspis and set off again about two months ago to start looking for things we need to look for, and then we found you."

"And what you are searching for is crystals, hunting for game and the Aspis—which you don't know the location of," I asked.

Brekt ground his jaw, but Nuo continued, "The crystals hold power, similar to magic, so everyone hunts for them. Magic itself is a power only for the gods, but the crystals are a natural power source. They can power weapons and machinery—if you can get your hands on any—and also be mixed in elixirs to make them extremely potent. The crystals are rare, though, so they're hard to find. When we do find them, we keep them. We hunt game and take on small jobs for coin. And the Aspis? Everyone wants it, friend and foe. It's a matter of who finds it first—Guardians, the Aethars or the Ikhor," he finished, getting serious.

His reaction when he spoke of the Aspis, making Nuo go quiet, highlighted that this journey they were on was difficult—one with a lot of danger and risk and that I was now tangled up in.

At the very least, I had to follow them to find safety. And if they did lead me to the Guards, would I find any answers?

If they've trained as long as they have and put all their faith into their skill and the Aspis—it had to be powerful. Did I want to be part of waking something like that?

Had I only walked away from one violent world and into another?

SIXTEEN

I climbed off the cart once we reached the river, muscles sore and stomach aching. Strong hands wrapped around my hips, catching my weight and steadying me. I turned to see Brekt standing there. He had reached for me as if knowing I might fall.

"Thanks." It was a stark contrast, this large man covered in blood and dirt coming to my aid. Especially a man so formidable.

"Kazhi will take you around the bend there." He nodded to where the river curved, allowing some privacy with tall grass and a few bushes.

We had reached flat land embedded beneath distant hills. The grass flowed back and forth in a breeze along the opposite bank, and the only sound was the water trickling. It was crystal clear, moving over rocks and collecting in deeper pools. The golden sun reflected off the ripples, making the water sparkle.

It called to something in me, some part of me that hummed with excitement that I had long since pushed down and forgotten.

"Here." Brekt passed me a black piece of fabric.

"What's this?"

"My last clean one," he said over his shoulder as he walked away. I was holding a new shirt of his.

I was surprised when my heart danced at the thought of wearing his shirts. What kind of reaction was that?

As I started toward the spot he had mentioned, I took a glance over to where he was walking into the sparklingly clear waters, pulling his clothes off and joining the other two boys who were already very, very naked.

I picked up my pace, rushing to find Kazhi, embarrassed to be caught gawking.

And maybe, yes, I peeked back, finding Brekt pulling down his trousers. My face burned as they reached his ankles, but I didn't look away.

I'd never seen anyone so toned. He was stunning. His muscles corded along his legs, and his physique would be an artist's dream with all the dips and ripples of sculpted muscle. I took in his black tattoo that curved around his body, down his back and along the right hip. It disappeared in front, which I knew travelled down the cut v-shape of his lower abdomen. Now I could see it wound around his right leg fading into smoke around the ankle.

Before he could catch me staring, I spun around and rushed away.

I reached Kazhi, who was already in the water, rinsing out her clothing while she was half-submerged, also nude.

I paused to take a breath. A powerful racket was pounding in my chest from what I'd seen, and I was also nervous about stripping bare. With all the tumultuous events happening in such a quick rhythm, I couldn't keep up with all the rules I was breaking.

But I joined Kazhi in the river.

In only underwear and one arm covering my exposed chest, I stepped toward the river's edge, dirty shirt in hand, reminding myself that Kazhi and Brekt had both seen me naked once before.

I dipped my toe in first and hissed. The water was frigid after being in the sun all day.

Kazhi raised an eyebrow while half submerged.

I was used to bathing in cold water—sometimes, I could heat it enough that it wasn't painfully cold—still, I wouldn't say I liked it. Stepping in further, I forced myself to sit as far as Kazhi so I didn't look like a wimp.

She lifted a hand holding a green disk and passed it to me, "Soap."

I grabbed it and got to work, cleaning myself and the shirt.

The water was clear, and the rocks beneath were tinted with blues and greens. There were little fish and other unrecognizable animals swimming underwater from rock to rock and behind weeds. Some shone brilliant colours when the sun touched their scales, making me think of Brekt's eyes in the dark. I ran the soap over my skin, fascinated with the abundance of life here and all the clean water.

I was watching the show of water animals when splashing sounded from around the corner, and a deep voice cursed, followed by Nuo's laughter.

I couldn't help where my mind took me—it wandered down the river and across the bend to the sounds of a water fight. I'd seen the powerful back side of Brekt, and now my imagination conjured up the other two, similarly powerful bodies, naked and soaked—my heart thudded in my chest.

I kept my face neutral. At least, I thought I had.

Kazhi was rolling her eyes.

"What?" I asked innocently.

"I know where your head is at." She curled her lip and pointed a finger at me. "Don't even think about laying your hands on my brothers."

"What? W-why would you even say that? Not what I was thinking," I lied, concentrating on washing the shirt. One spot was getting very, very clean.

"Bastane, I won't have to worry about. He'll just reject you. Nuo won't care who you are—he'll be in your bed in a heartbeat. And Brekt? Well, he's a surprise. Usually, he wouldn't take interest, being so focused on our goal, but he seems to give attention to you."

Her reptilian stare held mine as I tried not to think about that fact.

Her tattoos, previously hidden by clothing, were now on full display. Every inch of her was marked. Her legs and arms were pitch black. The tops of her hands and her stomach held scales like a snake and travelled up her chest.

No markings gave away her legacy, not that I knew what all the signs would be. Nuo had said her legacy had been kept secret, even from him. Did she really see them as brothers yet keep so much of herself hidden? Was her past that hard to talk about?

"Why would Brekt be interested? I'm very different from all of you."

She scanned me suggestively, glancing down at my exposed chest. "Aside from the obvious, I don't know exactly why—but it was his idea to drag you along, and he doesn't do anything without reason, certainly nothing that would waste his time. Brekt seems to know things, and his path is set on what he knows."

"How do you mean?"

"Just trust him. If he says to run for your life, it means you're about to die."

It must be the acute senses that Nuo told me about, that the legacies of Night had. I hoped I never heard him yell to run for my life.

But I had already faced that situation. Flashes of the Aethars blood pooling from his chest threatened to pull me under. I hadn't buried the images well enough.

"So you aren't—" I paused, not sure how to ask, but she understood what I implied, and her lip curled again.

"With them? No, thank you." She dunked her head under the water. Her long black dreads splashed as she whipped her head back out.

"Do you have anyone like that? That you're close to?" Did I say love? It was hard to imagine who this cold and unnerving woman would take to bed.

"If I did, Bones, they wouldn't be like those ill-bred oafs. And I certainly wouldn't share that information with just anybody. Especially bare-skinned women I don't quite trust yet."

"I'm bare as much as you are," I muttered.

"I don't mean nude." She stood up and rang out her hair. Her small breasts, tattooed as snake skin, were peaked from the chill. "I've never seen someone with such clean skin. Aside from the virgins who amble around the Temple of Day."

"Well, I'm not a virgin," I barked, then stopped. People were supposed to assume I was.

I checked for her reaction. She was standing there, eyes to the sky, drying off in the sun—my admission meant nothing to her.

"Here on Arde, if you aren't a temple virgin, then the bare skin means you are either a weak line in a legacy, inexperienced in life, or truly from a world far from here. *Everyone* marks their skin in some manner."

I passed her back the soap ignoring how her comments stung. I didn't want to be seen as weak. "Are there many Guardian women?"

"As many as want to be. I would say more men choose this life than women, but there are still many. One of the Guards is a woman."

"Really? One who will fight alongside the Aspis?"

She flashed me a look, naked for the world to see and uncaring. "I think I would detest your world, Bones. Women are natural fighters. Though we may lack the muscle, we learn faster, unhindered by ego. We fight dirtier and kill cleaner. But scorned, we have the capacity to become more evil than any man that could walk the earth."

A shiver went through me that wasn't from the cold river.

"Have you been scorned like that?" I asked, my voice whispering across the rippling water.

She faced the southern sky. What she was searching for, she didn't say. But when her attention returned to me, I saw something far older and wiser than the snake I often felt under her skin.

"I have been many things before. Sometimes trying to be good leads you to bad people, and they will use you while you remain oblivious. I walked a fine line once and could have become evil. I was given a choice, and I chose good."

"Who gave you that choice?"

"My brothers. Had they not intervened, my life would have gone down a dark path. Brekt offered me a place with them, and that hand that reached out to me changed everything. I barely came back to the light after the things I had done and seen. I would have become the cold hand of death and turned it on more than those who had used me. I once worked for people with sick aspirations and was close to becoming like them."

She moved toward shore. "Hurry up, sounds like the boys are done. We will need to plan our next stop and where to sell all of the filth we collected."

"Coming."

I finished cleaning the shirt, rung it out, grabbed the soap and stood. What awful things had Kazhi been forced to do? It gave me insight into Brekt's character—he was a man who offered trust first to prove yourself. I suppose he was giving me that as well.

I wondered about the female Guard and what she was like. Terrifying, would be my guess.

The sun was warm on my now-cold skin, and a cool breeze was drying me off. I stood for a moment, enjoying the fresh feeling of being clean and gloriously nude. It was thrilling. This was the skin —wild and curious at heart—that I never wore around others.

I closed my eyes and faced my free palm forward, catching the air and letting it slip between my fingers. The sun cast an orange glow behind my closed lids. My hair brushed across my shoulders as it danced with the breeze.

I felt something stirring within me. This new world was rousing something, awakening some slumbering piece of my heart.

I felt like I was coming alive.

Sighing, I turned to go find the others. As I took a step, finding my balance on the rocks underwater, I caught movement from shore. Brekt was stepping around the bushes and coming toward me. His dark eyes lifted to meet mine.

He froze in place, and his lips parted. His gaze darted up and down, stopping at my chest, which was not at all covered by the damp shirt I had flung over my shoulder.

I swallowed, only realizing too late I hadn't moved to cover myself.

He coughed, turning his back to me. He stood tense as if unable to move. One of his hands flung out to the side, holding a small towel.

"Kazhi said you were done. I was bringing this over. For your hair. I will leave it here." He moved to glance back over his shoulder again but caught himself, dropping the towel before he took off back toward the horses.

With shaking hands, I dressed.

When I finally returned to the others, Brekt was already sitting on the shore next to Kazhi and Bastane. They were passing the bottle of sour liquor between them. Brekt peered over his shoulder, eyes burning into me, then back to the river, lifting the bottle and taking a long drink.

I noticed Brekt's top was wet and forming to his muscled back. Because he had given me his last clean one.

Nuo was several feet behind them, going through all the bags he had lined up. He pulled out more clothing, bits of food and personal items. I went to inspect the haul, avoiding the temptation to sit with the man who knew exactly how unmarked my skin was.

Something stopped me as I walked toward Nuo. I was being pulled, a sensation settling like a cord stretched from one to the next. I followed that feeling back to the shore where Brekt was sitting, tipping the bottle up.

It was an echo of something long forgotten, a slithering of fate —as if I was tethered to the man looking out to the shining river, I could feel him there.

But that was silly. I was imagining things.

I continued toward Nuo.

I was romanticizing Brekt—he saved me, he was handsome, what woman wouldn't? Especially one who had been alone for most of their life. The battle must have affected me more than I thought.

Remembering what happens when you give into temptation, I moved to sit next to Nuo. I cleared my head of the warm obsidian eyes sliding up and down my body.

Nuo's hair was wet and falling in his face, and his glasses were back on. The blood washed clean off. He shoved his hair back unsuccessfully as he glanced down around him. I found the three slashes on his neck again, marking him for what he was—a legacy of the Sea goddess. I had already forgotten her name.

I wondered if, while in the river, he swam under the surface and used his second lungs. I also wondered if it was rude to ask, so I decided against it.

Along the ground sat many small objects—bottles, blades and various tools. He picked up a small carved box, opened it, and slammed it closed before throwing it to the ground.

I picked it up to peek inside. Several metal rings coated in blood clinked together as I turned the box from side to side, inspecting the contents. "What are these?"

Nuo made a face. "Trophies. May the guilty suffer the Endless Night."

They were identical to the metal rings Bastane wore. Grasping the meaning, my stomach rolled. "Are they from other Guardians?"

"Yes."

"That's awful!"

"Don't be surprised, BB," he said, one of the rare times Nuo was serious. "The Aethars are brutal and capable of causing much damage. They will kill any they think are associated with the Guardians and, in turn, anyone wishing to help the Aspis."

"Why do they hate the Aspis so much?"

"Because they worship its enemy. They want the Ikhor for their

THE GUARDIANS OF THE ASPIS

own purposes and will do unimaginable evil to get what they want. They're hungry for it."

"But you guys took them down, made it look easy. You laughed about it after."

"We are different. Trained differently."

"How so?"

He watched the others throwing punches at each other for hogging the drink, unaware of the conversation behind them.

"We had a tough teacher." He left it at that.

I found something sticking out from under the clothing Nuo had thrown to the side. It sparkled in the sunlight like a clear stone. I pulled it out—it was a hair comb, curved with a stone handle. The handle was clear, with bits of opal veining and moonstone-like reflections. I lifted it to the sun, and pastel tones caught the light.

"This is beautiful. What is it?"

Brekt turned to see what I held, locking eyes with me. A shiver ran through me. It took me a moment before I realized Nuo was answering my question.

"—the crystals are drained, and they become like this. Leftovers are usually thrown away, but sometimes a crafter will make trinkets with them. Cheap to buy, but I can see why women would like them."

I was only half listening. Brekt's jaw clenched, and his eyebrows drew together as if irritated. He turned away and went back to drinking.

I examined the brush, wondering if I had asked something wrong. My mind immediately went over all the things I had said.

Did I imagine the heated look before?

I didn't have a lot of experience where men were concerned. A man like Stephen was a world away, quite literally, from a man like Brekt. I never knew my father. I had nothing to compare.

Nuo snapped two fingers in front of my face.

"It's all yours."

"What's mine?"

"The brush." Small dimples in his cheeks appeared. He threw a bag at my feet. "This too. Fill it with your own things. Take any clothes you want. The clothes in the bags are being left behind."

"I'd rather not."

The discarded box that held the bloody rings was a hideous sight. I didn't want anything that belonged to these people. But the brush was beautiful, and the bag I could make use of.

Nuo found a notebook amongst the Aethars' belongings. The pages were old and stained, some with fresh writing scribbled within the last few days.

As I was putting my new brush in my bag, he shouted, "Yes!" making me drop the bag in front of me.

Everyone spun in our direction. The drink being passed around was currently in Kazhi's hand. Bastane's cheeks were red, and his eyes glossy. Kazhi's tattoos made it impossible to tell if she was drunk, and Brekt, well, I avoided looking at Brekt.

"They made notes of their travels, most likely to take back to their wastelands. They marked several spots with a drawing of a crystal." He gave his friends a triumphant smile.

"What does that mean?" I asked.

Brekt strode over, grabbing the notebook from Nuo. "It means we hunt for crystals."

"Meaning our weapons will get all that more powerful." Nuo's eyebrows went up and down, suggesting I should be impressed.

He lifted a small knife out of his belt, showing me several small carved-out spaces along the hilt and blade. A few of those spaces were empty, but the others held little stones of various colours.

The crystals! They mentioned before they powered weapons. Images of the strange riding machine in the Last City flashed in my mind—dents and coloured disks sat in and around the vehicle because crystals powered it! I hadn't understood what I was looking at before.

"If they found the location already, wouldn't they have taken the crystals?" I asked.

"No," Brekt answered in his deep timbre. "Most won't go into the caves deep enough to collect them all."

"Why?"

"You don't want to see the things that live deep in those caves, Bones," Kazhi warned, taking a peek at the book. "Did they have any maps of the Aethar side?" She leaned toward the pages.

"No." Nuo showed her. "Just of our lands."

Kazhi's shoulders dropped as if she had been eager to find something. She pointed at one spot on the page.

"This one here. We could reach it by nightfall."

"You know I'm game." Nuo grabbed the bags we were taking and left the rest for someone else to find.

We packed quickly. I was given a horse to ride and had trouble stretching myself to get up. I noticed I was not offered help this time.

That's fine. I hadn't had help since I was sixteen when Rebeka gave up on me. For nine years, I've managed. And for seven, I've been completely alone. I could handle taking on a whole new world all by myself, thank you very much.

CHAPTER
SEVENTEEN

"Why were the Aethars' skin so scarred?" I asked Nuo, who was sitting to my right.

"They do it to themselves," Brekt said from across the fire pit, ignoring that I hadn't asked him.

Even after riding next to him all day, I was still stricken by his presence. That something—that cord—often pulled my attention toward his imposing figure as we rode.

The sun had gone below the horizon before we reached the cave. It turned the whole landscape orange and navy blue. The sky was pink and purple, and the few clouds floating along were shades of rose to the darkest violet.

We had two tents set up close to the mouth of the cave, and a fire was going. A few logs found on the surrounding hill became our seats. The horses and carts were close to the edge of our small camp, and cushions were set up in the cart for whoever was going to stay awake and play lookout.

"It's supposed to be a testament to their dedication." Brekt was currently staring down at his soup. He was a far cry from the usual upbeat demeanour that Nuo carried around. "They live their lives in worship to the Ikhor. When it rises, they want to be chosen to be the host. They think the more they can withstand damage from the elements, the more they are worthy."

"That's a bit horrific." I thought the Law Keepers had been bad. What would they have been like, possessed by magic?

I sipped on the soup they had made. Vegetables were floating around in a cup, and as a second course—a stale piece of bread. It was better than most meals I had made back home.

"They *are* horrific," Brekt nodded, "Their practices are cruel. They burn, bury and freeze themselves. They strap themselves to high cliffs to face the brutal winds. They endure it to the point of death to prove they can be strong enough to carry the Ikhor's power. Prove their body won't be ripped apart bearing the burden."

It was difficult to picture people practicing such horrors, and I had seen some pretty awful things back home.

"So the Ikhor isn't a creature? It's a person possessed?" The idea was more frightening than I'd thought. I had imagined another giant beast, like the painting of the Aspis. But the Ikhor would look like a person.

"It might as well be a creature for all that the person becomes. Nothing is human about them once possessed with its magic. The power is not meant for a mortal body. The magic has become an evil thing."

"The magic has become evil?"

"It's old magic. Over time it has warped and twisted—tainted by the evil minds it possessed."

"So, you need to find the Aspis to stop it from happening?"

He nodded, "It's a cycle that happens in every era. The Ikhor returns, and the Aspis will rise to destroy it. Our texts say that the magic—elemental magic, to be specific—belonged to the gods. The first Ikhor was one of the first children of the gods. He stole their magic out of jealousy. Unable to control it, he became corrupted and the Ikhor began to burn Arde, killing other humans that lived around the world. The gods were not able to control or kill their first child. Out of love, perhaps, but no one knows why.

They created the Aspis, a creature born from the soils of Arde, to destroy the Ikhor. The Aspis became our champion."

"Why elemental magic? What does that have to do with the Ikhor or the gods?"

"The power it stole was the magic of the elements—the gods' magic. The gods created the earth with it. The Ikhor can control the elements as easily as a god can."

"Did the gods lose their abilities when the Ikhor stole it?"

Brekt cast me a puzzled look. A spark of interest ebbed away some of the darkness. I could tell from his face that no one had ever asked him that question.

"The truth is, BB," Nuo chimed in, "we don't get a lot of downtime with the gods. But I assume they didn't lose all their powers, seeing as they weren't defeated and have continued on."

Nuo sat on the ground, leaning back against the log behind him and had an arm propped on a bent knee. He raised his cup of soup to his mouth, relaxed. If anything, I felt more like Brekt at this moment—it was exhausting how much I had to learn about this place.

"Why is magic only for the gods? If it exists, why can't everyone use it?" I asked Nuo.

Reserving all the power for four beings reminded me of the power dynamics of home—the Law Keepers kept the weapons for themselves.

They forbid the talk and belief in gods, and now I could see why. If we had believed in a higher power, would we follow the Keepers as obediently as we did?

"The gods used to share their powers with the people in the Golden Age millennia ago. The first children—our ancestors—had the power to use magic. But one of them, in particular, grew too greedy, wanting more power and stole their god's magic. They have forbidden the use of it ever since."

"How *can* you steal magic from a god?"

Nuo gave me the same look that Brekt had—as if I asked something he had never considered. Did they not question anything of their histories?

Bastane and Kazhi, who were taking seconds of the soup heating over the fire, seemed uninterested in my history lesson.

"I suppose the legacies used to be much more powerful than we are now," Nuo shrugged. "If they could use magic, the first children were closer to the gods than any of us."

"You shouldn't question the gods or our legends," Bastane added, surprising me. He'd been paying attention after all. He was staring at me like I was being scolded by a parent. "They listen, you know. They won't appreciate you second-guessing their powers."

"What do they do if angered?"

Bastane only continued to eat his dinner, ignoring my growing curiosity.

I swallowed some more soup, redirecting my questions, hoping I didn't get another scathing look from Bastane.

"But it didn't work when they created the Aspis. It didn't kill the Ikhor because both are still alive," I stated, captivated by this magical history. Our worlds were both broken in such different ways. Why couldn't the gods kill the Ikhor themselves? Why did they give the job away to another creation of theirs?

"It did, in a way," Brekt answered, fixing on me. "The magic didn't return to the gods because it wasn't *given* back. It changed and became something of its own—it was reborn into a willing human who worshiped the power, raising the Aspis once more."

"So that's why it comes back? Because every time, the person the power inhabits won't return the power to the gods?"

"Yes. The Aethars, being the most willing hosts, are hungry people. So when the Ikhor's power chooses—and it always chooses one of them—they will not return it to the gods. They believe the power will bring their people to a higher status, leading the world under their command. Their mission is to destroy the Aspis first, hoping it never rises again. Though they have never succeeded. The Aspis has always won."

I shivered, not hiding how the tale affected me. Their people have waited almost a thousand years for the beast to protect them from the Ikhor.

"Now that you know more of our histories, Bones," Kazhi said, "Is your story of how you got here still the same?"

When I didn't understand, she added, "You say you were told to wake the Aspis. Now you know what it means to wake it, what every Guardian wishes to accomplish. For glory and honour, to save our people, to stop the Aethars. Do you want that too? Do you still deny you have no idea why you are here?"

"I have never wanted glory and honour. I've wanted many things. But not those."

"Tell me." She didn't blink, waiting.

"Kazhi," Brekt warned. But I didn't hesitate. I remembered her admission—these men had given her a choice to be good or turn evil. Now, she was testing me to see what I was made of.

Could I walk next to these Guardians? Should they take me to the Guards who would help save the world?

"I've wanted a full belly." I met her dead in the eye. "I've wanted company after years of loneliness. I've wanted my mother back from the dead. I didn't get any of those things. I had them taken away. So, I didn't *want* to be saved by that river. I didn't ask to be brought here. And I *don't* want to be a part of waking a giant beast."

The circle was quiet, my truth a messy pile before us.

"And what if you were sent here to do just that, to wake the Aspis? Would you do it to save the innocent lives relying on the beast if you were the only hope?"

"Kazhi," Brekt snapped. "Leave the girl alone. We don't need her, nor would the Guards need her. Asking her to follow us would mean her death. You know it. We all know it. Leave it."

Kazhi turned slowly to Brekt—a beast herself.

I was at a crossroads. I was telling the truth when I said I didn't want to be part of this. But to be a hero—had it been fate that had my mother training me in secret all those years? Was all of this the workings of gods?

"Has anyone tried to stop the Aethars before the Ikhor possesses one?" I wanted to learn more but also wanted to break the tension and stop Bastane from staring at me the way he was.

It was Nuo who answered, "Those who have gone to Aethar lands do not return. The land is as scarred as their faces, and the southern borders of our lands are a maze of canyons, impossible to travel through. If somehow you make it through the maze and the long desert, you won't go much further from the violent nature of the Aethars waiting for intruders."

Kazhi watched Nuo as he spoke about the violence of the Aethar. She slanted her eyes toward me, looking for a reaction. She was waiting to see if I would give away any indication I was lying, that I was really an Aethar myself.

Ignoring her, I moved on. "I'm confused about the magic."

Bastane signed and raised his hand to his face, pulling down as if it was taking a great deal of effort to be sitting here, listening.

"If the magic has to be given, how was it possible it was stolen? Wouldn't that mean a god gave it to the first Ikhor?"

"Olivia." Bastane's head cocked to the side. "This happened at the beginning of our histories when children of the gods only first began walking the soils of the earth. Rules and magic were different then. Time has evolved magic and evolved the evil within it. The first children were close to being gods themselves. The world you see now is not the world that once existed."

I shouldn't question these people on their stories. These four were my only friends—if they could be called that.

"Where does the Aspis go after it defeats the Ikhor? If it's always reborn?" I wanted to believe I was asking out of curiosity and not because the Light tasked me with waking the beast. Not that I had any plans to do such a thing.

Nuo regarded Brekt, who was turning the cup between his hands, travelling deep in thought. Did my questions have him spiralling down, just like me?

It was Nuo who answered once again.

"From what we can tell, the Aspis returns to the ground once its duty is fulfilled."

I didn't know what to say. So many more questions came to mind, but too much to take in.

Firstly, how could that light expect me to wake something like that? Was this the reason Brekt was so worn out and miserable? Because he, too, was hunting a beast that would only subdue the evil and not defeat it? For that's what the story suggested, the Aspis never *truly* won against the Ikhor if it rose again in the next several hundred years.

"Is the Ikhor alive now?" I worried about the answer.

Brekt's haunted stare bore into mine, and it took everything in my power not to turn away.

"It is rumoured that we will see it in our lifetime. Visions have been had," he said, almost reluctantly, as if he knew more than he was willing to say.

"What about you four?"

"What about us?" Shadows danced across Brekt's face when the fire crackled. He was all the more lethal, giving me chills where earlier I'd felt intrigued.

"You're searching for the Aspis, but what about the Guards of the Aspis? Will you fight with them too?"

If the Guardians were as formidable as these four, I couldn't imagine the warriors who would guard the black creature. What kind of person could fight beside a thing like that?

"What we are doing is not your concern. We are dropping you off in the next city. I am telling you our legends and history, knowing that it cannot be used against us, as everyone already knows this history. But I could yet find out you are lying about your story and are, in fact, an Aethar or someone who is not a friend of the Guardians."

"Did I not try to kill one earlier?" I was thrown off by his sudden turn.

I knew they didn't trust me yet, but to accuse me of being one of those people, and after the looks he had given me all this time, I thought ... I don't know what I thought.

He went back to his soup, ignoring my question.

Instead, Nuo leaned forward. "As you saw, the Aethars are not like us. Killing one of their own would not surprise me. So if you are one, no, I don't think attacking one would prove anything to us."

Guardians, Aethars ... on top of them, an Ikhor, Aspis and gods. These were powerful and dangerous people.

There is so much to this world I would have to learn if I planned to survive it.

And was that all I wanted? To survive? Not to give in to the curiosity of what the Light had said?

CHAPTER

EIGHTEEN

"Bones."

I turned, surprised Bastane was addressing me. He wore a scowl, clearly upset about something. We stood at the entrance to the cave where I was arching my back to soothe the kinks made from sleeping on the hard ground.

"It looks like I got voted out of the hunt to keep an eye on you."

The other three stood before us. The early morning light cast shadows all around. Nuo pulled out a long object made of the same stone material as the vehicle in the Last City. It shone like metal but had the texture of bronzed stone. One end was obviously the handle, and the other had a sphere near the top.

Noting my stare, he explained it was a crystal-powered torch. They only had one, so Kazhi lit a fire torch, and the three were ready to head in. I wanted to run to Nuo and ask if he would stay instead, but I shut the thought down. He would be mapping out the cave.

Anxiety twisted my gut as they journeyed into the dark, a blue light now glowing from the sphere at the top of Nuo's torch. Bastane followed, entering the mouth of the cave.

Curious, I did as well.

They didn't look back as they went, eventually hitting a corner and moving out of sight. Silence followed the absence of their footsteps.

"How long will they be gone?"

"Depends on how deep the cave goes," Bastane shrugged.

The mouth of the cave was well hidden in a low rocky pass. The opening of the cave was large, considering the cliffs surrounding it.

Small stone structures were placed at the entrance, making it apparent others had been there before. They were little shrines and had markings painted on and around them.

"Dragging you along is not something I agree with, so don't mess around today," Bastane's voice echoed off the rock, "And don't get chatty. I'm not interested in nonsense or other worlds. I intend to train while they're searching." A slow smile transformed his face. "So be prepared to be a punching bag. Let's see what you've got in your skill set."

My mouth went dry. Where was the man promising to protect me and pulling Aethars off my back?

Bastane wore his cloak with fur around the collar. His golden hair was combed, sitting along his sharp jawline, reflecting the morning sun. His stubble made him look more like a rugged prince today.

Flashes of Stephen tangled in sheets caught me off guard, making my heart race. Bastane was tall like Stephen, but where Stephen wore easy smiles, Bastane did not. Being under his scrutiny made me want to go back to the cave they found me in. Aspis and this world be damned.

But I forced my chin up, meeting his sharp blue eyes. The sun's light shone on the gold embedded in them, showing him as a son of Rem. Knowing what he planned, I wondered what was worse—being in the dark cave, dangers unknown, or out here.

But I was soon distracted by markings on the cave walls. I didn't see them at first. They were faint drawings that covered the entire cave and continued into the dark.

"What is this?" I walked closer to inspect the figures. It

reminded me of the painting on the ceiling of the inn back at the Last City. These, however, were a lot older. More primitive.

They depicted a battle. I moved further along the wall, where it showed a temple made of gold with a golden disk circling behind it.

"These paintings are our history," Bastane answered, "How we know what our past held. That one there, the gold temple, belongs to Rem—the Temple of Day. The temple lies in the south, near the desert. The little gold figures around it are the legacies of Day. The first of his children had skin and eyes of gold."

Many of the figures had crumbled away over time. There must have been three times as many children of Rem on this wall, now turned to dust. This world held a healthy population even thousands of years ago.

Other temples lined the walls further down into the dark and out of sight.

"You really don't know any of this, do you?"He was studying me, still not believing I came from somewhere else.

"No. It feels like a dream to me."

I glanced over my shoulder to the other side of the cave. Walking across, I stopped and gasped. The large black creature on the inn's ceiling was painted here and, unlike that one, intact.

Black scales and serpents were tattooed on all the Guardians' bodies, but I was wrong; it was not a serpent at all.

"It's a dragon," I whispered in awe, eyeing the very thing I was told I needed to wake.

I knew of dragons from stories. I was enchanted with the tales of dragons; their legends drew me in, captivating me, and I asked to hear those stories every time.

This dragon was black, with a long body like a snake, and its tail faded into a puff of black smoke. It had thin arms near the front of its body. Its head was more snakelike, with fangs protruding from the top of its mouth. Horns curled from its massive head above glowing golden eyes.

The dragon faced a luminous figure painted further down the

wall—*the Ikhor*. They were both hovering over a red sea, bodies of all legacies beneath them.

Bastane came up beside me. "I don't know what a dragon is, but that's the Aspis."

"This is what you're looking for?" I glanced from him to the image. "You mean in this world they exist? I could see a real, fire-breathing dragon?"

A hand suddenly clamped down on my shoulder, and Bastane twisted me, shoving me back against the wall. My head smacked against the stone, and his hand on my shoulder pinned me in place.

His eyes were livid, and his fingers dug painfully into my shoulder, down to the bone.

I struggled to push him off. "What are you—"

He leaned closer. Anger lined every angle of his face. "Never say something like that out loud again."

The knife in his free hand pointed toward me.

My own anger flared. I'd lived a long life of keeping thoughts in, knowing punishment would come with a single wrong word.

"What did I say?" I asked as calmly as I could.

"The Aspis is not a coward or a fool." His breath was hot against my face. "To suggest the Aspis would fall so low to use elemental magic is enough to damn yourself. The type of punishment you would face from a Guardian's hand is beyond your imagination."

He nudged the blade closer to make his point clear. "I will give you the benefit of the doubt this time, assuming you're smart enough never to suggest it would *breathe fire* again."

He jerked the blade away.

My back stayed against the wall, my chin tucked in. I peered at him through my lashes, fury coiling under my skin.

I'd seen the look in his eyes a hundred times before. I could see it in the villagers back home. It was pasted to the faces of every Law Keeper that walked through town—someone who unquestionably believed their truth and would take down anyone who argued against it. Someone who wanted to punish those they thought were wrong.

I haven't truly escaped, I seethed. I was still held under the thumb of adamant followers of rules and religion.

But I was too cowardly to say anything. I clenched my fists and shifted. Bastane took notice, eyes narrowing at my feet that I had placed for balance, ready to attack.

"Good stance. Should we try you out then?" His blade tipped up. He was ready to start his *training*.

"You're going to fight me while I have no weapons? Now who's cowardly?"

He laughed and nodded, leaving the cave to return with a sword.

He lifted the blade, passing it to me. I struggled with the weight of it. "I don't know how to use this, and I think you know that."

"I do know," he said, being cocky. "How do you feel about learning to use one? After the battle with the Aethars, it's obvious you haven't trained with a sword. I'll show you the basics if you like. Until we drop you off, that is."

And here I thought I was only going to get a beating. Nope, just cut to pieces. But he was right. I should learn to use a weapon. Freedom came with a price. You needed to defend yourself and protect what you had.

"Hold it like this." He showed me, lifting his own sword. Behind his arrogant smile was a watchful gaze as if this was a test. I followed his lead as he showed me how to hold it and balance my weight.

"What happened to your promise to hack off the arms of any man that laid hands on me?"

He paused. Remorse flashed across his face. "You're right." A hand went up to his hair, brushing it back. "I apologize if I hurt you. And for pushing you like that."

"Why such a reaction?"

He lifted his sword again, and I followed his movements.

"The Aspis is a hope held on to for close to a thousand years. Ever since the last one defeated the Ikhor. My entire life has been dedicated to training for its arrival. There's a lot of hatred between the Guardians and the Ikhor, along with the Aethars who worship the evil. The Aethars cause suffering, just as the corrupted magic has done throughout all of history. You spend a life living that way, and I think you'd react the same."

"Well, I haven't." Mine was a different enemy.

"I'm starting to accept that as the truth. Which is why I'm sorry, but I cannot stress enough to watch what you say around others."

"That's one lesson I should know by now. I've lived that way for most of my life."

"As much as I don't wish to build a cage for anyone, I suggest until you know more about our world, you keep to yourself. Not only are you unfamiliar with our histories, but you aren't a child of our gods. People already have a hard time trusting each other. I will refrain from attacking you, though, every time I hear something I don't like."

The corner of his mouth lifted. I nodded, ready to move on. His sword lifted, and we were past it.

Maybe Bastane was someone I could learn to like, just like Nuo. He was a pain to deal with, but he adapted quickly. He continued his instruction on the sword, going into great detail about how to move it across my body and how to move my feet while handling the blade. I rotated, holding the blade horizontally, my arms beginning to burn.

An hour later, the burn had turned into an ache, and sweat was dripping off me. I changed my mind—I didn't like him at all. He was a relentless instructor making me do the same movements over and again until my footwork was right.

"You need to build the strength to even carry a weapon. Do it again." He circled me, mirroring the movements. "Your confidence with your feet is good. You move without ever crossing them."

"I've only practiced in the dark with no opponents." In my

small home, there was little space to train, and not worth the risk of training during the day.

"Well, I think that settles it."

"Settles what?"

"Brekt wanted me to try and pick up any holes in your story while they were gone. I've never heard of a world where women were prevented from learning to fight, you talk of strange creatures like dragons, and your reactions to everything are all wrong."

"You mean all of this was to test me?" My earlier suspicion was right. He was watching my reactions.

"One of us had to stay with you today. We just made the time worth it."

I blew the hair out of my face. "So what? I get to live now?"

"I didn't say that." He motioned me to lift my sword once more.

God, how had so much happened in only a matter of days? Ready to die, then tasked with waking a dragon that would save a world of people. Now being tested for lies? I blinked several times, feeling a burning in my eyes, but no tears came.

I let loose a long breath, curbing my rising irritation. I wanted to learn how to release it all—the well that was buried inside me, overflowing with emotions. I became a speck of a soul trapped in a stone body. I longed for something to motivate me to let some of it —any of the pent-up feelings—bubble to the surface.

I simply didn't know how.

After losing my whole world, I still couldn't bring myself to cry. What would hurt me now?

There was one particular emotion I felt looking back to the last days of my life back home, an emotion that I had put in a box and stuffed into the darkest cavern of my heart—anger.

It was more than anger if I let myself dive deeper and honestly admit what was inside—it was a blinding, consuming, and suffocating rage. What had been done to me, forced upon me, made me hate.

If I were to open the lid to that box, to take a peek, I would be overcome.

I promised to keep that lid shut until the emotion inside would no longer be a heavy blow when it was released.

But for now, I needed to control my emotions.

I held my borrowed sword in front of me, wondering how long the others would take. Part of me wished to be saved from Bastane's training. The other part wanted to confront Brekt after learning he wanted to test me. I really wanted to know what was in the man's head.

CHAPTER

NINETEEN

Brekt

Brekt untied and retied his hair for the third time in the last hour. He moved through the dark cave, seeing nothing, while Kazhi and Nuo followed behind with torches.

He carried no light. He didn't need help seeing in the dark. His legacy allowed him to navigate the cave as easily as if it were day. All he needed was a little sound to guide him.

"Buh-reck-tuh."

Brekt paused, whirling around to face the two behind him, assaulted by the light of the torches.

"What," he growled.

They stood, wearing the same expression. An orange glow lit up one side of the tunnel while blue lit the other.

"I've asked you the same question three times," Nuo muttered, the side of his face awash in blue.

Brekt turned back to the dark, seeing no sign of the crystals. He ran a hand over his face. He couldn't recall any of the tunnel before now and wondered how many crystals he may have overlooked.

He was fixated on the mistake he was making. *I shouldn't have brought her this far. She could be put in harm's way. Who in the cursed*

140

Night is she? His thoughts had been on Olivia since he'd left her behind.

"You gonna talk or just be a pain in the ass?" Nuo groaned, "You know it's bad when *you* annoy *me*."

"What?" Brekt spun back to Nuo. Not even the gods were strong enough to shut his brother up. But nothing Nuo said registered. The racket of his thoughts were louder than the echoing in the cave.

Nuo and Kazhi exchanged a look.

"What?" Brekt demanded, focusing now. He folded his arms, waiting.

"This is worse than usual," Kazhi murmured to Nuo.

"He's not even drinking, and he's gone dark."

"If you're going to talk about me while I'm before you, have the decency to speak up." When neither said anything, Brekt faced the tunnel, stalking forward.

He needed a plan. He needed an outlet.

The day they found Olivia, they left her in the Last City and travelled back to that cave she was first in. With Bastane's tracking abilities and Kazhi's unique senses, they could say with certainty that Olivia had been alone, broken and dying. There were no tracks in or out, and nothing was disturbed around her.

So how had she arrived? She was too close to death to move on her own. None of them knew of glowing lights that could speak. The only glowing figure to exist was the god Rem himself. Bastane had seen him in the Temple of Day when he was a boy, the only one amongst them who'd ever laid eyes on a god.

But there was no word that Rem had left his temple. And why would the god deliver such a woman to Guardian lands?

"Brother!" Nuo's voice echoed. They had entered an open cavern, large enough for Nuo's voice to bounce back several times. Brekt couldn't recall which direction they had come from.

Nuo brought the light to Brekt's face. "If you don't tell me what's up your ass—"

Brekt whirled around. "*I* don't know what's up my ass, so how would I inform you? For once, can we hunt in silence?"

"Not until you get with it. Talk, or *I'm* going to talk this *entire* hunt."

"Ugh, I'm out then," Kazhi groaned, already walking ahead, raising her torch to the walls. "You two idiots are worse than the pricks at the north camp."

Brekt and Nuo had been raised in the blistering cold north, full of miserable bastards. The only warmth had been Nuo's relentless attempts to make others laugh. He loved an audience.

Brekt noted the shift in his small family since the arrival of this woman, Olivia. Instead of brooding, heading toward a daunting future, they'd recharged with purpose today. Except, perhaps, for himself.

Did they feel as he did? Like pieces were being set on a board, waiting for him to predict the next move?

But who had set the piece down?

A sharp stone bounced off the back of Brekt's head. He whipped around and reached for Nuo, who dodged. Brekt moved out of the torchlight, blending with the dark.

"Fucker." Nuo threw another, then another, trying to find Brekt in the dark.

"Dickhead," Brekt swore when a stone connected between his eyes, making Nuo laugh.

"I'm bored. There are no crystals here. You aren't talking. And I'm itching to get to Bellum. Let's head back outside."

"You just want attention. You found someone new who hasn't tired of your stories," Brekt grumbled.

"Well, obviously. You're terrible company."

Brekt was relieved he was not the only one captured by her intensity. She had a thirst for her new life. He saw it every time she found something new, touched something she'd never felt, or drank in their stories with wonder.

Nuo was watching her as well. He hid it with a charming personality and sarcastic humour. But his demeanour changed when he thought she wasn't looking, becoming observant and calculating. Brekt noticed the woman did something similar. She covered up what she wanted to hide from those around her. Offence and defence. They were two sides of the same coin.

"I'm dealing with shit. Remember?" Brekt lifted his hand to his hair again, stopping himself. He watched Kazhi's torch bob around the cavern ahead. She was making a circle back toward them. Brekt didn't elaborate on his thoughts for fear Kazhi would hear him.

"Why don't you explain what this *shit* is. The girl?" Nuo asked. "You said you wanted her to come with us, that you recognized her. But not why."

"Ignore what I said. I was wrong."

Brekt walked the edge of the cavern, looking for cracks in the walls and a glow that might give away a hidden crystal.

"Liar. I'll find out soon enough. Not often have you kept secrets from me. I'm the master of interrogation, remember?"

"And I'm the master of ignoring you."

Kazhi groaned, stopping before Nuo. "You two idiots are slowing me down. I'm heading down this way. Alone." She stood before a fork in the cave. The tunnel she pointed down was narrow, the air thick.

"You should let me go alone," Brekt suggested, "I can navigate the dark."

"No way you're making me stay with him," she spat, "He's too chatty right now."

Nuo simply shrugged.

"Fine. But be careful."

Kazhi rolled her eyes and swiped the crystal torch from Nuo's hands.

"Hey, that's mine!"

She shoved the fire torch at him and moved away. "If the fire goes out on that torch, Brekt can hold your hand on the way back."

Kazhi left Nuo grumbling, disappearing in the dark. She had the skill of becoming invisible, and Brekt had once thought she might be a legacy of Night, hiding her identity—hiding because the children of Night were mistrusted.

Brekt knew precisely what this world thought of the children of Erabas, and Sea-legs weren't better off. His teacher, a legacy of Day and former Guard turned instructor, had taken over North Aspis and practised his cruelty on Brekt and Nuo.

"This wouldn't be a problem if you hadn't left our second torch down in the desert," Nuo complained.

"What can I say? The Aethar hiding in the caves surprised me."

"And you didn't go back for it."

"Stop whining. It'll be there when we go back next time."

"Next time," Nuo let out a hollow laugh, "How much longer do you think we will live?"

Brekt avoided the dark question. The blue light of Kazhi's torch faded from sight. He could see every bump and groove on these walls, where his brother and sister would be left blind.

"Don't worry about Kazhi. She'd survive the cave crumbling around her," Nuo went on when Brekt didn't respond.

Brekt nodded, knowing Kazhi was far more capable than her small frame suggested. Kazhi was their scout and spy and a terrifying killer.

She had joined their group years ago and prevented them from being caught off guard on more than one occasion.

"So, you gonna elaborate on your dreams from the other night?" Nuo asked casually as they navigated down a new tunnel. Nuo assumed it was Brekt's dreams that plagued him.

"Wasn't planning on it."

"Let me guess. Aspis? No, you've had enough of those. Did you see my heroic death? Was it of a woman? Perhaps your dreaming mind has been inspired by our new company."

Nuo was goading him, and Brekt knew enough not to rise to it. It would only delight his brother more.

When Nuo opened his mouth to go on, Brekt cut him off by whipping around and grabbing him by the hair. Nuo laughed.

"You're annoying me more than usual. I think it's you that has something on their mind."

Nuo pushed him away. "Just trying to relieve some of the tension. You know I don't feel right after a hard interrogation."

The Aethar were invading their lands in more significant numbers than ever before, and Brekt had felt the changes in the soils of Arde. The magic in the crystals was glowing brighter. The tension between the people was tighter. Hatred and distrust were being bred into every child born.

Nuo was right to question what age the group would make it to. They had fought side by side for years. And they would until the end—until the coming war would claim their lives.

"Perhaps, your natural state is having your nose in a book and not your hand wrapped around a weapon," Brekt suggested, knowing that was only half true. Nuo was a natural fighter.

"Ah, but life has other plans for me."

As Brekt and Nuo travelled deeper into the tunnel, Brekt considered what they would do once they reached Bellum. For three days now, he had tried to come to a decision. He didn't want Olivia to suffer. This journey and the coming war would claim her life if she got involved. His goal, the goal of all Guardians, was to stop the Ikhor. And some magical force had sent her to be a part of that.

It was for Brekt's sake that Nuo had changed his mind about her that first night. He knew the things Brekt had seen, and Nuo thought the girl could help. But Brekt had shut down any conversation on the matter after their discussion in the Last City. He wouldn't be so selfish.

Nuo was blissfully quiet for a few moments before breaking the silence with, "She is beautiful, though, isn't she."

She was. It infuriated him how easily he lost his focus. Every time he tried to forget that Olivia was with them, that he and the others had a purpose, she would snare his attention.

"I know what you're doing. Leave it," Brekt grumbled.

"She could be a nice distraction before the battle begins."

"You're talking to the wrong guy."

"Well, I'm not talking to myself. You know my preferences."

"You'd say no to the new girl?" Brekt grinned. Nuo never said no to a willing woman.

"Gods no, never. But she's not eyeing me. Do you actually intend to leave her in Bellum? I'm surprised you've brought her this far."

Brekt had seen too much in his life to think it was a coincidence. The timing was too accurate. But still, if he had a chance to save one more life, he would let it be hers. She made him think of how life could be if they were successful. If the Guardians aided the beast and claimed victory, promising peace for another thousand years.

He veered around a corner, only to run into a large boulder and catch his toes. He placed his palms on the rock, chewing his lip. He wanted to get back outside. Searching the cave was giving him too much time to think.

Nuo groaned, and his words were lost in the clamour of Brekt's thoughts.

Brekt scowled, "What'd you say?"

"Seriously? I said we are never getting out of this cave."

A breeze fluttered against his skin as they rounded the boulder. This tunnel must lead to a second exit.

"You tell me what you want to do with her, and I'll follow," Nuo said abruptly.

Stopping, Brekt nodded, wishing they didn't have to get into this now. He wasn't sure what he believed or even what he wanted.

"Well?" Nuo lifted the torch, holding it to Brekt to get his attention. "I see you looking at her."

"And looking is all I'll be doing since the beast is soon to rise."

"Why torture yourself on missing out on some fun? This could be your last chance to be buried deep in—"

They both spun at the sound of rock crunching beneath a foot. Kazhi came around the corner. "Find anything?" she asked calmly.

"Walk louder, woman," Nuo spat.

Kazhi held the crystal torch in the air, and the blue light lit up the white strips of her skin. "I made a noise. Mostly so I didn't have to hear the last part of your sentence. You disgust me, Nuo."

Brekt held back a laugh, remembering the first and only time Nuo flirted with Kazhi. Brekt had found Nuo upside down in the training ring, naked while it was snowing. Nuo was laughing in the end, enjoying the attention, but he never spoke to Kazhi that way again. He had, in fact, been more polite to all women after that.

And since a Guardian's life is always cut short, Brekt worried his brother would never see the day he would feel more than lust for a woman. Not that Brekt ever had.

"What about you? Find anything?" Brekt took a seat on a smooth rock.

Kazhi pulled a large crystal from her bag, glowing with enough magic to refill their supplies. She shook her bag. A few others clinked inside.

"Nice." Nuo took a seat beside Brekt. The two were too large for the small rock, and Brekt was nearly pushed off. "That all?"

"Just this small collection. Wedged between a crevice. I think it was overlooked. The rest of the tunnel was picked clean."

Nuo pulled out a snack from his bag and began chewing, the sound rattling Brekt. This cave was growing too loud.

"Give me some," Brekt demanded, having worked up an appetite from stewing over his thoughts.

"Fuck off. Bring your own snacks," Nuo swore over a mouthful.

Brekt raised a brow, and Nuo shoved all the food in his mouth, anticipating an attack. He gave Brekt a brilliant smile.

Brekt punched him in the gut, making him spit his food out on the ground before them.

Nuo was left gaping at the wasted food. "I'm going to end you."

"Learn to share."

Kazhi took a deep breath, rubbing at her eyes.

As they made their way back to the camp, Brekt's stomach

worked into a knot, thinking of Olivia again—her face, her eyes, her mouth. She wasn't what he expected.

This woman was supposed to help wake the beast? He couldn't see it. He had been searching endlessly, as they all had, for answers on how to wake it.

Every answer was vague, shadowed in a thousand-year-old tale. The Aspis always won and brought the people peace, but the cycle never ended. The magic returned to the earth until it rose once more.

Nuo had combed through every library he could. He had spent months in the grand Guardian City where the Guards were meant to dwell, looking for answers about the beast and the Ikhor. Some tales said one would wake the other. Others said the first to rise would gain power over the people. History became unclear when a thousand years passed, and books were often rewritten.

Brekt peered over at Nuo, regretting not telling him the whole truth, knowing his brother would be upset once he learned Brekt had been keeping things from him.

"Nearly there," Kazhi informed, as the sounds of Bastane's laboured breathing echoed in the cave. Brekt worried for Olivia. Bastane was difficult to converse with.

When Bastane joined the north camp, their teacher reluctantly accepted Brekt and Nuo because they worked well with the Council's *golden prince*. So, he made a team out of the three (and eventually Kazhi) to create a force the north couldn't contain. Their skill then reached the attention of those in the Guardian City.

Brekt was reluctant to return to the Council, who had requested their presence in the city to the south. He didn't want Olivia going there either. He knew they would be tasked with searching out those who opposed the Council and eliminating them.

It was another task that Kazhi took on. Her past had given her the skill to hunt and disappear unwanted Aethar sympathizers.

That's what you were deemed if you went against the Council and the rules that governed Guardian territory.

The Council would hear Olivia's story and use her to find the Aspis. They would work her to the bone.

No, Brekt must keep her story secret for now.

They reached the opening, the light filtering in around them. Brekt strode toward the cart. Kazhi stopped to pass the crystal torch back to Nuo after he extinguished the fire on his.

Bastane was working line drills in the shade. Brekt searched for Olivia, worried Bastane had run her off, when her head popped out of the cart, hearing them approach. The relief Brekt felt from seeing her troubled him. He didn't need this distraction.

But his relief quickly grew to concern when Olivia jumped out of the cart, crossed her arms, and silently watched them approach. It was the first sign of anger she had willingly shown. However, she didn't come closer.

Bastane's feet stopped. "Find anything?"

"Yeah, a small bag full. How'd it go here?" Brekt replied, carefully watching the glare from Olivia. What had upset her?

Nuo and Kazhi were not far behind. And Brekt heard Nuo miss a step when Olivia rounded her narrowed eyes on him.

Bastane offered no information, so Brekt continued toward the cart, knowing Olivia wouldn't likely speak up.

"Why are you still testing me?" she demanded, surprising him. "Haven't I proven I've told you the truth?"

It was there, on her face, how her cheeks reddened. He could see the resemblance now. Her nose had scrunched in concern, making his head go blank. He felt himself harden, thinking she had looked adorable. And he hated that he noticed it.

Brekt tried to focus on what she was saying. She was angry.

"I asked him to watch you." He folded his arms. Anything so she didn't see them shake. "Because the direct approach wasn't getting much information out of you, seeing your face change every time someone asked you a question. Nuo's too friendly with you, but Bas doesn't go easy on anyone. I knew he would notice more than any of us if something didn't line up."

"And you thought holding a sword against me was the best way?" she fumed. Her face changed, worried, but she continued, "I don't appreciate being tested. You want to know something? Ask me, don't scheme behind my back." She stomped toward him.

How long had she been waiting to confront him? It was as if a fissure had cracked in her walls.

"It's not like I trust you either," she scolded him, "Should I be testing holes in your story?"

"You don't have the luxury of options right now, Olivia." Brekt was letting his already worked-up emotions get the better of him. He stared down at her when she stopped directly in front of him. This close, he could appreciate her grey eyes—stormy yet warm—flash with anger. He hoped and prayed he didn't give away his thoughts. His cold words were the opposite of how he felt. "You have no other help being offered to you at the moment, so you should take what you can get. We can leave you here with no change to our travels. It's you that needs us."

Nuo groaned next to Brekt and hid his face beneath a hand.

"Why are you nice to me one moment and so mean the next?" she didn't take her eyes off him.

"Good question," Nuo mumbled, and Brekt avoided the urge to strike at his irritatingly nosy brother.

"People can lie with words," Brekt's voice was low now, almost apologetic, "but eventually, they will slip. I didn't think it was *mean* to make sure we weren't harbouring an Aethar and taking her across Guardian lands with a free pass. It's called caution."

It was also called '*he needed to know who she was.*'

"The solution to finding those answers isn't to point a knife in my face."

Brekt's questioning gaze moved to Bastane, who answered with a muffled cough.

There was a snicker from the side, and Olivia ripped her attention to Nuo, who was hiding a smile.

"What?"

"It's maybe the first time I've seen Brekt berated by a woman."

"I give him trouble all the time," Kazhi added from behind them.

"You don't count," Nuo and Bastane said together.

Brekt felt uncertain about how to handle the situation. He stumbled over words. He was without practice when it came to arguing with women, probably because women didn't usually *berate* him.

But he lost track of the conversation when his mind kept repeating; *it's her.*

CHAPTER

TWENTY

Liv

"Well, what do you want to know anyway?" My hands flew through the air, trying to release my frustration. "Aren't you ditching me the first chance you get? There's nothing more you need to know about me. All I want now is to be left alone and free of my past. I don't want to be looking over my shoulder, making sure I'm careful with everything I say and do. Which now, thanks to you," I directed my anger toward Bastane. "I feel like I have to be on guard again."

Brekt stepped forward, getting further in my face, and it took everything in me not to cower before him. My first real confrontation was not going well. I wanted to tell him how angry I was. But my mess of emotions was scrambled with all the things I didn't say.

"I want to know what kind of person we might leave behind," Brekt growled, "I want to know if this image you're portraying is true. But I also don't disregard the fact that we found each other for a reason. Forgive me if I am trying to figure out the why of it while still following my duty."

Something was nagging at me—some itch under my skin, the pull on a cord I couldn't see. Brekt wasn't telling the whole truth. There were questions as he sized me up, waiting for me to reveal something—something he expected and didn't explain why.

"Don't be so upset, Bones." Bastane patted me on the shoulder.

I was about to turn my frustration on him when Brekt added, "It's a caution, not meant to be insulting."

"Whatever," I huffed, deflated. The mess of words in my head didn't form an acceptable retort.

"We should get packed up," he finished, taking the bag of crystals from Kazhi.

"Can I see?" I couldn't meet his eye, even when my curiosity about the crystals overruled anything I felt about the test.

Brekt's lips twitched, hiding a smile, and he nodded.

He strolled over to the cart, set the bag down, and lifted a purplish crystal out. He passed it over—it was heavier than it looked.

It wasn't like any stone I'd touched before. I expected it to feel cool to the touch, but it was warm. And there was a humming coming from it. I moved it to my ear to it.

"It's the magic," Brekt smiled. "This one is packed, making it hum with the power. The cave was mostly empty, but Kazhi found this deep in the tunnels. It'll power up some weapons, and we can make some more magycris from it. The liquid that healed you can also give you a boost of power and strength."

"And once the crystal is emptied of magic, you can make pretty things with it?"

He laughed. "Yes, but very few want an empty crystal. It's not a sign of wealth by any means. Empty crystals usually become trinkets. Things children collect and wear."

"Well, I don't care about that. I think they're lovely, like my brush."

I handed the crystal back, wondering what was next to come. They were loading up the horses again, and Nuo was in the front seat of the cart studying his map. I went to join him, interested in learning about their geography. I caught a quick glimpse of poorly sketched forests and caves, almost like a kid's drawing, before he folded his map, seeing me approach.

"Where to next?" I asked.

"Bellum is southeast of here. We can offload some of the horses and items we don't want there. I'll get someone to cut up the crystal for our weapons and an alchemist to make us magycris. Then we will find you a place to stay. This city should offer you some work and a decent home if the Guards decide not to meet you."

He said it like it was nothing. I knew it was coming, but I was stung by the casual way he mentioned leaving me. Even after such a short time, I was sad to say goodbye.

Perhaps I may yet find a way to wake the Aspis, but it would not be with these four.

Maybe I was lying to myself when I said I didn't want anything to do with the Aspis. I was waking up with a spark of excitement in the morning—a seed of hope planting itself in a long, dead wasteland—a feeling I never imagined for myself again. Yes, I was also easily upset by these people, but there was something about being pushed. I've never had that before.

Brekt was loading the bags on his horse. His hair was coming loose from the knot he'd tied. He seemed rattled.

Would I ever see him again once they left? The thought that I never would, bothered me.

"Does the Aspis talk?" I asked Brekt, who froze when I approached his horse.

"What kind of a question is that?" He stayed focused on his horse.

I didn't dare admit I hoped the Aspis could talk if I found it.

"I just wondered."

"The last time it roamed these lands was around a thousand years ago. I can't say any of us know what it is like. I do know, however, that there is no record of it speaking." He was fighting back laughter.

So I was back to hoping I met these Guards and that they had answers. And what if I came across the Light once more? What if it took away any choice I might have and *forced* me toward the Aspis?

Brekt tightened a strap holding his bags. "Did you see the cave paintings? They weren't as deteriorated as some."

I nodded, "I saw the Temple of Rem."

"What about the others further in?"

When I shook my head, Brekt left and approached the cart where Nuo sat, pulling the crystal torch from his bag. Nuo lifted his eyes from his map, giving me a smile when Brekt returned, leading me deep into the mouth of the cave.

Brekt led me past the Temple of Day. He shone the blue light on the wall, pointing to a black temple with a white star overhead.

"What is this one?" I asked.

"The temple for the god of Night, Erabas." He lifted his hand to the wall and rested it against the temple there.

The figures under the Temple of Night—Erabas's children—all had glowing eyes. They had varying shades of skin, but they all stood staring forward as if guarding the cave we stood in.

I peeked at Brekt, remembering his iridescent eyes, and shivered.

He pointed to another that was blue with a ripple over top.

"The Temple of Sea."

The figures under Mayra's blue temple looked like something I had seen before, like a drawing I had made in my childhood of a story my mother told. The story was of a woman with a fish tale who lived deep in the sea.

The hair on the figures here floated above them as if they *were* underwater. They had three gills along their necks, and some of their hands were webbed.

"These two, the Temple of Night and Sea, are long lost. No records for the location of the temples of Erabas or Mayra exist."

"Why do their temples no longer exist?"

"That is also lost in history. But one thing I know is their

SARAH L. ROSE

legacies are least favoured. Perhaps the gods were not liked, and
their temples destroyed."

I found him peering out toward Nuo. Were they unliked only
because of the blood they carried?

"It's said the gods of Night and Sea were terrors compared to
Day and Mountain." Brekt lowered his focus to me. My heart
kicked up under his stare. "They were cruel to their worshippers.
After a time, they did not find enough satisfaction in the peace
between their children. It's said that Erabas grew jealous of Rem.
Rem was seen as the most powerful of the gods, and his children
loved him dearly.

"Erabas wanted more power. He was said to be hungry and
cruel. He wanted his children to be as desirable as the golden
legacies of Rem. So he battled Rem himself, trying to destroy the
god of Day, but instead, he destroyed vast landscapes and tumbled
entire cities under the oceans. Erabas lost the battle, and it's said
he was never seen again.

"No child has been directly blessed by the god of Night since he
left, and the bloodlines thinned. Either the temples never existed,
or the children destroyed the temples and let them fade from
history. Only markings like this suggest they might be real."

I was enamoured with the sound of his voice, only partially
taking in the story. "So when did the first Ikhor steal the magic of
the gods? Before or after Erabas died?"

"The timeline doesn't specify."

"And no one has tried to find the lost temples?"

"Oh, many have tried over the years, groups who wish to serve
those two, but they don't have a huge following, unlike Day. The
legacies of Night have been nearly lost to time as Erabas is lost in
our histories. And Sea-legs? There are yet many, but their bloodline
has weakened severely as if Mayra has too left her seas." His head
nodded to the many golden figures standing around the golden
building. They did outnumber those under Erabas's dark temple.

Brekt moved further into the dark to the last temple with trees
all around it. "The Mountain Temple. The god Ouras blessed his

children to blend into the landscape of Arde. His temple lies to the east of the swamp lands."

"And all these figures are his legacy?" The people were drawn as half animal. Some had tails, spots or stripes. Some were crouching on all fours. "Some of them have wings!" I said, turning to Brekt.

He concentrated on the wall. "The bloodlines have changed over the years, but some still bear the full power of his legacy."

I returned my focus to the temples, wonder filling me. There was never a religion to learn about back home, aside from my mother's stories.

"So I will meet people who can fly?"

"Probably not." Brekt gave me a lopsided grin. "They are mostly stories now."

"Not true," Nuo boomed, coming up behind us and making me jump. He nodded toward the cart, pushing Brekt and I to follow. "You forget the Desert Eagle."

Bastane, who had been listening from atop his horse, snorted. Brekt coughed to hide his laughter.

Nuo looked affronted. "Don't tell me you don't believe in him, Bas."

Bastane fixed the reins in his hands. "Every little boy learns of the feared Desert Eagle, and each pretends they will grow to be him. If the legend existed, which I doubt he did, he's long dead and just another story."

"What's his story?" I asked.

"Hop up in the cart, BB. I will tell you on the road."

"His own mother tried to have the legend killed. But he flew far from home. To the desert lands between the continents—in the Canyons of the Lost."

Nuo sat forward, resting his arms on his knees, the reins tied before him and began to tell of the famed legacy of Ouras—a pure-blooded child of the Mountain god—who, out of spite, rebelled against his family's high status and cruel ways to become an outcast and help those in need.

"He's remained there ever since, never returning home, guarding the passage. He has become a vigilante, ferrying lost souls trying to pass between the continents. They say he is biding his time and will rise again and destroy the remaining members of his family who continue to ruin and rule the people of his homelands."

Suddenly I found myself wishing for a hero like that—one who could have saved us all from the Keepers.

"You said he flew from home. How did he fly?" I leaned closer, eager for more.

"With his wings," Nuo sang, eyes going wide.

"Like on the cave drawing?" My voice rose.

"They say his wings are bigger than any of his bloodline before. That even when he flies high above you, he will block the light of the sun. The only warning before your death."

"But wait, if he had wings, then why did he never leave the Lost Canyons—"

"Canyons of the Lost," Nuo interrupted.

"Right, Canyons of the Lost. If he flew there, couldn't he fly away?"

"See Bones?" Bastane interrupted, riding to my right, sounding like he was trying to hold in a laugh. "It's a silly story told to little boys who want to be heroes. The Desert Eagle is a favourite. Protect the weak by taking from the rich. Nuo's teacher threatened to send him to the Canyons dressed as an Aethar when he misbehaved as a boy. It's a perfect bedtime story and a warning for those who want to grow up to be a great Guardian."

"And why that didn't suit a boy like you, Bas, I can't imagine." Nuo leaned back in the cart. "Perhaps growing up being praised by the Council made it harder to find interest in such heroes. Poor little orphan boys, however, would eat it up every night before bed, hoping to one day be a legend like Desert Eagle."

I glanced toward Bastane to find his face neutral. Why was Nuo so offended?

"I like the story of Desert Eagle," I said.

Nuo lit up. "You've got fine taste, BB."

"Can you show me the Canyons of the Lost on the map?" I asked innocently.

Nuo pursed his lips, so I switched tactics, "I saw it already. Your attention to detail amazed me."

Brekt, riding beside the cart at Nuo's side, hid a laugh. Only Nuo fell for the compliment.

He pulled his map out, explaining as Guardians travel, they make personalized maps—where they've located crystals, stashed treasures, weapons and machines they can't always take along with them. A Guardians map is a very sacred item, and Nuo took charge of the map belonging to his team. He'd been building it for years.

I took note of how compliments easily swayed him.

He had drawn their large continent, Veydes, which connected to a second land mass of similar size at the southern point. A sea was between the two continents, and oceans surrounded the rest.

"Only two continents?" I asked.

"There are only two left. There used to be more, but they were swallowed by the ocean or destroyed long ago."

"Destroyed? How do you destroy a continent?" Then I remembered what Brekt had said about Erabas.

We exited the rocky canyon and hit a dirt road, riding as the sun lowered in the afternoon sky. Miles of rolling hills lay ahead.

"Depending on who you ask, there are different tales of the past. Everyone tells a different version of how lands were lost, but Erabas is mentioned in all of them."

Nuo was good at weaving a tale. I was mesmerized by the rising and swelling of his stories.

"At the time of his leaving—which may also have been his

death—many changes happened here on Arde, and much was lost. People don't like to talk about it because differing opinions drove a wedge between the legacies. They have been the cause of many wars."

"Why don't you have any symbols on the Aethar lands?" I wondered.

"There's nothing to mark down. It's all barren lands with small pockets of Aethars, mostly living in the south close to the canyons. As I said before, any to have crossed their borders have not returned. Some say that to leave Guardian lands is an insult to the gods. They say the gods will curse you by turning you against your legacy to become crazed like the Aethars. They worship the Ikhor, not their creators."

"How could you turn against your legacy?"

"It's only a tale to scare people from crossing the borders, but perhaps the gods can give as much as they can take away."

Brekt was watching as Nuo told me tales. I would peer over at him between stories to find his attention darting back to the road ahead.

The afternoon passed quickly, and before the sun was gone from the sky, Brekt stopped us to make camp for the night.

I stretched, jumping out of the cart, and helped unload the tents, listening to Nuo and Bastane argue about who they thought would win in a battle against the Desert Eagle.

CHAPTER

TWENTY-ONE

"I win again," Nuo shouted from across the fire. He and Bastane had been playing cards while I ate in silence. A strong wind whipped my hair around and threatened to take their discarded cards into the air.

Kazhi was out in the dark of night, scouting for more Aethar and Brekt was in the cart at the edge of camp, watching the dark. We had stopped on the top of a large hill, with enough rock to hide the fire and two tents already set up near the cart.

Before I went to my tent, which I would be sleeping in alone until Kazhi returned, I sought out Brekt, who had been assigned guard. He was slumped against the backrest in the wagon's front seat, with his giant sword leaning beside him.

I pushed against a growing wind, hoping it didn't worsen or my tent would be taken with it.

Hearing my footsteps, he tore his attention away from the night, his posture tightening. Our eyes locked, and I couldn't ignore the rush I felt seeing him framed against the black sky, gazing down at me like a god of Night himself.

The cool wind blew strands of hair across his face. The long scar running from temple to jaw was hidden in the gloom, but his tattoos were a stark contrast, the night making them come alive.

Something in his face changed—a shadow passed over him. Perhaps he wished to be left alone.

"Is it dangerous for her to be out in the dark, scouting for Aethars?" Why had Kazhi gone and not the legacy of Night? Would she be caught in the growing storm?

Tension in his shoulder eased as he chuckled, "*She* is the danger in the dark. Kaz is a unique warrior. She scares even me. Her strength isn't in muscle but madness."

"Madness? Is she not stable?" Who was I sleeping beside at night?

"In a manner of speaking, no. Her senses are unreal. She's not like anyone else. If someone ever tried to disappear, Kazhi would find them." He looked at me as if considering continuing. "She has been hired before for her skills and used in an unfriendly manner. She keeps to herself, and it's often hard to know what she's thinking. I'd stay on her good side if I were you."

"How do I do that?"

"Good question," he mumbled.

Had I already left her good side?

A low cooing came from the night beyond. I strained to see past the cart where it had come from.

"A night bird." Brekt pointed to a dead tree that was difficult to make out. There was movement and a flash of eyes from high up on a branch. The cooing came again, and I saw a faint outline of a large bird with pointed ears.

"It's terrifying," I whispered. "And large."

"Most people have never seen one. They do not typically show themselves. Their wings, when spread, reach further than both my arms. But they aren't interested in attacking you. They want the creatures that scurry on the ground."

"Why is this one here then if they don't show themselves? I think maybe it does want to attack us." I inched closer to the wagon and Brekt's sword, never taking my eyes off the black bird on the dead tree. Its long beak curled down below its hauntingly round eyes. Its massive talons, larger than my hands, wrapped around the branch.

"Night animals have never been afraid of me."

I quickly looked away from the bird, just in time to see the smirk Brekt was trying to hide. "If this guy scares you, I won't tell you what other animals I've found walking up to my tent at night."

This was one of those moments I wished I didn't have an active imagination.

"Has any of them tried to eat you?" I wrapped my arms around myself as a shiver went down my back.

"No, there is something about me that makes them curious. I imagine all legacies of Night have this reaction to night animals."

"Have you not asked the others?"

My focus was stuck on the bird, who hadn't moved. Maybe Brekt was right—perhaps the night bird was just watching him.

"I've never met another legacy of Night."

That surprised me.

"You haven't met any? How?"

Nuo mentioned something about how there weren't many legacies of Night. And their god was gone from this world.

"I don't know if there are any left. If there are, they have not wanted to make their presence known."

"That must feel lonely."

The look that passed through Brekt's eyes told me I was right.

"It can be. Then wouldn't you also feel lonely, Olivia? There are no others like you in this world."

He searched my face, again seeking some answer. For the first time in my life, I felt like someone was seeing under my mask and knew what lay beneath. Brekt's inquiring stare caged me and my heart skipped. He was a flame, and I was drawn to the bright kaleidoscope as it burned, unable to look away.

"I—I hadn't thought of that."

"But you aren't alone, Olivia. Neither am I."

When I didn't answer, he continued. "We are all different, and we don't choose our friends because they share the same ancestry.

We are more alike than we are different. If you need help, you can ask us."

My chest squeezed. The sentiment surprised me, and I turned back to the bird. Brekt's words reached a part of me deep within, to a loneliness that had existed for far longer than my few days in their world.

"Thank you," I said quietly. "I should get some sleep."

"I hope you sleep well."

His soothing timbre followed me as I walked from the cart. I squeezed my arms tight around me as the cold wind picked up.

As I neared the tent, watching the fire where Nuo and Bastane still played cards, I jumped when a form suddenly took shape out of the dark.

Kazhi walked into camp, steps steady and hair unruffled by the wind as if it didn't dare touch her. She truly looked like she was made of madness, that even the foulest wind would not set her off course.

Entering the tent and flopping down onto my furs, I eyed the gap in the flaps of the door. I could make out the massive form of Brekt sitting back in the cart. I smiled, laying back and closing my eyes.

I fell asleep feeling safe, full and a little less lonely.

TWENTY-TWO

I was restless all through the night with dreams of running through an endless forest, a woman screaming "*Stop*" echoing all around, while scarred men were chasing me. When I tripped over a root, fingers wrapped around my ankles. The hands were bloody, knuckles bruised from what they had done to the woman screaming. I gaped upwards into red, angry, scarred eyes. Blood started dripping onto my face. The neck of the Aethar split open before me, and a torrent of blood rained down, drowning me. Before the blood pulled me under, the Aethar moved his lips, mouthing the words *Wake the Aspis.*

I woke in a sweat, rubbing at my face.

My head swam, and I had difficulty remembering where I was. It was the dead of night, and snoring came from the tent next to mine.

My eyes adjusted to a soft glow from outside—a moon lit up the night sky. There was an outline of a small figure with lengths of hair sticking up at all angles in the tent beside me.

I took a deep breath, not wanting to fall asleep in case the dreams returned.

A shuffle from outside turned my blood cold. Dirt crunched under heavy feet. My breath caught in my chest as a large figure entered the tent and crouched down. Before I could react further, Brekt's deep voice broke through the racket in my chest.

"Kazhi." He reached out to shake her leg. She sat instantly with a knife in her hand. He must have anticipated it because he grabbed her wrist, whispering, "Next watch."

She nodded, grabbed something beside her bed, and crouched outside.

My pounding heart had nearly calmed when Brekt's massive form entered the tent. This time, my heart stopped. But he only leaned over Kazhi's makeshift mattress and flopped down.

Had I missed them changing beds the night before? I had woken up to an empty tent this morning, not realizing they switched through the night.

Brekt was on his back, and a large breath left him as he settled in, arms lifted above his head. A moment later, his breathing turned heavy, and he was asleep.

It made sense he took her bed as his was most likely taken. My nerves, however, did not care about sense—I was sleeping alone with a man.

A dangerous, sexy, and easily reachable man. This was against so many rules.

I concentrated on my breathing, slowing my pounding heart, reminding myself no one was coming for me. And moments later, combined with the sound of Brekt's heavy breathing, my eyes became heavier, and I started to drift back into my dreams.

And this time I was in a river, in a naked water fight ...

I awoke again in the early morning hours. The sun, having not quite yet broken over the horizon, cast the inside of the tent in a grey-blue tone.

I was on my side, my hands tucked under my head, facing Brekt's bare back.

His sizable tattoo stood out against his tanned skin. It was the body of the Aspis. Claws reached over his shoulder, and the beast was surrounded by smoke. Black characters ran along its form.

I was admiring the muscles built along Brekt's ribs, which were within arm's reach, when he moaned and shifted, turning onto his back.

My breath caught, nearly choking me, as he settled once more. The blanket was pulled up to his midsection, leaving his chest bare. I was not unaware of the hard planes of his chest, nor the muscles built along his side. But it was lower where my attention caught, how the blanket was pitched below his hips.

Pitched high.

I licked dry lips, glued to the spot where his arousal showed. A shocking amount of heat rattled me, seeing how significant this man was. In *every* way.

The fact that he slept so close I could reach out and touch him did not go unnoticed. A small part of me—okay, a massive part of me—wanted to do just that.

I forced my gaze away from the hard, swollen bulge under the blanket and took in his sleeping face. Sleep usually shows the softer side of someone's features, but not this man. Though the look of fatigue had receded, he was still intimidating and strikingly sexy.

His lips were slightly parted, inviting—

He moaned again, mumbled something incoherent, and his arm went down. A muscle tightened in my core as his hand went under the blanket—and *moved*.

The blanket shifted back and forth. I couldn't look away as he palmed himself slowly, asleep. I had never seen Stephen do such a thing, and I found it ... sexy. I didn't want him to stop.

I tried to stay quiet, not to wake him. I wanted him to continue his sleepy massage, but the fear crept in, the one that always prevented me from taking what I wanted. I went to turn, to avoid getting caught, but the movement triggered something in Brekt's awareness.

He stopped what he was doing, rolling to his side toward me. The hand that was seconds ago palming himself came to me, grabbing me around the waist and pulling me to him.

Even in his sleep, he was strong. I slid across the furs and the gap between our bodies closed. His hard length pushed against me, digging between my legs where warmth was building, turning it higher.

He felt unbelievable, and I closed my eyes to enjoy the sensation. I should not want his touch this badly. I should pull away. He was practically a stranger. But his warmth, his hard—

He tugged me closer, burying his face in my neck and whispering my name.

Hearing it on his lips sent me into a fever, razing my body. Was he dreaming of me? I shivered from the thrill even when I should have been stopping this.

I exploded with desire as his scent hit me, wild and masculine. I was surrounded by it, consumed by it. His lips moved against my neck, kissing the sensitive skin, and the stubble of his chin grazed along my jaw.

His lips were deliberate in their path down my neck. Was he not sleeping? I should be terrified. I should be scared of being caught. I should not be filled with longing for him to continue.

Most nights, I wished for a body next to mine, remembering how the warmth felt with Stephen. The feel of Brekt wasn't comparable. He saturated the space around us, filling it and drawing me in.

I reached up and grabbed onto his arm as his lips found my cheek. To hold him close or to move him, I didn't know because that was the moment I made a noise so tiny but so damning.

His eyes opened a crack.

But he wasn't awake, not really. The hand on my hip moved up my side, sliding under my shirt and branding my bare skin. He was almost to my chest as he muttered, "I can feel you," in a deep, gravelly voice. I put my hand against his shoulder to finally push. I would be mortified if he knew I let him continue.

His eyes opened fully then, dazed, taking me in. He glanced down to see his hand resting under the soft skin of my breast. His lips twitched, and I focused on them, hovering above my own.

"Looks like it wasn't just a dream." The twitch of his lips became a lazy smile. A sexy, sleep-filled smile.

He *had* been dreaming of me.

Slowly his hand slid back down, though he deliberately kept it against my skin, grazing my side. He kept his eyes on mine as his fingers reached my hip. I was burning from the indiscretion. I finally pushed him, weak against the size of him. But he moved away, throwing himself back down on the furs with his arms above his head, seeming perfectly unbothered.

Confusion and anger twirled in my chest. I grabbed the blankets, pulling them over my head with a moan of frustration.

He laughed outside my thin fortress. "Is it men you're not interested in, or is it me?"

"Excuse me?" I threw the blanket back down. "You're the one who got handsy while half asleep. I was trying to be respectful."

He was teasing me. A gleam in his eye showed he was trying to make light of the situation. But the tension lining the edges told me he also felt embarrassed—maybe he wasn't so unbothered after all. My anger dampened. Slightly.

The tent opened, and Kazhi's head poked in, "Breakfast. Pack up." Then she was gone.

Brekt sighed, facing the ceiling.

"Sorry," he muttered, not moving, sounding like he was saying it only because he ought to.

"I am interested," I said without thinking.

He looked over, brow raised.

"In men, I mean," I quickly added.

His laugh was low and deep in his chest. His attention wandered down below his hips, where he was still hard.

"I hate mornings in these fucking tents," he groaned.

He sat up, trying to cover himself with the blanket.

I caught his eyes sliding toward me before shifting away. There had been an emotion there I didn't understand—longing, but also something like sadness, guilt and confusion.

It was a fraction of a moment we sat there while I tried to figure out what it meant.

The smell of breakfast hit me, and my stomach growled, breaking the tension. Bastane had caught us something to eat today.

"Let's go," he grunted.

The strange look was gone—frustration taking its place.

Not needing much to be ready for the day, I scrambled out of the small tent. I didn't know what my appetite was craving more, the meal outside or the temptation I had just left behind.

CHAPTER
TWENTY-THREE

I turned my horse to follow Nuo ahead, the sun beating down above me.

"Olivia." My name was succulent in Brekt's deep tone. He rode up beside me, slowing to match my pace.

"About this morning, in the tent ..."

I kept my face neutral but what I felt inside was anything but. I withered in embarrassment.

"Mmhmm?" It was all I could get out.

"I wanted to make it clear it wasn't intentional."

"Of course, I—"

"At least at first," he interrupted. A ghost of a smile touched his lips.

My mask slipped, and some fevered emotion rose to the surface. "W—What does that mean?"

"Well, I *am* a man, and you are ..." He surveyed me while he found the words. It was like back in the river, I was exposed, my clothing doing nothing to cover me.

"I'm what?" I gritted.

He sighed and went back to watching the road ahead. "You're unanticipated. That's all."

"That's twice you've said something like that."

"Like what?" He was concentrating on the horizon, avoiding meeting my glare.

"Like there was something you did expect."

He gave the impression he was hiding something, and it frustrated me that I couldn't get a straight answer from him. Was he surprised when he touched me this morning? A woman who looked nothing like them?

"It's nothing."

I blew out a breath and kicked my horse into a run, irritated at the cryptic comments.

Perhaps Brekt didn't find me attractive—I had no unique gifts from a god, and the women I've seen so far all wore tattoos. Maybe he was confused about why he would want to touch such a 'bare' woman.

Whatever. I didn't need to care. I barely knew him. We might be saying goodbye soon. They might be handing me over to the Guards and forgetting I was even here.

But I was soon disheartened, for those were the last words he spoke to me for several days.

Nuo's map didn't portray how far their lands stretched. The others hardly spoke to me those few days on the road. They had their eyes ahead of them, and I caught them whispering to each other several times—Nuo and Brekt most of all.

Last night at a campsite close to a trickling river, I overheard them arguing about leaving me in the city. I couldn't tell, but it seemed Nuo was arguing against it.

Nuo had once claimed that he led the group. He most certainly directed them, with Brekt being a silent observer. But when I watched them closely, I noticed they all spoke to Brekt when it came to me, and Nuo often went to him to discuss other matters.

I retreated further into myself as the days passed. I didn't have anyone to talk to, although I wasn't making an effort either. They hadn't bothered to ask what I wanted, and I still thought it was a mistake that I was brought here to raise a beast from a thousand-year slumber.

If they were going to leave me, that was fine. I told them everything I knew. What use would I be now?

The problem was with all the quiet time on the horse, my mind wandered too often back to my world. Would the armed Keepers continue to search for me? Could that strange Light transport them too?

My worst fear manifested slowly over those quiet few days—if I failed to help wake the Aspis, would the Light come for me? Would it return me home?

I couldn't let that happen.

I squeezed the reins so hard my knuckles turned white. I held them as if I could tether myself to this world.

Brekt had been riding close to me this morning, but whenever I looked over, his focus was far away. Even when the other Guardians tried at conversation, he wasn't interested.

I needed a distraction. And I think he did as well.

"How fast do these horses go?"

Brekt's face slowly changed—a gleam in his eye made me regret asking the question. "Want to find out?"

He shouted something, and both horses kicked off, galloping faster than I thought possible. I stood off the horse's back as it sped down the sloping hill between the purple flowers and flowing grass.

My hair was a stream behind me, the air whipping through it. The horse was a force of its own—the power of its hooves hitting the ground vibrated through me. I'd never felt so alive.

I laughed in wonder. I became the wind chasing the shadows of clouds across the hills. I was a force that could not be stopped.

I let one hand go of the reins and held it out in the air, allowing the breeze to flow through my fingers. My eyes closed, turning off the world around me, heightening the sensation of flying through the air.

Something deep in me settled. A muscle relaxed, a thought calmed, or maybe a part of my spirit was reignited. A little bit of life seeped back in. Just like I had felt back at the river, days before, I sensed something stirring within me—something awakening.

We rode like that to the top of the next hill, slowing as we reached the peak. With the new landscape revealed at the top, I finally beheld the city of Bellum.

It was nestled in a valley surrounded by hills. One side was a wall of rock, cut as if a giant's blade had come down and taken half of the hill. The city had been built against the cliffs. Pathways cut into the cliff leading to the top, where there was a lookout over the city. The buildings were low to the ground, only a few going more than four stories high.

The city was large enough to fill the entire valley. Roads from all directions led into the center, and they were busy with riders and carts.

"What's it like?" I asked Brekt.

"It's mostly a trading city, but there's a lively community at night."

Would he ask if I wanted to stay here? Nuo had joked about sending word to the Guards, but when I asked him about it last night, he shrugged it off.

"So what now?"

"It's far from the dangers to the south where Guardian lands meet Aethar. Bastane, Kazhi and I believe it's best we leave you here."

"This is not Guardian territory."

"No. This territory is part of Veydes, they consider themselves free, but the people here do not side with the Aethar."

I looked back to find the others far behind, waiting for Bert to bring the cart along.

"I have to meet the Guards." My back straightened, and I looked Brekt dead in the eye.

He was taken aback by my sudden demand. "Why?"

"I know you don't believe me about the Light I saw. But I know what happened. It told me I needed to wake the Aspis."

"Olivia, you can't even hold a sword. How can I expect you to follow the Guards when you're a—" His jaw clenched.

"What?" I pressed. "I'm a what?"

"You are a liability," he growled.

I turned from him, hiding the emotion I couldn't mask. But he was only confirming what I already thought—I wasn't of any use. I had the title 'Bag Boy' and could barely help with that. I wasn't a legacy, I didn't have any valuable skills, and I knew they didn't trust me with their secrets. If I was supposed to wake the Aspis, I was the least capable of doing so.

But he couldn't stop me. I wouldn't allow it. I whirled on him. "I can't go back."

Having nothing to offer made me angrier at the life I had been given and the choices taken from me. It chipped away at any identity I might have made for myself.

"If I was brought here for a reason, I must find out why. If I fail to do so, the consequences might have me returning home. What if the Light finds me again and, seeing me fail, takes me back?"

He opened his mouth to argue, but I wouldn't hear it, "I will not go back there. I *chose* to run from those men. I will be the one to control how I die. If this journey is so dangerous, then it's the death I choose for myself."

He stayed silent. Something I'd said seemed to have sparked interest in his eyes.

"I have a second chance at life." I continued, "For some reason, I was brought here, and I want to find out why. I am meeting the Guards whether you take me or not."

He wasn't the only one surprised I had put my foot down.

A power in me was growing.

I kicked my horse into a run and left him behind. If they wouldn't help, someone in Bellum could tell me how to get to the Guards. I didn't care what he thought of my outburst, but perhaps he didn't mind it because I swear I heard laughter as he followed.

TWENTY-FOUR

The city of Bellum was alive and unlike anything I could have pictured back in my world. The movement and commotion were like a beating heart and people of all shapes, spots and colours moved like lifeblood through its veins.

Unfamiliar sounds and scents hit me. I relished every second of it. If people stared at me, I didn't notice.

Nuo suggested that if anyone asked, I should say I was a legacy of Sea and wasn't blessed with gills. Bellum was far enough from the sea that I could avoid proving I was a strong swimmer. The truth was, I hardly knew how to swim.

We walked down a busy street with carts full of food, furs, building supplies and weapons, all moving with no discernible pattern or order. We'd left the horses and cart back in the stables near the city's entrance.

My earlier anger had left me by the time the others had caught up. And Brekt had been ... cheery.

A finger came to my chin, closing my mouth. Nuo was chuckling at my expression. All around me were men and women with tattoos and painted skin. Those that didn't have tattoos had many piercings and wore jewelry all over their bodies.

There were people like Nuo with gills on their necks and some that had slightly webbed hands. Most often, the skin of the Sealegs was pale and some greenish.

There were more legacies of Mountain than in the Last City. Ouras's children came straight from a fairy tale. They were the easiest to find—spotted skin, cat-like features, scales, fuzzy pointed ears, fangs, and some with tails.

I didn't see any pure-blooded legacies of Day, but there were those with golden skin and some who walked close by with semi-golden eyes. They all looked as Bastane had described—tough people that could handle themselves in extreme conditions.

If there were any children of Night in this city, I saw none.

Nuo pointing us northward toward the market.

The sun shone down on buildings of pale stone, and others made of red wood. They were simple and packed tight together.

Market stalls had canopies dyed various colours with markings painted to display the symbols of their trade. People were on the streets yelling their prices and drawing you in with clever phrases. I smiled at those who caught my eye and tried to wave me over.

This was the most human interaction I'd ever experienced at once. Usually, if I was in a crowd, my head was down.

I soaked it all in, pushing down my fear of being so seen. The seed of hope I carried deep inside grew a little more. It cracked and sprouted a small root.

Brekt was walking ahead of me. His tall form stood out easily amongst the crowd. People parted for him and the other Guardians as they moved through the street.

So it wasn't just me who found them intimidating.

Two women stopped their shopping as our group made to pass. They both had raven skin, their eyes prominent, and they had small fangs on the top row of their teeth. As I got closer, I heard them whispering as they watched Brekt walk ahead.

"That's Erebrekt of the North. What's he doing here?"

"I hope there's no trouble. I thought he was supposed to be at the Guardian City."

Erebrekt?

He had once asked me if I knew him, saying some did. Was his reputation one that caused whispers as he passed?

Who was he? These four Guardians I travelled with were known.

My questions faded as we entered a square-shaped maze of market stalls. The commotion of the markets bombarded me.

Along the square's northern edge were stalls to buy and sell animals. The centre was for clothing and fabrics, and the southern end had endless stalls of food.

Kazhi walked past me, spoke quickly to Brekt and took off down a southern street.

Bastane said he was off to speak to a horse seller and headed north.

Brekt turned to Nuo. "Take Olivia to find some new clothing. I'm going to grab us some food and ask around for a good crystal smith. Kazhi will be back to let us know where we are sleeping tonight." He left us there, not saying a thing to me.

Nuo had a concerned frown as he watched Brekt disappear down the street.

"Is something wrong?" I asked. The two women's concern after seeing Brekt had me worried.

Nuo plastered a smile on his face.

"Nothing at all. Let's do some shopping Olivia. This is going to be fun." He finished with a wink.

He threw an arm around my shoulder and led us through the central markets, weaving through stalls of leather and furs.

"Now, BB, I happen to be what one would call a fashion connoisseur. Specifically women's fashion. I can tell you what would be perfect on any woman's body and, with one look, can have them sized up accurately for a fitting."

"One would think you stare too long at women."

"One would be absolutely correct. How do you think I end up knowing as much as I do? By asking?" He surveyed me like it was a ridiculous thought. "I will help you find something that accentuates all the right parts."

"I'm not sure I really want your help now that I think about it."
I tried to push him away but couldn't stop from smiling. "Next
thing I know, you'll have me dressing scandalously."

"Now we're talking." He squeezed my shoulder before he
released me and walked into a ring of stalls lined with women's
clothing. "See if anything catches your eye."

I walked along the stalls taking in the peculiar attire. I didn't
know where to start. One stall sold dresses that seemed bulky and
heavy, and I moved past those. I found another and lifted a piece of
fabric that was soft and flowing and meant to wrap around your
body.

"If you don't want to look scandalous, I wouldn't go for those
wraps," Nuo mentioned behind me. "What about these?"

I walked to the stall where he held up a simple top and loose
bottoms. They were, of course, black. "Is there something that has
more colour?"

"Not a black girl, huh? It hides all the blood and dirt," he
suggested, "What about this?"

"Pink doesn't seem the right fit either. How about this one?" I
held up an emerald-green set.

Lifting it to my chest, Nuo nodded his approval. "It brings out
your eyes. Perfect."

"My eyes have no colour. They're just grey."

"Your eyes are full of colour, BB. You need more imagination."
A half smile lit up his handsome face. His brown eyes were deep
and rich, just like my mother's.

"Are you staring at *me* now?" I said, nudging him.

"There's no man in this city that wouldn't. Now let's get you in
a stall to try them on."

I paused to study him. There was no laughter or trickery to his
voice. "Why would men stare at me? Because I don't have tattoos?
Or because I am not a legacy of a god?"

"BB," he said, arching his brow, "You're a beautiful woman.
You must be aware of that. You said you didn't have a man at

THE GUARDIANS OF THE ASPIS

home, but we all know that was a lie. Did he not tell you that you were beautiful?"

"He told me a lot of things that didn't end up being true," I said, remembering all the things Stephen said but didn't do.

"Well, you can ask as many men as you want, and everyone will give you the same answer."

"But Kazhi said I look like I belong in a temple."

"Everyone has their kinks."

I considered what he said as he led me to the changing stall. When he went to close the curtain, I opened my mouth to ask but then closed it, shaking my head.

Nuo guessed what I was thinking. "Yes, I know he thinks you're beautiful too."

"Wha—What do you mean? I didn't ask you anything."

Damn Nuo for being so observant. I took the curtain and closed it myself. I could hear him laughing outside as he waited.

Why did I even care? The man in question was leaving on a grand journey in the next day or so. Most likely without me.

I could admit to myself he was good-looking. I could accept it was more than that, that he was good-looking in a way I had never seen a man *be* good-looking. I was drawn to the dangerous weapons and his skill at being formidable and mysterious. And once he left, many others could fill those shoes. Right?

Brekt couldn't be the only man that drew me in like that, and I would prove it once he was gone. I had no reason to linger on thoughts of him. Instead, I should be happy I was getting out of this large top that didn't fit.

The new clothing was soft, and the fabric was thick. The pants were loose, almost like a skirt. They came up high on my waist, and thank goodness because the top didn't go very far down. It hugged my ribcage. The neckline cut into a v-shape, showing off the tops of my cleavage, and the sleeves sat low on my shoulders, going three-quarters of the way down my arms. I couldn't see myself, but I felt elegant. Yet it was very practical, and I could move around easily.

I eyed the boots I still wore. I wasn't offered new shoes. I was fighting to avoid the images of Stephen repairing them, his long fingers and strong hands working his tools and polish.

I opened the curtain to find Nuo waiting close by.

"Dear gods, BB." He grabbed his chest. "Blessed Rem. I think my heart has stopped. You'll notice men looking now."

"Not too revealing?" I glanced down at myself. The shirt was tight on my heavy chest. "What am I thinking? You're the worst person to ask that."

"You know, you're absolutely right. But I think you're decent enough. I only worry people will ask too many questions about your god, but you should be okay saying that your mother had very few signs of being blessed by Mayra and that she passed none onto you."

"Do any Sea-legs you know have missing gills?"

"No." He paused. "But Sea-legs tend to be ignored in most places, so you should be okay."

He paid the seller and bought me a long black cloak to keep me warm when needed. Nuo also said some might assume I'm a child of Ouras with a possible tail in my loose pants.

"You'll have to make do with the one outfit for now. We don't have a lot of extra coin on us."

"I will find a way to make my own coin. This is great. Thank you."

He nodded, his jaw set. He didn't agree with leaving me behind to figure this world out on my own, and I appreciated it. I really could be good friends with Nuo.

"Why do I feel you are the only one who would keep me around?" I said.

"You made my brother laugh."

And that was the only reason he gave me.

He headed east, opposite the direction we entered from. I wanted to ask him more questions, but he was moving too fast. How could making Brekt laugh be the reason he would help me find my answers?

Walking amongst the stalls, I *did* notice men looking my way, and for the first time in my life, it wasn't against any rules for me to enjoy it. A weight I had been carrying was chipping away slowly.

In some ways, I was still terrified of being seen, but I'd lived so long trapped behind the mask. I wanted out. If my first step was showing a little more skin, so be it. It felt *good*.

There was a whistle to my right, and I turned to see Bastane catching up with us. "The Median style suits you, Bones."

"Median?"

"The areas too high to be south and too low to be north. We group them in as the Median. These clothes are brought up from there," Nuo explained.

"My family farm sits on the northern borders of the Median," Bastane added, "It's a blend of Guardians and farmers, and in the east, you'll find many of Ouras's worshipers."

Nuo soon took off, heading back to the stables where Bert and the horses were tied. He was going to take the animals to the seller Bastane had found. Nuo was the best negotiator in the group, effortlessly charming people to agree to his price.

I followed Bastane, who was stuck 'babysitting' as he put it, and we reached an area selling weapons and tools.

I walked up to a table displaying all kinds of knives and swords. Some of the weapons were very plain, and some so enormous I don't know how Brekt could even carry them. A pair of thinner swords caught my attention.

I touched the hilt of one of the beautiful swords. It was curved and had symbols etched into the blade. The second blade was a copy of the first. There were three indents where crystals sat. The guard above the handle was a disk shape that circled the blade like a blooming flower. The handle was wrapped in purple-dyed leather and had empty clear crystals set down the length of it. The crystals shone in the light of the sun.

I picked one up, trembling as I held the weapon. Checking that I wasn't being watched.

An old man with stark white hair and pointed ears covered in white fuzz came over, thinking he had a buying customer.

"Those are twenty coins for the pair—a very reasonable price since they come all the way up from the Sand Cities. But if you are to buy them, my dear, I'm willing to let them go for fifteen. A beautiful set of swords should go with a beautiful woman."

Bastane scoffed, "I've been down there, and swords sell for much cheaper than that, old man."

The grizzly-looking man grabbed the sword out of my hand and countered Bastane.

"Thirteen coins and they're hers. They will go so well with your striking features, sweet child."

Shivers danced along my spine. It was not from the man who called me a *child* but from a presence behind me. I felt him there before I heard the timbre of his voice. The air around me was heavier.

"One lesson with Bastane, and you think you can handle two swords?"

I spun, craning my neck to find Brekt smirking, his dark stare fixated on me. The brightness from the sun made shadows dance across his features.

There was a pause in the world around us. All my senses focused on him. The scar running down the side of his face stood out in contrast against his tanned skin. He scanned my new outfit, but if he enjoyed the view, he didn't say.

His hand went to his hair. He stopped himself, lowered his arm, and he gave a soft shake of his head.

My hands ached to pull him close, to feel him as I did in the tent. It made no sense to one as inexperienced as me. I should be drawn to someone like Nuo, who was open, carefree and easy to talk with. But next to Brekt and the force in which he commanded my attention, Nuo was just a handsome man.

Brekt was wild, intimidating and terrifyingly beautiful. I had no explanation for why he made me feel breathless yet frustrated.

"Kazhi has found us a place to stay," he said to Bastane. "Two rooms for tonight. Go find Nuo and help bring back any items we haven't sold off today. I'll take Olivia with me to sell these furs."

I then noticed the bags hanging over his shoulders. My heart sped when Bastane left us alone.

I followed Brekt as he left the large square. He navigated us down smaller streets, weaving between buildings.

"Nuo has the shirt I borrowed from you. Thanks again for that." I wished I could come up with something more to say. My time with him was coming to an end. Questions I had about him would forever go unanswered.

"You're welcome." He walked stiffly beside me. Maybe he didn't want to babysit me, either.

"You've been to this city before?"

He nodded. "All four of us have travelled far. Part of our training is seeking out different instructors. This city is a great stop for trading and making money. People from all over the continent stop here with items to sell. You can find almost anything in the market back there."

His words were clipped, like he was forcing conversation.

"Will you be leaving tomorrow, or are you staying a few days?"

He stopped suddenly and faced me, a hand coming up to his jaw, rubbing the stubble from his day-old beard as he stumbled over what to say.

"I ... We—" He sighed and gazed down at me. "I am sorry to leave you like this, but we've got to keep moving. We have somewhere we need to get to, and I can't bring you along." The tension in his voice made me regret asking him anything at all.

"Because I'm a liability?"

His eyes scanned mine. "Something like that."

Every time I talked to him, I felt more confused and bothered by his hot and cold attitude.

"Olivia."

His hand lifted as if he would sweep the hair out of my face, and I didn't dare move. My chest thundered in anticipation of his touch.

Instead, his hand lifted to his own hair, moving some stray strands out of his eyes.

"This—it's not something I can handle right now."

"What do you mean? What isn't?"

His hand came down, and he was shaking his head. "Nothing." A strange emotion passed over his face before he turned to continue walking.

"You can call me Liv," I said to his back.

He looked over his shoulder at me. "What?"

"You can call me Liv. I don't usually go by the name Olivia. People close to me call me Liv."

His head tilted to the side. "I haven't heard you use that name before."

"I hadn't corrected you yet."

"Right." The strange look stayed on his face. What did *that* mean?

He continued down the street, no longer walking as if he was uncomfortable. His focus was now far away like I had given him something to think about when I mentioned my name.

I knew Brekt was hiding things from me, but at that moment, I had this odd sensation that he knew something *about* me. Was Brekt connected to that strange Light too? If he were leaving in the next day or two—which he never answered—I would never find out.

We reached a small shop. It was on the bottom level of a four-story building with a window that housed a large shelf you could walk up to and do your business.

"Wait here," Brekt mumbled before he approached the shop.

The owner was a bulky man. His skin was rough like he'd lived a hard life and his face was serious when he nodded to Brekt, knowing the Guardian who approached.

Brekt dropped his bags and proceeded to negotiate prices with the man. I couldn't hear what they were saying. I could only see when the man shook his head and then nodded when he finally came to a price he would pay. He filled up a small bag of coins and passed it to Brekt.

I followed Brekt as he headed back in the direction we came from. He was counting the coin as I watched the people on the streets. Men and women entered secluded patios with chairs set up and drinks being served. Couples sat close while they enjoyed the shade.

I realized today was the first time I had walked around in public alone with a man—first Nuo, then Bastane and now Brekt.

My sister would die from shock if she knew what I was up to. In her eyes, I always attracted trouble. But she was wrong. I was the one seduced by it—lured into the idea of doing something new and forbidden. She said I was like the pirates in my mother's stories who were lured under the water by the songs of the undersea women.

My companion elicited a new kind of thrill, calling something to me, and I wanted to dive in.

People moved out of Brekt's way as he strolled down the street. He didn't seem to notice the impact he had on his surroundings.

Erebrekt of the North.

Brekt stopped, focusing on his hand held out in front of him, considering something as he eyed the few coins in his palm.

He pursed his lips and passed the coins over. "Don't tell Nuo it was me."

I looked down at the pile of coins and back to him, wondering what I should use them for.

"Let's go." He nodded down the street and led me back to the markets.

Without realizing it, I was led back to the table displaying all the swords. I finally counted the coins he gave me. There were thirteen.

Something was caught in my throat, and my heart tripped over the thirteen coins in my palm.

"You're back," the white-haired seller said, coming over to us.

Brekt pointed to the two purple-handled swords. "She will take those two for thirteen, and that includes wrappings for them."

The seller looked over at me, and I nodded my head once, unable to speak for fear of my voice cracking.

"They will be a good fit for you, my dear, and they already have their own cases." He reached below the table, pulling two long strips of hardened leather attached to a belt. The leather was dyed a dark purple with silver threading throughout and jewels embedded along the side. They were beautiful.

Brekt was handed the swords as I passed over the coin.

He gave me a tight smile as he reached for me, wrapping the belt around my hips with a sword on each side.

His closeness made the air pulse around us, and the sun became hotter, warming my face. His breath fanned my cheek as he leaned down.

My hands shook. I wrapped them in the loose fabric of my pants to stop Brekt from seeing. Fear and wonder fused in my chest, undoing me.

I had my own weapons.

I was *free,* and I was *armed.*

Brekt—he had helped me get here. He had brought me out of that dark cave where I was dying and armed me with blades. He didn't just save me—he was raising me up so I could save myself.

When he was done, he stood back. My pulse quickened as he checked me over, lingering on more than just the swords. "Suits you. Learn how to use those properly, and you'll be a force ... Liv."

I blushed, hearing my name. It was sultry in his deep voice.

A gift—this new life was a gift.

"We should get going. Kazhi will be expecting us. And food." He patted the one pack he had left with him.

CHAPTER

TWENTY-FIVE

Everyone was waiting for dinner when we reached the inn. Bastane lifted a brow at my new swords, then rolled his eyes at Brekt. Nuo noticed right away.

"They suit you, BB. But may I ask how you found coin to buy those?" He scanned the room, stopping on the culprit.

"An admirer bought them for me," I said.

"Mmm-hmm. I suppose we won't be missing coin if I count it tonight?"

"How would I know?" I shrugged, moving to the table where dinner was being laid out. Brekt had bought a beautiful spread of new flavours for me to try.

Tonight might be my last dinner with the group before they took off. Where would I be in the next day or two, and what would I be eating?

Kazhi walked up and inspected my hip. "You'll need a good instructor to teach you how to use two at once."

"I'll ask around."

"Kazhi would've been able to teach you." Nuo flashed a look to Brekt.

Ignoring the reminder that Brekt didn't want me coming

along, I lifted a sword from its case to inspect the symbols. "What do these mean?"

Kazhi scanned the blades, which I noticed had different symbols on each. "They are old sayings written in the old language of Day."

"You can read the language of Day?"

She gave me a look, suggesting I shouldn't ask any further.

Nuo joined us to inspect them. "I haven't seen this writing before."

"Maybe you're not as well read as you like to tell everyone." She patted his shoulder.

He scoffed and returned to the table. "Who reads stuffy old proverbs anyways."

I smirked, trying not to laugh.

Kazhi read the first poem. "This one translates to, *You can move an entire mountain, but one piece at a time.*" She returned it and lifted out the next blade. "This one reads; *A broken crystal still holds power.* Looks like whoever owned these swords needed a reminder of the power they held."

I ran my finger over the symbols. I could swear they were more than just metal. A tingling sensation travelled up my fingers as I touched the old language.

"They speak to you." Kazhi's voice was low.

"What do you mean?"

"I think these were meant to make their way into your hands. Just as you were meant to make your way here. Hold tight to them and remember their words."

A shiver went through me. I felt like a piece of a puzzle was sliding into place. They did feel right, and the proverbs did speak to me. I had never felt like I had the power to move mountains.

I was thinking of Kazhi's words as we finished dinner, when Nuo announced there was a celebration tomorrow night in the courtyard behind the inn—a wedding. Guests were already piling into the rented rooms, and an early celebration was starting tonight. Meaning the group was staying at least one more night with me in Bellum.

The other two men were cleaning and sharpening their weapons. I watched as Bastane explained the technique to me. Brekt mentioned he had found a crystal smith and would head to his shop first thing in the morning, and Bastane would make an appointment with the Alchemist.

Nuo had his glasses on as he worked on his notes. His serious face was back. He had changed into a lighter fabric to get prepared for a night of fun—he would join the wedding celebrations downstairs.

His shirt was loose and open at the collar, and his sleeves were rolled up to show off the corded muscle along his arms. His vest with all the pockets was tucked away, transforming him from intellectual mapper to suave partygoer.

The inn was a four-story building sitting next to the rock cliff at the city's south end. Both rooms faced a grey stone courtyard lined with benches and tables for eating. A fountain stood in the centre, and tall trees along the outer perimeter created privacy from the businesses next door.

Pathways led up the cliff behind the inn lined with lanterns hung for the wedding. I was curious to see what a wedding even looked like.

Nuo invited me down to the tavern below to see the decorations and drink with the guests who'd arrived early. He told me it would be celebrated tomorrow through the night until the new day so that the Night and Day god could both bless the union. They would dip their feet in sand and water for Sea and Mountain's blessings, and when midnight hit, they would be husband and wife.

I considered going with him. I did wish to go. I wanted to experience for the first time being amongst a crowd with nothing holding me back.

But fear overrode the excitement and the temptation. It was one thing to try something while no one was watching, but to be in front of a crowd where anyone could see? It had my heart thumping just thinking of it.

Even earlier, while Brekt and I walked to the inn, I hid the swords with the cloak Nuo had bought me. How would I find and face the Guards of the Aspis? I couldn't even brave a party.

So, I decided not today—but maybe one day.

The rest of the group agreed to join Nuo. They left their larger weapons in the rooms, taking smaller concealed weapons, just in case. Bellum was a trading town, mostly neutral, but you always had to be cautious, Bastane had warned.

I grabbed my bag, holding my crystal-made hair brush, and headed to the second room that Kazhi and I were sharing.

I lit the candles spread throughout the room. I laid my purple-handled swords and my black cloak on the bed. I took off my boots and put my brush down as well.

I took stock of my few belongings. I was rewriting my story. These four items made up my identity now—the mysterious woman from a faraway world.

I didn't have many belongings back home, only a few weather-worn pieces of clothing to keep me warm. The only other items in my small shack had been a stained mattress with furs I had sewn together for a blanket, a foggy mirror and a pot and pan to cook with. Anything else I wanted, I had to make—even friends.

I never admitted to my sister or Stephen that I was lonely. Who wouldn't be in that forest? So, I used my time making myself little creatures out of acorns, sticks, bark and whatever other materials the forest provided.

None of the creatures made sense to look at. They weren't people or animals. They were all made-up beings from my mother's stories, each unique and magical. I gave them all names, and eventually, they all felt like they had their own personalities. I would talk to them when I was sad and yell at them when I was angry. And I knew they wouldn't leave me.

A pang hit my chest thinking of my creature Millie and the

others I abandoned. It made me feel silly, but nonetheless, I pictured them waiting in the same spots where I left them.

I had said goodbye to them before I had fled from the Keepers the day they had shown at my door.

I considered that keeping sculptures made from twigs wasn't the best company to keep oneself sane—let alone for seven long years.

I didn't miss home. I didn't miss my sister or even Stephen. But my little creatures I had made from nothing—I regretted leaving them.

Would anyone visit my shack one day and see them? Would a child find them and take one home?

Stupid things to think about in the situation I was currently in. Maybe in this world, I wouldn't have to make friends from sticks and acorns.

I had fallen asleep listening to laughter and music from the courtyard below.

By the end of the evening, I regretted not going. What would've happened surrounded by four Guardians? I'd lost a chance at trying something new and, instead, let myself stay in bed and stew over things from my past.

Somewhere between the bad memories and falling asleep, I decided I would make the most of this world. I might be terrified and hide from every new experience, but I would wake up and try.

Although, my dreaming mind had other ideas. Gruesome dreams plagued me before a loud banging woke me. It took me longer than it should to remember I was in Bellum in a cozy bed at the inn.

There was a candle flickering, and Kazhi's dark silhouette was sitting on her bed, looking toward the door where the banging had come from. She was still dressed, bed still made, meaning she must have just recently returned to the room.

Whispering came from just outside the door when Kazhi stood to answer. There was a knife in her hands, and her footsteps were silent as she crept forward. Another loud bang made me jump—it sounded like an entire body was thrown against our door.

I reached for one of my new swords, which I had put at my bedside before I had gone to sleep. Holding the weapons made me feel braver as I rose to my feet.

I braced myself as Kazhi grabbed the handle and yanked hard, whipping the door wide. A drunken Nuo landed hard on his ass inside the threshold.

"What are you idiots doing?" Kazhi scolded Nuo, who was now groaning on our floor. "I didn't think I would have to babysit you the entire night."

"I'm not the idiot," Nuo slurred, tilting his head backwards to look up at Kazhi. "That one is."

Around the doorframe was Brekt holding onto the wall.

"He insisted he check on Olivia. He's drunk and having one of his moments."

Brekt was flushed from the drink. There was a crease between his brows, and the circles under his eyes were darker in the candle-lit hallway.

"Why would you need to check on Olivia? She's been here all night. I'm in here with her." Kazhi's tone suggested she was not surprised by how annoying her brothers could be. She seemed more exasperated than angry, as if this happened often.

Brekt stepped forward, swaying, nearly joining Nuo on our floor. He grabbed the doorframe to steady himself. "I saw a flame. Flickering. I saw it under the—" The explanation was cut short by a loud hiccup.

Brekt moved to enter the room, but Nuo pushed him back with a foot in the air. He scrambled to his feet to grab onto Brekt before the man fell back himself.

"He thought the room was on fire. The man's seeing things." Nuo began to shove Brekt back toward their room.

"You thought the room was on fire?" I giggled.

Brekt looked up at me, just realizing I was standing there. He sobered up when our eyes met, standing straight, eyeing me up and down as if worried I had been hurt. Nuo threw an arm under him to lift him to stand.

"Like I said, he's seeing things." Nuo pushed him again, unable to get Brekt to move.

"You are okay, Liv?" Genuine concern lined his features.

"I'm fine. There was no fire."

Brekt nodded once, seeming to accept I was fine.

Why had the sight of a flickering candle set him off?

"Night, night, *Liv*." Nuo smirked before he closed the door behind him. He was muttering something to Brekt in the hall, too quiet to hear.

Kazhi was shaking her head as she returned to her bed.

"What did Nuo mean when he said Brekt was having one of his moments?"

I set my sword back beside my bed, next to its twin.

Kazhi twisted a blank expression toward me. The candle flickered behind her silhouette as she considered how to answer.

"Out of the four of us, only Nuo was set on becoming a Guardian. Nuo had no family and no prospects for a future. There was nothing outside the Guardian camps for an orphaned Sea-leg. He likes the challenge, he likes the travel, and I think he even likes the attention. He's known for his skill in battle.

"Bastane was pushed by his family as punishment. He never needed to become the Guardian he is now. His family is well off, and he could have become a politician in the Guardian City like his father. His family owns a large farming business that his older brother now runs, so he will always have things to fall back on. Why he stayed, I don't know.

"I was asked to join the three of them when we met at North Aspis. I was employed elsewhere before then—unsavoury work—

so I was happy to follow the three who became my brothers. Becoming a Guardian was the better option out of many bad ones.

"Brekt, however, like Nuo, had no other options. As a legacy of Night, you are not looked down upon like the Sea-legs are but rather feared. They call them the dark children. Night legacies are rare, and people don't trust what they do not understand. Night legacies have gone missing over the years, and I know only of one Guardian who is a son of Erabas. I sometimes think Brekt chose this path because Nuo did and wished to keep his brother alive."

"You said missing. You think someone has been killing them off?" I was shocked at how much Kazhi was willing to tell me. Even more so, that Brekt could truly be the last of his legacy.

"I know they have been disappearing."

"How do you know?"

She didn't reply. I had a feeling this was part of the many things she's done and seen in her life. Had she been involved? It was not information she was willing to share, so I asked, "Why did Brekt not want to be a Guardian then? If he had no other options."

"Brekt is good at what he does. He's the best. But something haunts him. I see it eating away at him—over time, it has worsened. Nuo was polite, saying he was having a moment in front of you. We usually say he's *gone dark*—fitting for a dark child.

"Brekt does everything in his power to keep us out of harm's way while Nuo leads us directly toward it. I think it keeps him awake at night. Whatever he's seen in his past, he does everything he can to prevent it from happening again."

"I know what that feels like."

"Do you?" Surprise flickered across Kazhi's face.

I nodded. "I have nightmares almost every night about things that I've seen. Many times it's my mother's face. Now I've started seeing the Aethars at night too. Maybe—maybe I should talk to him."

"You might not get answers, but it doesn't hurt to try."

I looked up at her in question.

"He doesn't want you to get hurt. He wants to leave you here to keep you safe. Nuo wants to take you with us. I think he sees how you could be of use, and not just for finding and waking the Aspis. They watch over each other. Nuo wishes for Brekt to experience more out of life.

"If Brekt knows you can handle hard times, maybe he won't worry so much. The two idiots won't stop arguing about it, and it's annoying. Maybe you and Brekt can talk about how you both go dark sometimes, and he can lighten up a bit."

I laughed, hearing the concern even through the insult. I envied Brekt and his *family*. He was lucky to have someone who cared enough to notice.

I asked Kazhi if she had anyone she loved, and I think I found my answer. Hers was a family she made.

I felt I understood Brekt a little more, but the way he looked at me tonight ... he was scared something had gone wrong.

Once more, I wondered if there was something important, something he knew about me, that he was keeping to himself.

TWENTY-SIX

Brekt

He was an idiot. An absolute idiot. How many ways would he embarrass himself in front of her? And he thought Nuo made a fool of himself for women. At least Nuo did it deliberately.

Brekt stumbled into their room, head pounding and stomach rolling. Drinking into oblivion did nothing to ease his growing concerns. Instead, it loosened his lips to the point where he'd told Nuo everything.

"You need some water," Nuo grunted, hauling Brekt across the room.

Nuo's eyes had gone wide when Brekt admitted he'd seen Liv before. That he knew her face as well as his brothers. Yet the woman they all were coming to know was nothing like the one he'd seen.

Brekt fell into a chair, smacking his head off the backrest.

"So when did she become *Liv*?" Nuo teased, handing Brekt a glass of water. The cool liquid slid down his chin as he gulped.

Brekt shrugged. "She told me to call her that."

Bastane was already passed out on the bed, looking as if he were about to fall off.

"But you didn't remember her as Liv."

Brekt shook his head, regretting the action immediately. He bent, putting his head between his legs. "Nothing is aligning with my memory. Gods. Damn them all. I can't take much more of this. Things were already too much before she showed up."

There was a loud thud, and Brekt lifted his head enough to see Bastane had crashed on the floor. Brekt covered his mouth because the desire to laugh was nauseating.

"Curse all you want, brother. The gods won't answer. You know I've tried," Nuo slurred.

Nuo cursed the gods in a multitude of colourful ways. He had been orphaned as a boy, his family slaughtered by Aethar. The gods answered by condemning Nuo to a life as a Guardian.

"She's going to hear about us on the streets now that we've left the north. Who we are and why we are here," Brekt muttered, holding his head. "I want to tell her."

"It was you who said not to." Nuo threw his hands in the air. "I can't keep up with you."

Brekt snorted. He couldn't either. "It's eating me up. Everything is happening too fast for me to make sense of it." Happening as fast as the room was spinning around him.

"You can't tell her anything yet. It's not just your secrets. It's all of ours. You argued that Bastane didn't want to reveal our mission yet."

"Fucking Bas. And Cursed Night. When she finds out, she will be angry with me."

But maybe he wouldn't mind seeing her light up with anger. How far he had fallen, to want to anger her so he could see a glimpse of the woman he knew.

She had been worried when Brekt stormed into her room. But he couldn't escape this feeling that she would meet her end because of him, because he couldn't let her go. If he could find a way to send her far away, he would.

"No, you wouldn't," Nuo answered the thoughts Brekt had said out loud. "She's in too deep now."

"Don't say that," Brekt growled, making Bastane sit up suddenly with a knife in hand. Bastane scanned the room, passing over the other two, then closed an eye, grimacing, before landing back on the floor.

Brekt would never tell Bastane about what he knew. The Day-leg would have little patience or imagination for such things. Bastane was eager to get to the Guardian City, where his father sat on the council, eager to please them all.

"Do you remember anything else about her? Anything that confirms it's her?" Nuo sat at the edge of the bed closest to the door. He, too, looked pale, and Brekt wondered which one would be sick first.

"The girl I knew wasn't afraid. She wasn't a stranger to this world."

He wanted to ask her, demand if she knew him, remembered him. He tried finding recognition in her eyes, but it was never there.

A small smile lit Brekt's face, one he hid while Nuo discarded his knives. Liv had caught him in the tent waking from one of his more colourful dreams. Thinking of the flush on her cheeks made him shift in the chair, hiding the signs of his desires.

It had been too long since he'd been with a woman. And this one—what god was toying with him, making his dreams become flesh and blood?

In that tent, her pale eyes were glazed when she looked up from beneath him—when he realized she felt too real to be a dream. He hadn't missed the longing hidden there, mirroring his own.

"What I don't get is that all of your previous dreams had been easy to understand. You knew what they meant. What's so different about her?" Nuo asked.

If only the woman who'd haunted Brekt's dreams all these years had been the one he'd found in that cave.

CHAPTER
TWENTY-SEVEN

Liv

I woke refreshed and ambitious. I drank some water and prepared to go outside and start my new journey.

I was alone in the room, Kazhi nowhere to be found. I strapped on my new swords, grabbed my cloak, went to the next room and knocked. No one answered. I tried again, and I heard a moan from inside.

I opened the door, which hadn't been locked, and found all three men passed out in uncomfortable positions. Only Nuo had made it to a bed. He was the one moaning.

He was sprawled across the bottom in the wrong direction. His head hung off one side while his feet floated in the air off the other.

"Bee-bee." Nuo's hand lifted in the air in a pathetic wave, and I couldn't help but laugh.

I stepped over Bastane, who was between the two beds on the floor. I put a pillow under his head, and even with the movement, he didn't make a sound. I grabbed Nuo underneath his arms and pulled him enough that his head was no longer hanging at a strange angle. He gave me a pathetic smile and fell back to sleep, snoring.

Brekt, however, I had no hopes of moving. He was sprawled across a chair. His head was against the backrest, tilted sideways, and one leg was hanging over the arm. I moved a water jug next to him and filled three cups.

It was strange that warriors would let themselves get to this state. They were utterly vulnerable to anyone who walked in.

As I turned back to my room, Kazhi was coming in the door with a tray of food. She jerked to a stop, finding me hovering over Brekt.

"I was looking for everyone and saw they're all passed out. I was just leaving." Why did I feel the need to explain?

"I have food for when they wake up. You'll want some, too, I suppose." She sat the food down on the table next to the water.

She was right, I was hungry, and I had no idea where to buy food. I grabbed a handful of bread and sat down on the empty bed.

"You're not hungover," I stated.

"One of us needed to stay sober in case of a threat." Her eyes found mine as she said threat.

"Me?" I questioned around a mouthful of bread.

One of her eyebrows shot up. "Hardly. Though I don't know you well enough to say you aren't a thief."

I rolled my eyes and took another bite.

"Why did you sleep in the other room then?" I asked.

"I didn't stay there. You passed out soon after the drunks were banging around, and I returned here to watch over them. They were too far gone to be of any use to themselves."

Meaning she had left me alone, vulnerable. I shouldn't feel insulted, but I did.

"What's on the agenda today?" I asked.

"We have yet to find a proper crystal smith, and one of the idiots will visit the Alchemist."

"Can I go?" I didn't even know what an alchemist was.

She gave me a sideways look. I was not invited.

I sighed, "Then I'm going out to walk the streets."

I stood, taking a strangely shaped fruit and pocketing it for the road.

"Don't get lost. I'm not interested in spending the afternoon searching for you."

"I won't go far."

"And don't get hurt. Brekt would kill us."

I halted, almost at the door. "And why would he do that?"

"Beats me," she shrugged, "Whatever you've done to him, I can't say. He acts like you two have known each other for years."

I left puzzled. What she said echoed this feeling I had been questioning. The more I thought about it, the more confused I was. Nothing could explain why he would care.

I mulled over what Kazhi said as I went back to the markets. I wandered for hours inspecting the items and foods of their world.

They had everything. The weapons stood out most of all, and I wanted to learn what each one did. There were many weapons made without crystals. Perhaps the crystal-powered weapons were less common than I thought.

The weight of my swords under my cloak grew. Brekt had spent their coin to buy me these twin blades, which I hadn't realized the value or rarity of.

It was past midday when I made my way back to the inn. Along one street, a glimmer of golden light caught my eye. I headed in its direction, curious if someone was selling something I'd never seen.

As I drew closer, I realized it wasn't a something, but a someone. A being covered entirely in gold stood on the corner of the street, speaking to those who passed by.

The man was bald. His skin was gold from head to toe. He wore gold rings in his nose, ears and other unique places—chains connected from ears to nose and jingled as he moved.

This was a pure-blooded legacy of Day—a child of Rem. Though his skin wasn't real gold, it matched his jewelry and the clothing draped around him.

Children sat before him, and several adults stood along the street. All had stopped to watch him speak.

I moved closer. The man's soft voice wove a captivating speech to the children. He was at the beginning of a history lesson. He paced before them, moving his arms and jingling his jewelry to make his tale more dramatic.

"Tens of thousands of years ago, our world Arde was ruled by the four gods. It is known that time began when the gods and Arde were made as one. One cannot exist without the other. And each god undertook a role.

"One god chose to rule the day, taking on the likeness of the sun. One decided to head the night and became an obsidian abyss. One took to the seas and became the ocean tide. The last ruled the land and became a mighty mountain, home to all manner of beasts.

"Together, the four made the world a harmonious place. Our world was prosperous, and Arde grew crystals filled with natural magic. The life of the planet powered the gods' magic. It flowed through their veins.

"They then bore children. The children took on their likeness and aided in keeping the land, seas, days and nights full of life. Time passed, and all was as it should be.

"But one day, a child of the Night—a dark child of Erabas— took it upon himself to ask the gods for more. They were powerful, and he wished to share their power. He wanted to serve his legacy, the children of Night, and make their lives more prosperous.

"The gods denied him. He laid blame on his father, Erabas, for his rejection. He thought of all the gods, Erabas would understand, that he would share the power with his children. But a god's power was too great to be in the hands of man.

"This dark child did not accept their answer. As the story goes, Night's son stole the gods' magic and fled back to his people.

"But the power was too much, just as they had warned.

"The gods were angry and demanded the power be returned, but the man refused. You see, the magic can only be returned if given. It holds onto the body, needing a vessel. Magic is a living thing, just as the gods are, just as Arde is. It was intertwined with the dark child and could not be taken. The man became so powerful that the gods could not defeat him alone. He was aided by his new followers, whom he named the Aethars.

"After his refusal, the gods, in their anger, created an incredible beast—one that could battle magic and destroy the man who wielded it. A great war began. Beastly powers against divine magic.

"The beast struck the man down, killing him when no other force could. The gods had their answer, their champion and Guardian. But the magic did not return to the rightful owners. Instead, it slumbered for a thousand years. It became twisted, taking on the evil desires of its first host. It waited, festering, transforming, to be reborn into a willing child of the gods. It would one day wake the beast once more, creating the endless cycle of war. You see, the gods found the punishment fitting. Every era, the lands would face war and ruin as a reminder of the sins of that child of Night. Even today, the magic sleeps, waiting to be reborn, and the beast will rise again to defeat it.

"The gods began blessing less of their legacies. As every era passed, fewer and fewer true children of the gods were born. Some say Rem battled Erabas for his failings with the dark children. I say the god Erabas, in his humiliation at the selfishness of his children, disappeared from history, never to be seen again. It is why there are so few children of Night left, why they keep hidden—they became outcasts. A cursed people to lead lives of suffering and endless unfulfilled desires. Only through pure bloodlines and strong families have the true images of the gods stayed with us."

As the gold man spoke, the children latched onto his story. The adults nodded, like they were hearing what they'd known their whole lives. But something about the tale bothered me.

A child of *Night* had been the first Ikhor—something the Guardians had not mentioned. Bastane said they didn't know if Erabas was around when the Ikhor took the magic, but the gold man's story said he was. Were there different versions of the tale?

The magic that was stolen—was it taken from all the gods? Maybe that was why they could no longer bless their children.

Kazhi believed Brekt might be one of the last pure-blooded legacies of Night. But the gold man blamed the children of Night and Erabas for their bloodline vanishing. Hadn't Kazhi suggested they were being killed off?

Were the dark children really cursed? Maybe I had confused Brekt's troubled look. I thought I could share my past with him to connect us. If his burden was a curse, then we were nothing alike.

None of that was what upset me about the story, however. No, it was how an entire group of people were vilified for the actions of one man—how the crowd nodded in agreement with the tale. I was reminded of the people back home and how I was vilified because I was different.

This was why they needed the Aspis awake. It had always saved them.

The gold man began to speak of Rem, the Day god, and what it meant to spend a life serving him.

The gold embroidered shawl flowed around his form as he moved his arms, speaking about the Temple of Rem.

He talked of serving the gods and forgetting the feuds of men. I wanted to laugh—his history lesson fanned the flames of those very feuds.

One man sat across the road listening to the histories. His beautiful face mirrored what I felt. He appeared troubled by what the gold man said, almost disgusted.

The beautiful man had long flowing white hair that was so light it almost looked blue. His skin was tattooed in blue, or was it blue markings from his legacy? I couldn't tell what god had blessed him. His face was flawless, with a straight nose and full mouth. He had vivid blue eyes that were watchful and intelligent.

He wore a grey cloak, hiding his clothing, but he had a very different look from the Guardians, who wore black clothes and tattoos. Not a Guardian, then.

"You see, after the Aspis rose to defeat the Ikhor and our

Blessed Rem formed the Council of Guardians," the gold man's voice interrupted my train of thought, "he directed the people to aid the beast to defeat the evil. After what the dark child had done and the reputation he had sullied for the children of the gods, Rem stepped forth to guide us.

"Since it has been formed, the Council has grown its city and spread the Guardians across the western continent, driving out those that would support the Ikhor and vanquishing the greed of the first child who stole the magic. This greed created the Aethars. They live in the lands to the far west—barren, cold and lifeless. You see it in their soulless faces, in their mottled skin. You see what would become of you if you prayed to and aided the evil that would ruin this world."

It was too fanatical for me. I surveyed the crowd watching him. There were a few young girls crowded together, laughing as they listened.

He explained that if you joined the Temple of Rem, you would be bathed in gold and shed your duty to your sex. You would become a cherished member of his temple. Those that came a virgin, untouched by mortal desires and with a pure body would—

"Ugh, enough of that," I muttered to myself, knowing I didn't want to set foot in his temple. Even this world was not immune to puritanical views.

Back home, all citizens were measured for their value. I was inexperienced when they tested me, but being a virgin hadn't helped me become more *marriageable*.

The examining doctor told me I could not have children—as if that one part of my system made me worth having someone or being loved. Part of me had felt sad, but it hadn't mattered in the end. I was denied a partner.

But now, I could carve out a new life. Would I be troubled one day when I could not bear a child?

Those thoughts were for another day. Perhaps a day once I had my answers, once I had found the Guards and figured out how I was to help wake the beast.

Others gathered to listen, some rolling their eyes once he started preaching about Rem's temple.

The beautiful man with blue tattooed skin was still listening. His face had shifted into a scowl. What part bothered him most? I knew he was not a child of Day like the gold man. Perhaps a Sea-leg, pureblood, unlike Nuo. It was hard to see from this distance if he had the telltale gills.

Children who had been listening were now moving, pushing, and whispering in each other's ears. The man's story started strong, but children had no interest in serving in a temple.

When I turned around, the beautiful man had his back to me, walking away. He, too, gave up and moved on.

I was ready to head back to the inn, but a hand grabbed my arm, halting me. The gold fingers wrapped around me belonged to the man who had just been speaking. I hadn't noticed him approach.

"My girl, you have the look of one who would serve well in Rem's temple." His eyes were wandering over my neck, my face.

"Why would you say that?"

"Your skin is clear of any markings. You do not have allegiances anywhere else? Perhaps Rem can find you a home."

"Because I am not tattooed? You think it means I should serve in a temple?"

"It is not just the skin I see but the empty look in your eyes. You have a soul yet to be moulded. You are an open vessel ready to become the one you were meant to be. Give that vessel to the Day god, and you will fill your lifeblood with purpose."

His words gave me pause.

"And what duties do you expect from your female worshippers?"

I was incensed, not unfamiliar with men like him. I was getting nervous about how much anger was shown on my face when I remembered I was done with that. I had promised myself I was going to change.

Let him see.

"There are chores to be done around the temple, but apart from that, we only ask that you spend your time loving the mighty god Rem."

I yanked my arm from his grip. "I plan to have fun in my life, thank you."

"Suit yourself. You will fall like the rest of them and become a part of the endless cycle of hate that many fall prey to. It means only an early death for you, child."

"I've prepared for an early death since I was thirteen, old man." I was tired of single-minded zealots running the lives of others. My earlier declaration to myself only gained a louder voice. I was going to experience life.

"What's your legacy, woman," he asked, searching my eyes.

I shrugged. "Maybe I'm a long-lost survivor of Night. But I wouldn't tell you."

The golden eyes widened as I walked away.

When I returned to the inn, Bastane answered the door and nodded, opening up to let me in. It was only him and Brekt in the room.

"How're you feeling?" I bit my lip to stop my laughter.

Sun was pouring in through the windows, lighting up the weapons littering the room.

Brekt lifted the corner of his mouth, "I heard you were nursing us this morning. We have recovered well, thank you."

"I'm surprised your neck still sits straight."

Bastane laughed. "I've seen this guy sleep in the strangest places and positions. There's nowhere he couldn't fall asleep."

"It's my best talent," Brekt shrugged.

Perhaps he was able to fall asleep in strange places, but the darkness shadowing his features told me he was never well-rested.

"What're you doing?" I asked.

I drew closer to inspect the long knife he was working on.

"I went to the crystal smith this morning. I had a few crystals cut, and I'm putting a new one in this blade. See here?"

The small glowing crystal was set in place. He pushed it in with a click. There was some sort of mechanics in the weapons. When it clicked, little arms came out to hold the crystal like a stone in a ring.

Once the crystal was set, lines began to glow, running down the hilt and up the blade. The blade itself started glowing like a thin film across it.

"What is that?"

Brekt smiled as my mouth hung open in surprise. I tried to ignore what his smile did to the rhythm of my heartbeat.

"The crystals power the weapons. Each weapon is designed to have different strengths. You don't really know what they do until they're powered up—the crystals in my knife power the blade to be protected from going dull. My sword is also powered to be stronger when it strikes. Some have arrows that are powered to find their target without fail. Kazhi's throwing knives are the same. Whoever made these weapons was nothing short of genius."

"You don't know who made them?"

"No one does. They just exist. Have for a long time."

Strange that they had so much history spanning back thousands of years, filled with legends and war, yet they still had mysteries like this.

I considered what the man from the Temple of Day said about being caught up with the Guardians and Aethars and their endless cycle of war. Were they so focused on their battle against each other that other critical histories were lost over time?

Brekt continued to put tiny crystals in his weapons. Was he like the gold man? Single-minded on his one purpose in life—his hate for the Aethars?

"I heard a man from the Temple of Day talking on the streets today."

Brekt looked up from his knife. He cut a glance toward Bastane on the other bed, also working on his weapons.

"A monk. What part of history was he teaching?"

He put his knife beside him and picked up another, placing more crystals.

"He started at the very beginning. He explained how the Ikhor was born and the Aspis created."

"I see. Saves us having to explain more, I guess."

"He said you were cursed."

The crystal in his hand hovered over the blade as his eyes shifted once more toward Bastane, who only ignored us, still working on his weapons.

When I went to question Brekt, his stern expression stopped me. He shook his head once.

What did that mean?

"Are you?" I whispered.

A shadow crossed his face, but he did not immediately answer. Could it be true?

"They say the children of Night are cursed, which is why we are all but gone." He kept his tone low.

"The monk said that Erabas deserting your world left his children as outcasts, cursed to live with suffering and endless, unfulfilled desires." When Brekt's eyes widened, I lifted my hands in front of me. "His words, not mine."

Brekt tilted his head back, and booming laughter echoed through the room.

"Dear gods, man, keep it down," Bastane mumbled. "I dropped my crystals."

Bastane shuffled around behind me as Brekt failed to control his laughter.

"What's so funny?" I couldn't contain my smile. His laughter was a deep and luscious sound. It did things to me.

"Don't worry about me, Liv," he finally said, "My desires are not unfulfilled."

My face heated as Brekt continued on his blades. "If the Day monk said anything true, it was that Erabas leaving ended the pure bloodlines. The rest is up for interpretation."

That didn't explain why he had peered at Bastane when I had asked the question. What was he uncomfortable saying in front of his brother?

I couldn't imagine he was like the cursed children the monk described. Brekt didn't seem like the kind of man hungry for power like his ancestor. He seemed worn out but not cursed.

I wanted to know what kind of man he truly was, but would I ever find out? The muscle showing through the tight black shirt said enough about his power. His sleeves were rolled up, showing his black scales and smoke tattoos.

Although none had voiced it, I knew the four Guardians cared for each other. That alone should say enough about his character. And he had been kind, at times, toward me.

"I don't have extra crystals for your blades if that's why you're sighing."

I focused, realizing I had been staring at him. Was I sighing? Did he know what I was thinking? He wore a half grin while he worked and slowly raised his attention to me.

"I wasn't thinking about you," I said quickly, realizing my mistake. "I mean, crystals. I wasn't thinking about crystals."

His smile grew, his teeth flashing. If hunting the Aspis didn't kill me, embarrassment would.

"I got you something else," he said, surprising me, "but maybe I will give it to you later." Another flick of the eye toward Bastane told me Brekt was not one for sharing information.

I nodded, curious about what he got me.

"I saw a man with blue skin today. What legacy has blue skin?"

Anything to make him stop smiling like that.

"He could have been legacy of Mountain. What did he look like?"

"He had a beautiful face, not like a girl, but beautiful for a man. His skin was blue, but he also had darker blue tattoos. They weren't tattoos like yours, more like lines and script. His hair was white and kinda blue, but I couldn't see anything else."

Brekt stayed focused on his knife while I rambled. He was setting a new crystal. It clicked in place. "What do you mean, beautiful?"

His tone was casual, but the way our eyes locked was anything but. The rush that went through me from what was written on his face was alarming—Brekt was jealous. But Nuo arriving with Kazhi saved me from explaining how the beautiful man was nothing compared to him.

Nuo had visited the Alchemist and put in their order. It would be ready tomorrow, and they'd be done their business in Bellum. Nuo didn't voice the question—*what would they do with me?*

I wasn't worried about taking care of myself. I'd survived harsh climates, both weather and political. I would be okay.

Then, Nuo announced he was going down to start round two of the wedding celebrations and asked if anyone would be joining.

"I will," I said, voice trembling.

The room went quiet.

"Are you sure?" Nuo asked. "If it's too much, we would ensure food and drink were sent to your room."

"Am I that bad?" I laughed nervously.

"When I mentioned drinking in the tavern yesterday, you went pale just thinking about it."

"It's—" It was silly trying to explain myself, "It's a new experience for me. But I realize it might be best to do something new with other people around. *While* you're still around."

"As a safety net?" he finished for me.

I nodded and the rest of the room filled with laughter. Nuo gaped at his friends, confused, as did I.

"If you plan to go drinking with Nuo and expect him as a safety net," Brekt said, "then you already forgot how we all ended up last night."

Nuo's eyebrows pinched, and he opened his mouth to defend himself. But Bastane cut him off, "He would throw the net over the edge and push you off. Then jump after you laughing all the way down."

Nuo was speechless. He pointed a finger at Bastane, opening his mouth to say something, but Kazhi interrupted, "And because you're a woman Olivia, you are the first target to go down when a drunk Nuo is in the room."

Nuo narrowed his eyes, then finally shrugged. "I can't argue that, BB. So," he shone with mischief while he rubbed his hands together, "are you in?"

I waited for more reasons to say no. But even with all their warnings, I couldn't come up with one.

"I'm in. Just let me clean up first?"

"Take your time. I will avoid any temptation until you are ready to go down. I am your loyal safety net," he winked.

"You're doomed," Kazhi muttered.

"I'm heading down now," Bastane said to Kazhi, who went to join him downstairs. Nuo sat, waiting for me. So I rushed to my room, wanting to feel fresh on my first night out.

It was getting dark. I grabbed the lantern that was beside my bed. I walked to the bathing room that connected the bedroom and the balcony to use the mirror while I cleaned up.

I washed up quickly. I didn't need to spend much time on myself.

I wondered if I would ever wear my hair in knots like Kazhi or tattoo my face like the other women I'd seen. On my walk today, I saw women who'd painted their eyes and cheeks. The effect was beautiful, highlighting the colours of stripes on their skin.

I was thinking of a woman who had bright red on her lips when two male voices trailed in from the balcony. The conversation was from the other room. I couldn't resist the temptation, so I walked closer to the divider between our balconies to listen.

The balcony was walled, so you couldn't see the other rooms. The railing was made of a few thin bars giving me a full view of the courtyard and the rock cliff behind.

The voices picked up in volume—Brekt and Nuo were discussing something, and they didn't realize I was on the balcony.

"What will it take to convince you to bring her along? The excuses you're giving me are getting weaker," Nuo said.

"They aren't excuses. We've talked about this."

"Yes, I get it. You have a lot on your plate. But you finally have an answer to all the dreams you've been having, and you're just going to leave her? It makes no sense."

"How do you not understand? We can't have her around when we go back to the Council, and you know we will be soon enough."

"Leaving her here is wrong. I believed you when we were kids, and you told me about your dreams. You've trusted me with your secrets and no one else. I know better than anyone. We can't leave her here. She's a part of this now. A big part. What if someone else gets their hands on her?"

There was a long, deep sigh.

My heart was racing. They had talked before about Brekt's dreams—the first night they found me. Did he see me in those dreams? Was I part of their search for the Aspis? Or would he be taking me to the Guards and the Council? I had wanted to follow them when they left this city, but if they were heading toward danger and war, I wasn't so sure. Helping wake the beast was one thing. The war itself was another.

Was this why Brekt acted so strangely? Why he gave me a look when I asked him to call me Liv? Him saying my name while he was asleep in the tent?

Brekt had seen me before.

Do you know who I am? He'd asked me because he knew who *I* was.

Their door opened and closed, and the room went silent.

The next moment a knock came at my door, jerking me away from the railing. I rushed to the bedroom and yelled for them to come in.

Schooling my face, I watched Nuo enter. He noted me brushing my hair and leaned against the door frame.

With no time to think over what they had said, I set my brush down and said I was ready to go. I needed to get my mind off these questions.

Or corner Brekt and demand answers.

CHAPTER

TWENTY-EIGHT

N uo and I travelled down to the tavern to find Kazhi and Bastane sitting at the bar drinking. Bastane talked quietly with a group of men, and Kazhi focused on her drink. Brekt was no where in sight.

The place was packed. Nuo grabbed my hand and squeezed. He gave me an assuring smile, and I took a deep breath.

Around me were all manner of people, just like the market. Tonight they wore fabrics matching their unique features.

Another child of Sea, like Nuo, with pale skin and hair so black it shone blue, wore a dark blue gown with white pearls—like bubbles rising in the sea.

The men Bastane spoke with had long ears, small black eyes and pointed noses like a rat's. They must have noticed my gaze as they all peered over at me at once and stopped talking. I felt a prickling at the back of my neck at the attention, and I moved on.

Nuo pulled me through the crowd and into the courtyard. He was searching for the married couple.

When he spotted the two, he got excited, tightening his grip and pulled me out onto the rock patio to get a better look.

He said usually, the couple would wear the colours black and gold, but this couple was celebrating a rare wedding.

"They're soul bonded," he whispered, and the excitement in his voice sent a thrill through me, seeing something rare and beautiful.

I stood on my tiptoes and tried to peek over heads.

His face lit up when he explained to me that it was rare for a person to find their soul-matched partner.

"Like a soulmate?" I asked with wonder.

He nodded. "Sounds like the same thing to me. Their souls are destined for each other, to find each other in this life. Tonight they are celebrating that reunion and marrying in the typical fashion, but you'll see these two will both wear white and silver."

Sure enough, the bride wore a flowing white dress with shining jewels and silver embroidery. The man next to her was the same. They were both legacies of Sea—pale-skinned, with their gills barely visible in the fading light.

I turned to Nuo, who searched the crowd. "You seem especially excited about a soul-bonded wedding."

"Of course, BB, a wedding like this will draw many single women. It's good luck for them to celebrate with a soul-bonded couple." His smile grew as he scanned the crowd.

The sight made me giggle. "You are hopeless."

His whole body radiated excitement, and it was contagious.

"Go. Find some of those women," I said, smiling.

"Olivia, I can't leave you here." He put a hand on my shoulder. "And as much as you're good arm candy, it won't do me any good to bring you with me."

"I understand. It's okay. I release you of your duty. I will go drink with Kazhi. If it's too much, I'll just go back upstairs."

He hesitated.

"Go." I laughed. "But don't break their hearts."

He smiled at that and left, winding his way through the crowd.

"That was fast." Kazhi drank as I took a seat next to her.

"You three did warn me."

The bartender, a horned Mountain legacy, walked up when he noticed me. "What would you like?" he asked in a gruff voice.

I didn't know. The only drink I knew was the sour drink found in the Aethars' bags.

"Give her the same." Kazhi tapped her glass. She flashed me a look of warning. "Sip slowly."

When the horned man dropped the glass in front of me, I took a sip and forced myself not to choke. It was strong like the Aethars' drink, but it was smoky instead of sour.

Aside from being difficult to swallow, it had a pleasant flavour. As I sipped, I watched the room. Men and women were talking and laughing. It was still so alien to me. I felt a pang of jealousy at their ease and familiarity.

Heat crept up my face as the drink settled in. The feeling wasn't new. Stephen and I would indulge in the rare drink his customers would pay him with. But I never drank more than a small glass. The worst thing would be the Law Keepers finding me walking home drunk.

I began to calm, the stress and worry leaving me. I decided to go out and join the music and laughter coming from the courtyard celebrations.

I left an empty glass and Kazhi behind. She watched me as I collected the courage to wander through the party.

I stepped out into the courtyard and hesitated, expecting some great catastrophe to befall me when I passed the threshold. Of course, nothing happened. No one even glanced my way.

The evening was warm with a cool breeze. The lanterns swung side to side, giving everything movement and warmth. People were drinking at tables while several couples were dancing around in the centre of the yard. The women wore dresses that spun out as they twirled in their partner's arms.

The party gave me no notice. I was just a member of the crowd, enjoying a night of celebration.

One couple was slow dancing, disregarding the faster pace of those around them. I tried not to stare as two women, arm in arm, whispered in each other's ears. One had arms of scales and smoke, which she wrapped around the second. This woman had fire-red hair and matching eyes.

I envied these two, who were free to be themselves out in the open. This couple wore no masks. They were not shunned or hated.

I had truly left home far, far behind.

I found an empty bench off to the side of the dance floor to watch while one song faded into the next. I let it all sink in. More people piled out into the courtyard, and I was joined on the bench by a couple taking a break from the twirling.

Night enveloped the dancers, the lanterns colouring everything golden. Jewels and adornments sparkled when they went past the soft lights.

A dark figure passed by on the dance floor, and my eyes caught Nuo at the same time he spotted me. He picked up his feet, striding toward me, smiling. This was not his friendly smile but rather a devious one—he was up to something.

"Olivia," he sang, grabbing my hands and pulling me up to him. His hands found my waist and held me close. I could smell the alcohol on him, and my stomach sank.

"W-what are you doing, Nuo?" My hands reached out to push against his chest. His fingers dug into my sides as he held me there.

His breath was hot on my face, "Changing the future," he whispered into my ear, "Follow my lead."

He grabbed my hand and pulled me onto the dance floor. We sidestepped a couple spinning toward us. We passed the two women, and red eyes glanced up at me, frightening me a little.

My palms were sweaty. He better not think I was going to dance. I've never danced with a partner and never danced in front of another person.

"Nuo ..." my voice shook as I pulled on his arm to make him

stop. I was dragging my feet to try and slow him down, but he was too strong.

"Come on, BB." He spun to face me. His arm came around my back, pulling me toward him. His other hand held mine in the air. "Trust me."

His body was hard, warm and much stronger than mine as he pressed against me. I stood stiffly as my heart thudded but not in the same way it did when Brekt was near.

His brown eyes warmed to a rich chocolate in the lantern light. His hair was swept back from his handsome face. Lines around his eyes crinkled as he smiled down at me.

"I—no, Nuo. I can't dance, not in front of others."

His mouth was to my ear. "It's not about them, Olivia. Just give it a minute."

I shook my head as he started to move side to side, hardly dancing at all. I stopped seeing him. The night air was feeling too warm. The lantern lights were sparkling and blurring as my head swam.

"Let me go—"

Nuo stopped us abruptly. I gave him a scathing look, but he wasn't watching me. He was focused on something behind me. I turned. Brekt's dark figure was stalking toward us, black eyes fixed on Nuo.

"She doesn't want to dance, you drunk asshole." A menacing shadow danced across Brekt's face.

Nuo eyed me with mock surprise. "Oh no? But Olivia makes a perfect dance partner. Look at her. She's glowing."

"I think that's the drink," Brekt grumbled.

"I think that's the anger," I gritted.

Nuo let go of me then and shrugged. "Well then, I best go find someone else to dance with. Good thing you're sober tonight, Brother. Even better that you were hiding by yourself over there, watching her." He gave me a conspirator's wink. "See you two later."

He strode away, leaving me gaping—what a scheming bastard. I wanted to laugh as much as I wanted to hit him.

I spun to Brekt, who was watching Nuo leave. A muscle ticked in his jaw. He was now stuck here, having to face me. Precisely what Nuo wanted.

I wondered again if I was in those dreams he spoke of. I was about to ask when he faced me and swallowed. "I take it that you truly didn't want to dance?" he said awkwardly.

"Are you asking me to?" I took a step back.

As much as I was afraid, I was intrigued.

He appeared to be battling himself, trying to come up with something to say.

"I do like to dance, but I can't dance with people watching. I'm ... not ready to try that yet," I whispered, saving both him and myself from the embarrassment.

He nodded in relief and regarded lively dancers.

Fingers wrapped around mine and pulled. I glanced down to see his calloused hand swallowing my own. He pulled me away from the dance floor.

CHAPTER
TWENTY-NINE

T he waiter carrying a bottle across the courtyard was irate when Brekt swiped the bottle from his tray and continued walking.

I was about to apologize when the waiter recognized Brekt stalking away, his face paled, and his eyes widened. The waiter didn't have the tattoos of a Guardian, which meant Brekt really was well known.

Brekt's grip was firm as he pulled me away from the courtyard. I was vibrating with anticipation as he led me to a pathway that wound up the cliff.

As we ascended, the music followed us up, just as loud as it was below. It was almost as intoxicating as the drink Kazhi had ordered me.

The music from the wedding was thrilling as it lifted and swelled. I wanted to spin and laugh. It brought joy and wonder and made me feel light—like if I twirled fast enough, I could float up off the ground.

The path's incline was sharp, but Brekt's hold on me kept me on my feet.

"Why are you like that?" I said to his back.

"Like what?" He continued to pull.

"You're so grumpy sometimes. Other times you can be surprisingly nice."

"When am I grumpy?"

"When you steal bottles from waiters. When you get mad at people who question you. When you are awake."

Brekt laughed, but didn't turn to give me his smile. "Guess it comes naturally then. Here I thought I was being quite nice to you."

"You are nice to me, sometimes. Other times you look like you want the world around you to leave you alone."

"I do want everyone to leave me alone, but somehow I get stuck surrounded by them."

We were nearing the top of the cliff, and the dance floor was now far below us.

"Where are we going? I can't walk that fast."

He inspected our hands as if just realizing he still had a hold of me. He let go and nodded his head forward. "A better view."

I followed him, quiet and apprehensive.

We reached the top of the cliff. The narrow path continued along the edge before it wound away down a long sloping hill, dusted with the purple flowers and long grass like the others we rode in on.

The moon was high in the sky, and the stars were out in full. Their luminescence reflected off the flowing sea of grass. The night was so brilliant you could see for miles in the dark.

The music reached the top of the cliff, and the grass danced in appreciation of the musician's song. It flowed across the landscape like waves.

Brekt walked out into the grass and sat, facing the cliff's edge and the city. He opened the bottle and offered it to me before taking a sip.

The grass tried to swallow him up, but he was formidable, and even the tall blades couldn't contain him. His arms rested on his knees as he nodded his head behind him.

"No one is watching up here but the stars above you," his deep voice rang out around me. He brought the bottle to his lips while he waited.

Had I stepped away from reality? "You brought me up here to ... dance?"

He nodded, looking away, jaw tense. "I'll make sure no one is watching you. Try something new."

My mouth hung open. The night wind kicked up my hair and flowed around my loose pants.

"Aren't you supposed to keep an eye on the others?" I asked, perplexed.

"They should be okay for a short time."

The drums and strings from down below pulsed with my heartbeat, matching the fast-paced rhythm. It echoed around me into the starry skies.

My heart swelled with this gift he was giving me. A gift which I was sure he couldn't understand the depth of. This free space he offered me to dance in the wild, under an open sky without punishment ... I had no words

I gawked at the man I had just accused of being grumpy. The one that didn't like being surrounded by people. His nocturnal eyes flashed when he stole a quick glance at me. He drank from the bottle, tilting his face away.

Tears threatened me as I strode out into the grass behind him. The top of the hill was flat, giving me a dance floor.

I heard a ruffle behind me, and found Brekt lying back, his arms under his head and his eyes closed. One leg was resting on his knee, and his foot tapped along with the beat. The grass nearly swallowed him but he was still too large of a presence to be hidden entirely.

I moved further away, hoping the grass would hide me completely.

I smiled, swaying back and forth as the music guided me. I had been envious of the couples dancing, wishing I could join them while they twirled.

The drink still in my veins released my nerves, allowing me to feel free to flow along with the song.

A low humming came from Brekt as he sang along with the music, adding words that were too low for me to make out. His deep voice was a pleasant addition to the drums below.

I grabbed my pants and let them flow in the breeze as I swayed back and forth. My head tipped up to the sky, and I twirled, the stars trailing above, making myself dizzy.

I laughed. Brekt's voice grew louder as he sang. There was a line about the gods and their lovers before his voice became muffled again.

The wind picked up, and I danced as if I knew what I was doing.

As I raised my hands, trying to touch the stars, the song swelled, and the drums pounded. I felt like the stars shone brighter as the beat pulsed. I imagined that if I turned around, I would see Brekt's voice lifting into the air and echoing around him.

I was intoxicated by the freedom, the movement, the sounds. All rare gifts.

The music started to slow, and Brekt's song tapered off as the strings rang out the last note.

I let my arms drop. I faced the night sky. Just like before, I felt a little piece of my soul come back to life.

The tiny seed inside me grew a second little root.

I thought of my swords and their poems. Maybe I was like a broken crystal—damaged but still able to hold power. I just needed to relearn that piece by piece, moment by moment.

I returned to Brekt, my footfalls light compared to the pounding in my heart. He watched me take a seat next to him but made no move to sit up.

The grass swallowed me whole. We were in a private little world that no one could see.

I grabbed the bottle from beside him and took a drink. The flavour stuck to my tongue, and I shuddered from the burn as it travelled down my throat.

"Thank you," I said once the fire subsided. I couldn't explain how much I appreciated what he did.

He was silent for a moment. I didn't think he would say anything.

"You're welcome."

We sat in silence for a moment as a new song trailed its way up the cliffside to reach us.

"Why do people call you Erebrekt? I heard it on the streets," I asked before thinking, breaking the calming silence between us.

"It's my name."

I rolled my eyes at him. "I'm not questioning that part. Why not Brekt like everyone else? And why do they say it with awe?"

His foot continued to bob to the music, with his leg crossed over a knee. "Only the others call me Brekt, and now you. Everyone else knows me as Erebrekt. It's the Night god's namesake, Erabas. I am a true child of his, a pure-blood. For some reason, that means something to people."

"Does it make you more powerful?" I was not familiar enough with his people to understand the differences between pure-blood legacies and not. "Or is it because they think you are cursed, as the gold man said?"

Brekt shook his head. "Erabas has not blessed a child for thousands of years. Children of Night had to keep their families tied to keep the gifts. It is rare to still have his gifts at all, let alone be pure-blood. What that gold fuck said in the streets is just prejudiced bullshit the temple monks like to ramble on about. They don't speak any better of the other legacies either. The followers of Rem can be extreme in their dedication to their own kind.

"It was why I was hesitant to speak in front of Bas earlier. Although he is not as bigoted as the other legacies of Day, he has his moments, and I don't wish to insult them in front of him. Being a pure-blooded Night does mean I have stronger gifts than others, but also, the people know me as a Guardian of the North. I have trained my whole life and earned a reputation, albeit an unpleasant one."

"Why is that?"

"North Aspis is harsh for training. It's rare for anyone to stay there for long. Nuo and I have trained there since we were boys, and I was always the strongest fighter. The teachers used my skills as a way of teaching the other students. They had us fight, to punish the ones who misbehaved or needed a lesson. That was the reputation that followed me."

"That must have been hard."

Brekt was used to punish other students. Was he forced to be something he might not have chosen for himself? I understood that lack of choice, but I couldn't begin to understand the feeling of being used like that.

"What's your last name then?"

"I don't have a family name. I have never known my family."

His foot was no longer moving to the music, but his eyes were still closed. I drank in the sight of the dark child. He let me call him by the same name as his friends did. That small act should not squeeze my heart the way it did.

"I'm sorry," I said, unsure how to comfort him. He appeared so strong and sure of himself that I doubted he needed it.

"Don't be. You can't hurt over what you do not miss."

Maybe he didn't hurt now, but it would have been hard as a child. "Did you ever search for them?"

"I asked about them. The man who trained me was the closest thing I had to a father, and he wasn't exactly loving. He told me I was simply left in the North near the camp for the Guardians to find. Nuo eventually looked into it and never found any record of pure-blooded legacies of the age to have children. So when we were a little older and travelled, we searched for more clues. I found none. I was told by anybody willing to speak to me that the legacies of Night had been gone from our lands for a long time. So that's why people react the way they do around me."

Brekt had already mentioned he'd never met another legacy of

Night. Kazhi had said they'd gone missing. The way she had phrased it made me think it was deliberate.

"You must have a family name, then?" he said, changing the subject.

"Olivia Dacla. It was my mother's family name. She didn't give me my father's name."

"Your father was not around then?"

"No. I was told he left because he was a coward. I believed my mother for most of my life."

"And what do you believe now?"

"That he was only human. Life has a lot of suffering that others will never understand. As you said, you can't hurt over what you do not miss."

I wanted to ask him about the dreams, but what could I say? That topic was hard to dive into without admitting I had been eavesdropping.

"What gifts do you have?" I asked instead. Perhaps the dreams came with his legacy.

He stretched his legs out and crossed them at the ankles. With his hands under his head, he seemed as relaxed as a cat bathing in the moonlight—a true creature of the Night. "Let's just say I am more deadly in the dark than I am in the sun."

I had seen how deadly he was in the day. But it didn't answer any questions I had about his gifts. Yet I wasn't willing to push. Something about the moment felt too peaceful.

"You know, I think you want everyone to be scared of you, but underneath, you're a big softy."

"Excuse me?" he grumbled. He had one eye popped open. "A few minutes ago, I was called grumpy."

I laughed. His face was definitely grumpy.

Even wholly at ease, he was lethal. It contradicted the man who sang along to the music, letting me dance privately under the stars. This man was an antithesis of himself.

"You cover yourself with tattoos and walk around like you own the world. You're usually grouchy and bossy, but tonight? A softy."

"There's nothing soft about me, Liv." He closed his eyes once more. A half smile began to grow. My attention snagged on his full lips and my face heated at his meaning.

I swallowed because he was right. I had seen him undress by the riverside—there hadn't been a single soft spot about him.

I forced myself back to the present. "Well, I haven't had anyone give me that before."

A heartbeat of silence. "Give you something hard?"

My attention flew to him. His smile was full now, eyes still closed. I could never admit how my whole body reacted to the thought of Brekt giving me something *hard.*

I shoved a fist into his stomach. His hands came up in defence as he laughed. When he smiled, the dark shadows that usually lined his face disappeared. He looked younger and even more striking, which I would not have thought possible.

I was unaccustomed to playful banter, yet it was easy with Brekt. The feeling threw me off and filled me with tingling curiosity.

I resisted the surprising urge to reach for him. "Soft and being a softie are not the same thing. No one would think you're soft." An eyebrow went up. "Not that I'm looking. I mean to say—What I meant is—"

My thoughts scrambled, but my voice was steady when I said, "I meant giving me the space, the respect, to be free."

"Well, I guess giving you this won't help my case." He sat up again, reaching into a pocket. He pulled out a small package wrapped in a large leaf.

"What is it?" I took the tiny bundle.

I forgot he had bought me something. I thought it would be an item to help me survive on my own. This would be the smallest weapon to exist if that's what was inside.

I opened it, and words failed me.

He remained still while I held the small pair of earrings.

"I know you can't wear them yet—you'll need to get someone

to pierce your ears," he said, low and stiff. "They are made from empty crystals. Like your brush."

I studied them closer, holding back everything my mind was shouting at me to say, to do.

They were little pendants held by a simple silver chain that would dangle when worn. I know if I held them up to the sun, the light would catch on opal-like vines running through the clear stone, just like my brush.

Brekt continued to look away from me.

"I can't describe how much I love them. Thank you."

Brekt had listened when I said I found my brush beautiful. He had remembered such a small thing. Now I had something else to add to my bag of belongings, and I think these tiny earrings would be my most prized treasure.

"Don't thank me. It's not an elegant gift. Children wear them. Bastane will laugh if he sees you wearing these, but he's a bit of an elitist."

"I'm learning not to care what people think."

I had to find a place to get my ears pierced because now I was absolutely going to get it done—another gift he gave me without knowing—a push forward to become the new Liv.

"And knowing how to respect others isn't being soft." He changed the subject, most likely to get my attention off the fact he had spent money on me twice now. "Those who seek power force their rule because *they* are weak."

"I've only ever known people like that."

"And did you give the power to them?"

"I didn't think so. But I wonder if staying silent was letting them win."

"It's hard to say what way is right. If staying silent was your key to survival, I don't blame you."

Dark eyes held mine. The beat pulsed from below as the moment held me captive. I became too aware of how close he was to me.

Again, that cord pulled, from one to the next, connecting us both. But it was stronger here, stronger than it was at the river when I first felt it. The pull was fierce—a legion of strings and bands tugging us closer. I peered between us, almost believing I would see something there. Brekt caught me eyeing the space. His eyes lit, dancing with questions of his own. Did he feel it too?

He moved to speak but stopped. A crease had formed between his eyes.

I waited but did not expect his next question.

"Do you like it here?" he asked.

"In Bellum? It seems nice enough," I said, disappointed that the moment was gone.

"I mean our world. Are you getting accustomed to it?"

"Not yet. Not really." Above us, a strange sky was staring back. "I still can't make sense of how I got here, and everything seems off —the sounds, the smells, the people. It's hard to wrap my head around the fact I'll never look up and see my sky of stars, not that I often saw them from my forest. I don't know your constellations.

"I had one back home that I found comfort in. I considered the arrangement of stars my secret. I wasn't supposed to have gone that far from home to see them. I found the stars when I ran away to the coast." I thought of the five bright stars high in the sky at the edge of my forest and the cliff that faced a sea of nothing and wastelands that lay beyond.

"I'll never hear the sounds of birds again, not the ones I know. I worry about what will become of my sister's children. I'll never see a familiar face—not one without the signs of their legacy. If I think too long on it, I feel lonely, even surrounded by others."

He was quiet, as I explained. His face changed when I said I felt lonely, turning thoughtful.

"And you like Bellum? Would you choose to stay here?"

"No, I meant it when I said I would leave to find the Guards on my own." I tried to hide my disappointment, fearing he would think I didn't appreciate his help so far.

"I want you to come with us," he said finally, as if he wasn't sure.

"Really?" I sat straighter. "I thought I was a liability."

"Yes, well, that wasn't quite the right word."

"What's the right word?"

I thought he leaned a little closer to me. The corners of his mouth tilted up.

But then he grew serious. "You are a distraction. Where we are going is dangerous. You could be put into situations threatening your life, and I know I will be on edge the entire time. I already am as it is without adding you to the mix."

He paused. I understood—he had a lot going on, and he didn't need to add keeping me alive to the list.

"But this city isn't a place for you. Kazhi can teach you the swords if you like. Bastane can instruct you on other weapons. Nuo will teach you about our world and most likely cause trouble for both of us, but at least you can get a better footing before we find you a safer place. If you are to help wake the Aspis, I will keep you safe until then. But once that happens and it draws the Ikhor in, you are to get far from it. I won't have you throwing away your life. Dying in this fight is someone else's job."

"Whose job?"

He didn't answer. But I knew who he thought. The Guards were supposed to be the ones who fought alongside the Aspis, but I felt Brekt had seen something different.

He was a warrior. He would be there when it rose. And he was taking me with them.

"And you? What will you teach me?" My voice became something I didn't recognize. I hadn't meant it to.

His eyes flashed, catching mine.

"There are a few things I can think of."

His lips, so close to mine, won my attention. I wanted to know all about the things he could teach me.

He leaned over, one hand reaching as he had before on the street—only this time, he didn't stop himself. The tips of his warm fingers brushed against my temple. A thrill went through me. He wasn't leaving me behind. I could explore what this feeling was.

I felt alive with Brekt.

A strand of my hair found its way between his fingers as he studied it. His face tightened a fraction as he dropped his hand, clearing his throat and looking away.

A chill crept over my skin. I liked his attention, but I was relieved when he released me from it, still scared of everything new. He was nothing like the men back home. What he made me feel was a force stronger than my fear of the Law Keepers.

He must feel it, too, that pull between us. But we both had a purpose now, and this was distracting him from it. There was something bigger out there than me.

When he forced his gaze back over the city, I focused instead on the excitement that would come tomorrow and the next day. I was going with them, I would learn swords, and Nuo would probably get me killed. But wasn't that part of the thrill that made life worth living?

Brekt stood, reaching down to help me up. I pocketed my earrings and grabbed onto his outstretched hand. When I was standing before him, he didn't let go.

"I don't always mean to be a hard ass. Grumpy, as you put it." His words were sarcastic, but his eyes were pleading, searching once again. "This will take time to get used to, having you around, trusting someone new. After a little pushing, I've agreed I will try."

I nodded. Yet, not understanding. Was it Nuo pushing him? There was more to it than just learning to trust someone new.

The luminescence in his eyes flashed as he scanned the hills. What could he see in the night that I couldn't?

Then he changed.

I took a step back, my pulse racing. I swore his figure darkened as if trying to blend into the black sky. Maybe my imagination ran away with the night, wild as the hills behind me. But he had been there, and then there was just a shadow.

The child of Night had disappeared with a thought.

Brekt rematerialized, turning south and pointing to the sky, and I had to pretend I hadn't just seen a glimpse of his powers.

"Those three stars are the crown of Erabas—Night's Crown. I look to those when I need to head out for adventure, to escape. Maybe just like Erabas did when he faded from history. I've often wondered if others like me were drawn away from these lands, like our god."

What had he run from? It didn't take me long to come up with an answer. I remembered running too. Was Brekt's home as suffocating as mine had felt? Was that why the others of his legacy had disappeared? Was there something calling them away?

I turned to the three stars that shone brightly in the southern sky and wondered about the lost people, feeling a kinship toward them.

"They're yours to use now, Olivia Dacla. When you feel like you have nothing here in this world, you can at least have a direction to go."

I had a new set of stars. But instead of having them as my own, I could now share them with someone else. I couldn't control the swell of emotion latching to my heart.

He spun and faced north. I moved with him and looked for the stars he now pointed to.

"Those five stars there are North Aspis—see how they're shaped as the beast? It's these stars our north camp was named after. I use them as a guide to find my way home. These two constellations are what I have to ground me. When I felt lost as a boy, I found comfort in knowing I had at least two options: head home or run away. If I could find the stars, I could keep going."

I stared at the five stars in the north, unable to process what I saw. Time seemed to slow down.

"Liv?"

Brekt's confused face stared back at me, and I could only guess what he saw on mine.

"What's the matter?" he asked, reaching for me.

I pointed north, to the North Aspis.

"What's wrong?"

He looked to the north, eying the five stars.

My stars.

The five that I had found on the cliffs back home. The home that was supposed to be a world away. But my stars, they were *here*.

I had never left my own world after all.

CHAPTER

THIRTY

It wasn't possible. How was it possible?

"Brekt, slow down, please!"

I ran down the path winding back toward the wedding below. Brekt was ahead of me. Anger was rolling off him—it saturated the air around me.

Panic flooded my veins and I tripped over my own feet. My hands scraped against stone as I reached out to stop my fall. Everything had turned upside down so fast.

Strong hands grabbed me, lifting me off the ground and steadying me. I was surprised at how fast he had made it back. I scanned Brekt's angry face as I struggled to control my breathing. The frenzied state of my mind was taking control.

"How did you reach me so fast?" I squeaked.

"You lied to me," he growled, his face inches from mine. The kindness I had seen moments earlier had gone.

Distrust—a look I had seen all my life—had taken over.

"I didn't lie. I didn't know. I don't understand how this happened."

I couldn't form an explanation fast enough.

"Who are you, Olivia? Tell me the truth, are you working with the Aethar? It was no coincidence we found you in that cave, was it?"

His hands tightened around my arms, and pain pulsed from his grip.

"I should've questioned you further. Your story seemed far-fetched, but you made me trust you. I felt better believing you were from another world. How did you trick me? What is this you're doing to me? Why are you in my head?"

I tried to squirm free, and the movement snapped something awake in him. He released my arms and shoved a hand through his hair.

"What is going on?" he said to the sky.

"I swear, everything I've told you has been the truth. You saw my reaction when I saw the stars just now. I am as confused as you are. I was told there was nowhere left in the world that was safe to live past our shores. I believed my people were the last of my kind. I've never heard of gods or magic or any of this. I'm not lying."

Brekt looked back to me, but it was there in his eyes—doubt, uncertainty.

"I don't know what to believe anymore," he said in a quiet voice.

He was opening up to me. He was going to take me with them. I was finally letting go of all the self-restraint ingrained into me over the year, and now I felt it all slipping through my fingers.

It was like back in my world, surrounded by strangers that didn't trust me.

"If your home is out there, Olivia, you can return. You can go back to your sister and the man you had before."

I took a step back from him. "No."

"You don't belong here. You said it yourself. You don't fit in. It's dangerous. No one will trust you now."

I took another step. "I will *not* go back."

He searched my face, and I held my ground.

"Please." It was a demand.

I hated that I needed to ask for help, that I needed him or

anyone to determine the outcome of my life. I hated that I lost control—I was as helpless now as I had ever been. I still needed just one person to trust me.

"Please," I whispered.

Brekt turned from me but didn't move to leave.

"Think about it; I have understood nothing from your world. From *this* part of the world. I have no legacy, no knowledge of the gods. But those stars are the very same as mine. I never left Brekt, but I didn't lie."

I could see him trying to work it out. But I was faster.

Something clicked—some important information I'd tucked away that could be a clue. "Nuo told me there was once a war between gods. Where your own histories say continents disappeared!"

"Those wars happened millennia ago if the history is even accurate." He moved to leave. I grabbed his arm to stop, yet he still did not turn to me.

"A millennia could be enough to wipe away traces of a legacy. That might be it. Don't you think?" I couldn't keep up with my own thoughts. All I needed right now was for him to stay and listen. "There has to be an answer in your history. There has to be some lost connection between our homes. Please believe me."

When he glanced back over his shoulder, a crease had formed between his brows. I let go of his arm, hoping.

"I'm taking you back to your room. I need to think."

I didn't move.

Brekt released a breath and closed his eyes. He began to rub his temples as I stood there waiting for a sign of the man who had been on the cliff's edge.

"I was brought here for a reason," I tried again.

"By a light? You think anyone believes you?"

I couldn't stop the sting of his words.

"I'm supposed to wake the Aspis." My voice felt small.

"You don't even know where it is."

When he dropped his hands, I could tell he had accepted some part of my story was still the truth. Or at least, he accepted that *I* believed some part of it was the truth.

"Don't tell anyone. Not until I've figured this out. Even Nuo. Especially Nuo."

"Why?"

"Because everyone will pin you as an Aethar, and the Aethars are the reason Nuo is an orphan. There's a part of him that demands loyalty, and if he suspected you were one or that you lied to him—no, keep this to yourself."

"But how could he believe I was an Aethar?" Could he not see the truth in front of him?

"You come from a land controlled by strict rules. You don't have access to knowledge of our gods and histories. You have never heard of the Aspis or the Ikhor, and you don't look like any of us. Some people say to cross to Aethar lands is to shed your legacy and your god, cursing you to a wasteland. It would seem to them like you've been secluded from our world."

"But I didn't even know what an Aethar was!"

"It's what makes the most sense, Olivia. It's what I am trying to rationalize *against* right now. Because you being from some continent lost from a war between the gods at the beginning of time is a bit too much to accept."

I was back to being Olivia. I was back to a stranger. I hated how, when he explained it, he sounded right.

Could I be one of them?

I pictured the scarred faces and their hatred and rejected it immediately. I would never be Brekt's enemy, or Nuo's, or any of the people I saw walking the streets.

"Let me return you to your room."

"Why would you? You think I'm an Aethar," I spat, unable to hold back.

"I am not sure what I think." Frustration filled his tone. "Just let me return you to your room. I'm trying to give you the courtesy of not forcing you or making you go back there. I'm trying to remember everything you've already been through. But I need to think of my brothers and sister. I need to think of what all this means. This all feels like there is some purpose I am missing."

Part of me relaxed. He wasn't going to push me toward home. I was grateful for the small kindness even if he thought I could be a danger to the others and himself.

"Thank you."

He nodded and moved to leave. "Why did you say I was in your head?" I blurted.

"Now is not the time to be asking me for truths."

So there was something he wasn't telling me. There was a truth I was missing.

He continued to walk away.

"The stars—" I said, remembering how I saw them in the north sky.

"What?" His eyes swam with suspicion as he turned back to me. "Do you remember something else now?"

"They're in the north."

"Yes. I know where they are. I'm not following."

"When I saw them before, from the outskirts of my own lands, they were not in the north."

"So maybe you're wrong, that this is not your world."

"I wish that were the case. They *are* the same constellation, but they're in the wrong spot. If I were from the west, in the Aethar lands, the stars would still be in the north, right?"

"I suppose. I've never been there."

"My stars were in the sky *above* me. Meaning my lands are not east or west. My home is north. I'm not an Aethar." I crossed my arms, standing by my logic.

He searched my face looking for signs of deception, but he would find none.

His shoulders slumped. "Let's go. We will talk more after I've had some time to think."

He began walking down the path but made no indication I was not to follow. I picked up the pace and reassured myself over and over I was not an Aethar. I was not his enemy.

As he led me back to my room, another thought surfaced—what if Brekt found a way to return me home? I had been brought here against my will. I could be returned just the same.

Brekt had brought me to my room and left without a word. I had no idea where he had wandered off to.

And I didn't get to ask him about his dreams.

People were still dancing well past midnight, and I was still wide awake. My breathing was under control, but my fears were spiralling.

I needed to find that Light. I needed to know, yet I wanted nothing to do with it. It could take me home—a home that was far closer than I had thought.

I leaned against the balcony railing as I watched the party continue into the morning, wondering about their lost god and how it may be his fault my lands were lost long ago.

I'd been touched by Brekt's gifts—the earrings and the two constellations. Then it all went so wrong, so fast.

The sounds of movement from the balcony next to mine caught my attention. Someone came into view from around the divider.

Nuo grinned at me. He had not been to sleep yet and looked like he might've just returned.

"How was your evening?" he asked, insinuating his plan had worked.

"Fine, thank you." Nuo was an orphan because of the Aethars, and if he knew I was from their world, would he do to me as he had done to the Aethar who first attacked us?

"Something seems off. I thought my brother would have opened up a bit. I saw him take you up the pathway. Did nothing happen?"

"He mentioned something about me coming with you when you leave the city. I don't know if it will happen, though."

His eyes widened, and his face lit up. "Blessed Rem, BB. What miracle is this? You convinced the big guy when even I couldn't." He frowned. "He'd better not start listening to you over me."

I laughed despite the sadness I felt inside. "Don't worry. He's still moody and cryptic toward me."

"I think it means he's starting to trust you." He passed something across the space separating our balconies. It was a piece of fruit.

I grabbed the fruit, hoping I didn't give away my emotions concerning Nuo's brother.

How had Nuo and Brekt turned out the way they had? Their teacher had shown them no love, yet Nuo was bright and exciting, and Brekt ... well, Brekt was precisely what you would expect from an upbringing like that. But inside, there was depth to him.

"I know when you're hiding something, BB."

"You do?" I said as if he was being silly. There was no way he could guess what had happened tonight.

"Your face goes blank. I've seen you do it when trying to hide from people. What do you not want me to know?"

I shuffled to the edge of the balcony, closer to him.

"I don't want you to know how nice I think you are for sharing your fruit. I was told you don't share food."

I popped it in my mouth as he grabbed one for himself. Citrus and sweetness exploded, making me want to moan. It was very delicious.

"I don't share my food often. But for close friends, I will give *one* piece."

Nuo gave me more than one piece, and my stomach turned on itself—I had begun to think he was my friend too. Would Nuo hate me when he found out the truth?

Under the lantern light on the dance floor, spinning dresses swirled round and round. The cool night breeze reached us as we ate. A comfortable silence settled in, and I began to relax. Things had gone wrong, but for now, I could enjoy this moment and hope for the best.

"Did you find any single women looking for luck?" I asked.

"Do you really want to know?" His voice suggested I really didn't.

"No."

He smirked. "I'm guessing nothing exciting happened for you on that end?"

"Nothing like that. No." Heat swarmed my face, though I'm sure he couldn't see. I thought of the earrings and how maybe I could consider that *something*. Or perhaps it was just a friendly gesture.

What would have happened after the cliff if I hadn't pointed out those stars? Surely Brekt would not have come to my room. There was something between us, but that might not be what he wanted from me. He was a Guardian, a famous legacy of Night. The more I thought of it, the more unlikely it seemed Brekt would want such a thing with me.

"Hmm, better luck next time. I thought my plan might get some things moving along."

"And what things would that be? That wasn't very nice, by the way. You nearly gave me a heart attack. I've never let people see me like that."

"Well, I won't apologize, BB. You need someone to push you a bit. I think there's a wild, playful woman underneath all those layers. I hope to bring her out. And we needed to get his attention." He gave me a cocky smile. "I was right. It worked, as usual."

"You're hopeless." But I was grateful for someone to even try. "Why do you need him to talk with me anyway?"

Nuo was quiet, looking out at the crowd below, but his eyes seemed very far away.

"Time is a funny thing, B."

I saw it then—the face Nuo rarely showed. The one that grew up in a cold northern camp filled with very little love.

"Time?" I asked, confused at what he meant.

Nuo shook himself, snapping out of whatever thoughts he was lost in. "Brekt has wasted too much of his," he finished, smiling.

"I know when you're hiding, too," I said, repeating his words.

"Maybe you and I have much more in common than we think."

I felt that way too. Like we understood each other, even with all the hiding we did.

"Nuo ..." I was curious about something.

"Yes?" His earlier look was long gone. Back was the carefree, handsome man.

"Do you have a family name?" I asked, knowing that a family name wasn't given to orphans.

"I did once, but I don't remember it. I don't remember them."

I heard the lie. He gazed, unfocused, out at the fading party. Nuo remembered having a family and losing them. I wondered if it was worse than never knowing anything at all.

"We should get some sleep. My muscles are a little sore from—"

"Ya, ya, I don't need to know," I interrupted.

He laughed as he headed back inside, and it didn't take me long to return as well. As I went to my bed, I considered that if Nuo was anything like me, he didn't forget a thing. He remembered his family.

It took a while for sleep to come. Once it did, the nightmares were filled with more sorrow and loneliness than they had been since I had come to these new lands.

CHAPTER

THIRTY-ONE

I woke late the following day with the sun high in the sky.
Food was left on a table, and I ate as I admired my new
earrings, hoping Brekt wouldn't leave me behind.

The crystal pendants were beautiful. Held up to the light from
the balcony, I found the veining in the clear stone. Rainbow
colours danced across the room.

I couldn't wait to wear them. I shivered, thinking of a needle
piercing my ear. How did they stand to have as many piercings and
tattoos as they did?

I examined my swords, convincing myself I was not
procrastinating. I needed to find Brekt and know what conclusion
he had come to after finding out I was from his world. Part of me
wanted to know what he thought so I could come to a conclusion
myself.

I pulled my swords out of their hard leather case.

I laid the sword containing two clear, empty crystals across
my lap.

Running my hand up the blade, I examined the symbols. '*A
broken crystal still holds power.*'

I wondered what power my swords would have once I acquired
magic-filled crystals. Would they never dull or be spelled to always

find their target? It was strange how quickly I adapted to this new part of my world—accepting magic and dragon-like beasts and evil spirits reincarnated into vessels.

Last night, before seeing the stars, I felt alive. I was finding myself. I knew parts of me were broken and aching—I had memories buried deep that I still hadn't faced or dealt with. So much rage existed in me, caused by the Keepers.

But I was ready to accept that even broken, I was moving forward. I was even *living*.

Brekt would understand. He would accept I hadn't lied to him. I would make sure of it. I would make a life here, and I would be free.

As my fingers swept past the two empty crystals in the blade, a faint glow materialized. I gasped and pulled my hand away, leaning closer to see which crystal the glow had come from. But they sat empty and colourless.

I put my hand back over, and nothing happened. Could the glow be similar to the Light that brought me here? I leaned closer to the sword.

"Hello?" I whispered, feeling ridiculous. The crystals they found in the cave had glowed, but they weren't the same blinding light that brought me here.

I must have imagined it, or maybe some magic was left in them. I should ask one of the others.

I grabbed my cloak, strapped on my swords and headed to the other room. I needed to face today and see where I would be going if Brekt had decided to leave me behind.

I knocked twice, waiting for several minutes before I realized they were all gone from the room.

A jolt ran through me. Did they leave this morning and not tell me? Did Brekt change his mind?

I raced downstairs to the tavern. The room was full of people enjoying a late breakfast or early lunch. I couldn't tell. I didn't see any of the Guardians in the crowd. I walked out to the courtyard and sighed with relief, finding Nuo sitting on a bench next to a blonde. Gold flashed in her eyes, and she had a beautiful golden tan. She was laughing and blushing, her hand resting on his arm.

I snorted and turned back to the tavern. I didn't have any money to order a drink, so I decided to head out for a walk. I would ask them about the crystals later.

The day was cloudy and colder than yesterday. I stepped out onto the dirt-covered street, glad to have brought my cloak. It covered me, hiding the swords. I kept the hood down as I walked, watching people shop and run their businesses.

I figured the others must be selling the last of their items and visiting the Alchemist to pick up their order. I had wanted to see the Alchemist, curious about their shop and how they made magycris.

I lifted my face to the sky, appreciating the wind and watching the clouds, looking for signs of home. I still couldn't believe this was all part of my world.

I passed numerous vendors, thinking of the hilltop. How many more chances would I have to spend time like that with Brekt?

I came to a crossroads where moving carts filled the square. One path headed north out of the city. I could see down the long road as it eventually travelled a hill up and out of sight.

I walked up the north street, inspecting storefronts, catching bits of conversation. The conversation was about the mundane and the everyday. It was reassuring to hear women gossip and men talk business. I didn't feel so lost knowing people were the same no matter how far I travelled.

A commotion that was stirring further up the street caught my attention. I weaved through carts to hear what was happening and caught a few words that made my blood run cold.

Aethars.

Eastern road.

Guardians.

I didn't think before I ran. I hurried for the eastern road. My heart picked up as fast as my feet.

What did I think I was going to do? I would give Brekt more

reason to leave me behind if I put myself in danger. But I needed to know what was going on.

When we faced the Aethars before, they were no match for Brekt and the others, but what if there were more this time? Maybe it wasn't even the Guardians I knew facing the Aethars. There had been many in the city when we'd arrived.

I panted, trying to make my way through people and wagons.

My questions were answered a few blocks later as I came to a large square. It was full of people, maybe fifty, dressed in drab, frayed clothing. Their skin was scarred and mangled, just as I had remembered several times in my dreams. The scarring made it impossible to tell what legacy they were under their misshapen faces. How could Brekt even wonder if I was one of these people? Some were even missing limbs.

The Aethars stood together in a circle, facing the growing crowd. A man in the centre of the group stood taller than the rest. He was on a crate, screaming at the citizens around him.

Several Guardians were spread through the square. Their weapons were drawn, ready for a fight, though the Aethars made no move to engage. These were not the Guardians I knew. I let loose a breath but quickly remembered they were still outnumbered. The two groups watched each other. Hate sculpted the Aethars face. That hatred was what made them ugly, not the scars.

The man in the middle caught my attention as he spoke of legends, a topic that I knew something about.

"The Aspis *will* fall. We will see to it as the Ikhor faces it once more. The time of the Aethars has come. We will rise from the embers of the burnt earth and claim the power that has been rightfully ours since the dawn of mankind. The Ikhor will lead the way, and you will all see a better world for the children of tomorrow."

A Guardian to my right stepped forward. "Stop spreading lies, Aethar. The Ikhor will destroy you as quickly as it will us. Leave this place before we make you leave. Or stay, and you'll never be able to leave again."

"You have no power here, Aspis whore. We are in neutral territory. As you see, no one's stopped us. You are outnumbered today, Guardians. We will be heard. The Ikhor will promise us a new Era with power finally on our side. The time of the Guardian Council ruling these lands is over."

The mention of a council caught my attention. Brekt didn't want me around the Council, for what reason, I hadn't heard. I had thought the Council ruled over only the Guardian territories in Veydes, which Bellum and Aethar lands were not a part of. So why did the Aethar care about them?

The Guardians continued to push back, "You can't think to know what an evil creature desires. Leave. Now. We won't hear of these theories and dreams that will surely be your death. Not that I'll complain."

The Aethar laughed. "You think these ideas are mine? The Ikhor has led us himself! He promises the fall of the Council."

Silence slammed down like a weight on the crowd.

"Led you?" Someone demanded, fear contorting their voice. "Do you mean to say the Ikhor has awoken?"

"That is exactly what I mean. He is awake, and he is leading his people to battle. We hunt for the Aspis, we will find it, and we will destroy it along with our leader."

My heart seized as the Aethar's eyes met mine. Hate and cruelty sneered back as he smiled at me.

"The Ikhor is coming," he warned, sending a thrill of fear through me.

A scream in the crowd echoed like an alarm, causing panic. People began pushing, running from the square.

I was shoved forward and backward. I moved to the edge of a building and stood in a doorway as citizens rushed by, screaming for their loved ones to get to safety.

"Is the Ikhor here?" Someone asked as they ran by.

"Run, pack. We must go into hiding," a man shouted.

"The Guards! The Guards of the Aspis are here!" a woman screamed. Shouts echoed, alerting that the Guards had arrived. Citizens pushed away from the Aethar and slowed to watch. The commotion eased when only Guardians remained near the circle of scarred faces. I craned my neck to see where they pointed.

The Guards of the Aspis. The appointed warriors. The strongest of all the Guardians who would aid the Aspis in defeating the Ikhor and the very people I needed to find. Already their presence calmed the people and cast nervous glances upon the enemy.

But if they were here at the same time as the Aethars ...

I searched for signs of an evil-possessed being and a giant black dragon. All I found were terrified faces. I'd been stupid, wanting to see what was happening in the square.

My heart raced. Would the Guards be like the other Guardians? Or would the legendary warriors have shiny armour and wave banners?

The crowd thinned as more citizens fled the square. The two groups faced each other, taking positions to fight. The Aethars parted, revealing to me the Guards facing off with them—the ones I needed to help wake the Aspis.

I gave an audible gasp. My thoughts spun as I took in the group before me. They were terrifying and dripping with power, exactly like I thought they would be. They stood side by side with their weapons drawn and more strapped to them, ready for the fight. Their focus darted from one Aethar to the other.

Death looked out from their eyes, promising that nothing would stop their path of destruction.

My heart thudded so loud in my chest that I could hear the pounding in my ears.

And I tried to understand why I hadn't guessed. Out of every Guardian I'd seen, they were the most terrifying.

Nuo, Bastane, Kazhi and Brekt stood in the square, armed and ready to take on the Aethar.

"The Guards are here now, you scarred-up scum. I'd run if I were you!" shouted a man from the crowd.

THIRTY-TWO

My thoughts were screaming.

They were the Guards? *The* Guards who were destined to serve the Aspis?

It made sense now. Why they were so secretive, why they carried such a burden, why they were so skilled.

Brekt's dark eyes scanned the crowd, landing on me. They widened a fraction, realizing I was in the line of fire.

Great. This is why he didn't want me following them. He'd definitely leave me behind now.

I slowly pulled up my hood to cover my face, not that the Aethars knew who I was. But if Brekt didn't change his mind, if the Guards were to take me with them, I didn't want my identity to be known. I didn't want anyone to know I was travelling with the most experienced warriors of this continent—maybe even the world.

I began to feel great reverence for the people I'd been travelling with and the man I had danced next to last night.

And I had been entirely unaware.

Brekt was no longer looking at me as he stepped toward the Aethars. His movement was feline, smooth and lethal. His head was cocked to the side, contemplating how he would end the

Aethars before him.

"The Ikhor is coming for you, Guards. He knows of you already and has sent us to find you and give you a warning. You will die by his hands. You will die before you ever reach the Aspis."

Brekt's features transformed as he took his next step. His tattoos became shadows crawling along his skin as he stepped toward the group facing off with him. He smiled, "You're warning has been received, and I am eager to send a message back."

The darkness under his eyes had vanished, and he was more alert and alive than I had seen before. This was his element—not the travelling and finding crystals, not helping lost women. Fighting and winning was what he was trained to do.

"Take down the bitch first!" an Aethar yelled from the hoard.

Kazhi cast a bored glance toward the Aethar. Bastane was smiling as if this was some fun game to him.

But it was Nuo who scared me. He wore a new mask, one of pure unwavering hatred. Cold. Cunning. Powerful. He embodied everything I pictured in a god of death.

Brekt raised his sword. Strong jaw set, no hint of emotion on his face, only cruel calculation. It was hard to believe this was the same man I had thought could feel something toward me. Could someone so frightening care for someone so meek?

His eyes flickered over to me for a heartbeat, and I nodded. It was time for me to run.

The other Guardians advanced on the group of Aethars, and screaming tore through the square.

Chaos erupted.

I turned and ran.

Guardians fought Aethars as I made to escape. The remaining citizens, once again fleeing, knocked me back and forth. Someone's shoulder caught against mine, jarring and painful, but finally, I reached the exit.

I looked back, seeing nothing but bodies moving in and around like a swirling sea—the sounds of weapons were a clashing tide against the rock. I caught sight of Nuo. His eyes were on the

Aethars—the eyes of death. He fought as if he felt nothing, facing off with a crowd of fifty or more scarred faces.

I continued running, not caring where I went or what direction I was going. I worried for my friends, worried about Brekt. However, I knew without question they would walk away from this fight. They had to.

As I reached the end of the block, I stopped short and nearly screamed.

More Aethars came around the corner. They grabbed and shoved people, some beating citizens to the ground.

Gold caught my eye. The golden monk was hiding in an alleyway. Our eyes met, and he shook his head and sneered—he wouldn't share the space with me.

Another group pushed past me and tried to find shelter between the two buildings—a mother with her two children who all had bushy brows and furry tails—but the gold man shoved at them, telling them there was no room and to find somewhere else to hide.

Coward. People were being hurt, and he just hid there.

I spun in a circle. Returning to the square was not an option. Standing in the middle of the street with enemies on both sides was not an option. I remembered the weight at my side. I parted my cloak.

My swords.

I had forgotten them.

I couldn't use both of them—I barely managed the one—but with no hope of escape, it was my best option. Innocent people were screaming for help. We needed every weapon we could use against the Aethars.

Grabbing the handle of a sword, I brought it out of the leather casing and held it up in front of my face.

A few running citizens made a wide circle around me. Maybe I could bluff my way out of this.

The mother, who'd tried to hide with the monk, was frozen in terror, eyes glued to my sword.

"Stay with me," I said, hoping I could help them. "Let's try to find somewhere to hide."

She nodded, and we moved further from the square where most of the Aethars fought. I tried a few doors along the side of the street, but none would open.

An Aethar, who had rushed out on the street to block those escaping, took notice of me and began stalking toward us. Their eyes darted behind me to the three following.

"Looks like you're ready to do battle with that pretty little sword, girl," a horribly disfigured woman said. She had cuts down her face in deliberate patterns, and the same cuts ran down her arms. There were no apparent signs of her legacy.

"The Ikhor sends his warnings. This was not supposed to be a fight, but you can thank the fucking Guardians for enticing a battle."

"It wasn't them that started this," I said through gritted teeth. The woman and her two children stayed back against the wall of the closest shop.

I tightened my grip on my blade.

The Aethar pulled a long blade out from her side. She raised it above her head and yelled as she came forward, bringing the weapon down on me.

I lifted the blade as Bastane had shown me back in the cave. Everything seemed to slow down as fear left me, adrenaline taking its place.

She moved to the side, dancing around my block. My mother's voice swam from the depths of my mind, breaking the surface, which I hadn't heard so clearly since before she died. Something snapped then, and my vision tunnelled, as a strength I'd forgotten I had swept through me.

Look into your opponent's eyes when you fight Liv. Anticipate where their feet will move without looking down.

I stepped sideways with the Aethar and moved my blade to block hers.

Our swords clashed.

The woman behind me spoke to her children, and from the corner of my eye, they ran away, across the street and out of sight.

The Aethar moved again, and she screamed as she brought her sword around to attack me from the other side.

Watch the negative space around your opponent and strike there.

My mind quickly noted where her sword was. I needed to attack where it was not. Her side was left exposed.

As our swords clashed once more, I brought my leg up and twisted it around to kick her in the ribs.

She stumbled back with a grunt of pain.

I fixed my stance and prepared for her to attack again. The force in which her blade had come down had shocked my arms into going numb. I wasn't going to last long. At least the family had gotten away. I tried not to think of how similar it was to my past—a mother protecting her two children.

Don't wait for your opponent to attack. Control the fight.

I stepped forward and brought my blade down on the woman.

She was quick, raising her sword to meet mine. My aim was sloppy. I would not win this fight with a blade.

She pushed then, slamming me back, and I stumbled, unprepared for her strength.

My feet failed me, and I fell to the ground, my tailbone screaming as the woman moved forward to bring her blade down again. I brought mine up as fast as I could, but not fast enough.

I flinched, knowing this was where I would lose, where I would fail at everything my mother had ever taught me.

But her blade never reached mine.

Instead, it met another.

The screaming of metal against metal rang in my ears and I found Brekt standing above me. His shadow cast me in darkness, and the woman's face gave away her fear. I felt it as well. But she feared the death he would deal, and I feared the man capable of it.

He came for me. Who knows how many he had to fight through to do so.

He took the woman down in two strikes.

I was still processing it as I stared at the body motionless on the dirt road before me, her scarred face turned away.

Pushing myself up, I stood awkwardly and went to thank Brekt. But he was already taking down a second and a third Aethar who had rushed him. He circled me then. I was in awe of his speed, his fluidity. He was a shadow, swiftly moving like smoke through the light around me.

It was brutal, yet beautiful.

More Aethars who had blocked the road ahead started toward us. Brekt held out an arm to push me behind him.

I shuffled back, hitting somebody. The sword I held was snatched right out of my hands. I spun around to find Kazhi scanning the crowd before her. She held my sword in her hand and, with the other, grabbed a knife from her belt and held it out toward me.

"You're too sloppy with the swords yet. Hold this and stick it in anyone who grabs for you."

I nodded even though she was not watching me.

"The square ..." I began to ask.

"Is well protected with Guardians. We left them with very few to take care of."

Blood coated her visible skin, the very little that was white. Brekt was already facing off with the Aethars, and Kazhi stepped ahead to join.

I pushed myself back against a wall. Guardians had piled in and were taking on the Aethars flooding the street. Citizens hid amongst doorways, behind crates and under wagons.

Across the street from me was the mother holding her children —they hadn't escaped. My fear demanded I not watch, the scene awakening a horrible memory.

The woman held her youngest, a son, while the older sister held tight to the mother's waist. Their bushy brows were tilted up, and their tails were tucked behind them. They were standing near a doorway with no way to escape. I considered the knife in my hand, thinking there was no way this small thing could make a difference.

The mother was terrified. But not for herself. She scanned the streets, hoping for a way to get her children to safety.

Not again. I can't let this happen again.

I took a step toward the family, set on doing whatever I could to help. I knew what it felt like to lose a mother. I knew what it was like to watch it happen and how it felt to carry that around with you for the rest of your life.

I dreamt of it almost every night—blood-filled memories that, no matter how hard I tried, would never let me forget.

"Olivia, get back against the wall!" Brekt yelled, who had been ensuring I was okay.

A scream tore out from across the street.

A Guardian was dead next to the family. The Aethar, who had taken the warrior down, advanced, seeking an easy target. A moment was all it had taken.

The Aethar struck out, taking the youngest boy and pulling him away from his mother's embrace. The scarred man had bronzed skin and grotesque round holes in his head that looked as if they were once horns. He pulled the boy to his chest and held a knife to his throat. The little boy froze, his pleading eyes on his mother.

CHAPTER
THIRTY-THREE

The woman was frantic, pushing her eldest behind her and screaming for help, searching the street for a saviour.

"No. Please," I whispered.

I stepped forward. I heard nothing around me. Saw no movement. Everyone stopped when they saw the knife against the boy's throat.

I found Kazhi next to me, warning me not to move. Past her, where Brekt had been moments before, the street was vacant.

The Aethar scanned the crowd. "The boy will die. Our warning is clear: war has begun, and none will be spared that try to stand in our way. The Aethar are done with the control of the Council. The Ikhor will see to it—a new era will begin with the downfall of the Guardians."

The boy in his arms was frozen, though tears streaked down his dirty face. His mother sobbed to the side, begging for him to be released. He was innocent, after all. He could be spared.

Take her instead.

The eldest daughter held onto her mother, begging her to make it stop.

I searched once more for Brekt. I couldn't find him but noticed Kazhi was closer to the Aethar holding the boy. I hadn't even seen her move. She had two knives in her hands, ready to throw. I held my breath, knowing how accurate her aim was. Could she kill the Aethar before he hurt the boy?

The man was still talking to the crowd. A shadow caught my eye as if something were blocking out the sun and moved across the street behind the Aethar. I lifted my face to the empty sky, finding nothing. Looking back to the street I couldn't focus on the shadow-of-nothing moving closer.

The mother shifted to speak quietly to her daughter, who then moved away and pushed herself against a wall.

I didn't grasp at first why she had pushed her daughter away. My heart plummeted when I understood what the mother was about to do. What every mother would do when her child was in danger. What my mother had done, what had killed her.

A scream tore from me, ripping at my throat, as she dove for the Aethar, trying to grab her son to push him out of the way.

The Aethar was trained and too fast for the sobbing woman. He pushed his knife forward, away from the boy and toward the woman advancing on him.

I ran toward her, screaming for her to stop. Tears welled up in my eyes, making my vision swim.

A hand stopped me, grabbing me by the arms and halting me in the middle of the street. I didn't turn to see whose hands were on me as the woman went down, facing the ground.

I struggled in the stranger's grip as I tried to get to her. The eldest daughter cried out as the boy screamed for his mother.

I thrashed against the strong hold. Not again. I would not let it happen again. I would not stand there, held back and watch another mother die.

"Please," I begged the world around me, for anyone who would listen.

The shadow in the street, the one I had seen before but not understood, moved once more, and I tore my eyes away from the body beneath the Aethar's feet.

Horror became amazement. The shadow became a physical

darkness. The darkness became a back swirling mist taking form, moving under the shade of an awning behind the Aethar and the boy.

It was hard to comprehend when the black mist formed obsidian eyes and a cruel mouth. A blade appeared in a hand. The hand materialized into the arm of a tall, dark, tattooed warrior.

Brekt became whole. The dark child himself struck out and plunged the sword through the chest of the Aethar. At the same moment, Kazhi threw her blade into the Aethar's throat, and Bastane appeared out of nowhere to snatch the child from the Aethar's grip.

The Guards moved as one.

They were incredible, fast and accurate. The Aethar went down, and Bastane held the crying boy in his arms as Brekt pulled his sword free.

The grip on my arms subsided, and I wasted no time dropping the knife in my hand and racing toward the woman lying on the ground.

I reached her just as her eldest daughter did.

The girl grabbed for her mother, pleading for her to be okay. I helped her turn the woman, lifting her into my arms and checking for signs of life.

Tears streaked through the dirt on her face. The skin underneath was losing colour.

I pulled her toward me, and I heard the sucking and squishing sounds of her blood-soaked clothing. The sounds I heard in every nightmare.

I pleaded with her to wake up, just as her daughter did beside me. Her son knelt down on the other side and reached out for her face.

"Olivia," came a faraway voice.

No. I wouldn't let go this time. I wouldn't let her go.

"Olivia, let me get to her wounds."

I found Brekt casting a shadow above me. He was holding a bottle of magycris in his hands, but his eyes were on me.

"Can you heal her?" I asked. "Please, please heal her. Don't let these children grow up without a mother." My voice broke.

"That's my plan. But you need to put her down. You're blocking the wound."

I set the woman down as gently as I could. She made no sound as I let her head rest against the dirt.

"Erebrekt, don't be a fool. You're bleeding out, man," Bastane's voice called out. "You need the magycris. We need to keep fighting."

"Please," I whispered down to the woman. "Please. Don't leave."

I knew she was not my mother. Somewhere in the far corners of my mind, I knew. But I could not bring myself back to the present. I could not see a stranger's face when I peered down at the woman. I saw my mother and her beautiful smile fading as the light left her eyes. I knew bringing this woman back to life would not change what had happened, would not fix that I did nothing while my own mother died, but I pleaded anyway.

"Please, god, any of you, help her."

The box I carried inside me was carved with the names of those I hated. It held my hatred captive. But living amongst my hatred were worse things. Worse memories. Worse pain.

Strong hands pulled me to my feet, and I locked eyes with Brekt.

The fierce look of bloodshed was gone, and the blood that was splattered across his face hindered none of what I saw churning within.

He didn't offer me comforting words or try to embrace me as I stood there fighting to keep myself tethered. He just stared at me, *into* me, and I knew he was searching for answers in my eyes as much as I was searching his.

I hadn't seen him since he found out I was from his world. No other answers were revealed as we stared at each other, but the one that mattered—he knew I wasn't lying to him.

He tilted his head down once in a silent acknowledgment.

"Bastane is right," came Nuo's voice from somewhere beside me. "You need to be healed, brother."

Without looking away from me, Brekt passed the magycris in his hand. "That is for the woman. I'll take Liv to the Alchemists now and join you in a moment." Then he yanked his head to the side, telling me to follow.

I grabbed his arm, pulling him to a stop, worried for the woman on the road. Nuo knelt beside her and used the liquid, pouring it into her mouth and some onto her side.

"Nuo will do everything he can for her," Brekt's voice was low and pained. "We need to get out of here, Liv."

I was Liv again.

"I can't leave her. You don't understand. I can't let her go."

"He's saving her for you. Many are in danger of losing their lives at the moment, but he's saving this one for you. Let me get you to safety so we can save more."

I nodded. Sounds of swords and screaming rang in the distance. The fight was still going.

Brekt took off past the family being patched back together by Nuo. He led me down the road, reaching an alleyway tucked between two tall buildings. He checked up and down the street, making sure no one was watching and pulled me into the shadows before winding down the tight alley filled with crates and barrels. There was a grey door hidden so well that I almost missed it.

He pulled me toward the door. He was breathing heavily, and for the first time, I noticed the dirt streaking across his exposed skin. His black shirt was ripped and soaked.

Blood.

Nuo was right—black hid the blood well.

Pain etched his face like each breath was hard to take.

He knocked three times, and the door opened a crack. A single eye peeked through, filmy and white.

"My boy," a gruff voice said. "I heard the screams. Is there an attack?"

"Aethars. I need to access our order if it's ready to go." Brekt stepped through the door the old man now held open. "Only open it again if it's one of us you hear."

With surprising strength, the old man grabbed my arm, pulling me in behind Brekt.

I felt relief, panic, and shame as the door closed. I had failed to protect myself or anyone around me. I had caused more trouble for Brekt and gave him more reason to leave me behind.

I turned to see the old man staring. Both of his eyes were glazed over, fading into white. I thought he might be blind, but when he faced me, I had an eerie sensation that he was looking right through me.

I was thinking about how creepy it was, this old man gazing into what felt like the darkest parts of my soul, when Brekt collapsed on the floor.

THIRTY-FOUR

"Hurry up, girl. Help me get him to the stool over there."
I rushed to help the old man who was reaching for Brekt. Brekt was trying to push himself back up. Blood was pouring from an open wound on his back—the gash travelled from his neck to his hip.

I grabbed his arm and pulled with the old man. Brekt was so packed with muscle it made him nearly impossible to lift.

He swayed when we got him to his feet. He must have used the last of his strength to help that boy. And this wound was given to him before then.

That mother—watching her had cleaved me in two. I was doing my best to keep it together as I hoisted Brekt's arm over my shoulder.

We got Brekt to a stool and sat him down. He pushed the old man away, saying he was fine, just a little dizzy.

With a huff, the man went to a table near the door, grabbed a bottle of magycris and brought it to where I stood.

"Don't just stand there, girl. Pour it on the wound."

I grabbed the bottle from him. A strange-coloured liquid flowed inside, swirling with colours of white and sky blue. I had swallowed this stuff?

It shone as I moved it around, glowing from inside the bottle. I held it up to Brekt. "How much do I pour out?"

He gave a weak smile, his face turning pale. "Try a few drops and see if it closes it up. I just need the bleeding to stop."

I hurried around him, distraught by the opening that split his back down the middle. Blood coated every inch of visible skin. I couldn't tell where to start pouring.

"I know you're seeing a lot of blood, Liv," Brekt moaned, "but if you could hurry, it hurts."

"Sorry!"

I pulled the stopper, raising the bottle above his back. I tilted it, letting a few drops fall. The liquid hit his skin, and a faint glow came from the wound, seeping into the blood and disappearing. I would have marvelled at the sight if it weren't for the sound that came from Brekt.

He moaned, swaying forward. The old man was before him and pushed him back upright.

I was awed as his skin healed where the liquid touched. I continued a path down his back, using a little more than he instructed. I was astonished this wound hadn't killed him.

"How did you get this?" I questioned when the last of the skin had closed. A nasty pink scar was left.

"In the square. There were a lot of them. I was trying to push through to get to the streets."

"This is my fault then," I whispered. "Hey! Sit down."

Brekt moved for the door, "There's more out there, and I've got to help the others. Stay here."

All the emotion crashed down on me when the door closed. Worry was inching its way in. It wasn't something I was used to—worrying for others.

Would Nuo save the woman? Could the magycris heal someone that far gone? I had been near death from starvation, and it healed me—I could only hope she was all right.

I found myself beside the stool in the dark shop of the

Alchemist—the shop I had wanted to see—with a pair of milky-white eyes on me.

The old man was short in stature. His coarse white hair, the little that he had left, stuck out at all angles. His skin was wrinkled in every possible place, and his eyes made me wonder how he could see anything at all. However, he stared at me with the confidence of someone much younger—and the knowledge of someone who wasn't blind in the least.

He squinted as if looking for something more than what was shown on the surface. His eyes widened a fraction before becoming dull once more.

"Well, girl, are you going to say anything? It's rude not to introduce yourself."

I stood straighter, wondering what he'd seen. I was still too raw to allow myself a retort. The Alchemist just watched.

I schooled my features and put on my mask. *Don't react.* He had to be a friend of Brekt's. But *I* didn't have to trust him.

The man tilted his head to the side. His hand came up to his chin. He scratched at his whiskers while he scrutinized me, and the rasping noise took my focus away from the shop.

"Yours is not a face I've seen before," he said in a low voice. I didn't know if that was a question or not.

"We have never met."

"I sense—" his attention wandered to the ceiling, "A growing power."

Was the Alchemist's mind addled?

"What do you mean?"

He shuffled away from me, moving through his shop.

I studied the place, finding work tables and shelves full of jars, liquids, plants and some smoking objects. The room was awash with warm lights from candles and little glowing orbs set on tables.

The areas of the room that weren't in shadows were bathed in an orange or purple glow. It was eerie yet not unwelcoming. It was exactly what I pictured when the Guardians—no, the *Guards*—had described an alchemist to me.

When the man reached a table, he put a pair of small glasses on the end of his bulbous nose and began turning dials on a contraption. He pushed and pulled knobs and poured liquid into jars. Smoke billowed out of some. One, in particular, was glowing, similar to the orbs.

He wore a white linen shirt that was clean considering his surroundings and, over it, a leather apron that went down to his bare feet.

"Your face, girl, is not one I've seen in my life."

"You mentioned already. I'm Liv. We haven't met before."

His milky eyes focused back on me. How could he even tell he'd never met me?

"I don't need to meet someone to know their face. Look past someone's eyes, and you'll find who the person really is. You meet the same people time and again if you live as long as I do. But I haven't met the likes of you."

"What is past my eyes?"

Maybe he was just crazy. He certainly appeared crazy. Even his surroundings were chaotic.

He picked up a tiny metallic stone and added it to the smoking jar.

"Your face is deceitful." His milky gaze tore into me. I could feel the mask slipping away, but not by my doing. "You try to be someone you are not. Too many secrets run this world—yet they are the key to survival. They are also the reason nothing ever changes."

"And what am I lying about?" My voice shook, and I wondered if the man was more cunning than unhinged.

"Your real eyes, girl, are terrified—terrified to be seen. You want to blend in, but you do not. You should not. You should burn bright."

Maybe not so addled after all.

He was focused on his work when he added, "You are not from these lands. I wonder what else you are hiding."

I jolted. I couldn't think fast enough to ask why he'd said such a thing. He picked up a crystal with a metal pair of tongs and lowered it slowly into the smoking jar. It turned a brilliant purple, and the bright glow lit up the planes of this face.

"I am not hiding anything," I stammered.

"And if I asked, would you say you are from Veydes? You won't fool me," he chuckled to himself.

"Where do you think I am from, then?"

"Do you not know?"

I hesitated, but curiosity got the better of me.

"I know where I am from—just not where that is," I prompted.

He paused his work. "What a strange thing to say. Lost lands, is it? I've heard of them." He nodded casually before focusing on his jars of steaming liquids.

"You have heard of lost lands? Where are they? Has anyone been to them?"

"No. I have heard stories over the years. Islands plunged into the sea, and others lost in the mist. Disappeared as much as the temples of Mayra and Erabas. My eyesight is not so good, but my ears are always open." The liquid before him pulsed and glowed brighter, lighting up his table.

"Well, if you've heard of these lands, then they aren't exactly lost, are they," I muttered.

It reminded me of the Canyons of the Lost. A place everyone knows of, though, according to Nuo's story, no one has ever escaped. "You're making magycris aren't you."

"At least your lying eyes can see. Mine tell me that perhaps you are not from the lost lands but an Aethar who's lost their legacy. Are the tales true, child? Do the gods scorn those who betray their own?"

"Don't just assume. You don't know anything about me. I wouldn't be an Aethar and be left alive by Brekt, would I?"

He chuckled, and it sounded like gravel rolling around in his chest. "So there *is* some personality hiding behind there." He lifted the jar in the air to inspect it. "Might keep you alive a little longer around here."

"Why did you say secrets run this world?"

"I've been alive for over three hundred years. I know and see many things. I see how everything changes, yet all stays the same. Many secrets lay behind closed doors. Be careful, girl. No one is as they seem."

"Who do you—wait, you're over three hundred years old? How?"

He shrugged as though I had asked him a simple question. Like it held no interest to him. "I handle magic crystals all day long. Probably did something along the way."

"Are there other alchemists? Ones who have lived a long life?"

"Don't know." He went about his work, not bothering to look up at me. "Don't get out much."

He was too busy to see me roll my eyes. Clearly, his mind had aged more than his body, and anything he said couldn't be taken seriously. I walked over to one of his shelves to inspect some of the plants he was growing.

"Careful with some of those. Don't let them touch your skin."

"Poison?" I asked.

"Mmm-hmm." He was mixing a new jar.

"What legacy are you?" I couldn't tell from his plain and aging features.

His hands paused working. "If I tell a secret, will you tell me one of yours?"

"I don't think I have any interesting ones, but sure."

"I am a son of Erabas. Much like the one you travel with— though I keep it to myself. I see best in the darker light and have a keen sense of hearing."

"I thought they were all gone!"

"Do not tell the golden ones," he whispered, making me pause.

"Why?"

"I told you one secret. Now tell me one."

"Well ... the only thing I keep secret is that I don't have a legacy at all."

"As you should. Tell no one—they will see you for an Aethar."

"Great, thanks for telling me *after* I just told you. Will you tell anyone?"

"No. Besides, I knew. You are from lands that are lost to the people here."

"That you know nothing about?"

"Correct."

My patience was waning as the conversation went on. I was still studying his shelves, careful not to touch anything, wondering how the Guards were doing.

God, the *Guards*, I still couldn't believe I had been travelling with the ones who were supposed to fight beside the Aspis.

"Do all legacies of Night have the ability to ... shift?" I remembered Brekt on the street, turning from shadow to man.

"A pure blood is the truly gifted child. Their blessing can form in many ways. I hear that Erebrekt of the North has rare skills indeed. He can see in pure darkness with the sound of his voice. He can hear through walls. I have been told he can even become the night itself. My gifts manifest in similar ways, but also different."

I noted that he hadn't quite answered my question.

He can even become night itself. Is that why I thought my eyes had played tricks on me? Now that I thought about it, I remember many times thinking I saw shadows pass over him, but I had just played it off as seeing things that weren't there.

"Why is it a secret you are a legacy of Night? What's been happening to them?"

"They are disappearing."

"Yes, I know. I mean, have there been others?"

Surely after three hundred years, he'd met more.

"History suggests as much."

"You haven't seen them?" Why couldn't this man give a straight answer?

The Alchemist sighed, "Those are not my secrets to tell. You travel with four Guards tasked to take down the magic-possessed Ikhor—it is in your best interest to keep things to yourself. I take it you haven't learnt that lesson, legacy-of-none."

I huffed out a breath. He had no idea how well I had learnt that lesson.

"Is that the same magycris the Guards ordered?" I walked closer to his desk.

"Yes. What your Guard ordered is already done on the counter over there. One slightly used by yourself."

My Guard. My heart did a little flip at his insinuation, which was ridiculous.

"So you make them for a lot of people?" He nodded in response. "What's your name, by the way? And how long have you known the Guardians? I mean the Guards, Brekt and the others."

He gave me an exasperated look. "I am working, you know. I'm not paid to answer a million questions to lost women."

I rolled my eyes again and took a seat on the stool Brekt had used. It was next to a table with small metal tools, all shiny and well kept.

I sat, taking in everything and nothing. My thoughts were running wild.

"Can you stop thinking so loud?" the old man grumbled, and I stopped tapping my foot and biting my nails. "They will be fine, and they will be here to get you in no time ... I hope."

I couldn't get my mind off the battle going on outside. What if more people were getting hurt? What if *the Guards* were?

Kazhi had taken one of my swords, its twin still strapped to my side. I pulled out my second one and laid it across my lap.

Today had been gruesome, showing what I would be up against if I travelled with the Guards. No wonder Brekt had been against me following. I had put them in danger as much as myself.

I studied the crystals adorning the blade on my lap.

"Once a crystal is emptied, can it be filled again with magic?" I asked the Alchemist.

"Not by anything but the earth itself, and no one has figured out how to ask the earth to fill them."

"So the answer is no."

"Careful, girl. Someone might think you are interesting underneath it all."

I scoffed. The old man got under my skin almost as much as Brekt. But I found I enjoyed the bold behaviour.

I wanted to be bold too.

The well of anger I stomped down inside me flared to life. I had a sword in my lap, yet I was still weak, proven on the street before —the weapon might as well be a blade of grass for all it could be used.

I concentrated on my sword—a good distraction from where my emotions were leading. I ran my finger over the blade, hovering over the old crystals. Like before, a light glowed in the empty stones. They hummed under my touch and I quickly pulled my hand away.

My chest tightened, and I glanced at the Alchemist to ensure he didn't see this strange reaction.

Only he had. And his eyes widened in surprise.

CHAPTER
THIRTY-FIVE

Brekt

B rekt returned to the fight. The Aethar hoard had spread throughout Bellum. Their numbers were difficult to determine, but nowhere had he seen so many together.

He found his team further down the street where he had left them. The trail of bodies was his guide.

He dove into the fight.

He had been sculpted for battle—he revelled in it. And right now, he desperately needed it. He was unravelling. The sounds of blades striking and bones crunching were more familiar to him than the sound of laughter. Taking down an enemy was more thrilling than the attention of a woman.

Except for her. His mind raged against the weak emotions while his heart betrayed the warrior he'd been before that cave.

"Nuo," Brekt roared. A group of Aethar collected to rush Nuo. Nuo spun, blade ready. Bodies fell.

Brekt moved next to Kazhi, who had her back to a tall building, facing several enemies.

Their eyes met. Plan made. Kazhi moved in that way of hers. None would see, but she would end up closer with each breath.

She was mouthing some silent prayer. She often did this before attacking, though Brekt had never asked what prayer she spoke.

Kazhi was almost as skilled as he at moving undetected. She was closing the distance to the Aethar, two knives now in her hands.

No one would see her throw them. It was Brekt who they kept their eyes on.

Bodies fell. His blood rushed.

Kazhi pulled her knives free of the fallen Aethars neck, cleaning them. Her snow-white skin had turned red. "What of the mother?" Brekt asked.

Olivia had broken down while holding the woman. Brekt could still hear the strangled sob she had made.

"She lives," was all Kazhi said before nodding toward Bas, who was circled by three scarred men.

They took the last Aethar down. The street was empty of civilians, save those strong enough to fight. Brekt cursed the trading city for not having their own soldiers.

Bellum was not in Guardian territory, and those here were outnumbered. Nevertheless, the city had been fortunate the Guards arrived and were eager to cut down the enemy.

"Look who put their dick away and came back to fight," Bastane muttered, standing straight. He gave Brekt a sideways glance.

"Ever the rule follower, Bas. It was you who demanded we practice for unexpected scenarios," Brekt reminded him, smiling.

"*We must never be unprepared.*" Kazhi imitated Bastanes rough voice, "*If one of us should fall.* You made me sit out the most."

"You guys know Bas," Nuo added, joining them, "Everything by the book. Don't waste time. Don't waste emotion."

Bastane pointed the tip of his blade toward Nuo. "You were why we practiced so many times. I figured it would be you throwing our game off when a girl came along, not the dark one." He tilted his head toward Brekt.

A lone Guardian, a golden Day-leg, ran toward them on the

street. She was bloody and panting. She slid to a stop, and Brekt noted the hand she held was missing fingers.

"I don't understand how there are so many. We need your help, Guards. They've swarmed the market, destroying everything."

The Guards were running before the Guardian could finish. The market was several blocks away.

Brekt's heart had almost stopped when he had found Olivia in the square earlier. How could he keep her from death when she ran toward it?

She had demanded meeting the Guards. Brekt had laughed when she had revealed the fire hidden beneath her fear. He welcomed it, wondering where that fire had gone since he first found her.

He believed her story now and wanted to tell her that today. He wanted to tell her all of it.

He had kept his identity from her for safety's sake, but it had been nice being looked upon without fear. Or even worse— reverence. The Guards hadn't deserved the kind of adoration they sometimes received. His team was a symbol. They had not yet proven their worth.

But Olivia had learned who they were as people, not Guards. He trusted she was ready to know more.

But maybe not all. Not yet.

The Guards ran behind buildings, through an alley and to the opposite side where the street opened to the market.

Chaos, everywhere. Dust floated through the air, kicked up in the riot. Brekt couldn't see far enough to know what was left standing.

"Do we split up?" Nuo scanned the market stalls close to them.

"I say yes," Kazhi answered, "the debris will cover our backs, and the dust will hide our approach."

Bas put away his long sword. Nuo held two short swords. Kazhi would use her knives, and Brekt would use his ability to shift. Precision weapons with little visibility.

"We each take a side. Drive them to the centre." Bas looked to each Guard, nodding. "West."

"North," Kazhi claimed.

"East," Nuo finished.

Meaning Brekt would move ahead and take this side of the market. He nodded to his fellow Guards as they vanished into the battle.

The square was a chorus of cries and blades. Brekt took a deep breath, welcoming the feeling.

He stood at the corner of the building, where no one could see him, in the shade of the ally. Figures fled past.

He reached out with his senses, feeling the shadows throughout the square, learning them, embracing and becoming them. Once he was ready, he knew precisely what colour of shadow to become.

Even in the day, he could become like the night. His skill was not bound to the darkness as most assumed. Where the day could not reach, he found shadow to form himself to.

The familiar feeling poured over him, like a warm body plunging into a cool stream. The sensation travelled over and through him as he became a shadow himself.

He did not become black as night or the shade of a tree. He became the movement you saw out of the corner of your eye before you looked, and it was gone. He became the absence of light. He took on the colours of the shadows and dust surrounding him.

He was light as air, moving around the corner of the building, advancing through the market.

The shadow-of-nothing inched further. Brekt sensed that the other Guards were in place, already moving. They knew how to act and what positions the others would take in any given scenario. They had trained for years, never stopping, constantly learning from mistakes, no matter how small.

They became invincible.

The screaming grew louder as the Guards cleared the market of

SARAH L. ROSE

Aethar. The others could be as invisible as he, dealing death before the enemy knew they were there.

Brekt became whole and plunged his sword through the back of the Aethar. And in a flash, he was mist again.

He scanned the market, searching for targets, but he was distracted as he went. The market stall where he'd bought Liv's earrings was in shambles.

They were the first gift he had ever given a woman. He had been willing to walk off that cliff to avoid embarrassing himself, giving such trinkets. But her reaction had been more than he expected.

His heart squeezed. *Damn it all. Concentrate!* He scolded himself.

How had this woman taken hold of him so quickly? He was so close to his goal, the Aspis waking, and never in his life had he let a woman in. Why her, and why now?

Brekt saw a form moving in the dust and shifted past the wreckage to find the back of a Guardian. The Sea-leg nearly screamed when Brekt materialized before him. The man's eye was swollen closed, and a gash across his throat. Luckily it was survivable.

"Time to get out, friend," Brekt growled, "we will finish the rest."

Brekt rested a hand on the man's shoulder. Relief transformed the man's face. Then Brekt was a shadow once more.

He spun, listening for footsteps. The market grew quieter as he went along. He found several more Aethar and ended them swiftly.

He stepped over a fallen body, turned, and bumped into a tall figure behind him.

That never happened. *You're distracted*, he chided himself.

Both of them spun, backing away and raising weapons. Brekt froze as he faced ... not an Aethar. Not a Guardian.

A man with white hair and blue skin stood, frozen as Brekt, deciding if he faced friend or enemy. The man had markings on his skin—dark blue, just as Liv had described. Her *beautiful blue man.*

280

His cloak was too clean. His face unmarked, body too lean. Not a warrior.

"Guard." The man backed away, lowering a knife, nodding.

Brekt shifted back to shadow as someone grabbed the blue man. "Let's go. We have our escape," a high female voice said.

The dust cleared as the battle neared an end, and the two people disappeared.

Brekt was close to the centre market when silence settled. The air was clearing of dust when he finally put away his weapon. He found Bastane counting his arrows and cleaning the tips of those he'd recovered. Nuo was sitting on a fallen stall, hands on his knees.

"Well, that felt good," Nuo smiled. Brekt let his ability fade, making himself shiver. The transformation always felt like water running down his back.

"Kaz?" Brekt wondered how she had not arrived first. She was the fastest of them.

Bastane nodded his head to the north, where Kazhi strode toward them. She grinned, showing two rows of blood-red teeth.

"Did you bite someone?" Bas scowled.

She spit blood at his feet, laughing when he jumped back. "Don't mess your boots, prince."

"Ugh!"

"You get a bit distracted?" Nuo asked. It took Brekt a moment to realize Nuo was talking to him.

He looked down and noted all the new gashes. He hadn't noticed how sloppy he had been.

"Told you," Bas muttered, "His mind isn't in the fight today."

"Fuck off." Brekt was unable to hide how much it bothered him.

Olivia had become a distraction he was not willing to leave behind. Not that bringing her along would give them time together.

Did she guess he would lose her one day soon?

Did she see him seeking her forgiveness for his selfishness? He wanted to tell her it would all be okay. But he knew the lie that it was.

More screams. The Guards rose and ran to the next street.

"This was a planned attack," Nuo shouted as they ran. "This is not how the Aethar behave. Somethings up."

Nuo exchanged a look with Brekt. He knew they were thinking the same—the time for the great battle was coming.

Brekt dove back into the bloodshed—to feel confident, sure and in control. Because lately, the battlefield was the only place he felt as if his feet were on solid ground.

CHAPTER

THIRTY-SIX

Liv

The Alchemist's eyes were on me, glued and searching. I knew what his look meant—that shouldn't have happened. The crystals should not have glowed under my fingertips.

"What—"

Someone banged on the door. The old man reluctantly broke eye contact with me.

A second loud bang shook the room, and a deep growl came from outside.

The Alchemist opened the door a crack and peeked through.

"Cursed Night, kids, I'm not a shelter. I'm trying to run a business here." He opened the door wide for the two Guards. Brekt was hanging off Nuo's shoulder and was limping once again. More blood was splattered across his face.

"I thought you were supposed to be a fearsome fighter," the old man huffed as Nuo led Brekt across the room.

"He is usually." Nuo's eyes glanced toward me. The guilt had me looking away. "Something is up with him today."

SARAH L. ROSE

Nuo spotted the stool I was on and headed over. I got up and helped him set Brekt down, who grunted in pain.

"Is he badly hurt? Has the wound on his back opened again?" There was so much blood. I ran to his back, but the pink scar remained closed.

"*He* is right here," Brekt grumbled. Blood was trailing down his face, his neck and under his shirt. His right leg had a brutal gash across his thigh. Any other wounds were hidden under all the blood.

"Brekt was trying to show off. Took on over ten Aethars at once."

"Twenty. I wanted to end the fight faster. And how did they make out?" he growled at Nuo, whose attention was on the Alchemist. The old man was bringing over the bag with the rest of their order.

I searched Brekt's face for signs of greater pain. His nostrils flared, and he was focusing on everything but me.

Nuo rolled his eyes. He appeared *mostly* unharmed. He grabbed a glass jar out of the bag and opened it. Hovering above Brekt's leg, he poured a few drops on the wound.

Brekt hissed and grabbed the edge of the nearest table, his wound slowly closing up. I was mesmerized by the power of magycris.

Nuo put the jar back in the bag and pulled out a small container. He dropped it in my hand.

"It's all you now, BB. Make him use it." It was a balm he passed me. "You can't enter a fight like that again," he said to Brekt. "What's up?"

"Nothing. I get to have one bad day, don't I?"

Nuo waited for Brekt to say more.

"I know why," I said reluctantly. "It's not his fault. It's mine."

"Liv, keep it to yourself," Brekt warned.

He missed the look I gave him, still not facing me.

"No," I snapped, making Nuo's face light up, and Brekt finally

284

turned my way. "I don't want any more secrets. Nothing changes that way," I repeated what the old man had said.

"What did I miss?" Nuo was still grinning. He enjoyed it when Brekt was scolded.

"Last night, I saw a constellation I recognized—one that I saw when I lived back home. I guess I'm from your world after all and was somehow transported from my land to yours. By that Light. Brekt is worried you'll think I'm an Aethar and didn't want me telling you."

Nuo's eyes widened. "You—"

His head swivelled from Brekt and back to me. I waited, holding my breath for him to turn on me like Brekt said he would.

Nuo surprised me by laughing. "Well, of course, she isn't an Aethar. You, idiot brother, should be the first to know that."

"Why is that?" I asked Brekt.

Brekt stayed silent. Because he saw me in his dreams? Did they tell him where my home was too?

"Nuo, you told me stories about the gods fighting and lands being lost."

Although the Alchemist pretended not to listen to our conversation, his keen hearing would miss nothing.

Nuo nodded. My revelation was keeping him quiet. He thought Brekt should know I wasn't lying.

"I don't know much of these lands other than old histories. I can't say I have a good theory."

"I wonder why they have not been found," I said, defeated.

"That will be one of the things we need to figure out. But I think even you can agree that it will have to be put off for now," Nuo sighed. "Clean up the wound on his back, BB. You two need to talk. One of us will be back to collect you as soon as we've got a way out."

"A way out of where?" I asked Nuo as he headed for the front door. He closed the door and left without answering.

I forgot to ask about the mother.

I was still holding my hand up with the container. Brekt was avoiding my gaze. "Talk about what?"

"Is everything cleared on the streets?" The old man asked Brekt.

"They're taken care of or have fled," he grumbled. "Don't know if they'll come back, but I'm guessing not with the numbers they lost."

"I've got deliveries to make then. I imagine a few customers will need this sooner than later. Don't touch anything, boy."

Brekt nodded. I was still watching him as the door opened and closed, leaving us alone in the Alchemist's shop.

Silence fell like a blanket over the store.

I opened the jar up to see a green lotion—the same balm that Brekt had used on me after that first Aethar attack.

"Where else are you hurt?"

"I can do it." He reached out for the container, but I moved my hand so he couldn't take it. He narrowed his eyes—maybe he believed I wasn't an Aethar, but he was still upset with me for some reason.

"What's wrong with you?" I demanded.

He glanced away. "What do you mean?"

"Why are you avoiding looking at me?"

He was quiet a moment before he slowly turned back. His face was void of any emotion, watching me, waiting for something.

"Well?" I asked. "Is it because of last night?"

"I—" he released a long breath, "I'm angry, and I'm— You know who we are now. The Guards."

"Oh. Yes, I heard on the street." I fidgeted with the jar. "Is that bad?"

"Yes. No. Both. I'm waiting for you to be upset or scared of what that means. I wanted to tell you myself. And also, I'm trying not to lecture you for being in that square."

"I see. Well, I didn't know what was happening until I was in that square." I should feel ashamed, but I would be lying to myself. I wanted to know what was happening. "As for finding out about you four, I was surprised. I'm *not* surprised you didn't tell me. As you said, you didn't trust me." Even if I didn't like being kept in the dark.

He nodded.

"I was mostly shocked because the Guards were not what I expected."

"What do you mean?" Curiosity erased the anger lingering on his face.

"In my head, I had pictured the Guards to be a little more glamorous than you four."

A ghost of a smile appeared on his face. "I had once thought the same."

"Where else are you hurt?" I put some of the balm on my fingers.

He seemed apprehensive but then stood up. He towered over me. His hands came down to his waistline, grabbed the hem of his ripped top, and pulled it up and over his head.

I expected heat to rush through me, but it was quickly overshadowed by shock. His torso and back were nothing but cuts and wounds.

"Oh my god. You're covered!"

"I was surrounded." He flashed me a quick smile. "They, however, are no longer on their feet."

I swallowed. "Sit down, show off. I'll start on your back. And stop looking so smug."

He did as I said. The cuts on his back were not deep, and I got to work.

I leaned close, rubbing the balm in as softly as I could.

"You're a lot better at that than the others. They practically make the wounds deeper with how rough they are."

I smiled, picturing Bastane or Nuo rubbing balm on a topless Brekt. My stomach twisted, thinking about Kazhi doing it.

"What did Nuo mean when he said he was finding a way out?"

"There were more Aethars here today than we have seen

before. Something is up. We don't want to be seen departing the city and leaving a trail to follow."

"Do you think the Ikhor has really come back?"

"After today—I do." A chill went through me.

This meant a war was coming. An evil spirit inhabiting the body of an Aethar would burn the earth, which my new friends were to stop, and I was part of it somehow.

"So, how long have you been a Guard and not just a Guardian?"

He tensed for a moment. "We were chosen a few years ago."

"Mmmm." I worked my way down his back and along his ribcage. "That's why you didn't want me to go with you?" I asked nervously. He didn't answer right away.

"Part of it." His voice was deeper than usual. "It means a lot of danger."

"What are the other parts? Nuo mentioned we need to talk. I agree. There's something you aren't telling me. He made it sound like you should *know* I'm not an Aethar. How?"

He didn't answer. I huffed a breath, trying to get my hair out of my face.

Brekt spun in his seat, no longer avoiding me. A small smile transformed his face, and a brow went in the air.

"What?" I demanded.

He turned back around, and a deep rumbling came from his chest. "I'm starting to figure you out, is all."

"What do you mean?"

"You tend to keep a lot in, but your mannerisms give you away. Right now, you're annoyed with me." I could feel his shoulders shaking.

"And you think that's funny?"

"Yes, actually, I do. Women don't usually get irritated with me. They tend to feel admiration before anything else."

"Well, it's not funny." I ignored his comment. "It's aggravating. I never get any answers out of you."

"And you're any different? Let's make a deal, Liv. You want me to talk, then give as much as you get. I'm not going to bare it all to a woman I hardly know."

Irritated, I pressed, "Why do you act as if you know me then? You chose to take me with you, and you—" I faltered, not wanting to admit more.

"I what?" He faced me fully. I couldn't hide from his piercing gaze, so black in the dim lights. The glowing objects in the room cast deep shadows across his face, and his scar stood out more than usual.

I stumbled over my thoughts. Did I mention that morning in the tent? That he looks at me like he's interested? That he bought me earrings?

What did any of that mean?

Nothing. It meant nothing, and he was right—he knew nothing about me, and I knew nothing about him. Whatever I felt was most likely just a result of loneliness, a need for some kind of attention.

"Is this because you still believe I was lying to you?"

"No. I decided today I trust that you've been telling me the truth, that you did not know you were still in your own world. But that doesn't mean I know you or that you're any less of a stranger. You still haven't told me much of your past." His hand came up to grab the jar. "I can do the rest now."

"Let me do your face first," I said quietly.

I was about to dip into some more of the medicine, but his attention was glued to me. The temperature of the room grew uncomfortably warm.

"We could at least try working together to wake the Aspis." I tried, ignoring the growing tension. "I've been waiting to meet the Guards to discover my role in finding the Aspis and how the Light brought me here. And now here you are, and I fear I will learn nothing. You four aren't exactly forthright with information."

"We were telling the truth when we said we didn't know how you travelled across the world. But we can try to help you find answers—if there is time. As for how the Guards locate the Aspis, even I won't reveal our biggest secret. I can't risk that. If others found out—no. Give it time, and trust us. With Nuo, we can find it and, hopefully, discover why you are here at the same time."

I clung to the hope he would stick by this decision.

"I shouldn't bring you with us," his eyes were searching, "but I feel like there's a force pushing me to do so. Tell me something, Olivia, anything. Just tell me something real, and I will do the same."

He was offering me an opening, one that I was free to take or leave. I wanted to take it. The feelings I had for him—I so badly wanted to have a reason behind them. Perhaps he wished the same.

I was being pulled to him. He had to feel it—because why else would he admit he felt forced?

CHAPTER
THIRTY-SEVEN

H e was stern yet eager as he waited, and I stood stupidly holding the jar, biting my lip.

His attention snagged on my mouth, and I knew he could see the warmth spreading across my face. His eyes darkened as a smile broke through his harsh features, making me lose my train of thought.

He was so beautiful in such a dangerous way.

And he wanted to know something real about me.

Right.

"Why did you beg that woman to stay alive?" he asked in a low voice.

I wasn't prepared for that question. I shook my head as if my will alone could erase it.

"Something happened to your mother. Something bad that you saw today."

There was a breath stuck in my chest. I nodded once, unable to say more.

"I see. I hope one day you can tell me the story. For your own sake, not mine."

"Thank you. For not pushing."

"The woman you wanted to be saved is breathing."

"She's okay?" I hadn't wanted to hope, only to be hurt if she'd died.

"Nuo healed her well enough. She will live."

"Thank you. I know you risked your own healing for her to have the medicine. Thank you."

The urge to reach out to him surprised me. And I wasn't sure he was someone who accepted that kind of touch. Instead, I gave him something else, something he had asked for. "Someone betrayed me," I said quickly.

His eyes flew to mine, and a crease formed between his brows.

I hadn't been ready to accept the truth. I still wasn't ready. "The men who showed up at my door were brought there. Because I didn't fit in, I wasn't acting as I should and following the rules. They wanted to teach me what I'd done wrong and how to behave."

"They were going to take you away to a prison."

"Yes. But they don't let you out after—at least I've never heard of someone being let back out."

A hand came up to my face making me flinch. I hadn't expected the contact. But as his fingers touched my cheek, brushing away moisture, I relaxed. Although his hands were gentle, his demeanour changed. He was stiff, agitated—maybe even angry.

"Do you know who betrayed you?" he asked gently.

I was terrified to answer this question. His fingers left my face and took my hand, which shook while holding the jar.

I tilted my head down once. I knew—and I would never forget.

He nodded. "You can tell me more another time if you need to." His hands dropped down to his lap. "I tried to grasp why you were so cautious about opening up. You had told me what your world was like, which would surely affect you. But to know you were betrayed, now I understand. Betrayal is not something you can easily move past."

"The day I opened the door to the armed men standing outside, *she* was there," I whispered, my voice cracking.

My eyes were on the jar, his wounds long forgotten.

I couldn't focus on anything while I relived that moment when the last piece of my heart had broken. "Rebeka, my sister, stood outside with the Law Keepers. They passed her payment right in front of me."

Brekt stayed quiet. It was difficult to admit that my last blood relative had tried to put me away, betraying any love that had existed between us.

"I had visited Rebeka several days before and hinted that I had sought the company of a man from our village. It was strictly forbidden. The Keepers gave high rewards to anyone who had info on those not following the rules. Rebeka had her second child on the way, and her man was a farmer on lands that grew a pathetic amount of crops. I tell myself she had reason to betray me, only so it hurts a little less. She needed to feed her children. And my misdeeds could have been used to punish her family, as well as myself.

"She had her hand resting on her swollen belly as a Keeper passed her the reward. I did understand. I truly did. Living was harsh, and as a mother, she would do anything to give her child the best chance possible. But she also understood that when she raised her eyes to mine, she was no longer seeing her sister. We were done in that moment. Every bond we ever had was severed when the bag of coin landed in her hands."

I continued to study the jar. Whether it was anger, pity or worry on his face, I didn't want to see it. It was hard enough opening up to someone about a truth you tried to hide from yourself.

"It's your turn," I said, ready to change the subject. I grabbed more of the balm for a gash across his forehead. This way, I didn't have to look him in the eye.

"What do you want to know?" he said evenly. I was grateful he understood not to push for more.

"Let's start with this massive scar on your face. Did an Aethar give you that?"

He laughed and rested his hands on his knees. "That's what you choose?"

My hands were shaking for a different reason as I pressed my fingers against his skin. I spent a lot of time with Stephen alone, but with Brekt, everything was more intense.

I could feel his warmth this close, smell the leather and pine along with blood. I was so aware of my senses, heightened in his presence.

The tattoos along his neck were so black against his tan skin. I reached out and brushed my finger along one. When I first saw their tattoos, I wondered what they would feel like. I was surprised they were as soft as skin.

I noticed him smirking and quickly pulled my hand back.

"Were you trying to feel my muscles or my tattoos?" he purred, "You're welcome to touch either."

I swallowed my embarrassment as fast as I could.

I rubbed more medicine in, dabbing across his face, trying to concentrate on the wounds, not the muscles he didn't need to point out. I was relieved when he changed the subject.

"The scar is from Kazhi."

"What? Did she do that to you in training? No wonder you guys are so scary."

He made a face at my comment. "No, it wasn't in training." He eyed me for a moment, considering. "She gave it to me when she tried to assassinate me."

I froze, fingers dipped into the jar.

A rumble came from deep in his chest as he laughed again. "She didn't start training with us until after."

"You let her in after she tried to kill you?"

"She had a rough past, one that I understood. She was used for her skills with hunting and killing."

He *would* understand—he was also used to punish other students in North Aspis. "You know about her past but not her legacy?" I probed.

"I've long assumed she is a child of Ouras. When I was young, a clan of Mount-legs came through the north camp to trade. Nuo was terrified of them. They were from the far north, and I had wondered how anyone lived in a place *colder* than our home.

"The clan had behaved half animal. Their skin was deathly pale with spots like a snowcat. Their skill and movement were unearthly. Nuo had nightmares for an entire week after they had left," he grinned.

I brushed a finger across rough skin as he continued, "Some legacies have been hurt because of who they are. As a Night-leg, I know that well. Kazhi didn't want to say, so I let it be. When she first came to the Guardian camp and tried to take out the best warriors, Nuo, Bas, and I captured her, and we got certain information out of her. Her past is hers to guard, as you should understand, Liv. I knew she was skilled and that her future was with the Guards."

"You *knew*?" I asked casually.

He shifted in his seat. I still wasn't going to admit I had listened to him talking about his dreams. We both understood that trusting a person with our secrets took time.

"Who sent her?" I asked instead.

"There are people in powerful positions who try to control the public. Many are pure-blood families. Even within the Guardians and their council, not everyone is on each other's side. Wealthy lords, who want power and glory, try to control who is chosen for the Guards. I believe one wanted his eldest son to be chosen. Knowing I was in the way, as well as Nuo, they sent Kazhi to take us out. She was a hired killer long before being chosen as a Guard. We convinced her that she was worth more than that. Although the pay isn't as good, it's a different kind of value."

He laughed, but there was no real humour as he talked of the conflicts for control and power. It explained why he appeared exhausted at times. But I was even more enthralled with my world —so much history, so much at stake. And now that I was growing close to people within it, I wished I could do more to help.

"Why do you keep going?" I asked.

Brekt seemed confused at the question, so I continued. "Why did you accept being a Guard if it makes you so miserable? Couldn't you stop?" Perhaps I was not asking for his sake but to answer my own reservations.

"I've never even thought it was an option. It's not an option." He shook his head, more to himself than for me. "I do it because of them. They are my family, the only family I've ever had. Bastane and Kazhi are recent additions, but I would do anything for them. And I will."

Guilt swarmed me like a howling wind. I was still convinced the Light had got it wrong—picked the wrong girl. Meanwhile, Brekt pushed himself forward to a future he may have never chosen for himself, all for the sake of those he called family.

"I wish I had family like you."

"I thought your mother was good to you."

"She was, and then all I had left was Rebeka. As you now know, she was the opposite. She had given up on me long before she handed me over to the Keepers."

I allowed myself to look at him this time. All I saw on his face was understanding.

"Not all family is worth having," I said quietly. "Your friends are what everyone should have, but not everyone gets."

"You get them too, Liv," he claimed, surprising me. "Nuo especially. He has already adopted you."

I couldn't stop the smile that bloomed. "Thanks. I accept, as long as you're not my brother."

His face went blank, eyes boring into mine. I just admitted I was attracted to him. How embarrassing.

"I saw you on the street," I said so quickly that it made it even more apparent I had been flirting. "I saw you come out of thin air."

"Did I scare you?"

"Yes." When I noticed his expression hardened, I added, "I'm not scared off. I'm just amazed at what you can do."

"I don't like people to be reminded of what I am," he admitted.

"I understand."

The old man admitted he was also a Night legacy. I didn't tell Brekt—as the old man said, it was not my secret to tell.

"I'm done now." I passed the jar to him.

"Thank you." He dunked his fingers into the jar and smeared it carelessly across his chest. I wanted to roll my eyes.

He stood, grabbing his shirt and pulling it over his head. I tried not to stare as his muscles flexed. He was so close. He was a magnet, and I was helpless.

I moved to make myself busy, but before I could, his hand reached out, and I stopped. We stood awkwardly while I waited for him to do something. But his eyebrows came together, and he put his hand back down.

"I say I don't know you," he whispered, his breath fanning my face, "but I feel like I've known you for longer than I have. There are things I want to share with you because I *do* trust you."

I couldn't move. All the while, my stomach flipped.

"I don't know how to act around you," he continued, "And I've *never* been unsure of myself."

I could hardly manage a coherent thought, "I know—not that I've felt very sure of myself, but that I feel like—I feel more than I should."

My throat went dry, and my stomach went into acrobatics. Why did I say that?

But he didn't back away. He didn't react in any way at all except continue to stare down at me.

I decided to be bold then. The feeling in my stomach travelled lower until it became something else, something I had become familiar with only after meeting Stephen—I wanted this man. And the way his eyes burned, I think he was feeling the same.

I lifted my hand and let my fingers brush his cheek. His eyes flashed with an unknown emotion. His skin was rough but warm, and the excitement sent a current through me. So I let my hand lower to his chest.

He stepped closer, pushing against my palm. The hard muscle flexed as he took a breath, which was as jagged as my own.

"You're not at all what I expected," he said, mirroring what he said to me the night by the camp.

"What did you expect?" What did he see in his dreams, the ones he hadn't yet admitted to? Would he tell me now?

His eyes lowered, becoming hooded.

My heart raced, and I wet my lips and his attention darted to my mouth. I felt foolish. Like I'd never done this before.

Before I could find out if he would lean in, voices sounded outside the door. I jumped, pulling my hand away from his chest.

The door opened, and Bastane came in with Nuo, who appeared to be in a foul mood.

Brekt stepped away from me, straightening his back.

"Wait till you hear what this guy has to say." Nuo walked into the room. He moved right around us, plopped down on the chair, and threw an elbow onto the table beside him. Little metal instruments clinked together.

Bastane was unloading a bag off of his shoulder. "If you don't like my mode of transportation, next time, you figure it out," he practically growled at Nuo. He was in a bad mood too.

Brekt had his arms crossed, waiting to hear what was happening, looking unaffected by what had just taken place between us. The moment was swept out from under us so fast that my heart was still racing.

"You got the worst airship we could possibly get a ride on," Nuo complained.

Brekt raised an eyebrow in question.

"Yeah," Nuo replied, "that one."

"An airship?" I asked. I knew what a ship was. But an Airship? Nuo had forgotten to explain what it was the first time he mentioned one.

"A flying machine," Brekt confirmed.

Our eyes locked. His mouth was set in a hard line, but it was in his gaze, burning with emotion, that I saw what his posture was hiding.

Maybe he wasn't so unaffected after all.

"And we are going on it?"

"Don't get excited, BB. It's flown by the worst, overbearing narcissist you'll ever meet."

"And you don't get along with him? That's hard to believe," I teased.

His face hardened. "It's a she."

That had me stunned. There was a woman that Nuo didn't like?

"We need to get out of this place fast," Brekt said, "The Aethars that left might inform the Ikhor we were here, putting the city and the people in more danger."

"*If* they were telling the truth," Bastane countered.

"I think they were," Brekt said.

Nuo sat up a little straighter. As if Brekt knew something. Apprehension sunk in. A war was coming. And I was going on my first trip in the air.

"If the Ikhor is awake, it means our time has come. It will call for the Aspis and wake it," Nuo said to his friends—to the Guards. Brekt shifted his gaze to me, worried.

"Where's Kazhi?" I asked.

"She's going to meet us at the launch site. She went back to the hotel to grab our things," Nuo answered.

Nuo reached around his side, remembering something. He pulled my sword out from his belt and passed it to me. I put it in its leather casing, thankful he had remembered it.

"Let's get to it then." Brekt moved to pack us up. My chest tightened—the giant black beast would wake soon.

I could no longer avoid the path set before me by the strange Light. The Guards had found me, the Aethars were moving in, and the Ikhor had awoken—fate had led me here. I only had to figure out how to follow through.

"Olivia, keep that hood up like before," Brekt said. "Now that we've been spotted, I think it's a good idea fewer people see you travelling with the Guards. I don't want you to get unnecessary attention. Falizha is enough." He gave Bastane a look.

Falizha—it was a name I'd never heard. The captain of an airship.

Bastane threw his hands up in the air. "How am I to know what specific women you need to avoid? They're everywhere, especially with this one." He glared at Nuo, who simply shrugged.

Was that why he hated this woman? A past lover? Or maybe he was denied.

But Nuo was watching Brekt, and worry etched his features. Did that mean ... was this woman Brekt's past lover? The thought slammed into me like a brick wall.

"Do you still wish to come?" Brekt's voice was low. The others headed to the door. "I told you on the hilltop I wanted to bring you. But that was before you found out we were the Guards."

I could only nod. I didn't know if I was ready for this.

CHAPTER

THIRTY-EIGHT

I followed the three Guards through the streets with my hood up and my head down. I focused only on keeping up with their long strides.

I heard crying as we passed groups and shouting as we turned corners.

The energy of the city had changed—they were scared.

I ungracefully maneuvered in the crowd, thinking about how this world was violent, divided—not unlike home, but here it was so very much *alive*. Only someone from a life of solitude and imprisonment might see it that way—see this chaos as a sign of living. I felt a thrill along with the fear.

The world was full of magic. Even my mother's stories could come true—I could see beasts and monsters, princesses and villains. I no longer had the luxury of being the girl who feared the world.

It took us time to navigate the city. Brekt was in the lead, checking streets, trying to avoid lingering Aethars. People got out of his way, recognizing he was a Guard—Erebrekt of the North, the feared legacy of Night. They gave similar looks to Nuo and Bastane. Luckily no one paid any attention to me.

I followed behind Nuo. It was impossible to miss the blood soaking the dirt below. Motionless forms lingered in my peripheral, and I refused to focus on them. I knew they were either fallen friends or defeated foes, but it didn't matter—death surrounded me and triggered memories of the past, just like the Aethar had when he captured the boy.

The still form of my mother flashed through my mind, and I quickly focused once more on Nuo's black boots trudging through the blood on the streets.

"Too many died today." Nuo offered a kind smile to those he passed.

"May they enter the halls of Eternal Day." Bastane touched his chest, his brow pinching as he took in the dead.

"And may the guilty suffer the Endless Night," Nuo finished what must be a prayer.

Families like the ones the Guards had saved were looking for loved ones not yet located.

The Guards tried to assure the people as they passed that help was coming. The Guardians were here and would chase down those who caused the destruction today. Every time they were stopped only made it more likely for us to lose our chance of getting out of the city, but I understood why they did it. These people had no one else.

After a long journey, we reached the northwest side of the city. The worn-out wood buildings were spread further apart. This area was for storage and shipments. Men carried barrels and crates through large doors and loaded others on carts pulled by more angulas. Bert had been small compared to the other leathery, striped skin creatures.

We were reaching the corner of the street when gold flashed from across the road. It was the monk. The same one who had been 'educating' people on the street and who had hidden in the alley during the attack. He was walking away from the direction we were going. He glanced our way, and his eyes widened when he noticed the Guards.

I was surprised when he zeroed in on me. Did he remember who I was? He was probably wondering why I was shadowing the legendary Guards. But why would he care?

We rounded the corner, entering a large open area at the city's edge. My mouth hung open as I took in the behemoth before me.

Hovering a few feet above the ground and larger than several houses was the airship.

It was made of the same metallic stone as Nuo's torch and the riding machine in the Last City. The top of the ship, which was three or four stories up, was open and surrounded by a gold railing. People walked around on the deck, carrying large items. They looked so small from where I stood below.

There were two long sails on the ship's side, reminding me of the pirates my mother told me stories of. However, unlike the vessels from her stories, there were no sails on top—they were instead tucked in down the sides. A strange fabric was folded in on itself, emitting a faint glow.

There were also glowing strips through the airship's metal—lines and patterns that flowed around its surface.

The lower half had windows throughout, and the front of the ship was made of a single large piece of glass. Here, more people stood inside talking over the top of a table. When the ship was in the air, was this where they stood to navigate?

The Guards headed to the lower back of the airship, where a step ladder made of rope hung, trailing on the ground.

There was no sound coming from the craft as it hovered there. If the city were quiet, would I hear a humming like I could from the crystals?

We reached the ladder, walking into the shadows under the ship. I brushed my hand along its bottom. The metal was warmer than I'd assumed. It was rough yet looked smooth, almost polished. Brekt was watching, and I pulled my hand back, embarrassed.

Bastane climbed up first, with Nuo passing up the few things we carried with us. I was about to head up when Brekt grabbed my arm.

"Maybe, for this journey, *do* keep to yourself."

When I tilted my head in question, he added. "I trust you ten times the amount I trust the captain of this ship."

That was saying something. "Why? Who is she?"

"Not now. This ship isn't a place we should talk openly."

He nodded to the ladder, and I grabbed ahold of it. The rope swayed as I placed my foot on the first step. My fingers closed tight on the wood, knuckles turning white. I let myself rock in place, unaccustomed to climbing, especially on a moving ladder.

There was the slightest rumble of laughter behind me, and a pair of hands reached my sides to steady me. That didn't help in the least, because I was now distracted by Brekt's grip on my waist.

Nuo glanced at us from above. "You really are a pain in the ass, BB." His hand shot out, and I climbed another step to reach for it. "But I must admit I enjoy the look on Brekt's face when I take your attention."

I turned my head, which was now level with Brekt's.

"Deck him in the face for me when you get up there, Liv. He's grown too accustomed to me doing it," he said.

"No. I enjoy your brooding face too much." I gave him a taunting smile.

Both pairs of eyes were on me. Nuo was failing to hide his pleasure. "It feels good to have her as my teammate, brother."

I reached the top and had to crawl on my hands and knees. Brekt was already pulling himself over the edge as I got to my feet.

"I think I might have a move or two to sway her over to my side." His wolfish grin made my stomach tighten.

"It's a game then." Nuo draped his arm over my shoulder. Brekt stood straight, eyebrow going in the air.

A lilting voice echoed in the small corridor we were huddled in, ending the fun.

It belonged to a woman walking down several steps and entering the long passageway in which we now stood. She floated toward us, past the ropes and lights that hung along the brown metallic walls.

She was beautiful and a notable legacy of Rem. This daughter of Day was gold perfection—perfectly put together, perfectly golden blonde, perfectly tall and symmetrical.

She wore dark clothes like most Guardians, contrasting nicely with her golden-tanned skin. Her clothes hugged her figure in the most flattering way. Was this what all pure-blood legacies of Day looked like? She reminded me of the gold figures in the cave, painted under Rem's Temple.

The smile she gave the two men was welcoming and a bit *too* friendly. She knew them well.

The lights reflected off her bright yellow irises as she ignored me.

"Hello, boys. I was so happy to hear you asked for my help to get you back to the Guardian City. I didn't hesitate to tell my crew to set up a room and get you some new clothing prepared."

Brekt nodded, and Nuo's face was wiped clean of any warmth. This must be the woman Nuo wasn't happy about seeing—the Captain.

Nuo stayed silent with his arm around me. It was Brekt that stepped up.

"Falizha. Thank you for the assistance. We were planning on returning to the city on horseback. With today's events, we were lucky you were in the area."

He stood stiffly, and his voice was clipped. He wasn't a very good actor. If I ever teased him about being grouchy, it was nothing compared to his current tone.

"It's been too long, Erebrekt." She approached and wrapped her arms around him, embracing him like they were intimate. Nuo's hand squeezed my arm to keep me still.

She offered a heated smile to Nuo. "And I'm glad to see you as well. I hope the Aethars didn't give you too much trouble," she teased.

"They wouldn't, would they? I'm a Guard," Nuo replied flatly.

Brekt gave him a warning look.

I was surprised at Nuo's hostility. Besides the hug I didn't enjoy watching, she seemed only pleasant toward them.

What had happened?

She turned to walk away as if there wasn't a third person in the hall to greet. My jaw clenched as she chimed, "Come, I'll have someone show you to your room."

"My name is Olivia." The sarcasm was not lost in my tone. "I'm sure you meant to ask. It's a pleasure to meet you."

I don't know what came over me. Nuo's reaction? My anger at her embracing Brekt? Or the fact she then just turned and pretended I didn't exist? I was done with being treated like that.

She stopped and slowly forced a smile. "Of course, welcome. It's been a hectic few hours preparing for the Guards of the Aspis to join my ship. Sorry for my rudeness. I'm Falizha."

It was subtle, but I didn't miss the warning when she said *my ship*.

The pleasantries contrasted the look she speared me with.

She continued out of the corridor, expecting us to follow. Nuo grabbed the sides of my head and planted a kiss on my forehead. "You damned hostile goddess, BB. You just made my day."

Brekt smacked Nuo across the head as I tried to push him away. "Lips to yourself, bastard," he growled, making Nuo laugh.

Nuo linked his arm with mine and pulled me forward, following Falizha.

However, I was focused on the woman, not the humour on Nuo's face. Falizha wore a mask too, and I could only guess that under hers was a villainous snake coiled and ready for attack.

"I've never seen anything like it," I wondered aloud, meaning the ship. We followed the stairs up, which led into a larger hallway. There were doors leading off both sides, all made of the same material.

"You won't see many like it," Nuo whispered in my ear, his arm still holding mine. "Ships like this are very rare. Only the extremely wealthy can keep one." His head nodded toward the woman leading us down the hall. She was just far enough away to avoid hearing us. "Daddy's money."

So, she came from wealth, which explained the ship but not the connection to the Guards. Brekt had asked me to keep to myself, so I didn't press further. I would wait until we were alone. I already had her attention against his warning.

She led us up another wide metal staircase that took us through a door into a large open space.

It was a war room. A massive round table in the centre was covered with papers and maps. Surrounding the table were numerous women. They all wore shades of black and had tattoos and piercings, some even as tattooed as Kazhi. Everyone here was a Guardian.

The wall opposite the door was made of glass. This was the room I'd seen earlier.

In front of the window was a raised platform with a table sitting on top. It wasn't quite a table, as it was angled, but I had no other word for it. A few chairs sat behind this table, and the women in these chairs pressed buttons and moved handles.

That must be where they controlled the ship.

Beyond the window the city vanished below us. It sent shivers down my spine and made me tighten my hold on Nuo's arm—I hadn't felt us moving.

I snapped my head to Nuo. "What about Kazhi?"

At that moment, Kazhi stalked forward, away from the table, having blended in with the women in black. She nodded to us, and I noted Bastane also at the table, talking with some of the women.

Falizha turned back to us. "Kazhi, why don't you take the others to your room, and you can all clean up? The trip across the continent will still take us a few days. Might as well get comfortable."

Falizha's eyes were on Brekt, making a trail up his form to stop on his face. She appeared to be sizing him up as much as she was checking him out.

"Captain," a woman came up behind her. Falizha's gaze lingered on Brekt for far too long before she returned to her work and let us escape the war room.

CHAPTER

THIRTY-NINE

The room we were given was small, with four sets of bunk
beds. Each bed had a set of clothing for the men, Kazhi
having already changed. A noticeable pair of clothing was
missing. It wasn't that I needed to change. I wasn't covered in
blood and gore. I just noted that I was to be treated like I wasn't
even here.

"There's a bathing room through there." Kazhi pointed to a
door to the side of the room. "Running water on this ship. We
lucked out catching a ride with them."

Nuo scoffed, Brekt stayed silent, and Bastane sighed before he
took the first turn using the bathing room. The negative energy in
the small space was suffocating.

Kazhi's hands went to her hips. Her black eyes bore into her
brothers. "You guys are still letting all that shit bother you? You
need to hide your feelings better."

Nuo sat on the edge of a bed, playing with his new clothes.
Brekt folded his arms and leaned against the wall. Neither seemed
willing to admit they felt anything at all.

Kazhi huffed. "Fine. I'm going to say hello to some of *our*
friends. Supper is in a few hours, and Falizha wants us to join her."
She looked at me, considering. "I don't know if that invitation was

extended to you." There was no guilt in her tone, only stating a fact.

Nuo lifted his head. "B and I will take dinner together. Here."

Brekt crossed his arms, and a shadow moved under his skin. "If I have to suffer it, so do you."

"And leave Liv alone down here?" Nuo tilted his head, knowing Brekt wouldn't argue.

Brekt's nostrils flared. "Fine."

Kazhi left, off to find the Guardians they called friends. It took some time for the boys to get cleaned and changed. I sat on one of the bunks, leaning back against a wall and fidgeting with my hands.

I was hidden in shadow, watching Nuo towel dry his hair, when my situation sank in a little too deep. I felt trapped, watched, and claustrophobic—like a mouse hiding from the cat waiting outside, watching the hole. Similar to walking through town back home—too many eyes watching, too many chances for me to slip up. Maybe I could hide down in this cabin for the entire trip.

"Who is Falizha?" I asked.

Brekt was in the bathing room, and Bastane had gone to find Kazhi. Nuo was the only one present, sitting across the room from me. He looked up, and his dark, wet hair fell around his handsome face.

He was freshly shaven, and a lovely citrus smell was coming off him. His arms rested on his knees, and he was back in plain black clothing. His shirt was tight across his chest, showing off his muscular form.

An unwanted emotion swept through me. Nuo was attractive and easy to be around. He was a Guard—powerful and fierce when needed.

It could be easy to fall in love with him.

Being here alone, it hit me how strongly I already felt. My heart pounded a bit harder, but a certain substance was missing. I pushed the thought aside, happy to accept that I could call Nuo a friend and that it was enough.

"Falizha is the daughter of the Governor of the Guardian City."

"That's a mouthful."

A smile touched his serious demeanour. "Isn't it."

"So, she has money and power, and she owns this ship?"

"Her father has money, a lot of it, and he holds the power. He lets her pilot this ship. She runs a crew of only women. For whatever reason, I don't know. She's not a very strong Guardian, but my guess is daddy had to find some use for her, a position of power. She gets one of his largest ships and hunts for crystals and Aethars."

"So why don't you like her?"

"I don't like the entire family, but especially her."

"Did you guys, ugh—" I tapered off.

"Gods no, and never will. Her exterior doesn't fool me. She's an ugly woman inside."

"Because?" I pressed, "Did she and Brekt ...."

A bit of the animosity left him, and some humour returned, "No. Not that I know of. Though she's tried and will continue to do so. The Guards symbolize power, and power is all she craves."

He shuffled back on the bed to lean against the wall across from me. We mirrored each other.

"Her father arranged her marriage to Brekt."

My heart flared with fury. He was engaged? To her? How could he accept something like that? And how could he give me gifts and look at me the way he does—

"Settle down," Nuo laughed, "Brekt declined, and when the Governor turned to Bastane and myself, and the two of us also declined, they were furious. I think Falizha is determined to change our minds, to show us her prowess with the big ship and crew. She has never stopped."

"How long ago was this?"

"Maybe a year or so."

Long before I showed up. "But that doesn't explain to me your reaction. You could be civil after declining. Why the hate?"

"Give it time, Olivia. You'll see."

He never used my full name. It made me all the more nervous.
The cords along his neck stretched, showing off the thin, near-
invisible lines of his gills.

"When we declined, we were living at the Guardian City. We
were the Guards—symbols of power and safety—but we were
tools more than that. We left shortly after the failed proposal to
train once more at the north camp, the home to Brekt and me. Bas
hated it up there. Kazhi is immune to all suffering, I think, so she
didn't complain out loud as much." The corners of his mouth lifted
at whatever memories he saw. "We were biding our time, training
and collecting ourselves before everything began. We knew it
would be us that would find the Aspis, that the Ikhor would wake
while I was chosen. I knew it would be during our time as Guards."
He was gone far away in thought.

Sadness saturated the air, soaking in after seeing some of what
lay underneath Nuo's mask. It was a heavy burden.

"I've trained my whole life. I wanted to be a Guard. I wanted to
have it all, and now? I am mapping the path for my friends to meet
their deaths."

I traced the lines on my palms while he spoke. I knew, without
asking what he meant. They would fight alongside a giant beast
and face off against the Ikhor. They were strong, but they still were
just mortal men—even with their strange abilities given to them
by gods. This battle would most likely claim their lives.

"I know I was avoiding it all as we trained up at North Aspis for
the last year, but it was nice, you know? I was back to where Brekt
and I grew up. We were free of this burden. We threw ourselves
into training. No fate of the world, no power plays and marriage
proposals, no obligations." His attention whipped to the bathing
room door, which now stood open. Brekt was leaning against the
frame.

Brekt's face held some of that sorrow, lining his striking face as
he listened. He folded his arms, chewing on his lip. "And now we
are headed back to the city full of Guardians and our
responsibility."

"And isn't it poetic that dearest Falizha is the one to drag us back?" Nuo finished.

The room was quiet, allowing them to settle their minds and find the right things to say.

It was revealing, the silence, almost like a moment of calm before the storm. I saw the life they were mourning, the one they would never have again—boys growing together into men, training and learning in a blistering cold camp, wanting glory and power and hating it when it finally became theirs.

The glorification of being a hero was very different from the reality of living as one.

My breath caught in my throat as I was again reminded of my mother. She had been a hero to me, a hero no one else had known.

Bright colours blinded me as memories pulled me from the room—flashes of her tear-streaked face. I sat up, trying to control my racing heart. I wiped my mind blank, stuffing the emotion down and focused on the two men.

They both shifted as well—as if a sheet of ice blanketed the room, and we were all shaking it off, letting it crack and shower to the floor.

"I was enjoying being on the road with you guys," Nuo sighed, "You too, Olivia. It was fun. Very entertaining watching you fumble around."

"You say that like it's over," I remarked.

He raised an eyebrow at me, so I continued, "We haven't found the Aspis yet. I'm not done fumbling around." I lowered my voice, "I'm not going anywhere. I am definitely not going home, and I'll be damned if we stop having fun now. I'm just waking up."

"Waking up?" Brekt asked, watching me.

I nodded once. "You guys have shown me things I never thought I would experience. I've spent most of my life holding back, avoiding responsibility. Yes, maybe by doing so, I avoided death, but I also avoided living, and that's more of a waste than anything. I'm ready to get my hands dirty. If we are going to die fighting, then fuck it. And fuck Falizha too." I swallowed.

Swearing in front of others was something I needed to get
used to.

The energy in the room lifted. Nuo's humour surfaced, Brekt
was still terrifying and grumpy, but at least I sensed hope again.
When his eyes found mine, there was even light in them.

My lips twitched, hiding a smile. New Liv was going to have a
colourful vocabulary.

"Fuck Falizha." Nuo sat up. "But if you think you are dying in
all this BB, you haven't noticed how much we are trying to prevent
that from happening."

"I want you to show me it all. Show me your whole world. Let's
live until we don't."

Every kind of emotion passed over Nuo's face—sorrow,
loneliness, fear, but also acceptance, excitement, and finally, he
landed on mischievous.

"You might regret telling me that, BB," he said in a silky tone. "I
know how to live quite well."

My smile grew. "Good, 'cause I never have."

I wasn't afraid. My heart thudded, and my veins felt on fire.
Brekt was contemplative, almost sad, but he nodded in agreement.

We would live. Until we didn't.

Brekt took a deep breath, "Looks like it's just me facing
responsibilities tonight. I should head to dinner. With Falizha."

"Fuck Falizha," Nuo chanted, grinning like a fool.

"If you're ready to face the world, Liv, why don't you join me?"
Brekt asked seductively.

I froze and retreated on the bed, "Well, maybe I'll just start
tomorrow."

A low rumble came from his chest as he headed for the door.
"You two stay out of trouble." He pointed a finger at Nuo, "And
keep your hands to yourself," he growled.

Nuo lifted his hands. "No promises. A beautiful girl tells me she
wants to experience it all. How can I deny her?"

My laughter was quick and too high-pitched. Even though I

had put Nuo firmly in the friend category, I still wasn't immune to his charm.

"You just remember how much you like your favourite part still attached to your body," Brekt threatened before closing the door.

"Ouch." I crinkled my nose.

Nuo's wicked eyes were on me. "So what naughty things should we get up to first, BB?"

CHAPTER
FORTY

I t was my idea. It was a stupid one, but I didn't regret it. Nuo wouldn't deny me anything. He was ready for any scheme set before him.

We were creeping through the halls, hunting for their supplies. Nuo warned that it wouldn't be taken lightly if they found me stealing from the crew, but he was a Guard and could talk his way out of anything. We agreed this was his idea.

We found the storage room on the lowest level of the ship.

A woman from the crew had shown up at our quarters with some food—a plate for the Guard Nuo and nothing more. So we were hunting for snacks and for something to drink.

"Aha!" Nuo shouted, his triumph lit up the dark room.

"Shhh," I giggled, inspecting his discovery. It was a large barrel full of alcohol.

He squatted, making a show of reaching down to lift the whole barrel, straining as it didn't budge.

"Not the whole thing," I squeaked between gasps for air.

His grin was infectious as he stood again. "Are we going to drink down here then? More likely to get caught."

"We didn't plan this very well. We need something to put it in."

We searched for cups. I found two flasks instead.

We headed back to our room with our stolen drinks and our pockets full of fruit and dried meats. The metal halls were all the same, and I was quickly lost. They were lined with red carpets, gold sconces and doors every several feet.

We were passing a staircase. Nuo whistled, his eyebrows wiggling up and down. "Follow me."

He headed up the staircase, away from our room and I followed. At the top of the landing, there was a large door with a bar across the middle to bolt it shut. However, it was not bolted at the moment. Nuo twisted the handle, and a strong wind hit me, blowing my cloak open. My hair whipped around my face.

We walked out into the open night sky.

It was the most surreal and dreamlike view I had ever seen. We were floating in the stars.

"Come on," Nuo called as he turned right.

There was a short staircase off the side of the open door leading up to a higher platform.

I would have been scared of falling off, but the thick gold railing was there to stop me.

"The ship's magic stops the wind from being too harsh up here," he threw over his shoulder. "If it weren't for the shield, we would be blown right off the edge."

The thin layer of shield glimmered in the air above like a translucent butterfly wing wrapped around the whole deck.

Nuo led us to the tail end of the ship and sat behind some crates tied down by ropes. They sheltered us from the wind.

He splayed his feet out before him, and so I mimicked him. My wide emerald pants fanned out around me.

Nuo pulled out a flask and handed it over. "Ready to get drunk? I promise, BB, I won't take advantage of you," he winked. I didn't believe him at all.

I grabbed the flask and brought it to my lips. When the flavour hit, I was surprised—I was expecting something strong or sour, but this one was soft and almost sweet.

Nuo noted my surprise. "That's the kind of drink you get with money."

"I like it."

"It also goes down quicker, so pace yourself. If I'm going to take your drinking virginity, I want to do it respectfully. No hangovers."

I blushed, thankful for the darkness up on the deck. Even though it was well into the night, the moon lit everything around us.

I'd admitted to Nuo I hadn't been truly drunk before. I needed to always be in control of my actions. He was helping me shed some of my old habits.

We sat in silence for a time while we both sipped from our flasks. When Nuo grabbed a piece of dried meat, broke it off and passed it to me, I finally asked, "What is this material that the ship is made from? I've seen it several times now. There was a large thing for riding in the Last City when you first found me."

"That would have been a racer. They work similarly to the airship but stay low to the ground. They're made from rare ore. We don't really know where you can find it or how to craft it. This ship, along with other tools and machines, are ancient relics. Usually, only the rich can get their hands on anything made from it, or lucky sons of bitches like me—a legendary Guard." He raised his flask in the air.

The sarcasm was not lost on me. He didn't think he was lucky at all.

I wished I could offer some comfort. Nuo was a good friend. He was loyal to Brekt, keeping his secrets, and part of the reason Nuo was quick to help me was for Brekt's sake. He was keeping an eye on me. But he didn't have to make it fun, and he didn't have to indulge me.

"I think you're the first real friend I've ever had." I hadn't meant to say it aloud, but the honesty just slipped from my thoughts.

He turned to me, brows in the air. "The first? Then poor you,

you're getting the crash course." When he turned back to the sky, I saw his face pinch with concern. Was it for him or for me? "You're doomed from now on, BB. No one will compare."

"You might be right." I took another long drink from my flask.

My body relaxed as the drink took effect, and I enjoyed the easy conversation with Nuo. But the comfortable silence was pleasant too.

"Does it bother you that you don't remember your family?" I asked. His face changed slightly. Maybe this drink was making me too bold with my questions.

"I don't forget everything. But I wish I did. Aethars killed my family. Those are the only memories that stuck with me. I wonder what life would've been like had they lived ... if I would have chosen to become a Guard. But then I would be missing what I have now. I try not to think on it too long."

Would I be different if I only had memories of my mother's death and not her life before? Would the comparison make a difference?

"Do the others have family?"

"Kazhi, no. Although, maybe she just hid them from us. Bastane's last name is Armel. His family are well-off farmers."

Nuo took another drink while he watched the night sky.

The moon was above us. I leaned my head back, trying to remember if I'd ever seen it this clearly back home. The forest did its job of keeping me secluded from the sky, and the Keepers had done their job of keeping me secluded from the world. I wondered if any of the Keepers knew that there was something more out there.

I didn't let those thoughts take my joy. The drink filled my veins, and my face held a sloppy grin. I was sitting next to a real friend and getting drunk on the top of a ship in the sky. I snickered at how ridiculous it sounded. Nuo had a smile tugging on his lips, his eyebrows lifting in question.

"Life can take you to crazy places."

He nodded.

I hiccuped.

He laughed.

I turned to him then, not wearing a single mask. "You're beautiful, Nuo. I like even the serious, sad parts of you. I think they're beautiful too."

His eyes widened before his shoulders started shaking. "And that, my friends, is a drunk Olivia."

"I'm serious!"

"Oh, I believe you, and I agree wholeheartedly." His arm came around my shoulder, and I leaned my head against him. "But don't go falling in love with me, BB. The big guy said he would chop off my cock."

I smacked him, but he only squeezed me tighter.

"Don't you two look cozy," a deep voice said from Nuo's side.

When our gazes clashed, I hiccuped again. Brekt stood overtop us, a strange smile on his face.

"Is she drunk?" he asked.

Nuo lifted his flask. "Sorry, brother, I popped that cherry. The girl cannot hold her liquor. She's professing undying love for me, and we've barely been at it an hour."

"You're mixing up your women. I said you were a self-obsessed, backstabbing ass—" A hiccup interrupted me.

Brekt grabbed my flask and came to sit, crossing his legs in front of me. He started to down the remainder of my drink.

"Hey!" I complained, reaching out to grab it. He pulled it away and continued to down it, eyes on me. He was full of cocky pride, daring me to take the flask.

"Dinner was that bad?" Nuo took his arm off me and passed Brekt his flask as well.

"Yeah," he groaned, downing Nuo's drink. "I got updated on every event in Falizha's life since we left, as well as who has married who and who's taken what position in the Governor's office. She wanted me to know how many Aethars she's killed and how many crystals she's acquired."

"Insufferable woman," Nuo mumbled.

Brekt swayed in front of me.

I pointed to him. "You're drunk too."

His body tilted to one side. "The only way I could make it through that entire thing."

"Kaz and Bas?" Nuo asked.

"Gone to bed already. I think they felt drained as well. I came to look for you two to make sure you weren't thrown overboard."

"What a waste that would be. Who would poor Falizha fall onto next once you're no longer her target." Nuo stood up, passing a piece of fruit down to me. "I'm heading to bed as well. Maybe I'll bump into some fun on my way down there. Now that I've kept my favourite parts," he winked at me.

Nuo left, and the heat from my face spread further—I was alone, drunk, with Brekt.

He shifted to sit beside me, leaning where Nuo had been.

I eyed him from the side, trying to hide the fact I was staring at him. His eyes darted toward me, flashing in the moonlight.

We sat in silence for a moment, tension building. Yet, it felt thrilling, wild and freeing. I had a million things to say and nothing good enough for the moment. I thought of everything I'd admitted in the Alchemist's shop and everything I had seen before that, the powers he had displayed.

He was the most powerful man I'd ever met.

His dark hair was pulled up behind his head, as usual. His tanned skin was flush from the drink, and his full lips were tilted up below a straight nose.

His features darkened as his attention snagged on my mouth.

"I don't get to be told I'm beautiful?" he teased.

I went to draw breath, shocked that he heard that part, but another hiccup came out. I put a palm to my face in shame.

"That word doesn't suit you." I peeked between two fingers. His eyebrows went up, and he looked a little hurt.

"You're more than beautiful," I hurried on before he mistook my meaning. "Beautiful is too gentle a word for you."

"What word do I get then?" His head tilted to the side. His tone had turned seductive, and it put the most delicious spell on me.

"Devastating," I breathed, regretting it immediately.

He stared. I thought I had said too much when his eyes turned hungry.

But he didn't lean in. He didn't ask for more. He didn't *take*.

A coldness swept through me. The heat melted, and uncertainty took over. I should know by now—he held back everything. While I may be determined to live and be free, I could not say the same for him.

I got to come along, but I may never get more than that. Especially where he was concerned. There was so much he had to focus on, that he had to do, then to think of things like that.

I pulled away, but his hand moved to my jaw, gripping my face and forcing me to look at him. His touch sent a shock to every surface of my body, causing my back to go straight, my lips to part.

His eyes swam with emotion, still glossy from the alcohol. I couldn't tell what he was thinking, but a crease formed as he studied me.

I blinked, worried that the moisture in my eye was visible. I was drunk. I was emotional. It was all rushing to the surface, and I was unable to hide the hurt of rejection.

I didn't know how to navigate this—or him.

His hand travelled up and cupped my face, and when he leaned in, he kissed the top of my cheek.

His lips were warm after the cool night air. A shiver went through me, and my skin felt tight as I drew in a shaking breath.

His kiss was so soft and tender—far from what I was feeling inside. So different than what I came to expect from him.

"We are both drunk on a vessel surrounded by people I don't trust. If I don't stop myself ... it's hard to not think about what I want to do with you right now. It's hard every day. But I can't, for many reasons."

What he implied—hearing those words, how his voice deepened to a growl when he said it, made my heart fracture and reform. I wanted to know what things he wished to do with me. I wanted to explore this heat I felt burning in my core.

I swallowed, not knowing what to say, not wanting to move in fear he would let go.

"Why?" I whispered. His eyes bore into mine. "What's the reason?"

Perhaps it was wrong to press, but I wanted to be bold. I wanted to know more.

"I'm—" he faced away from me. His hand left my face and took the warmth with it. "I'm afraid."

"Of me?"

His head came down once in a nod. "And for you."

It bubbled up from deep inside of me, and drunk as I was, I couldn't contain it—my laughter burst into the night air.

The crease between his eyes returned as he faced me.

"The mighty Guard of the Aspis is afraid of me?"

Humour gleamed in his eyes. "You are probably the most terrifying thing I've ever faced."

His demeanour was lit, and the joy made him more handsome. I'd even call it bashful, the way his eyes were cast down for a moment. "And you missed that I said I was also scared *for you*."

"Can you elaborate?"

A smile was still on his face though it was slipping. Would he be willing to admit his dreams? That he saw things that were going to happen?

"I am afraid of what it means that we've crossed paths at this point in my life. It now means danger for you and a distraction for me." His eyes softened. "Not that I mind this distraction, but it could lead to bad things. I want to avoid those bad things. I think people will come for you."

"Like Falizha?" I asked.

"Or my enemies, which Falizha technically is not."

"So, if you don't touch me, they won't come for me?"

"When you say it like that ... But yes, something along those lines."

"And what if I refuse to play along with this plan?"

I was acting in a way I wasn't used to. Was it the aftereffect of hanging around these fierce warriors?

"I don't know how long I could guard myself against you. I'm losing the battle after one drink." He rubbed a hand down his face. "I could fight off twenty Aethars at once, but you? Wanting to know the feel of your lips ... fuck."

His head leaned back and hit the crate with a thud. He took a long breath.

A small part of me felt bad for putting more on his plate. The selfish part wanted to jump onto his lap and find out all those things he wanted to do with me.

I can't say his explanation helped, but I didn't press him further.

I stood up, dusted off my cloak and reached down a hand. "Let's get some sleep then. I'll form a new plan tomorrow."

He glanced up at me through his lashes. "Inviting me to bed, Liv?"

The desire hadn't left me, so it was only kicked up at his suggestion.

I made a face, pulling my hand away, unwilling to take the bait. I turned toward the door that led to the inside of the ship. Deny me and then taunt me—Brekt was ruthless.

A rumble of laughter and footsteps caught up to me. Brekt reached my side before I got to the stairs, and I decided I wanted to be a little more curious tonight. I moved to the golden railing.

"What are you doing?" Brekt questioned from behind.

"I want to see how high up we are."

"I wouldn't if I were you."

I grabbed the top of the railing as I peeked over, seeing the ground below lit up by moonlight. The tops of trees and rolling hills were beneath us—far, far beneath us.

Everything spun, and before I lost the contents of my stomach, I squatted down, curling into a ball and holding onto the bars for dear life.

Brekt's face swam before me as he crouched down on his heels.

"So ... What are we doing down here?"

"Panicking," I whispered.

"Does it help to crouch?"

"Yes. Panicking at a lower level is safer."

"Hmmm. I wouldn't know. I've never panicked at a lower level."

"Have you ever panicked about anything?"

He lifted his head as if thinking. "Maybe if my bottle is running low. Otherwise, no."

He reached out a hand to help me. I didn't want to take it. The mocking gleam in his eye wasn't helping. But when I finally gave him my hand, he didn't let go as I steadied myself.

"Why did you lean over the edge if you are scared of heights?"

"I feel too adventurous around you."

"It's my fault?"

"Yeah. It's not *my* fault you make me feel safe," I muttered. "You could be pushy, you certainly have the muscles for it, but you aren't. And look what happens," I shrugged.

"And here I thought I was the one experiencing new things."

"What new things do you experience with me? I don't know anything."

"You react in ways no one else would. Everything is unfamiliar to you. Like when you run your hand across a piece of metal, feeling it for the first time."

"It's weird you remember that."

He was unaffected by my teasing. "I've started to feel jealous of the different things you touch. I've seen you do it with fabrics and food as well. But really, it gives me a different perspective, considering things I've never thought twice about. As if I'm experiencing them for the first time. I'm doing things I never thought I would miss. I'm thankful you've come along with us."

"Why would you miss them?"

Brekt's gaze shifted away from me. "I don't want to get into that tonight. Tonight is different—hopeful. I don't want to ruin it."

I chanced another peek over the bars and knew right away it was a bad idea. I felt dizzy all over again, but a strange light caught my eye before I moved away.

It appeared in the sky, then disappeared behind a massive hill in the distance—a glow like the crystals.

Brekt sought what had stopped me.

"I think I saw another airship." I spun to him.

"I doubt that's what you saw. They aren't common to see flying."

There was nothing in the distance but black now. I didn't push it, but the glow was the same as the sails on this ship. But Brekt was blessed by Erabas, the god of Night. Of course, he would see better in the dark.

We walked in silence back to the room. A million thoughts ran through my mind, but I decided to just enjoy the moment alone with him.

Brekt led us, knowing the way, and eventually opened the door to find the room already in darkness. Snoring came from one of the bunks. But the second set of bunks were empty, so I headed there. The door clicked shut behind me, leaving me in near-darkness.

I figured Brekt wouldn't sleep on top, so I grabbed the ladder to climb when a hand touched my hip.

My hands squeezed the ladder, and my foot froze on the first rung. I tried not to make a noise.

But when his hand moved, it was only to help me take my cloak off.

"Sleep well tonight," he spoke into my ear, and I savoured the feeling of heat, the tightening of skin and the pressure building inside.

Tease.

He made sure I got up the ladder. I was still a little wobbly from the drink. The bed shifted below me a moment later as he sunk into it.

I rested my head on a flat hard pillow and stared into the

darkness, thinking about the warmth of his hand. The looks he gave me...

A loud crash sounded from the hallway, and hushed laughter echoed down the corridor. It was quiet for a moment before I heard a moan reaching our room from down the hall. I put my hand to my mouth to stop myself from making any noise.

A sort of tapping started as something hit the wall repeatedly. The moaning grew louder. It was a woman's voice followed by a low timbre of a man saying something incoherently.

I knew in my gut it was Nuo in the hall with the *fun* he went searching for.

I groaned. Brekt had sparked a desire that left me wanting and needy. Now the sounds of passion were coming through the door. Nuo was making it so much worse.

I grew irritated. Nuo didn't seem to mind going out and having fun despite the serious nature of their mission. Why was Brekt so hell-bent on holding back?

There was a louder moan, and then the hall went silent. I wanted to scream. I wanted someone to touch me like that. I had finally decided to let loose, and look what it got me.

The door crashed open, and sure enough, Nuo stumbled through, whispering, "Oops."

He shut the door, and as he walked toward a bed, he tripped on something, crashing into the floor, moaning from the pain rather than pleasure.

"Oops," Brekt rumbled, and I bit my lip, knowing he tripped Nuo on purpose.

He deserved it, though.

Another bed shifted, and Kazhi's sleep-filled voice filled the cabin. "Shut up and go to bed. You're a bunch of idiotic assholes." Minutes later, her snoring echoed Bastane's, who hadn't woken up at all.

Finally, Nuo found a place to sleep and climbed in. Another thud echoed through the room as he hit the ground, thrown from the bed.

SARAH L. ROSE

"What the fuck, man?" Nuo slurred.

"Stay out of my fucking bed, drunk bastard," Brekt growled.

"Was that your dick, or were you happy to see me?" Nuo laughed from the floor.

"You think my dick felt hard, wait till you feel my fist. Now fuck off." The bed creaked, and I think Brekt rolled to face away.

Nuo mumbled something and giggled before going quiet. I didn't hear any more before snoring came from below.

It took me forever to fall asleep. All I could think about was something hard lying right below me.

CHAPTER
FORTY-ONE

Nuo's hopes of avoiding a hangover were a waste. My clothing was soaked with sweat, sticking to my itching skin. But thankfully, I slept through the night and was not woken by the painful cries of my mother screaming, blood dripping from her nose. Instead, I had dreamt of Brekt, and the dreams had been vivid and detailed.

"Ugh." I sat up in bed, and the world tilted. I wanted to lay back down and play dead for the rest of the day. Maybe for the rest of my life. Then I wouldn't have to face the Captain of this ship or the man who had appeared in my dreams.

Being horny and hungover was a disgusting combination. I cursed the gods of this world.

I peered down from my bunk, a mistake I hadn't anticipated. I grabbed onto the railing. Too high up—it was just like leaning over the side of the ship.

All the beds were empty. I was wondering if they'd all left when the bathroom door opened, and Brekt stepped out, rubbing a towel on his head.

His thick, black hair was wet and hung loose down his shoulders. He was too wild to be in the simple black clothing he wore. I could easily picture him in the north, surviving and training in the cold temperatures.

I could curse him, too, for the cocky grin he gave me as I groaned and grabbed at my head.

He swiped a jar from the side of the bed and passed it to me. "Drink this. It will take some of the pain away. Then drink lots of water. After lunch, Kazhi wants to train with you."

"I take back everything I said. I don't want any of it, adventures or training."

"One hangover and you're defeated? Come on, Liv, I was excited when you said you would fight me. Gave me something to look forward to."

"You're a masochist," I groaned.

"The shoe fits."

I lowered my hands to see him pulling his hair up.

I couldn't appreciate the ways his arms flexed when I was incensed at his teasing. Everything was push and pull with Brekt. It wasn't fair. I'd lived a secluded life—he didn't understand he was playing with a caged, hungover animal.

There was a pounding in my ears that wasn't from the headache.

I focused my anger and headed down the ladder. I almost slipped on the last rung and he reached to steady me, making me angrier.

His words and his actions didn't line up. He pretended to be chivalrous and then taunted me with insinuations.

"Where are my change of clothes?"

He smirked like my anger was cute. "Sorry, they only brought clothes for us."

I narrowed my eyes at him. "Fine. I'll make do."

The smile I gave him wiped his own from his face. His brows drew together, wondering what the shift in my attitude meant. I basked in it.

I walked past him, grabbed the hem of my top and pulled up.

He groaned a curse as I pulled the fabric over my head, freeing my breasts from the tight fabric. Even though my back was to him, he would've caught sight of something.

An old part of me wanted to scream and run before I was caught. But she was not in control right now—the angry, hungover, horny one was.

I threw my top to the ground. I reached down to my pants, giving him a knowing look over my shoulder.

A low, pained moan came from behind Brekt, "BB, please tell me your topless, and I'm not still dreaming."

"Shit." I covered myself. I hadn't seen him. Nuo was lifting his head off a pillow on a lower bunk. Brekt's smile turned wolfish as he crossed his arms to see what I would do next.

"You're dreaming," I spat at Nuo.

I tried to ignore Brekt. "And you're dreaming too, whatever it is you're thinking." I walked into the bathing room, shutting the door behind me.

Swearing came from the main room, and the door was slammed shut as he left. I smiled in triumph. If I had to suffer, then let him suffer too. He was a big-bad-Guard. He could handle it.

I took my time cleaning in the small bathtub. It felt great to be soaped and scrubbed but not so pleasant when I had to slip back into dirty clothing. But I reminded myself I'd lived through worse.

I tackled my knotted hair. Even though I was practically pulling it from my skull, I could only focus on the memory of his warm lips on my cheek, his calloused hand cradling my face.

It's hard to not think about what I want to do with you right now. His voice alone had me aching, clenching the muscles closest to where I wanted him to touch.

What was I going to do?

When I returned to the main room, Nuo was up and holding his head. I grabbed the bottle Brekt had given me to drink and shared it with Nuo, trying to calm myself. Anger, frustration, desire, hunger—I was a boiling pot of overreactive behaviour. Is this what most people felt? If so, living was messy.

The drink settled in, toning down my headache to a

manageable level. Nuo didn't bring up my little show for Brekt, and I was thankful. He was eyeing me with a suggestive smile, but he kept any comments to himself.

"So, are we hiding in here today?" I asked.

He made a face. "No. I don't like being on this ship, but I am not a coward. Let's go find some trouble to stir up."

"Stirring up trouble with you always has side effects." I rubbed my temples.

He chuckled. "Everything worth having in life always does."

Wasn't that the truth?

We ended up in the navigation room, where the crew mapped out their trip. I was glad to have Nuo with me as I faced these women again.

On the other side of the room was the large window. We were flying through mountains covered in trees.

I forgot all my worries, gripped by the shocking colour of the jungle. The blue sky was a stunning contrast against the hues of green spread across the sharp angles of mountains and cliffs. We soared high enough to coast through the saddles of the mountain peaks.

Nuo was walking to a table where a black-haired woman stood, studying a pile of open books. He leaned in close, whispering in her ear, making her blush.

I would bet anything that was his *fun*.

I went to the front window, passing the large table and the raised platform where women sat pressing buttons on the long panel before them.

Across the mountains were bursts of florals decorating the hillsides. Next to the ship, there was a flock of strange, bright-coloured birds flying in unison.

I wondered briefly about the airship I *thought* I saw last night. I prayed the Aethars didn't have a ship of their own.

Footsteps approached, stopping when they reached my side. I turned to see Falizha standing straight, facing forward. She was gazing out at the landscape, gold eyes scanning the trees below, looking every bit like a wealthy woman with power at her fingertips.

Her bright golden hair was swept back, and her tight leather clothing showed off her lean figure. She wore a clasp on one shoulder where a glowing crystal was displayed, and a long deep purple cape flowed out from behind her. She wanted people to see who was in charge.

Her attention moved over to me, expressionless, searching for some answer as to who I was and why the Guards would be dragging me along.

"Olivia, you said your name was?"

"Yes. You remembered," I said evenly.

"Hmm. It's a strange name. I wouldn't forget it." Her tone suggested she would keep it tucked away, information being power and all. "I am having a hard time discerning where you are from. You don't look like a Guardian, and I can't see any signs of what legacy you are, so I can only guess a watered-down line. What business do you have with the Guards?"

Her glare travelled down my body, coming back up slowly, suggesting she could only think of one reason I might be dragged along.

I wasn't worried about her assuming I was a plaything. If she wanted to make a power play, then keeping her in the dark would be mine. I didn't want further questions about my legacy, so I pretended to blush and tucked my hair behind my ears.

Back at the main table, Nuo was finishing writing something on a piece of paper, folding it, and stuffing it into his front pocket. He turned to see my eyes pleading, wishing to be rescued.

What Falizha didn't know was that I'd spent years of my life blending in to be what other people wanted to see. I wore that now on my face. I was the quiet, unassuming mistress of one of the Guards.

And she was going to assume the wrong one.

Nuo came up beside me and draped an arm over my shoulder.

SARAH L. ROSE

"You're making my friend here blush, Falizha. I hope you're not bragging about Daddy's money and false accomplishments."

I stiffened as Falizha's calm exterior shifted. It was like a layer peeled back, her face contorted, revealing the true woman underneath.

"I don't have to brag about anything, Nuo, my dear. All you have to do is look around. This is my ship, my crew of Guardians. Your whore here will see when she reaches my city."

If Nuo was surprised at Falizha's assuming my profession, he didn't show it.

"You mean the city your father has a cushioned ass on? Your claim is a little far-fetched, don't you think? It belongs to all Guardians."

She took a step toward him.

Nuo didn't budge. "Ah-ah, sweet Falizha, don't you forget who I am, who you have boarded on your ship. There is power in a name, and then there is power. We both know which each of us possess. And that I have both."

I shivered under the weight of Nuo's arm. His threat was effective.

"I would never forget that, child of Mayra." She dared a step closer and put a hand on Nuo's other arm. "Don't forget, Nuo, who you rely on for aid in your search for the great Aspis. Don't forget the children of Rem hold power in my city. My father is happy to lend you what funds you need. For now."

"I have all I need." He squeezed me tighter.

"Estal would say differently after last night, I heard."

Falizha's poisonous smile landed on me, expecting a reaction. When I only blinked, it vanished.

She gave us one last look, satisfied knowing I was nothing more than a waste of space on her ship and left us alone to head back to the main table for planning.

Nuo turned us to the window. His body was tense next to mine, his arm holding me close. I rarely saw this side of him. Usually, it was saved for the Aethar.

"I was asked to help review their maps and translations of old texts. The Guardians are constantly trying to find new caves and where more ancient machines might be buried."

"And they want your help? Or maybe Estal wishes for more of your time." I put my arm around his waist, squeezing.

He pretended to be confused. "I would never cheat on you, BB. And this cover will work to our benefit once we reach the city."

"How will playing a whore work to my benefit?"

"Because, if I'm walking around like I own you, the people in the city won't zero in on you ... but Brekt might." His eyes twinkled with mischief.

I sighed and took in the landscape through the window. "I don't want to play games, Nuo. If he is not interested, then I'm not going to push. Bigger things are going on."

He was quiet for a moment. "The seriousness of our lives is all he's dealt with since a young age. He never goes after anything for joy, just relief. If you don't do it for him, do it for me. I want my brother to experience something good before his end."

"And are you so sure guarding the Aspis will be your end?"

"The odds aren't in our favour, B."

I frowned, knowing I would have to deal with the future and accept it. The threat of death wasn't new for me, but people I cared about? That was going to be hard to watch.

"And how does it work in *your* favour?" I asked Nuo.

"Because I think your presence will make the other women want me more."

I smacked him on the chest. But he was right because Estal was shooting daggers in my direction. So I squeezed him a little closer. "You'll owe me, Nuo. If I'm helping you get laid."

"And what is it you want?"

"Right now? Surprisingly another drink," I groaned.

FORTY-TWO

I didn't go for another drink.

Instead, I asked for Nuo's help. I wanted to be more proactive with why I was sent here to find the Aspis. I wouldn't be welcome to browse Falizha's library, so Nuo was seeing if he could find anything about speaking lights.

Nuo spent the rest of the morning on the bridge of the ship, translating old books. They turned out to be stories of the gods bringing ships and weapons to Arde. It sounded more like tales my mother would tell rather than histories.

Nuo was at ease amongst the books—glasses on while he jotted things down. The women watched, fascinated with how fast he could translate.

He was not only adept at translations but also at manipulating a room—the way he would stand over a book or lean toward Estal —it was as if he knew when people were watching him. He was a master.

But nothing was written about lights that spoke. He said we would search the Guardian City library next.

I was eating lunch in the cabin when Kazhi came to find me. I'd barely seen her since boarding the ship yesterday, and Bastane had been missing, too. Maybe he had found his own fun amongst the crew.

Kazhi picked up my swords from the bedside and tossed them to me, "We start training today. No use wasting time in the air. Follow me."

I scrambled for the door. She had already left the room, not waiting for a response. I caught up when she was turning a corner at the end of the hall.

Her pace was hard to keep up with. We were already going down another level. "We aren't going to the top?"

She raised an eyebrow at me. "You think you can fight with two swords while battling the sun in your eyes and the wind blowing you around?"

"No," I shot back before she thought it would be fun to watch me try.

She didn't alter her quick pace for our conversation. She was always in Guard mode, never relaxed. Even her free time was spent away from the group, scouting.

"Looks like we are a team now, in search of the Aspis," she said dryly.

"Let me guess; you heard I'm from your world and are against trusting me now?"

"Yes and no. But I'm curious about your insights on finding the beast. If you have any information that we don't."

"What information do you have? You all mentioned that you were searching for the beast, but not the method on how you find it." I didn't mention to her that I had already asked Brekt, who had refused the information.

"The Guards have their ways of searching. I agreed to bring you along, but I am unwilling to share the Guards' secrets. The walls have ears on this ship."

"I'll ask Nuo later, then."

"You can try. Brekt reminded us, especially Nuo, to keep that bit to ourselves."

"From me?"

"Yup." Brekt still didn't trust me, even if he believed me about my homeland.

"So I tell you my information, but you keep yours? Seems fair."

"Life's not. So do you have information on the beast?"

"No," I mumbled. "I never lied to you guys. I am in the dark. I'm going to search the library in the Guardian City. Maybe there are answers to how and why I was brought here."

"Hmm," she grunted.

"Where have you been lately, anyway? Even in Bellum, you were gone more often than the others."

Her black eyes shifted to me. She didn't like my noticing her absence.

"I collect secrets, Bones. I watch everyone. Everything. Always."

I shivered. It was the creepiest non-answer I'd ever heard.

Before Bellum, she had roamed through the dark, searching for Aethars to avoid an attack. What threats was she looking for on this ship?

We reached a long open room that had weapons and tools displayed on the walls. The floor wasn't metal, as it was everywhere else, but a softer material, good for falling on.

It was a training room.

My mother had once hoped for a place to train. All we had was a thick forest floor, and I often returned home covered in needles and sap. She would spend hours with me on technique and footwork, teaching me to stand my ground against an attacker to dominate the fight.

I only had her as a fighting partner, and she was much bigger and stronger than me.

Kazhi stood before me in the centre of the room, hands on her hips. I rubbed my sweaty palms against my pants.

"What kind of secrets do you try and collect?" I tried to fill the silence.

"The kind people would kill to possess. And kill me for knowing. Take a stance."

I moved my feet, feeling clumsy when I shouldn't. But next to this woman, I think even my mother would feel intimidated.

"Is it all to fight the Ikhor? Your collecting?"

If she were just collecting information on her enemies, why would she be spying on Falizha's ship?

"The Ikhor is enemy number one, the Aethar along with it. Sometimes, however, essential information doesn't reach the ears of the Guards—like a mass of Aethars heading toward Bellum."

Oh.

Falizha had a ship—and eyes—in the sky. Falizha missed the chance to warn the people and Guards in Bellum. Could she have saved more lives?

"So even the Guardians don't fully trust each other," I stated.

"You should never fully trust anyone. You never know who's shifted alliances."

"You think some Guardians align themselves with the Aethar?"

"It has happened. And the Council is always trying to find traitors. But it's rare. Hatred for the Aethar runs deep in these lands."

"Do you hate the Aethar, like Nuo? Are they all that bad?"

Luckily, Kazhi didn't accuse me of delaying our training. Which I was.

"That's how the scarred fuckers have always been when they come to these lands. I don't question my orders to take them out. Plus, it's what I'm good at."

There had been so many bodies left on the street of Bellum. I hoped that the mother and her children would recover from the horrors they faced. I wanted to hate the Aethar too, but ...

"Where I come from, everyone I met was bad. They were like the Aethar," I muttered, "They don't look like the Aethar, nor have their beliefs. But they are unloving and cruel like them. And they hate everyone else."

Kazhi's gaze was probing, as if wondering where I would go with these thoughts, though I couldn't imagine why she would care. When I hesitated, she lifted a tattooed brow.

"I wasn't like the Keepers or the villagers," I continued, "so there has to be some in the Aethar lands who want to break free as much as I did. Next time—next time you are asked to kill them, if you and the others go into Aethar lands, judge them first. For others like me."

I waited to hear the condemnation, but it never came.

"You'd make a good Guardian. Maybe not for the Council, and not with those sword skills, but otherwise, you'd do well."

I was about to ask what she meant about the Council when the door opened, and Bastane walked in.

"If you're training here, take that side of the room. This side is ours," Kazhi barked, motioning to the centre of the mats.

So this is where Bastane had been hiding.

"I'm also going to watch." He jerked his head toward me. *Great.* "In Bellum, you used some of the moves I showed you outside the cave. I'm impressed. Better than us having to watch over you."

I searched his face for mockery, but he was being serious.

I had been ashamed of how I fared against the Aethar woman. But now—I felt a boost in my confidence, eager for another lesson.

"Don't get too cocky, girl. Not yet. Raise your swords," Kazhi demanded.

I fumbled, trying to get two of them in my hands.

Kazhi palmed her face. "Looks like we are starting from the very beginning. Grip."

The lesson continued like that—Kazhi expecting more and pulling back to explain the simplest things. How to draw two swords, how to hold them, and ways to swing them. We hadn't even gotten to moving around.

Much later, Kazhi sighed, "My head is starting to hurt." She had barely moved while pointing at me and barking orders.

"Mine too," I grumbled.

"Let's call it for the day. Small steps. But go over in your head what you've been taught before we pick it up again tomorrow."

Bastane had been training on the other side of the room,

shouting at me throughout my lesson. He now dared Kazhi's wrath by coming back to our side.

He pushed his golden hair back from his face. He had stripped down to a plain shirt that was soaked through, and yet he seemed like he could go for hours still.

"Olivia hasn't even broken a sweat." He stopped in front of me, his breathing hard. "Throw those to the side. We fight for real now."

"Wh-what?" I felt my stomach bottom out.

"I know you've trained before. We can work on some of that. Plus, I want a partner. The other Guards all think they've trained hard enough that they don't need to keep it up. I need someone to use as a punching bag." He rolled his shoulders.

"And you choose the girl who can barely hold a weapon?"

He made a face. "I'm not *actually* going to hurt you. Come on. Part of your training—working up the muscle to hold the swords."

I huffed the hair from my face. He had a point. I was too soft around the edges.

And perhaps, a little muscle would come in handy when around Brekt. Not that I was thinking about fighting him.

I put those thoughts away for later consideration.

Bastane grabbed a long square pad covered in leather and held it up in front of me. "Use this for now. Let's see your striking."

I took a step back.

"What's the matter?" he asked, seeing me worry my bottom lip.

My mother's voice had rung as clear as the crystals when I fought the Aethar in Bellum. But I wasn't used to opening up to Bastane, so I couldn't express my concerns. I blocked thoughts of my mother for a reason. I hid that she trained me, only relying on my mother's instructions in extreme circumstances.

No, I thought. I had made a promise to myself. To move forward. I would do as Bastane said. My friendship with Nuo was a blessing I never thought I would have. Maybe Bastane and I could be friends as well.

"My mother used to train me," I said, my voice a whisper.

"I remember." He inclined his head, trying to encourage me to continue.

"The memories are painful, and I had to hide that I'd trained after I lost her. I'm scared to face that."

He lowered the striking pad a fraction, contemplating what I said.

"My opinion? It's time for you to face these things head-on—work through them. But if you aren't ready to do that, let me know. If you are," his gold and blue eyes were on me, "we go slow."

Bastane's intensity, his focus, showed a different power than the others. He was quiet, keeping most things to himself, but I noted that he respected space. He didn't push me around. And he was also right.

He had held a knife to me when I had assumed their version of a dragon breathed fire—but we all made mistakes.

I shifted my feet and lifted my hands in the air. I could do this. I *would* do this. He raised an eyebrow, tilting his head. He gave me a slight nod, and that was all I needed.

I struck the bag with a fist.

It was sloppy and felt foreign to me. My wrist bent the wrong way.

"Again," he prompted.

I struck again, the same fist, shifting into the punch, feeling better. I did it again. And again. And again. Each time I was becoming more sure, more aware and more focused.

A smile spread across my face as the muscle memory sprung from where I had tucked it away. It coursed through me, settling into each limb. Another piece of me awakening after a long sleep. Another layer I had built falling off.

The tiny seed planted deep within me grew a third root, spreading further into my veins.

And finally, I blossomed.

Bastane fixed his stance as he held the pad up. My punches

were growing stronger. Kazhi leaned against a wall, watching as I let loose.

My breath started coming faster as sweat trickled down my back. Bastane stopped me and stood up straight. "You've been holding back, Olivia," his smile grew. "This is getting fun."

"It is. How about some kicking," I panted, hands resting on my hips.

"Show me."

I shot my foot forward and slammed into the pad near the top of his chest, knocking him off balance. He cursed as he flew back several paces.

"Damn, woman. You've been hiding that this whole time? Your technique is foreign, but it works. More."

He dropped deep, spreading his feet out to brace himself.

So I did it again. I practiced the strikes my mother had taught me all those years ago. I allowed the pent-up frustration I had been carrying around to be released. I let myself feel how to move, remembering how to shift and pivot, to put my whole body into the attack.

I stopped, wheezing. I had no strength in me.

"Thank you, Bastane. That felt good." I wiped the sweat from my brow.

"Call me Bas. And we train like this after the swords with Kazhi. You've got enough that we don't have to start at the beginning. I think we can use this knowledge in some of your sword training. Right?" He turned to Kazhi, whose face was blank, watching us. She nodded once.

"Why would you help me?" I asked him.

"Why wouldn't I? We have the same goal. If you're tagging along, we shouldn't have to watch you. We are Guards of the Aspis. Not Guards of Olivia."

I gave a nervous chuckle at how he missed the insult there.

"How about one more round? For a little fun?" a voice from the door said. A few women from the crew had entered the room to do their own training.

"We were just finishing up," Bastane said.

One of the women grabbed a second striking pad, and the other grabbed a long stick leaning against the wall.

"Just two minutes. Let's do a drill of multiple attackers for a final push before you finish," she encouraged. "We like to finish strong, to push out that last bit of energy."

My chest constricted at the thought of someone else watching me.

I'd been so built up from Nuo's animosity toward Falizha that I went on immediate defence around these women. But judging from their faces, they were genuinely interested in helping me finish for the day—this was something they must do to train.

"I asked the girls to come and train with me after Olivia," Kazhi mentioned. "If you're up for it, Bones, it's a good exercise. Block the attack from Tessi," she pointed to the russet-skinned woman with the long staff, who had small antlers curling from her hair, "while throwing punches at Bas and Cali while they move around you. Go slow."

Sweat was trickling down my back, multiplying my discomfort. Could I do this? In the spirit of moving on from my past, I was willing to find out.

"Slow then," I agreed. "I haven't trained for a long time and never with more than one person."

"At your pace," Cali said. She was shorter than me, blonde and holding the second striking pad. Her eyes were a rich brown rimmed with shining gold—I immediately knew what legacy she was.

They circled around me. The temperature of the room dropped. Bile rose in the back of my throat. I went hot and cold.

In the back of my head, flashbacks of my mother threatened to be released from their vault.

I stomped them down. I was on an airship, surrounded by people trying to help me, not harm me.

I took my stance, and the others followed, moving around me. I struck out at Bastane first, trying to push him back. Cali moved to my side, and I flew a kick toward her.

"Good," Bas encouraged. Why did he sound so far away?

"Keep your focus around you at all times," Kazhi called out from the side of the room.

I whipped my attention to the russet-skinned woman, Tessi. She pushed her staff toward me, but I quickly blocked. Then Bastane was closing in again.

I couldn't catch my breath. It was too much. My mother's voice came back, clearer than before. Not the voice of the teachings—but her screams.

I threw a sloppy punch at Bastane, hitting the pad. My entire body trembled.

The staff came at me again, and I jerked, swatting it away. Cali came behind me with the pad, bumping into my back. I threw my fist and bent it the wrong way again.

"You're getting sloppy, Olivia. Reset, concentrate," Kazhi's voice drifted over to me from far away.

The room shrunk, my legs unable to hold me upright. My eardrums pounded, drowning out the sounds of the room.

The pounding turned into painful grunts and struggling moans. I heard muffled words and curses. I wasn't seeing friends surrounding me—they were sneering faces. Their words of encouragement and suggestions turned into taunts and insults, accusations and threats.

I spun, trying to focus. Who was around me? Why were they coming at me?

Swarming me.

Attacking me.

Trying to take me down to teach me a lesson.

One that would be the last lesson I ever learned.

The room was gone. We weren't on a training pad but on a cold, wet street. Mud was soaking my feet, and blood was streaming down my face.

They were going to pin me down. They were going to hurt me. I kicked out. Dark eyes were wild on me, ready to strike and take me out once and for all. I batted the woman away, a sob escaping me.

She paused and pulled back the weapon, glancing from me to the wall where Kazhi stood. It was an opening. But I felt a presence behind me. They were going to blindside me—a cheap shot. So I spun, my fist flying and landing with a loud crunch on a scratchy jaw.

I saw blood, and it undid me.

Tears flowed, breaking free of the dam. I clutched my head and pulled at my hair as my heart exploded. Pain and agony filled every crack I had in it.

There was a grunt and a curse as I fell to my knees, gasping for shallow breaths. Wetness soaked my face, running down my neck, and I thought it was blood.

The pain was unbearable. My mother's face swam before my eyes—bloody, beaten and lifeless. Images I had spent years repressing.

I scratched at my eyes. "Make it stop," I pleaded.

Two large hands landed on my shoulders, and I looked up to find a bloody face. Bastane's lip had split open, just like my mother's had. I pushed him away. I had nightmares of it every night.

Worry etched his features—the only thing I could differentiate from the day I watched my mother die.

"Go away. Stop," I begged. "I don't want to remember this."

Bastane said something to Kazhi, and I heard the women's footsteps leaving the room.

"Olivia," he said, staying back from me. "I don't know what's happened but listen to me—I'm going to take you out of here, okay? We are going to find the others, and you can talk, or not, whatever you need. Let's not stay here, though. Is that okay?"

He was talking to me like a child, like some broken thing. I wasn't a broken thing. I had made sure of it. I made myself strong and durable. I swayed on the floor, holding my head as I convinced myself of the lie.

He stepped closer and touched my shoulders once more. "Can I take you from here?"

Blood was smeared across his cheek, where he tried to wipe it away. I nodded. I wanted to apologize, but I couldn't speak.

He reached down and lifted me off the floor, holding me at arm's length and steadying me on my feet.

"I've got you. You're with friends."

And, at his kind words, the little control I had left vanished. I buried my head in the fabric of his chest and let the tears come out.

I hid my face from him, not wanting anyone to see. But there was no hiding the sounds of my gulping for air between sobs.

He held me and shushed me, and told me I was safe.

I wanted to punch him again. I wanted to kick him. I wanted to do anything violent enough to get the images of my mother's death out of my mind.

CHAPTER

FORTY-THREE

The pressure inside my chest fractured me.

I hadn't cried for years. I didn't know how. The last time was when my mother died, and since that day, I'd bottled it up and spent years keeping it caged.

It was like a deep well was exploding.

Bastane moved us quietly through the ship. I barely took note of where we were headed. My heavy feet moved on their own. The only sound in the long hallway was the air I was gasping for. It grated inside me like a sickness, as if I were fighting for my life.

A door opened with a crash and seconds later, Brekt was coming around a corner, stopping when he saw us.

"What's going on? Kazhi said something happened to Olivia."

I couldn't meet his eye. I didn't want to see any of them. Because for the first time since I was thirteen years old, I was crying, and everyone saw.

But I deserved it. I could see her body, lifeless on the ground. I forced myself to look at it—truly look at it and face the memories I'd neglected. I deserved this pain for forgetting. She was my world, and I cut her out of it the day she died.

She didn't deserve that.

348

Brekt was next to me now. "Olivia. Liv. Tell me what's going on." I couldn't give him a response. "What happened, Bas?"

A new pair of arms grabbed onto me. I panicked, swatting out, ready to strike anything that wanted to hurt me.

"Don't touch me," I growled.

Both pairs of arms froze. I finally took in the face that drew me in like a gravitational force. Seeing the concern in the darkness there made me crumble all over again. My knees gave out this time, but Brekt kept me from falling.

He glared at Bas as if it might have been him that had hurt me.

I sunk into his warmth, his strength. The feel of him was calming. I gripped his shirt, hiding my face in it and letting out another loud sob.

Brekt reached down to lift me, and this time, I let him. I let him pick me up into the air and hold me close as he walked us away from the others. A door opened and closed again, and silence fell around us.

He sat on one of the bunk beds in our room, cradling me in his lap. A hand came up to my hair, stroking it.

His mouth was close to my ear, and his deep voice soothed me. "It's okay Liv. We are alone. You don't need to hold it in. No one will see."

So quickly, he understood me. What I needed. I was engulfed in his scent, which today was citrus soap, food and his own earthy smell. I filled my lungs, and my breathing began to calm.

I could feel his heart pounding. I lifted my chin, and our eyes met. His darkness soaked me in.

My heart went soft. There was something powerful in the way he looked at me. There was a sureness about him—he could handle my tears, pain, and weaknesses if I were willing to let him.

His arms loosened while I slumped in his lap and pressed my head against his shoulder. I wasn't yet willing to leave his embrace.

He leaned over and passed me one of the flasks we had stolen last night—it had been refilled.

A hint of a smile touched my lips. I swallowed, letting the alcohol soothe some of the tension that had built up. He stayed quiet, giving me time, so I drank a bit more before handing the flask back.

"Thanks," I rasped.

"Gonna explain why you needed it?" he asked slowly, as if afraid to spook the animal.

Tears threatened again. But I sat up, facing him. Since I was still planted on his knee, I was at eye level. His breath fanned my cheek. If I wanted to, I could trace the lines of his scar from temple to jaw.

I soaked up his strength to use as my own. "Bastane and Kazhi were training me."

He stiffened. "Did they hurt you?"

"No, nothing like that. They were doing a training exercise with me in the middle—multiple attackers."

"It's a common exercise we use."

I nodded. "Only, I stopped seeing the training room, and everything started resurfacing after the Aethar attack in Bellum."

"Oh." He remembered what I had felt after the attack and the mother who had gotten hurt.

I balled my fists in my lap. "Today's training reminded me of how my mother died."

His posture relaxed, though his face remained the same. I swore I saw shadows moving around us. He returned the flask, and I took a long drink.

I wanted to tell the story. It had stayed within me for so long, and I wanted it out. He waited, knowing I needed to tell it.

"It happened in the village when I was thirteen years old. Rebeka was fifteen. Everything had always been so hard for my mother, who was bold and outspoken. She had never fit in. My sister and I adapted much easier. Maybe a trait passed on from my father's side.

"The village always posted papers of new rules and demands —work was dished out, homes were taken, belongings confiscated. People were suffering heavily, and my mother was overcome by anger. She didn't try to hide her thoughts on the constant changes," I paused, taking another sip. I was getting to the part of the story I had locked away.

One of Brekt's hands was pressed against my lower back. The other rested on my thigh, holding me close to him. I didn't feel the thrill of his touch as I spoke. I did, however, feel grounded.

"We were shopping that day the Law Keepers were in town—with new laws and more restrictions. They were taking away more rights from women and people who didn't have the right skin colour, according to them. My mother snapped—she let loose on the Keepers, yelling complaints about them taking too much. How was she to raise two daughters in this world when they had no choices left? She was crazed.

"The townspeople gathered to hear, nodding with her but making no move to stand next to her. I blame them as much as I blame the Keepers and myself.

"One of the soldiers, worried she was getting a crowd riled up, struck her down. No one stepped in to help her.

"I screamed for her, but Rebeka held me back. She was always calmer and more sensible than I was. But this time, Rebeka was too restrained. I never forgave her for holding me back—she held me as I watched the soldiers swarm my mother, who tried to stand, to confront them further. But she was outnumbered and surrounded."

"Fuck," Brekt growled, seeing where my story was headed—the similarities to the training and my darkest memory.

I nibbled on my bottom lip to stop it from quivering.

"I watched them beat her to death. Screaming from the side, Rebeka held me weeping while the townspeople did nothing. Many ran away. We outnumbered the Keepers by ten, but the people were already conditioned, afraid, and unwilling to fight back."

Brekt's fingers tightened on my thigh.

"They left her there, on the street. When Rebeka finally

released me, my mother was no longer breathing. I remember looking back to Rebeka, who had tears streaming down her eyes, shaking her head no. She wouldn't approach our mother. She wouldn't let others see she was on my mother's side."

Brekt stayed quiet, letting me get lost in the past. In the silence, I thought of the months after. We never once spoke about our mother's death. Rebeka changed after that, becoming colder, never showing emotion or letting me do anything that wasn't allowed— not as my mother had.

Rebeka took care of me until I was 18. She was a model citizen and a good worker. They found her a husband, and I was forced to leave my home. I was told to try to find some work because I was on my own. I wouldn't get a husband. I couldn't make a family, and I allowed myself to accept that—I was to live as a prisoner inside my own mind with a blank face on the outside. I let them see what they wanted because the alternative was becoming like my mother.

The door to the room squeaked closed, breaking me away from the past. Nuo stood there, his mouth set in a hard line. He came across the room and sat on the bed opposite us. He reached his hand out for the flask, also taking a drink. "I heard. Wanted to make sure you were all right."

I nodded, happy to have him here too. He provided a different kind of comfort.

Brekt moved his hand up my back. "That's a lot to keep inside, Liv."

He wasn't saying he was sorry or that he understood how I felt. Maybe he thought those kinds of things were useless anyways. What he said next was all I needed to hear, "You have us here. Don't forget that. You don't have to be afraid of anyone doing that to you. I won't allow it."

I shook my head because he was wrong. "No, I told you I made my decision not to hide. I avoided thinking about my mother and tried not to share her fate, but I was wrong. To live is to face that consequence. She was my hero, and I forgot that. I have a new focus in life—to live as she did. I would rather risk death to be able to live as I see fit. I want to fight for what I believe in rather than spend years hiding and filling my heart with regrets and missed chances. A short life that's full will be better than a long life that is empty." I wiped more tears away. It felt good to finally cry.

Nuo gave Brekt a strange look as I spoke.

"Until her dying breath, she fought to be herself—even if she lost that battle. What she taught me that day was a lesson I should have never buried."

Nuo nodded his head. Though he hadn't heard the story, "I get that, and I've got your back," he said. "We live to the fullest."

I was grateful. I didn't want them to protect me from everything. And they couldn't. As Bastane had pointed out—they were Guards to the Aspis, not to me. I wanted to make as many mistakes as possible to feel it all. "No matter the bad side effects?"

Nuo considered and then laughed nervously, "Our side effects are still most likely death. But that won't change for us even if we play it safe."

Brekt's grip tightened. "Olivia's fate doesn't have to be tangled with ours."

"But our fate is tangled." Did he still not believe I was asked to help them?

Nuo frowned at him. "It is, whether there was a message given to her or not. Are you really willing to deny her the chance at a life she's finally been given?"

"After what I've seen? I feel like I'm the only one being sensible."

"What have you seen?" I asked. His mouth clamped shut. "Should I not know? It might help me discover why I'm supposed to help you."

His face was a sea of shadows. For a moment, I thought he would reveal his dreams. But he shook his head. "I've seen much the same as you have of our world."

I tried to understand. My choice to live as I wished was not something I could force on someone else. Doing so was as bad as the people back home.

I patted his shoulder. "Maybe some other time you'll tell me."

When I stood, Nuo's expression hardened, upset that I wasn't pushing Brekt around. He may be fine swaying people to his ideas with his charm. But I couldn't do that because I knew how it felt to be caged in.

Brekt stood behind me. I was ready to move past the fact he didn't want to talk when he asked, "Do you want to keep me company a while longer? I don't feel like keeping myself busy with this crew."

And I knew who he meant, so I nodded.

FORTY-FOUR

T he view from the deck was impossible to take in all at once.

The sun was low in the sky, grazing the glowing mountain tops. The jungle below was cast into dark shadows, while the vast expanse above was turning amber.

The brilliance of the gold railing reflected the sun, fashioning colours I'd never seen. I ran my hands across the cold metal.

Brekt rested his forearms on the rail before him, looking at the landscape, but I had a feeling he wasn't seeing any of it.

Something was bothering him.

Our side effects are still most likely death, Nuo had said.

Brekt had seen gruesome and horrible things, so my story couldn't be what was bothering him. What ate him up? Besides the weight of everyone relying on him, along with the other Guards, to find the only thing that could defeat the Ikhor—who was now awake and coming for them ... I turned back to the sunset. Everything was bothering him.

The cause for the shadows lingering behind Brekt's eyes was no longer a mystery.

The wind kicked my hair up and around. My loose pants flowed behind me, showing off my curves—which were too soft as my training had shown. I was going to fix that. I wanted to be strong like the two women who tried the exercise with me. I wanted to speak to them—to apologize or explain. I didn't know which. I was embarrassed at what they had witnessed.

I inhaled the cool evening air. I would face this with the Guards. Next, I needed to find out *how* they searched for the beast.

"I have always known what was going to happen to me," Brekt said, startling me.

He was a statue, cold and unfeeling, watching nothing of what was in front of him. He looked down at his hands as he linked his fingers together. "I've known what was going to happen since I was a child."

I held my breath, hoping. As far as I knew, Nuo was the only person he'd told of his dreams.

"I can see things. I saw becoming a Guard, along with Nuo. I saw Bastane showing up and training to fight with us. I saw Kazhi's attack on me and her becoming part of our circle."

I didn't dare speak. What kind of power allowed you to see such things?

He tilted his head toward me, though he was still very far away. "They're flashes in dreams, but they always come true. I don't know where it comes from. As you are aware, I don't know anything about my family. North Aspis took me in and raised me. The staff members were my mothers and fathers, Nuo becoming my brother.

"Nuo has researched endlessly for clues to where the gift comes from, perhaps part of why he is so well-read. But nothing ever surfaces. His best guess is that my family once held an Oracle or a seer in its bloodline—but it doesn't seem like the right answer. Oracles can pull images toward them. Mine are sent to me in dreams. I only see images of things happening to *me*. Things I'm present for. I have wondered if it's a rare gift of the legacy I was given."

"Did you see me?" I asked.

He finally came back to reality, eyes roaming my face. His attention was probing as he considered his answer.

There was a battle going on inside him, one I couldn't begin to understand. But I was learning to read the shifting tones of his skin as he struggled to keep the moving shadows at bay.

"Yes." He squared his shoulders. "I saw you for over a year and a half before we found you."

My heart gave a hard thud as he turned away from me. A year and a half? This was why he always gave me strange looks. He seemed confused when I told him things about myself, like calling me Liv instead of my full name. Because I wasn't what he expected.

He'd known of me well before we ever met.

Facing the sky, he drifted back into his own thoughts. I wanted to press for more, but I understood that expression. He was closing himself off. There was yet something he wasn't willing to tell me.

Nuo wanted to push Brekt to live before it all ended—before they fought the Ikhor. I was beginning to understand why.

My heart began to slice open, and all the little cuts were from truths I didn't want to believe. Brekt had seen how this all played out. And I was somehow tangled up with it. Had he seen my death?

"Do Kazhi and Bastane know about these dreams?" I asked.

"No. Only Nuo. And now you."

I knew a secret that he was not even willing to tell two of the Guards. "Thank you for telling me. Trust is a gift I have never been given. I promise to keep it to myself."

He nodded, still gone somewhere in his mind.

"Tell me more about the north camp. What was it like growing up there?"

It was like he shook himself, something falling away as he turned to me, half of his face glowing golden from the sun, the other half blue from the night sky catching up to us.

"North Aspis was not a comfortable upbringing, and it was miserable until Nuo showed up. Although, he made me miserable for a long time, too—always talking, always trying to show off that he was the smartest. Back then, he hadn't grown into himself. He was whiny and desperate to be heard."

I grinned, picturing a little Nuo and how much of a handful he would have been.

"You mentioned before you had a tough teacher."

"Yes, he was not loving. There were many teachers, but the one training us in combat was particularly difficult. He didn't like me. When I was older, I became the one that was tough on my team. Because of what I'd seen, I knew we had to train harder than any before. I pushed Nuo relentlessly.

"We grew up alongside each other, becoming brothers, and one influenced the other. I don't sleep much because of the dreams, and I do everything I can to prevent them from happening in my waking hours. I made sure we became the most feared. We were each other's greatest competition and closest allies. I wouldn't be who I am if it wasn't for him."

"You mean you would have been worse?"

A genuine smile changed his face. The wind itself could have knocked me over—his smile was *sexy*. His teeth were straight, his canines slightly pointed, and his full lips parted, creasing off to one side. His shadow of a beard didn't at all hide the hard lines of his jaw.

He lifted a hand and pushed the loose hair out of his face. "I don't think you realize how horrible I can be. You're getting the nice version."

"How about you start giving me a seductive version?"

What was wrong with me? All the rules I made—give him space, don't be pushy—I was doing the exact opposite.

But he met me full-on. He pinned me in place, my insides clenching. It made me inch closer to him, closer to his mouth. Closer to the curve of those lips.

But he didn't reach for me.

"I don't know if you could handle the seductive version, Liv. Most can't." His smile was playful, but he wasn't fully invested. So I backed off.

"I can be quite seductive, too," I boasted, making a face. "When you get past the tears and inability to control what I say, it's quite charming." I tried and failed to hide the embarrassment and how my face flushed.

"You don't need to say anything to be seductive," he coaxed, his deep voice snaring me. "Just get angry and start stripping. That'll put me in my place. I'm happy to get you going at any time if that's the result."

My arousal quickly turned to anger. "Well, you won't be getting any more of that. Tit-for-tat, Brekt." I spun away from him.

"I've never heard that saying, but I like the sounds of it."

And I liked the feeling of what his voice did to me—the low timbre reverberating in all the best places.

I sighed, and my stupid mouth went off again. "It's tough for me to focus around you. Especially when I finally decided to let loose. And I'm trying not to be pushy, but you make it impossible. Should I say something? Should I not? It's driving me nuts."

God, I sounded whiny. I was always so flustered around him.

"Don't hold back for my sake."

I cocked my head, and he continued. "I have my issues to deal with, but that's beside the point. If you have something to say, say it. If you want to do something, do it. You get one life. Others aren't afraid to live as they wish. Why should you be?"

I gripped the railing, leaning back. "I figured—I thought I might make you angry or something, pushing you. I don't want to drive you away."

"Well, by living and breathing, you'll eventually hurt someone's feelings. It's the bad side effects, right?" he said softly, repeating Nuo's words.

I nodded, understanding what he meant.

"You can't predict or control others, so don't bend to your assumptions. Don't hold back in fear. Most won't hold back on you."

He was right—the world was harsh. Why avoid enjoying your life and giving in to the fear of bad consequences?

I was still considering his words when the metal door leading inside the ship opened behind us. Guardian women came out onto the landing.

They headed to the sides of the deck where ropes were tied to the golden posts, hanging over and dropping out of sight. I hadn't noticed them before.

Next through the door came the Guards, spotting us and heading over to the front where we stood.

Bastane reached us first. "They're stopping at some caves. Half the crew is going down and want the Guards to join them."

Bastane—Bas—gave me a tight smile. I returned it, thankful he didn't ask how I was. I wanted to apologize for punching him, but I felt it wasn't needed. He nodded as if to say it was okay, moving on.

"Shall we go?" Nuo asked, his face lighting up. "I could use an adventure away from this ship."

"One of us would need to stay here with Liv," Brekt pointed out. It sounded like he wasn't excited about cave hunting.

"We were all asked to go. She will have to stay here," Bastane said.

"Not a chance." Nuo folded his arms. "Falizha is staying on the ship. I don't trust her to leave Olivia alone."

"I'll go with you." I couldn't tell if the pounding in my chest was excitement or not.

Nuo scratched his chin. "I think Falizha will be confused at why I bring my whore along to hunt crystals."

There was a pause of silence before Brekt's voice grew deadly quiet, "You're what?"

I had forgotten our ploy. Nuo gave a half-shrug, "Falizha has already decided I pay Olivia for her nighttime services and that she's my carry-along-whore."

Nuo was pleased with the look on Brekt's face, as if it was for his own entertainment. The growl deep in Brekt's chest only made Nuo smile more.

Bastane raised his eyes to the skies, and Kazhi surprised us all with a laugh of her own. It was one of the few times I'd heard her laugh, and I found it unnerving.

"We should have gotten our stories straight," Kazhi sighed.

"Why do you have to have stories in the first place?" I asked. "Aren't you guys the top of the top? The Guards of the Aspis?"

They all made faces, like reminding them was an unnecessary pain.

"Falizha will have to assume you don't want her out of sight," Brekt decided. "Sorry, Liv, but this cover Falizha has created might work for the best. We don't understand, yet, how you're to aid in waking the Aspis. Best to avoid any unwanted questions. People won't care about the purpose of a paid woman with us. But I suggest keeping a low profile and not speaking around people you don't know." His mouth pressed into a hard line. "And I guess you're sticking by Nuo's side—safer than staying on board."

"What would Falizha do to me if I did? I need to know these things if I'm coming along with you guys."

"Falizha is not our enemy." Bastane looked to his team, "You would all do well to remember that. And we have a mission to accomplish, in case you've forgotten. We need to get back on track. I think Olivia's arrival took us off course for far too long. You've done nothing to figure out why she's even here. No offence Liv, but I am having a hard time seeing the reason for following along with this. We need to get serious."

It was Nuo who answered. "Trust me that there are many reasons to bring Olivia along." He gave Bastane a dismissive wave of his hand before leaning toward me. "And Falizha might harm you if she thought it got her closer to us. Or she might use you to take one of us down."

"You need to be aware of the power hierarchy in our world." Brekt ignored Bastane's rebuke. "The Guards are symbols to the people and, as such, are respected. But we are not at the top of the food chain. We are replaceable." His eyes shifted toward Kazhi.

Right. She was hired to assassinate him. Meaning someone out there didn't believe the Guards were untouchable.

Brekt and Nuo shared a wordless conversation, ending with a nod from Nuo.

Brekt's voice was quiet when he said, "We believe it was Falizha's father who tried to have me killed—who hired Kazhi."

"You told her that? About the attempt on your life?" Bastane asked.

"We trust her. As should you," Nuo said.

Kazhi's reaction was curious when she simply looked at me and shrugged. "I never actually knew who hired me for the kill. I just accepted the job, not knowing what I was getting tangled up in. But The Governor would gain the most with a position free for a new Guard."

"And we are going there, to the city, and will face him? The man who tried to have you killed. Theoretically." My head was spinning with all the new information. There was still so much I didn't know about this world.

"We are going to be staying in the same palace as him," Brekt corrected.

No wonder I was to play a role. I was heading into the snake pit itself.

"Wait, so why would he try to marry his daughter off?" My mind was reeling.

"We think he planned to kill off one of us and put his son in their place," Nuo explained, "It was known—before we were chosen to be the Guards—that we were more qualified than anyone. The Governor must have heard the rumours of our skill and sent Kazhi to take one of us out before we could take the coveted position away from his son. But when the most notorious assassin didn't return from the mission, he switched gears, pushing his daughter in our path. He wants his family to be seen as a symbol of power, more than it already is.

"The Guards of the Aspis have always lived in the Guardian City, training with its people. But the city became too political for us. The Governor and his Council are tasked with running the City and the Guardians beyond, but they seem to believe they control the entire continent of Veydes. It can be suffocating, having their influence wherever we go, always assuming everyone is spying on you. We have bigger issues on our plates than playing mind games."

"So the Guardian lands aren't run by the Guardians?" I asked.

"The lands belong to the gods. Technically, they are not supposed to be run by anyone. However, the gods seem to have taken a back seat for a very long time. Most of us have never even seen one."

More voices sounded from across the deck, stealing our attention.

Falizha now stood there. The crew had been pulling up ropes from the sides of the ship. The Captain now surveyed what had been dragged up on deck—bodies. They had hung them from the side of the ship.

There were so many. The women were lining them up. My stomach swam at the sight. Their skin was rotted. Blisters had formed around their necks from the weight of the ropes. Had they been alive when strung?

"What are those?" Bastane choked.

"Aethars," Brekt growled. "Another power play, I'm guessing, to anyone looking up from below."

"She's sick." I glared at the woman in charge. I had a new respect for Nuo's hatred. And I would be staying in Falizha's home.

Cruelty was a curious thing. Where did it start, and where did it end? Was it the Aethars who began this cycle of hate?

No. It was neither Aethar nor Guardian. It was the first evil to roam these lands—the Ikhor did this. Its evil magic had caused more rot than Falizha ever could.

CHAPTER

FORTY-FIVE

W e'd been given crystal-powered torches, ropes and supplies to help Falizha's crew search the caves. I tried not to appear too amazed at how the torches worked.

Kazhi found me clothing suitable for crystal hunting. I was in soft leather pants that hugged my behind and a long sleeve top that was snug. Thankfully, she found an undershirt that held some of my other, more significant, curves.

The five of us gathered above the ladder leading to the outside of the airship.

Brekt was helping me put some supplies in a backpack— magycris and extra food. My swords were strapped around my waist, a last measure *in case of trouble*. I hadn't asked what kind of trouble we might find.

I was bouncing up and down, anxious to head out.

"Are you nervous?" Brekt asked in a low voice behind me.

"No, not about the cave." I bit one of my nails. The others were almost done strapping on their numerous weapons.

"Then what for?"

I gave a shy laugh. "I've never worn such tight clothes," I said quietly over my shoulder.

He was silent for a moment before he whispered, "I feel jumpy about that too."

I spun to find his lopsided grin. He caught his lower lip in his teeth, stealing my breath. I couldn't think of anything clever to throw back at him with that mouth so close.

"Should I try making you upset?" he teased, a hopeful gleam in his eye. My face warmed, thinking about stripping for him.

My nostrils flared.

My hand was halfway toward smacking him when a hand grabbed my wrist. "Now, now, BB," Nuo said quietly, "I know you two want to stay behind and get handsy, but there are people in the corridor with us."

The women down the hall were also getting ready to head out. No one was watching us, however.

Instead, I made a face at Nuo.

He returned it, "It looks like Bag Boy and Bag Leader are on duty tonight. We have important work to attend to, so let's get our serious faces on."

Brekt was smug as he went down the ladder. It took me the longest to get my footing on the shifting steps.

I descended into the night, which was entirely upon us now. Lights from both fire and crystal torches sent flickering colours of orange and blue across the ground, lighting up long blades of grass and strangely shaped bushes. We were in an open area surrounded by jungle. Trees were visible just outside the sphere of light.

I moved away from the airship hovering above my head, breathing in the humid night air. I had only ever lived in a cold climate, never warm enough for the air to feel damp from the heat.

At Falizha's request, Nuo mapped out a path to an extensive system of tunnels under one of the mountains. It suggested several entrances, so we would split into groups and head in different directions. The groups would be divided further once inside the caves.

"Stay with me, no matter what." Nuo's tone was serious as he led me into the black sea of trees.

He held a map in one hand and a torch in the other. It was so black under the canopy of trees I could see nothing past the leaves that reflected our light. Brekt was upfront with Nuo, removing the brush as we went. They became part of the night with their black clothing—Brekt even more so with his unusual gifts from the Night god. I, too, followed like a shadow in their wake as if I were a Night legacy myself.

The jungle sounds were a symphony of buzzing and cawing, like everything living was protesting the dark. I was glad I had my thick boots. It was too easy to picture creatures darting out of the bushes to bite my ankles.

The group of women following behind set me on edge. They had gathered around Nuo when he explained the route, giving me looks and trying to decipher why I was standing with them.

A particular woman with a heavily tattooed face and hair shaven to her scalp had been more watchful than the others. The way she eyed me—she creeped me out.

It took us less than an hour to find the cave. Even when we reached the mountain's edge, I couldn't understand how they found the small opening. We could only fit through two at a time. I passed into the cave through thick stone, leaving the open air and wild jungle, switching the living darkness for a still one.

Inside the cave, the combination of our lights lit up the area, gleaming off large cavern walls with multiple tunnels leading off it. The stone was dark, the air was damp, and stalactites hung from the ceiling.

Oddly, I didn't find it scary. I thought a cave would be claustrophobic and that I'd be terrified of what kind of monsters we would find, or rather, would find us. But something was calming about the static, quiet darkness—so different from the wild, loud sounds of the jungle creatures.

"What's this?" I whispered to Nuo, who had joined me near the wall of the cave.

Like the first cave I visited, this one had drawings. Legacies were painted beneath the temples—gold figures under Rem's, haunted figures with white piercing eyes beneath Erabas's. The blue figures under Mayra had three slashes on their necks, appearing as if they floated underwater. Last was Ouras's temple —figures with animal patterns and wings.

Under each of the temples, amongst all the figures, were a select few with circles around them like an aura.

"I'm not sure what those halos are." Nuo folded his map and tucked it away. "The cave paintings are said to be older than many of our written texts. My best guess is the legacies circled like this are the pure bloodlines."

"But all the bloodlines would be pure so long ago, would they not?"

"As I said, it's my best guess."

On a separate wall, a village had been painted, but much of it had crumbled away. The few figures were painted in different colours, and their clothing was very unlike the Guardians.

"How about that wall? They're different than the legacies on this one."

The people on the crumbled wall didn't look anything like the watered-down legacies—which Nuo was. Something about them seemed peaceful, though, and it roused emotions I couldn't understand.

Nuo didn't have an answer for me, so I formed my own.

"Could these be my people?"

Nuo eyed the wall with new interest.

Though the serenity and peace between the figures here were so unlike the people of my world, I couldn't help but feel I was right. Nuo was quickly called away by the Guardians, and I tucked the thought away to question later.

Nuo picked a tunnel off the back of the cavern for us to explore. A group of women broke off to follow us, including the scary woman with the shaved head. Her skin had a leathery texture, and down her back were thick scales similar to armour. When she finally noticed my gaze fixed on her, she smiled, showing rows of sharp teeth. I stepped closer to Brekt and Nuo, resisting the urge to hide behind them.

We took off down the tunnel. Our footsteps echoed around us. No one spoke.

With nothing to distract me, my mind replayed the fact that Brekt had seen me in his dreams for over a year and a half. I could understand if he didn't want to talk about private matters, especially if he saw things that were to happen to his friends, but what if he had answers as to why I was here and why they took me with them? Had he seen the Light that brought me here?

I was sure the answer was in his dream.

He had confided in me something that Kaz and Bas didn't even know. The warrior prowling before me buried a considerate heart within. There was a harmonious combination of his brutality and humanity. He'd bought me earrings and swords. He let me dance without the worry of being seen. He held me as I mourned my mother. But he was equally deadly. He elicited fear but, yet, took mine away.

I followed him for what felt like an hour, maybe more. My appreciation gave way to irritation.

We had to backtrack countless times, turning around to take different routes. We marked each turn with oblong stones. The Guardians were all trained to work as a team, even if some of them had never travelled together.

Some tunnels broke into two, and our group split further still, yet the shaved woman continued to follow us. I'd hoped she would choose another path.

Eventually, we were down to five—the shaved woman and a tall, young girl with braided red hair and gills.

We rounded a corner, coming upon a long tunnel. Nuo stopped. I halted, my heart booming in my chest. A faint glow came from around the corner at the end of the tunnel. Nuo held a thumb up to Brekt.

He led us toward the light to a low-hanging opening. We all crouched to enter.

The large cavern was painted with strange ethereal hues— colours you couldn't find anywhere else.

Crystals of all sizes jutted out of the ground, the walls, and even hung from the ceiling. Some were larger than me. They lit the entire cavern with a blueish-purple light, each one a slightly different colour.

A soft glow outlined Nuo and Brekt's features. They were stunning. I lifted my hand. I was also radiant with the ambient light as if my skin sparkled from within. There was no longer a need for torches.

My mouth hung open as the two Guardian women walked past me. The shaved woman bumped into me, not bothering to apologize as her leathery skin scraped my shirt sleeve.

The young red-haired woman went up to Nuo. "Let's get as many as possible into our packs and head back. We will point the others in this direction if they haven't come across any. We can fill our ship with this cavern alone."

Nuo agreed. "Let's split up and pick away at smaller pieces."

The others took off, and Nuo nodded for me to follow him. But I paused when the shaved woman stopped to scowl over her shoulder at me. Her face changed when she looked at Nuo. I didn't know how many women he had *fun* with, but I guessed a few. Perhaps she was one of them.

I kept close as we walked further into the never-ending cavern. Nuo explained that we would take smaller pieces instead of trying to mine larger crystals which would weigh us down. He also warned me to keep an eye out above. Any vibrations we made could loosen the crystals overhead.

After searching, trying and pulling crystals to see if they would come free, he found a small cluster far from the entrance and began to slowly pull them apart. He motioned for me to grab my bag. My Bag Boy skills were being put back to work.

The large crystal jutting out from the wall beside me was almost as tall as I was. As I reached to grab the strap of my pack, the crystal caught my attention. It glowed like the rest, but this one had a strange pattern. Several reddish rings circled one another, spaced apart like they were caught in the prism.

I peered closer, trying to see what the rings were made of when they flashed as if they were blinking on and off—or rather, open and closed.

I pulled back with a gasp.

"Nuo, are there big animals in this cave?"

His eyes met mine before focusing behind me, widening.

"Liv, get down now."

FORTY-SIX

I didn't hesitate, hitting the ground and scrambling toward the crystal behind me. Nuo grabbed a large knife from his side.

Scampering up the wall and peering down at us was a humongous, white-skinned lizard. It was as long as three people, and its feet were larger than my chest. It stuck a pink tongue out in the air. Its round eyes with tiny black pupils moved back and forth between Nuo and me.

The colour of its skin glowed the same colours as the crystals, making it blend into the wall, becoming a crystal itself.

Nuo stepped slowly in front of me.

Triggered by Nuo's movement, the lizard raced back down the wall, rushing toward us.

Nuo shot out with his knife, but he miscalculated the lizard's attack. It swiped out with its tail, knocking Nuo off his feet. He landed on his back, his breath exploding from him. His knife dropped to his side, out of reach.

I scrambled to my feet, pulling out a sword to defend us while Nuo recollected.

The lizard spotted me, and its tongue reappeared, tasting the air. It moved in.

Before I could react, it sunk its teeth into one of Nuo's legs. It held firm, dragging him as it started crawling away faster than I had thought possible. Nuo grabbed at the lizard, trying to pull himself free, his face contorted in pain. The lizard was moving so fast that Nuo was out of reach in seconds.

"Nuo!" I shouted, forgetting his warning too late—my voice echoed back and forth across the walls and reverberated in my chest. The cave moved. Dust fell from the ceiling.

Crystals fell as Nuo was dragged across the cave floor back toward where we entered. Within another heartbeat, he was out of sight. The muffled sounds of him being taken faded while the echoing of my voice still rang around me.

I stumbled in my haste to follow. It was easy to see his trail—dark spots glistened on the ground. His blood. Seeing it made my heart stagger. There was already so much. Grunts echoed, but it was hard to tell where they came from.

When I came around another corner, I ran hard into someone and bounced off them, falling back to the ground.

Above me stood the shaven woman. When she noticed Nuo's absence, a smile spread across her face. Her dark eyes narrowed in on me. She must have come to investigate the sound. Had she been hoping I was alone?

"Nuo, he's hurt. We have to help the Guard," I sputtered, hoping to direct her attention to one of the chosen Guards, her symbol of hope—someone much more important than me.

"I wasn't asked to help the Guards." Her voice was deep and rasping. It suited her chilling features.

"What—What were you asked to do?" My mind was whirling. Is this the outcome the others had feared, that someone would use me to take advantage of the Guards?

Panic was the only source of strength I had. I brought the sword, still in my shaking hands, up in front of me.

She laughed at it, and her sharp teeth flashed in the low light. "I heard you don't know how to use that thing. I also heard that master Nuo, for some reason, thought he would train a whore to fight. I'm here to remind you of your place in the world; the dirt, the sewers, the run-down shacks in the slums of the city. Watered-down legacies like you aren't worth a thing. No one will miss you."

She kicked out, striking my hand. The sword flew out of my grip. I gasped at her speed and accuracy.

I sprang up and ran. Nuo was fighting that giant lizard alone, and I needed to reach him. But I also needed to focus on staying alive. I didn't look behind me as I swerved through crystals, the reflecting lights making me dizzy. I came to an open area and skidded to a halt.

Dust clouded before me. A gaping chasm split the cave floor, spanning several feet across. The missing ground was black as pitch, an endless pit—an easy death.

I considered jumping it when a pair of hands came around my neck, pulling me back against a curved body made of steel.

"You don't deserve the attention of a Guard nor their money. I'm just throwing away the trash so they can get back to focusing on the goal. Much is at stake, and your life is nothing compared to how many will die if they fail."

The soft skin of my neck was too close to her dagger-like teeth. Her hold on my neck tightened.

I struggled for air as her raspy voice cracked through the violent storm inside my head.

I grabbed ahold of her wrist while shifting my hip toward her, just like my mother had taught me. I pulled forward, sending her flying over my shoulder. She landed square on her back.

Shocked that I had succeeded, I rushed and landed on top of her, throwing fists into her face.

Rage and terror and all the emotions I'd gotten so used to holding in were coming loose. The box I had hidden deep down inside, holding in the feelings I didn't want to face, slipped open a crack, and for once, I let them out. I carved the woman's name into that box, next to the Keepers. I had a target. My emotions were alive, crawling out of me and down my arms as I sent fist after fist to her face.

My rage lit the cave as bright as the crystals.

Everything was glowing brighter. The lights around me started to pulse and shift from blue to purple and then a bright white. Even the woman's scales reflected the glare.

I paused for the smallest second. The crystals were definitely brighter than before. That moment cost me. She rotated, catching my torso and rolling me so that she was on top. I panicked, noting we were less than a couple of feet from the vast chasm.

She scrambled to get the dominant position, and it was my turn to eat fists. Her knuckles came down with a sickening crunch against my jaw. I tried to buck her off, with little success. Another punch landed against my temple, and the lights swam.

The glow around the cave faded. I don't know if the crystals stopped shining so bright or if I was losing consciousness.

Her hand shot out and caught me in the throat. I coughed, trying to catch my breath around what felt like a collapsed windpipe. I couldn't move. I could only lay there, gasping air as lights faded in and out.

I was aware of the slide of metal and the glint of a knife but I could do nothing but watch as she raised her blade above me.

No one will miss you.

All this because I was distracting a Guard.

The world was cruel. Always cruel.

Was this what Brekt saw? Was this the outcome he was worried about? Why he wouldn't get close to me, wouldn't kiss me, because his own people would turn on me?

As she moved to bring the knife down, a shadow formed from nothing behind her. I only briefly saw the look on Brekt's face. It was the one he had warned me about, the version of himself he hadn't let me see, even in the street of Bellum during the Aethar attack. This was the face of a deadly, pure-blooded legacy of Night.

His features were hard to focus on, shadows of night. His

tattoos swirled beneath his skin, and his eyes flashed iridescence as they reflected the glow of magic. He seemed larger, deadlier.

The god of Death.

He's finally come for me, I thought. But not to claim my life. To save it.

He grabbed the woman by the back of her shirt, pulling her off me. She lost grip of her knife. It fell and sliced across the top of my thigh. I finally got air my lungs and gasped at the pain.

Brekt wrapped an arm around the struggling woman, bringing her to his chest. His eyes were focused with a killing rage as his knife flashed. He brought it forward to her throat, slicing sideways in a single confident stroke, spilling blood down her chest and out in front of her.

The woman made an awful gurgling sound, and I felt nothing. I watched, frozen.

Brekt showed no remorse, no reaction whatsoever, as he held that woman bleeding out in his arms. His eyes flickered as he checked to see if I was okay.

His lip peeled back, showing his teeth a moment before he drove his knife into the side of the woman. She jerked from the contact. She was already fading as she felt that final, vengeful plunge of the blade.

Brekt had let something slip, allowing me to see the darkness under his skin. The kill was not clean or peaceful—it was sudden, feral and brutal.

This was the man that most people saw. This was the Guard people feared on the street who moved aside as he walked down the path—Erebrekt of the North.

"You killed her?" I whispered. It came out like a question without meaning to.

A cruel smile formed on his lips. "No, I didn't."

I jerked as he pushed her body away from him and down through the crack in the ground.

There was no sound as her body disappeared, answering my earlier questions about how deep it might go.

My hand shook as Brekt reached down to help me up. My thigh burned from the open slice as I put weight on it. I thought he might ask if I was okay, but he gave me a quick once over and turned, saying nothing and expecting me to follow.

CHAPTER
FORTY-SEVEN

I was still shaking, still coughing as we searched for Nuo. I couldn't speak. I didn't know what had scared me most, but surprisingly it wasn't the near-death experience.

Three things played on repeat in my head. First was how the whole cave *glowed* as I tried to hurt that woman, just as the crystals in my sword glowed when I was studying it.

The second was that there was no sound as the woman fell down the crevice. Her body just faded from sight, her life blown away, a whisper in the dark. And I had considered jumping that gap.

And third—the precision with which Brekt had taken her life and thrown her in the pit. He was terrifying, cruel and lethal.

I was in step behind him as we hunted for Nuo. Brekt's pace was hard to keep up with as we followed the trail.

We rounded a corner and almost missed the young redhead lying face down in the dirt. We wouldn't have seen her if it wasn't for her bright hair. It was stupid to wear all black in a dark cave.

Brekt rushed to her side, crouching down, checking her pulse, then shaking his head. He was up immediately and continued forward to find Nuo. No time wasted.

Had the other woman killed her? She said she wasn't asked to help the Guards. She didn't want them dead; she wanted *me* out of the way.

A groaning sound echoed as we closed in on the cave's far end. Only minutes had passed since Nuo's attack, yet so much had happened.

Brekt picked up his pace. The sounds were getting closer when the end of the lizard's tail came into view from around a crystal near a wall.

The lizard's head moved up and down like it was tearing flesh from a body. I covered my mouth, feeling queasy. Would we find Nuo already half-eaten? I didn't know how I would be able to handle that loss.

But the grunting sound came from *under* the lizard.

Brekt rushed to the head of the creature, angled in an unnatural way against the cave wall. A booted foot was visible from under its neck.

I fumbled to help Brekt lift the dead weight.

Nuo moaned as he slid out from under the lizard, gulping air as he was finally released. He held his chest as he braced himself, trying to refill his lungs.

"If you had taken any longer, I would've suffocated under the weight of that thing. What use are my friends if they can't follow me being dragged through a cave by a half-blind lizard?"

Nuo had open wounds on his legs—gashes from the lizard's teeth. He was covered head to toe in blood. His shirt was ripped, and his face was sliced open in several spots. He had fought tooth and nail, literally, for his life.

As he stood and balanced himself against the wall, I noticed another one of his knives missing from a belt. I guessed he'd freed it and used it against the frightening creature.

Relief washed over me, and I rushed to wrap my arms around his waist. I knew I was covering myself in blood and possibly causing his wounds to sting. But I have only once before felt that kind of fear—of losing someone you care for.

He was stiff, holding me for a moment as I slumped in his arms.

I leaned back. "You'll be okay?" I croaked. My voice was lost after the woman had punched my throat.

"You can count on it, BB. I told you I'm a legendary warrior." When he tried to laugh, it came out in a coughing fit.

"The other two are dead," Brekt said in a low growl. "We need to get out of here. Let's find our stuff and get back to the entrance. Olivia doesn't leave our sight."

I put a hand on Brekt's chest. "Back off. Nuo didn't leave my side by choice. That thing tried to eat him and dragged him away."

Brekt's fury was turned on me. A storm raged in his eyes, and something more I didn't understand.

"What happened to the other two? What happened to you, Liv?" Nuo noticed my leg, the swelling on my jaw and around my eye.

"We are wasting time. Let's go," Brekt snarled. He spun on his heel.

I opened my mouth to question him when Nuo grabbed my arm. He was shaking his head. *Later* he mouthed. But he looked as confused as I felt.

We found our packs after a quick search, and I collected my dropped sword. We passed the redhead again, and Nuo eyed her but didn't ask questions. He snatched her pack and torch and followed Brekt silently.

It took us longer to make it back through the tunnels to the entrance of the cave. My one eye had nearly swollen shut, and my throat burned from where she hit me. I struggled to keep up as I limped from the slice in my thigh.

Nuo was far worse—his entire lower leg was in pieces from the lizard, but he didn't complain. I was angry at Brekt for not noticing how much the two of us needed to take it slow. He was silent ahead of us, blending into the shadows more than usual, fading in and out of sight. His gift was usually deliberate. Right now, however, he seemed to be losing control.

Nuo threw worried glances between the two of us, and I shrugged in response. I didn't understand his anger.

Once we neared the main cavern, Brekt stopped before we rounded the last few corners. Faint voices were echoing in the distance.

Brekt didn't turn as he spoke, avoiding looking directly at us.

"You two stay here. I need to get a message to Kazhi. I'll explain after." He vanished out of sight.

Nuo stared at the spot where Brekt last stood. His brows pinched.

"Somethings happened. What's going on? It has to do with the other two Guardians back there, doesn't it."

"I don't know why he didn't tell you." I chewed on my lip, considering. "I want to trust he has a reason or a plan. Let's wait for him to come back."

"You won't tell me what happened? Olivia, you're bleeding. Your face—" he paused, thinking. "Huh."

He rubbed the bottom of his chin, watching me. "You'd keep things from me for his sake."

I nodded, worried I was risking Nuo's trust, but I was still reeling from Brekt's anger and didn't know what to say.

Nuo's face relaxed. He leaned against the wall, bracing himself and dropping the bag on his back.

"Are you mad at me now too?"

"Oh no. Relieved, actually, that you care for him enough to stay silent. He's impossible to deal with at times, so I know it's not easy to always be on his side. Although, I do hate not knowing."

He was rummaging through his bag, looking for medicine. I remember it was in my pack, so I rushed to help. He smiled in thanks and continued. "You're a loyal person. It's rare. Especially for us. I'm happy you would stick by him even if he doesn't deserve it right now."

"I don't understand why he is acting that way."

"I don't know either. But, when men are upset, the last thing they are likely to do is talk about it. So hang tight. Hopefully, he doesn't plan to leave without us." He gave a husky laugh.

I helped Nuo get magycris on his leg. I opted for the balm on mine, saving the expensive liquid for when we might have a more dire need of it. I ignored the blood on my knuckles—stains from the woman's face.

Nuo struggled to sit down. I felt heavy, thinking I had lost him. The emotions were crushing. It put into contrast my old life and now. For years, I feared being hurt or punished for acting differently. It was nothing compared to losing someone you loved. My mother's death had been sudden, with no time to feel panic.

I could handle bad things happening to *me*, but my friends? I couldn't go through that kind of pain again.

I felt another layer coming off, maybe several, realizing what real fear was. When I left this cave, it wouldn't be the same woman that went in. She would be stronger and more capable of handling life. I kept an eye on my friend, thankful I had been brought here, even though sometimes it was much more complicated than before. Friends were something worth living for.

I was willing to face it for them.

The quiet, cold cave would soak up the detritus of all I was leaving behind. And I was ready to soak up the world waiting outside.

CHAPTER

FORTY-EIGHT

Brekt returned not much later, Bastane with him this time. I struggled to my feet, Nuo grunting alongside me—our pain was equally growing as time passed.

Bastane whistled when he saw us. "What the hell happened to you two?"

Nuo was kneading his shoulder. "I'd like to know as well. I only know half the story."

Confusion flashed over Brekt. Probably wondering why I hadn't told Nuo. "We aren't going back on the airship," he said.

All of us stared at him, surprised.

"I spoke to Kazhi. She went ahead with everyone to grab our belongings and sneak off the ship. She will throw our stuff overboard and find a way off without being seen."

"What for?" Nuo stood straight, back in Guard mode, gathering information for the new plan. "Why are we hiding now?"

Brekt finally faced me. I couldn't tell what emotions I saw swirling in his eyes while he spoke, "I think Falizha tried to make a hit on Olivia's life."

Nuo's eyes widened, taking in my wounds with a new horror.

Bastane lifted a brow while taking in my swollen eye.

With everything happening so quickly, I hadn't considered it might be Falizha who ordered to take me out.

I wasn't asked to help the Guards. No one will miss you.

"They'll question why we aren't on board," Nuo stated as I tried to calm my racing heart.

"Falizha will hear how, just now, I asked Bastane to come to help me search for something before we left. I also told them to go ahead of us. Falizha will think we are looking for Liv, who is dead."

Brekt was emotionless, his words clipped. I knew enough to recognize he was caging what lived beneath his skin.

Bastane was making a face at my bruises. "May the guilty suffer the Endless Night." It was the prayer I heard back in Bellum. Then, he said to Brekt. "So what should we be doing?" He, too, was calculating and making a plan.

"We head back out to the landing site, no torches. We make sure it's gone and call for Kazhi. Then," Brekt sighed, clearly not happy at the next part, "We make our way to the city on foot."

"Fuuuck." Nuo raked a hand through his hair.

Bastane gave me an exasperated look.

I returned it. "If you want to kill me, Bas, I guess there's a line now. This is not *actually* my fault," I spat.

"The jungle is miserable, *Liv*. It won't be me killing you. Wait for the blisters on your feet and the bugs." He smiled, but it was all teeth. "I will be blaming you the entire way."

"Kazhi will navigate." Brekt ignored us. "She knows this jungle well. We have to make tracks tonight if, for any reason, Falizha's crew decides to come back for us. Grab some food if you need it now. We aren't stopping until morning."

Bastane walked up to me, stopping when we were toe to toe. "Next time we train, I will repay you for this. I hate bugs."

I trembled while his gold-rimmed eyes bore into mine. He was just as terrifying as Brekt when he wanted to be.

The Guardian women were all gone when we finally braved leaving the cave and snuck into the roaring jungle. They had left crystal markers at the opening, which Brekt quickly stuffed into his pack.

I was limping, following behind Nuo, who was in worse shape than I was. I tried a bit of medicine on my swollen eye but couldn't manage the sting. So it remained closed. Not that it would make a difference to my vision—the darkness was so absolute. I didn't know how they navigated to the clearing where the ship was.

The crystals in Nuo's bag glowed faintly through the fabric, allowing me to know where he was. He was my beacon in the dark.

We hadn't collected many crystals, considering the amount we'd found. They were integral to their lives, and I was part of the reason the haul was cut short.

As I followed the glow in front of me, I weighed the reasons for Brekt's anger. I'd screwed up their mission, sure. He had warned me of the dangers.

You are a liability, he'd told me.

I was also battling my feelings about seeing him kill that woman. It unsettled me unlike anything had before.

I wasn't prepared for what it revealed—a killer, a hardened warrior, something abhorrent and formidable. Was this something he locked away as I did my box of anger? A trait of his legacy—the cursed children?

I would have compared him to the Keepers if I hadn't seen his other side, the kinder side.

I'd begun to trust Stephen when I was swept away from my forest and was disappointed when he didn't save me. Was I romanticizing Brekt, hoping to find a man that would? Or at least be capable of it?

But Brekt *did* save me. He killed that woman and threw her in the pit.

Although Brekt came to my rescue, it wasn't in shining armour. It was on a black steed with wings made of night. It was bloody and sharp and gruesome. I didn't feel warm and fuzzy. I felt cold and hollow.

I couldn't see him ahead of me, but I could feel him. The pull was a physical thing now. It was constantly there, humming in my body. I no longer pictured him gliding through the forest on two feet but slinking around on paws with sharp fangs. It was no longer the dark I was afraid of.

I thought I'd leave the cave stronger, but I was still just a coward, afraid of what I couldn't predict in others. I was the last person in this group that would be a hero.

When we reached the airship landing site, the space was empty, and the sky was clear above it.

The stars gave us enough light that I could see the shapes of the three men and the outline of the trees.

Brekt whistled, the sound carrying across the space and swallowed up by the jungle. A rustling came from behind us, and a soft whistle returned.

"Kaz," Brekt said in a low tone.

A shape came around a tree toward us. "The place has been cleared," Kazhi informed us, not bothering to whisper, "I overheard some of the women telling Falizha that we were staying behind, that we must have lost something important."

I would have tried to hide in shame if I wasn't already in darkness.

"Were you able to find the rest of our belongings?" Brekt asked.

"Yes," she replied, "and luckily, we didn't sell our tents. That's one blessing."

"And the fact we've rid ourselves of Falizha once again," Nuo added. I was grateful he tried to add a bright side. Not that any of them would see the difference. There were a lot of bad sides.

"Let's combine our packs. We get as far as we can on foot tonight. Kazhi, are you able to navigate us in the right direction?"

"In the general direction, yes. Come morning, I will need higher ground to know exactly where we are and go from there."

"Let's move then."

After a few moments of repacking in the dark, we were off.

"Hold onto my pack," Nuo whispered, "don't want to lose you in the dark."

I nodded, forgetting he couldn't see and grabbed onto his pack, following them into the darkness once more.

FORTY-NINE

E very sound in the dark put me on edge.

Not only were creatures different back home, but so was the climate. It was cold for most of the year, even when summer came. Here, the heat stuck to me. My already tight clothes itched against my skin, and my hair stuck to my neck.

Bastane was right to be angry with me. Walking like this was miserable. What would it be like when the sun came out and more creatures awoke?

The bugs weren't as bad as I had feared. They would fly around you and land, but none bit.

I was dragging my swollen feet when Kazhi stopped us near a large rocky overhang. The stars were still out. I could see them between the leaves of the trees above. The overhang allowed us to hide a fire with two tents around it.

Nuo lit the crystal torch while they made a fire. He gave me the second torch he had swiped from the redhead. I held it uselessly to the side, unsure of how else to help. We didn't have any furs, so we would sleep on the hard ground. Bastane told me the tents would keep most of the bugs away.

The four sat in front of the fire, unprepared to sleep, and Bastane decided to cook us food.

"I'll take the first watch," Kazhi said, "It will only be a few hours until the morning, and Bas can go for a quick hunt."

Bas nodded and leaned back against the rock of the overhang. And being a legacy of Day, he was immune to the harsh jungle climate. He still wore all his weapons while the rest had all removed theirs, trying to relieve themselves from the heat.

What I wouldn't give for a bath. The cut in my leg was still open. There was enough of the balm in the gash that I wouldn't have to worry about infection, but it didn't close up like magycris healing.

"I'll take second watch," Brekt offered. He was sitting across the fire from me, staring into the flames.

"No need," Kazhi said, "we won't get much sleep tonight. You get as much as you can. I'll be fine to go another day. Nuo looks like he could use some time to recover." She eyed Nuo's wounds. Her focus then shifted to my bruises, and her eyes narrowed on the cut on my leg.

"Did the woman say anything to you? Before she tried to kill you?" So she was already told about the incident.

I nodded, trying to recall what she had said. The memory was blurry, overshadowed by Brekt's appearance. "She said she wasn't sent there to help the Guards and that I was in the way. I was distracting you from your goal." I wasn't brave enough to look her in the eye.

This was the confirmation they would need to leave me. I was a liability, as Brekt had said. I would never make it to the Guardian City with them.

"Well," Kazhi said, "seems like enough proof to me that Falizha was responsible."

"It could have been someone else on the ship. Who knows how they all felt about Olivia at our side," Bastane suggested.

Kazhi's lip curled. "Get your head on right. You have too much respect for the power the Council holds. You're too loyal to your legacy. The golden pricks from the Guardian City are heartless. You've seen enough that you should know that by now."

"We just don't have solid proof. I don't want any of you getting the idea we can storm the city demanding answers from the Governor's daughter. And might I remind you I am one of those golden pricks, and my father has a seat on that council," he spat.

"No one thinks that we can storm the city," Brekt interrupted, "but Kazhi is right. We know you grew up amongst the elite, but it's time you accepted that what they do behind closed doors is not as respectable as how your family operates."

Nuo nodded in agreement. "Falizha is certainly capable of this if she is anything like her father."

"You are still assuming you know who tried to get a hit on one of you two," Bas waved a hand toward the two of them, "And therefore you're assuming who tried to harm Olivia."

"We aren't going to do anything once we get to the city but be cautious, " Brekt said, "If she thinks Olivia is dead, we go with that story. Then we can get in there, get supplies and head back out."

"How will we convince her father and the Council to hand over more weapons and an airship to travel?" Nuo's eyes were glued to the flames burning before us.

"I'm not sure yet, but a lot of acting on our part. The one thing we have is that we haven't found the location of the Aspis yet, and the threat of the Ikhor is now very real. The Council will have no choice but to offer aid. Or at least make the public see it that way. They need us for their good image."

"How *do* you find the Aspis?" I asked. It was something I should've known by now. I wasn't going to accept Brekt's excuse about the Guards' tightly held secrets.

They all stared at me and, one by one, looked away, staying silent. Kazhi was staring up at the sky, unmoving. Nuo turned to Brekt, who was captured by the fire. Bastane was also gazing into the flames and heaved a long sigh.

Nuo rolled his eyes, and I leaned forward, hoping to be let in on this well-kept secret.

Nuo mimicked Bastane's sigh before he mumbled, "We don't know."

I was stunned into silence. My eyes darted over them, hoping that he was joking. No one moved to correct Nuo. No one offered up any clue as to what they were searching for.

I stumbled over what to say.

"You mean this destiny you were given—the one that could save the world and be the very thing that prevents thousands of people from dying, the one you have trained your whole lives for—came with no instructions on how to complete it? There are no books or stories on how you even find this mythical creature that saves the world?" My voice rose as I continued. "You mean you're running around on horses and airships and through caves with no idea what you are doing?"

"Pretty much." Nuo looked back into the fire just like his brothers.

"But—I—I thought you'd be able to help me figure out why I was sent here. I thought you could find it or had clues. You said this was your biggest secret."

"It is. We *will* continue to search for legends of talking lights, but as to how to wake the beast ... we are all in the dark together on that one."

I couldn't believe it, I thought them all so strong with a grand purpose, yet they were all moving forward with no idea what they were doing.

"Well fuck," I said, finally.

Nuo and Bastane laughed, Kazhi stayed silent with her eyes skyward, and Brekt finally cracked a smile after hours of unbroken hostility.

"Does anyone else know you have no idea how to find it?"

"No." Nuo tensed. "They assumed when we became Guards that the knowledge would come somehow. We never corrected them. We've been playing a dangerous game for a very long time to keep that secret. If that information got into the wrong hands, there would be panic and less trust in us than there already is. That I am telling you, Liv, means that you're part of this now. One of us.

THE GUARDIANS OF THE ASPIS

You hold that truth inside of you. It could do a lot of harm out in the open."

"You should have told me sooner."

"We first had to believe you were not an enemy. After that, we needed to trust that you could keep things to yourself. You proved that in the cave. Plus, I was kind of hoping your purpose in coming here was to give us the answer. I was just going to let you solve it." He rubbed the back of his neck, giving me a weak, crooked smile.

Brekt lifted his head to peer at me over the fire. "Letting them assume we have the knowledge allows us to get what we need while we search. We are still the best suited to fight with the Aspis, so let them believe the rest."

"But you're running around aimlessly. You don't know what you're looking for."

"Sure we do—a giant, black, snake-like beast with horns. How well hidden can it be?"

I opened my mouth to argue but had no idea what to say. It was absolutely ridiculous. I was back to square one.

Brekt continued, "We believe the Aspis is slumbering in a human body. It will sense the Ikhor and awaken." He drew his hand through his hair, pulling it away from his face.

"A human body? How?" The idea that it was inside a person was insane. "So the title Guard is just a title then? There are no special powers that come with it?"

Nuo cut in, "We were the strongest fighters, the best working unit. That was all. They assumed the rest."

I thought being a Guard would explain the monster swimming underneath Brekt's skin. There was a monster under all of them when I thought about how they fought and killed. I wanted to believe it was because of magic and destiny. But they were just flesh and blood killers.

Was it wise I followed them? What other dangers would be drawn to these four? Oh, right—the Ikhor. The worst of them all.

"So what about the Ikhor then? It's awake. Won't everyone wonder where the Aspis is?"

"Another reason to avoid the city," Brekt said, "the questions. We hoped that on our travels, we would hear whispers of anyone who might have information for us. How to wake it. As Nuo mentioned, we hoped you might give us that answer."

"How to wake it and where it might be," Bastane added, "I theorized it was slumbering in your lands, and you would lead us back there. We all assumed the Ikhor would wake the Aspis immediately. It appears as though that's not the case. Perhaps it needs close proximity. Meaning we have work to do. We mustn't stay idle."

"Is it not wiser to leave me behind then?" I didn't realize they had no direction.

"Yes—" Bastane said.

"No—" Nuo said at the same time.

"You're not staying behind now, Olivia. It's too late for that," Brekt growled. He was back to not looking at me. And calling me Olivia.

I stood up and dusted myself off. "I really hate that name, you know. You can all stop using it. My name is Liv."

I stomped off to the tent. Perhaps childish, but I'd had too much. I pushed aside the opening and sat beside my pack that was already placed inside.

"You could ease up," Nuo whispered to Brekt from outside, "a lot has happened tonight."

"No kidding," Brekt mumbled.

"Well, I'm getting some sleep. Before I start acting like *you*."

Footsteps shuffled in the direction of my tent. The flap opened, and Nuo poked his head inside. "Mind if I sleep here? Everyone else is acting like an asshole while we both almost died tonig—"

He didn't finish his sentence because he was ripped away from sight.

"What is wrong with you, man?" He hissed from the pain in his wounds.

"Fuck off," Brekt spat before he pulled aside the flap and crouched in. He gave me a withering look and sat opposite me. He grabbed a pack on his side and puffed it up like a pillow. Without saying another word, he lay down, facing away.

Muffled voices whispered outside the tent, and the fire was snuffed out. I fluffed up my own pack and laid down. I wouldn't sleep easily. The pain in my leg and my face still throbbed. My throat hurt from where I was punched, and the heat made me feel twice my weight.

Brekt's breathing evened out. He had already fallen asleep.

I lay there angry, frustrated, and scared for the future. I thought they knew what they were doing.

But they were running around as lost as I was.

FIFTY

The following day my body was stiff from sleeping on the hard ground. That, and from almost being beaten to death. I woke to find the sun up and food cooking. The tent was already empty.

I had dreamt of Brekt again. The dreams were vivid and more intimate—a tough thing to wake from when he was so standoffish. I used to have horrible dreams. Now my mind seemed determined to focus on what I couldn't have rather than on things I had lost.

Outside I found the other tent taken down and everyone dressed. Bastane had found a small animal for breakfast, and its meat was smoking over the fire.

Brekt was on a log facing away from the flames, watching the jungle for movement. Kazhi was nowhere in sight.

Nuo was leaning against his pack with his map out and glasses on. I joined him, sitting down, hearing all sorts of joints crack and pop as I hit the ground.

Today there was no humour about him. It was one of the first times I'd seen him this serious for this long.

"What're you looking for?" My voice was even worse than the night before. I rubbed a hand over my throat.

His eyebrows met in concern, but he didn't ask me how I was. "I am marking the areas where we found the caves. It was Falizha's maps we found them on, so I am updating mine."

The new ink on the page was dark and easy to find. He had written *Nope* next to the caves from last night and a distorted image of a lizard.

Nuo didn't pull the map away as I read all the names of the places he'd written. His map was huge, but so much was yet blank. The world was massive, more than I had ever thought could exist beyond my borders. I still had a hard time believing I was home, that I was made like these people were.

"I've been wondering ..." I began, not sure how to put my thoughts into words. Nuo waited for me to continue. "I know now that I am still in my world, not transported magically to some mythical land. What's bothering me is your tattoos."

"Don't tell me you're still scared of them."

"Not like that, no." My swollen eye ached when I grinned. "But I wonder, why did the Keepers forbid them?"

"I imagine they wouldn't want you to express yourself in any manner."

"Definitely. But how would they even know what tattoos are? I never saw one before coming here, but I knew they were outlawed. How did the Keepers know?"

"Maybe some did have them?"

"I doubt it. The people back home loved their rules and abided by them with a passion. I wonder if someone once knew of the Guardians, knew of your lands and forbade us from any knowledge or allegiance to the outside world."

"Someone would have to go very far to hide that much information."

I nodded. And why would they bother? "Maybe I'm overthinking it."

I admired his map, which he was still scribbling in. "What's with all the stains?" I pointed to the corner of the page.

"I have been known to have a drink while mapping." He shrugged.

"The diamond shapes?"

"My favourite ladies."

I ignored the urge to hit him.

There was a roughly drawn outline of a large stretch of water, with a coastline on the opposite shores. The Aethar lands were vast and completely blank. Nuo had never stepped foot in the wastelands.

What if the Ikhor was currently over there, burning the earth and his worshippers? Would that mean they would flee over here?

"Will you follow the Aspis if it travels to those lands you haven't mapped?"

"We will have to. We will go where it goes once we find it. I want to ask you, Liv, that you never go over those borders."

He pointed far southeast of where we were now, where desert land faded into nothing.

My heart ached. I didn't want to say goodbye. Would they return after?

"Past that, it will be impossible to keep you alive. Stay on Guardian lands."

I said nothing. I made no promises to watch my friend walk off to his death, leaving me behind. But I had to admit I was useless if I followed them. I would put them at risk and lead them to a sooner death.

But there was yet time to figure this all out.

Brekt was still ignoring us. His back, already drenched in sweat, faced me, his hair pulled up high off his neck.

Would I be able to figure him out before it was too late? Did I still want to?

My heart told me yes. Something still drew me in, even though I now feared what he was capable of. I shivered, remembering the soundless fall of the Guardian woman.

By the time Kazhi returned, having scouted out the way, we had already eaten and were packed to go.

Bastane told me that Kazhi had spent time in this jungle before she became a Guard. She knew the mountains, the beasts, and the villages. We were going to find one of these villages tonight.

The walk should have been better after resting, but it was so much worse. The leaves blocked the sun, but they trapped the air around us. It was heavy and hard to breathe. I was soaked from sweat within the first hour.

Kazhi was unfazed. She led our group, and her hair was caught in a breeze that didn't meet us behind her. Her wild hair and full black tattoos suited this forest. Bastane complained the most about the bugs buzzing around our heads, yet didn't have a drop of sweat from the heat. Brekt and Nuo stayed silent, walking, sweat-drenched, with a distance between them. I worried I had done something to cause this silence, but I couldn't figure out how it was my fault.

Hours later, when I thought I couldn't walk another step, the others paused ahead of me.

"What is that?" I whispered

A shape moved ahead of us, behind a gathering of leaves. Fingers peeled back the foliage to reveal a woman.

It was hard to pinpoint her age. She had brown skin, like the bark on the trees. Her long white hair came down over her shoulders in hundreds of braids. Gold beads and coins were weaved into her hair, and a gold band sat around her neck. Golden fabric flowed from the band, coming down in a swoop that barely covered her breasts. Her dark nipples were visible through the sheer fabric. She wore several belts with beading and cuffs around her hips. They held a small, sheer piece of cloth in front to cover her sex and another small piece behind, but she may as well have been naked.

She stood straight and sure of herself, unsmiling.

"Oracle." Brekt bowed his head. "What brings you to find us here?"

"I wander my jungle looking for the future. But I am always looking and never meet it. Why is that?" she asked. Her voice was dreamy. Young and old at the same time. She faced us, but I felt she was seeing something else.

She waited, but no one answered her.

"Because once you find it, it becomes the present?" I said hoarsely, unsure if she was actually waiting for an answer.

Her eyes found me, and a smile touched her face.

"And yet, I think I *have* found it today. Legendary Guards—like me, searching for answers they have already found. Come. I know you wish to rest with my people tonight. You are welcome, but your feuds are not. Leave them behind."

She gave a dismissive wave of her hand, disappearing into the thick brush.

"I guess we follow," Nuo said, moving ahead.

We were all broken from the spell she put us under and pushed on.

As I fell in line behind Bas, I wondered what she had meant about the Guards finding what they had been searching for. What else could it be if not the Aspis?

But I failed to care about having more questions with no answers. I just wanted out of my boots. My feet had blistered as Bastane promised.

Fortunately, it did not take long for us to reach her village—the very one Kazhi had been aiming for. The sound of rushing water reached us before I saw the homes.

The last time I had heard rushing water like this was when I had come upon the waterfall while running from the Keepers. Only this time, when the waterfall came into view, I wasn't sure if I was heading toward danger or away from it.

A small village was built along the banks of a river below the tall, flowing waterfall. Arching bridges connected the town, split by the flowing blue waters. Villagers like the Oracle with deep chestnut skin walked atop them. Though more modest, their clothing still left much to be seen.

On the bank opposite us was a group dressed in black and

covered in snake-like tattoos—Guardians. Kazhi had mentioned they passed through the jungle on their hunts.

For the first time, I wondered if I was seeing enemies or allies. Falizha had put a divide in her people without realizing it.

And when had I started to think of them as my people?

It was a simple village of a hundred homes or so, the small round huts made of materials from the jungle. But the surrounding landscape was anything but simple. The mountains curved up on either side of the river, and the tops of trees spread miles ahead. Sounds of laughter and conversation paired with the thunderous waterfall.

The Oracle stopped before a bridge. A few women coming toward us waved, recognizing Kazhi.

The Oracle turned to our group. "Kazhi, take your warriors to the hut we have prepared for you. You must stay with us for a night or so. Rest."

"Thank you, Oracle. As always, your hospitality is appreciated."

We moved to follow Kazhi, who was already approaching the women on the bridge.

"Olivia," the Oracle stopped me.

How did she know my name?

"Yes?" I swallowed. I didn't exactly know what an Oracle was. I think it meant something like a witch.

She smiled as if she knew what I was thinking.

"Follow me." She turned, walking past the bridge and toward the waterfall.

The others were already walking away. Brekt was the only one who had stopped to wait for me. He eyed the Oracle and nodded once, motioning me to follow her. His face held that never-ending darkness. Perhaps he was still angry.

I pleaded silently for his help. I didn't want to be alone with a strange woman, not so soon after the last one had tried to kill me.

His chest rose and fell as he took a deep breath. His mouth was a hard line.

Like this is my fault, I thought. But he stepped off the bridge to follow the Oracle.

"Get moving," he whispered as he passed me.

He was definitely still angry.

If the Oracle was aware Brekt was following, she didn't make it known. She led us between huts with men and women doing laundry or cutting up fish and game. Children were running near the river, chasing each other with sticks and yelling words I didn't understand. As we drew closer to the waterfall, the houses gave way to the forest once more.

A well-used path wound between trees leading toward the falls. Bright-coloured flowers bloomed along the pathway, and the green of the trees was breathtaking. Beams of sunlight hit the forest floor and exploded around me as I walked through them.

I couldn't see any more structures ahead to guess where she was taking me.

When we reached the falls, Brekt stopped, "Give me your swords." He reached out a hand. "She doesn't allow weapons inside."

"Inside where?" I asked, removing the belt holding my swords. The Oracle disappeared behind some more trees and was out of sight.

Brekt pulled out a coin and passed it to me. "Give this to her when you're done."

He left me to sit down on a fallen tree, ready to wait.

"What does she want?"

"Mostly to give you riddles," he muttered.

He wasn't interested in being helpful, so I huffed out my frustrations and left him there.

I followed the path toward the rushing water. As I came around a few trees, I discovered the opening behind the falls.

The roar of the water was deafening as I approached. The water turned to mist around me, the sensation a welcome one after the heat of the jungle.

The mist sparkled in the sunlight, dancing over my head, and I reached up to run my hand through the rainbows. Swirls moved and formed around my fingers.

I passed through the mist, tucking my head in and closing my eyes, laughing as the spray soaked me through.

When I opened my eyes again, I was in a large cave behind the falls. It was lit with crystal torches and filled with all things gold.

Piles of gold treasures lined the sides of the cave, and elaborately woven carpets led up a staircase to a raised section where the Oracle stood waiting for me. When she saw I had entered the cave, she disappeared into another room in the back.

I rushed up the stairs. My footsteps were muffled as they moved across the damp carpets. At the top of the stairs, on a flat area covered in gold relics, were more crystal lights hanging on the walls. The door leading to the room behind was covered with thick fabric.

I entered the room, folding the fabric back, and was met with an open living space.

The room was tinted purple from all the crystal lights, and a large chandelier hung from the center of the ceiling. The Oracle blended into the walls with her dark skin, but I could track her around the room by her white beaded hair and golden necklace.

"Come, child." She sat down in a woven chair covered in furs and motioned me forward.

I sat opposite the Oracle, seeing her face clearly in the light of the crystal chandelier hanging above our heads. It cast a glow on her cheeks as if she'd painted them. She watched me, concentrating like she was working out a puzzle.

Was she going to put a magic spell on me, as a witch would do?

She laughed. It was a cold and haunting sound. "I am no witch. However, our abilities might seem the same. A witch has never been known to this place." She waved around her.

Fruit and dried meats were spread on a dining table behind the sitting area. There was a glass and a pitcher I wished to reach for.

This room was like being in a dream. A strange dream I would have a hard time waking from.

I paused at her words. Just like the Alchemist—was she assuming I wasn't from here?

"What is an Oracle then? And what is your legacy?" I coughed, trying to clear my throat.

"I am a simple child of Rem, who sees more than others."

I slumped in my seat, puffing the hair from my face. "I don't understand. No one ever gives a real answer to my questions."

"Give *me* a real answer, woman-of-the-other. Why have you not heeded your call to wake the Aspis?"

I froze. How— "You know about the voice. That told me to wake the Aspis."

She passed me a glass of water. "You were brought here for a purpose. Yet you run around as if you know not what it is."

I took a swallow and shivered. It was not water but magycris. My throat itched before the pain disappeared completely, the sensation spreading to my sore legs and feet.

"I don't understand my purpose here when there are the Guards. I don't know how to find the Aspis."

"I think you do," she whispered. Her eyes scanned mine. "The Guards were asked to find. You were asked to *wake*. You have seen things."

What have I seen? "I haven't seen any signs of it. Only pictures in caves. Do you know where it is? I have no clues."

"You have seen other things. Things that have made you pause. A pause that almost risked your life."

I searched my memories and halted on one in particular. "The crystals. They glowed before the woman tried to kill me."

Her head tilted down. "You have seen. You know more purpose surrounds you than you are willing to admit. But you remain idle. A new future lies ahead. You must take it."

"What do I take? What purpose? You must know something you can tell me. Anything. What do the glowing crystals mean?"

The back of my neck prickled in frustration. What was it she was trying to insinuate?

"Do I have powers?"

"Many of this world hold powers. The blessed are like gods. You are not a god's blessing. Yet the magic of the earth stirs when you are near."

The Oracle closed her eyes, and they moved behind her closed lids as if she was searching for something.

What was she seeing?

"My vision has never been so sporadic or hasty as it is with you. I see many things. Quick glimpses into what could be. What is. Your home is chaos. The world is chaos, made from the chaos that still sleeps."

"You can see my home?"

She nodded. "You must not return there. Do not seek it. I see suffering. I see death and shadows. And hate is in your heart. If you return home, it will mean your failure. If you should fail, look north for the darkness, not south."

What the hell did that mean? That I wouldn't find the Aspis? But that might mean— "If I fail to wake the Aspis, will the Light come to find me and return me home? *Can* I return? Where is it?"

"They call it the Lost Lands because they are lost. They were *meant* to be lost. I only see the trees but not the forest. It is hidden from me."

"What about the Light? Do you know anything about what brought me here?"

Her eyes opened then, wide and questioning. "It was not a light that brought you here."

"Yes, it was. It was painfully bright, and it spoke. It's what told me to wake the Aspis."

"That was not what I saw when the fates showed me your face. You were carried by chaos and darkness."

Chaos and darkness. She can't have seen how I was brought here then.

Her eyes closed again and shifted back and forth—this time, faster and faster.

"I see no Light coming to find you. I see scarred faces smiling, and I see yellow eyes in pain. A broken heart, full of new hatred. Hold your secrets tight. Survive. Do not speak of where you are from, even if it's the gods asking. Trust the woman."

She touched a hand to her temple, concentrating on whatever she saw. Was she asking me to trust Kazhi? Did Kazhi hold secrets that would help me?

"You have not truly known darkness. None of us have. Many things could happen. I see many futures. But I will not risk swaying you to one path over the other. Your choice must be yours. That will matter one day."

She stood suddenly. The beads in her hair clinked together as they moved. "Powerful beings are coming for you. You will try to get in their way. I see death, but I also see hope."

She moved around her room. She was picking up things and putting them back down. Her frantic movements had me wondering if her mind was all that stable.

A breeze moved across the room, raising the hairs on my arm. I glanced to the door to find the fabric stiff and unmoving.

The Oracle paused her search, turning to the door as well.

"Magic."

"What do you mean, magic?" I asked, worried.

"It feels like power, like humming. Vibrations. Shivers. I think it hunts for you."

That's what magic felt like, what I had mistaken for a breeze? Had I felt it before?

"Where is it coming from?" But the Oracle didn't answer. She only continued her search around the room.

"It is interesting you travel with the Guards." She moved away from me and out the door, leaving me alone in the strange room.

I quickly followed her.

She was now rummaging through things in the cave behind

the falls, picking up items and throwing them aside. She touched her face and spun in a circle.

"Do I have anything to do with the Guards?" I asked, a terrible suspicion building. "Were they meant to find me?"

"Oh yes. They were meant to find you."

A feather could knock me over. Or was I the feather caught in a terrible storm?

"Why?" I needed answers like I needed air, though I feared the answers would suffocate me. I needed to know there was a purpose to soldiering on after leaving home, willing to open up, fight, and become more for the sake of my friends.

"What am I?"

She halted, turning to me. "Interesting choice of words. That's not what someone would normally ask. Shouldn't you mean *who are you*?" Her smile said everything she didn't. I had a bad feeling I was figuring out the answers all on my own.

She finally held up the object she'd been searching for—a small crystal bracelet. When her eyes connected with mine, I felt something change in the air around us, making me alert and on edge.

"You will be the end of everything," she said dispassionately, and her voice echoed in the small cave behind the falls. I felt that breeze once more, the tickle of magic across my skin and a deep-rooted panic began to form. Where did it come from?

She walked up to me and put the small bracelet on my wrist. The strangely shaped crystals were tied and bound in leather. And they were all empty.

"To match your lovely earrings," she said, patting my wrist. "Now I am tired. I must sleep. The visions take a toll."

I looked down at the leather-bound crystals.

Great. This will help.

The Oracle scoffed, somehow knowing what I had thought.

She held out her hand. "I believe you have a coin to be given to me."

"That's it? You've told me nothing."

She put a finger against my forehead. "Use that girl, I have told you plenty. It is you who must put the information to use."

I didn't hide the scathing feeling I had toward her. Her riddles would haunt me. They would begin to carve out my future while I stood and watched with little control.

I shoved the coin into her hand and left her cave as fast as I could.

CHAPTER
FIFTY-ONE

I raged back toward the forest. The Oracle had succeeded in baiting me with truths while telling me nothing. Yet I was afraid she had just told me everything, and I didn't *want* to understand.

I had finally broken free of a cage, only for the Oracle to build me another with her warnings of more suffering to come.

I wanted to help the Guards. I wanted to find the answers to all my questions and learn how to wake the legendary beast. Then I wanted to live and experience my freedom with Brekt after they defeated the Ikhor.

I didn't want darkness and magic and end-of-the-world prophecies.

But not everything she said was inexplicable. She saw the trees of my forest and told me I should never return—not that I wanted to. She saw the crystals glowing and said they reacted to me. She felt the magic at the moment I had felt it.

Like Brekt, she knew things. But it wasn't dreams; she looked and the images were there.

I stuffed the panic into the box inside me, next to the pain and the rage and all the other emotions that wore me down. My survival had always counted on hiding it all away.

Brckt was pacing the small opening where I'd left him, as if he were on edge too. Good. I needed an outlet.

"Why is it that anyone who has information on me thinks they can keep it to themselves?" I stopped in front of him, steps away. "Why am I left in the dark when it's about me? You've held so much information back. What else are you hiding?"

He glared at me, clearly on board with us directing our anger at each other. "Not everything is yours for the taking, Olivia."

"Stop calling me that," I said through my teeth. "Tell me what your dreams are about. What happens to me?"

"You might be in them, but they're my dreams, *Olivia*. You don't get to demand information. That's not how the real world works."

He wasn't pacing anymore. He squared his shoulders, looking furious.

I wanted to push him. I wanted to hurt him back. His condescending comment about not understanding the real world struck a nerve.

I took a step closer.

"Why are you so angry with me?" I shouted. "What did I do? And not only me, your closest friend Nuo. You're beating down an injured man."

"Don't tell me where I should direct my feelings."

"You've been angry with me since the cave. I deserve an explanation, at least."

"I'm not angry. And I don't want to talk about it," he seethed, stepping in with me.

Oh, he was angry. He was a breath away, and I could see his dark lashes framing his furious, shadow-filled eyes.

"At least tell me what I did. I'm tired of this morose attitude all the time and leaving me in the dark!"

"I watched you nearly die, Liv!" His hand flew in the direction of that cave. "Am I not allowed to be upset about it?"

My nerves faltered, and I took a step back, but he didn't allow it. He followed me, coming forward. "I held her in my grip, one of my people, and slit her throat."

I almost stumbled at the brutal force of his words. The image of her blood spraying out in front of her body slammed into me as I tried to fight back.

"She was going to kill me," I said weakly. Was Brekt as disturbed by the killing as I had been?

"I know." His hand went to his hair, pushing the strands out of his face. "But she was likely told to do it, lied to. In a panic, seeing you like that, I reacted."

"So you're mad at me because you killed her." I was grateful, I really was, but at this moment, I was so mad he was laying it all on me. "I didn't choose to be her victim. I didn't choose for you to react that way!"

I finally lost control, and I shoved him.

Hate is in your heart.

My hands slammed into his hard chest. He didn't budge. Instead, he grabbed onto both of my wrists and pulled me closer. He held me like that, gazing down at me. It wasn't a lover's embrace.

"Never start a fight you can't finish, Liv."

His lip curled back, a rumble coming from his chest. Shadows swirled across his skin. His hands were tight around my wrists, but they weren't hurting.

He leaned in closer. His dark eyes bore into mine as he said slowly, "I wasn't expecting thanks. But I also wasn't expecting a stab to my gut. You just stared up at me like I was something you should be scared of, the way everyone has always stared at me." It all settled in what he was saying. "I saw the fear. The one person I didn't want looking me that way. And what was the first thing you did when you saw Nuo? You ran to him with open arms, embracing him, worried for him. You didn't see him as a killing monster. Not as you saw me. I killed one of my own for you, and you pulled away."

He let go of me, pushing me away from him.

I was speechless as I stumbled back. I never guessed that he was upset because ... was he jealous? Had I insulted him?

No. I had reminded him of everything he's faced since childhood—an outcast, a legacy of Night that was unwanted, used against the other kids to punish them.

He was right—after what he'd done, I was afraid. It was different when I ran toward Nuo, happy that he was safe. Part of me was opening up for Brekt, a part far more vulnerable. Finally seeing what he was capable of and knowing I cared for him—I didn't know how to handle those feelings.

I stepped closer, reaching out to explain.

"Don't, Liv. I don't want to hear it. I know it's easy for people to want Nuo," he cursed, coiling that anger and releasing it. "Maybe you ran to him with open arms because he's willing to give you anything you asked. Maybe I don't get that treatment because I haven't given you what you wanted yet, is that it?" His words hit their mark.

I shook my head, unable to speak. There was a sickening pressure building in my chest and moisture gathering in my eyes. How had I missed it?

He dipped his chin, zeroing in on me. "But he wasn't there. Nuo didn't kill one of his own. He didn't throw her body away. He didn't have to watch as she held a knife over your chest."

Brekt turned and surprised me by walking away. I rushed to follow him and nearly ran into his back when he stopped. He spun to me, running his hand down his face. "Fuck, Liv, you're making me unhinged. I don't know how to handle myself anymore or how to handle this pull to you."

"You *do* feel it. What is this?"

"All this grief I put myself through to keep my distance, hoping that'll help keep you safe." He lowered his hands.

Something changed. The darkness ebbed, the anger cooled, and new warmth appeared. "I'm tempted to say fuck it."

The forest disappeared, and all I saw was Brekt. These growing feelings between us were hard to ignore, and this pull I couldn't explain—he *felt* it. I wasn't running from this, even if it scared me.

He stepped closer, and he leaned in, "I want you. I want to feel every part of you, and I don't want to think about the bad side effects."

Without my control, I was pulled closer. My back arched, trying to fill the space between us.

I reached for him, needing to touch him. He didn't stop me as I rested my hand against his beating heart. His chest rose and fell as fast as my own. I hated that I had to push him, for us to fight, to be able to say such things to each other. I hated that in anger, we chose to open up.

I leaned in. Aching.

His eyes widened once he realized I was so close. His hands came up to my arms, holding me in place. "This can't happen, Liv. I mean it. You'll get hurt." His fingers dug in.

He was fighting himself as much as he was fighting me.

"I've already been hurt, Brekt. Some things are worth the risk."

I held in a breath, waiting for his response. I was about to move away when he cursed.

His mouth lowered. His breath fanned my face.

Then he kissed me.

With the lightest touch, the sky opened up, and lightning crashed around us. Maybe it was the anger. Maybe the draw I had to this man. Maybe it was all the anticipation—but one touch of his lips, and I was explosive. My body was filled with a hunger for more.

My skin burned where his hands held my arms tight. He anchored me there, moving his lips against mine with sinfully light kisses. The feel of him—

My hand on his chest moved.

His body tensed underneath my touch, and I was worried I got it wrong—he didn't feel what I felt, and he was going to pull away —but then he groaned, and the sound of it rattled through me.

He pulled me closer. He reached behind me and ran his hands

up my back, leaning into the kiss, consuming me. One of his hands came up to bury into my hair.

His body shuddered against mine, and the current inside me bundled in my core. He was coaxing out a feeling that I had never truly felt before.

I buried a hand into his shirt, pulling at him.

The hand in my hair pulled my head back at an angle, and his mouth ground deeper. His tongue began exploring, sliding across my bottom lip and drawing it into his mouth, sucking on it. His other hand trailed a path down my back as he deepened the kiss.

His tongue found mine, warm and demanding. It was intoxicating. He tasted like sin, like heaven and every flavour I never dreamed of. The feel of him, the energy surrounding us, vibrated.

His fingers flexed against my skull, pulling at my hair as he tried to pull me even closer, welding our lips together. His mouth moved against mine with such skill and knowing—I needed *more*.

I moaned against him, trying to pull him closer. I leaned my whole body against his firm chest.

A rush of excitement went through me when I felt how hard he was against my stomach. I ground against him, wanting to feel the length, causing him to hiss.

His lips left me, but his grip stayed fastened.

"Liv," he breathed, his forehead against mine.

Even in the warm air of the jungle, both of us lost for breath, a cold chill swept across my mouth where his lips had just been. The chill went down through me, knowing I was missing something— missing his warmth, the heat of his kiss.

"Don't stop," I whispered.

He let loose a long, shuddering breath. "I can't. We can't do this."

But he didn't let go. He held me, our bodies pressed tight, trembling, his lips a breath away. I savoured the taste of him still on my tongue. But I could feel his grip slipping. I could feel the pull between us dulling.

"I can't," he said firmly as he pulled away.

His eyes held longing. He was searching, as he always did, and I wished I knew what the question was.

We were suspended in a moment outside of everything around us. I was a moon spinning around him, drawn to his pull. I couldn't let go.

But he was no longer pulling—it was clear when his eyes shuttered that he was pushing.

He moved away from me to grab his belongings, and I stayed there, wrapping my arms around myself.

I was shaking. It happened and was over so fast. The most intense I had ever felt in my life. I felt more from Brekt's kiss than when Stephen had taken me to bed.

He swung his pack over his shoulder, looking out toward the path. His eyebrows were bunched. On his face flashed guilt, regret, and other emotions I wasn't willing to admit to myself.

"We need to meet up with the others. Let's get some food and rest. You're not fully healed yet," he said as he walked away.

CHAPTER

FIFTY-TWO

Brekt

As Brekt pushed himself away from her and headed back through the jungle, he felt like he was bleeding out on the dirt below.

The waterfall's roar had compelled the storm inside him to crash and boom even louder than before.

Nothing could have prepared him for that kiss. Not even the dreams he's had of her for over a year. Dreams she only knew half about.

His lips tingled, and his back still stung from where her nails had dug in. He liked the scrape of them and wished to feel them across his skin.

He balled his fists, letting his own nails sink in, trying to forget. He wanted to curse whichever god had done this to him. He wanted to go back and finish what he had started. He wanted to do the things he had dreamt about doing to her.

He reached the bridge that went across the river, but he couldn't go there quite yet. Kazhi was on the bridge, and she was watching him, giving him a questioning look. Ignoring her, he continued into the jungle. He needed to be alone for a while.

He followed a small path leading away from the village. He didn't care where it went as long as it got him away from her.

A terrible hollowness had always dwelled inside him—it was dark, bleak. It was nothingness. He had been born to fight and die for a future he would never see.

He had learnt to cut off emotions and avoid attachments. His death was looming, so why was this woman brought before him now? He had seen her in dreams. She wasn't supposed to be real.

His dreams had been an escape over the past year while he trained and waited for the Ikhor to rise. He could fade away and think of the woman who bore no tattoos. He could forget for moments at a time that everyone around him was afraid of him, that they jumped to get out of the way when they saw him —*Erebrekt of the North,* the cursed child.

He would think of her and forget that he'd seen how his friends die, how he would die.

But she wasn't a dream. He had found her in that first cave. He'd known she was there by some magnetic pull. She had crept through the black and colourless landscape inside him and found his heart.

He was angry with her, but more than that, he thought he was falling in love with her. He wondered if she had noticed how strange he acted, always trying to hide it.

He had loved the woman in the dreams. He would wake from them, mourning someone who didn't exist. He knew her, had felt her, had made love and fucked her. She was wild. She was like fire. She turned everything into a torrent of colour.

But the woman he found surprised him—she had depth and character the dreams hadn't warned him of. She was curious about everything and asked questions relentlessly, but she was also reserved and frightened.

While he compared the woman in the dreams to the woman he left at the falls, Brekt found a small stream in a secluded part of the jungle. A large tree was growing from a split rock, and he sat, leaning forward, while he gathered his thoughts.

He tried to relax so his cock would stop throbbing, but telling himself not to think of her only made him remember the things they had done together.

He thought of how she told him about her past, ripe with pain and loneliness, something he understood well. If it weren't for Nuo, he would've had a terrible childhood with no one to care for. The real man under the skin, behind his iridescent eyes—no one would have cared about that man. He was orphaned as a babe and remained unwanted throughout his life.

Liv had told him she had been betrayed by her sister, who should have loved her more than anyone. She'd had a man back home, and he was struck with pangs of jealousy when he thought too long on it. The fiery woman in his dreams was not the same as the closed-off woman in reality.

She hid her emotions and desires, but he saw that fire growing. Like earlier, when she stomped toward him, ready to battle. Brekt wondered if she noticed his immediate excitement, seeing the woman he had fallen for.

But one emotion he hadn't been ready for was her fear. The way her eyes had gone wide when he killed that woman. He wanted to see affection. He wanted to see, on her face, what he felt in his own heart.

But how could he love her? He knew nothing about her. He hadn't realized she preferred to be called by a nickname ... But he was learning.

He learned she liked pretty things and bought her earrings to match her comb. The silliest thing he'd ever done in his life. When he saw her eyeing those swords in Bellum, he worried he'd made a mistake, that she wasn't a woman who was fond of jewelry.

He was thrilled, giving her the money and seeing her face light up when she held her swords. And then, on the cliff, when he decided he'd give her the earrings anyways, worried she would laugh at him for being a lovesick fool, she looked at him with an unexpected emotion in her eyes.

Like no one had ever given her something so precious.

He was caught in a downward spiral thinking about her. He had come to this spot in the jungle to try and stop, with zero success.

He had seen her naked in the river before Bellum. She was exactly how he remembered. Her breasts hung heavy on her chest, dripping water off peaked nipples as pink as her luscious mouth. Her green top came down so low on her chest that he could see them bounce when she walked too fast. The pink that had dusted her cheeks when she was drunk was the same as when she was riding on top of him.

It was all too much.

Unable to stand it anymore, Brekt pulled down the top of his pants and freed himself. He began stroking the hard length of his cock. He was constantly at war with himself to keep her out of his thoughts. The ghost of her kiss was still with him, causing an overwhelming need for release.

He'd been with many women in his time. He would take what he needed from them and move on—no need to linger when a greater purpose was put upon him. He could never offer them a future.

But none felt like *her*.

He leaned back against the tree behind him. He thought of her stomping toward him, pushing against his chest. He liked her anger. He liked how she looked with no walls up. He stroked harder as he thought of her pulling herself to him and the feel of her warm tongue against his, the taste of her mouth. He wanted to go back and find her and take her now. He was tired of pretending he didn't want it. He wanted to hear the sounds he knew she made when he was inside her.

He thought of his hands tangled in her hair and pulling her mouth toward him at just the right angle, his other hand holding her lower back so he could push his hard cock against her. The feeling was overwhelming, and he almost lost complete control, holding her like that. He was ready to go so much further than just a kiss.

He wanted to feel her mouth on him in other places. He'd seen it already. He'd seen so much of her.

His muscles tensed as he came, thinking about her pushing her hand down under his belt and stroking him just as he was now.

As he sat there breathing heavily, reeling from his release, the other parts of his dream surfaced again. Her frightened face lingered in his thoughts. Her screaming in pain. Her tear-filled eyes.

How could he protect her from pain while fighting his growing feelings for her?

Brekt felt lighter as he walked back to the village.

He saw Liv sitting near the riverbank with some village women. They were bathing in a pool connected to the river. Liv looked terribly uncomfortable. He couldn't imagine how they convinced her to get in with them. They had given her a towel to cover herself with while they passed around a bottle and talked. The rest of the women were bare as the sky above them.

He headed off to find Nuo and clear some things up.

Nuo had been aware of his dreams since they were young. Nuo didn't believe him at first. Not until things started to come true. The dreams most often were repeated images—Nuo losing a fight, Brekt getting a black eye, the both of them stuck doing extra chores because they were showing off—until eventually, it came to pass.

At first, Brekt didn't want to tell Nuo about the woman he had continuous dreams about. When he did, Nuo was sure they should keep her close.

Why would he find a woman he desired so strongly at the time he was set to fight the Ikhor? He knew he would not survive this. He saw many horrors when he wasn't dreaming of Liv. He tried to leave her behind, knowing she would get hurt, but he couldn't do it. He wanted to be there for her when she did.

He had seen Kazhi try to kill him and then stand beside him as a Guard. He dreamt of her surrounded by smoke and ash, being swarmed by the Aethar—a dream that hadn't yet come true.

He'd seen Nuo, cold and blue on the ground, covered in blood.

Bastane smiled so few times, but Brekt knew he would smile before his death.

And he saw only blackness sometimes and wondered if it was his own end.

Then there was her. Almost every night. Sometimes it felt like paradise, and other times it was agony to watch her suffer. And she will suffer the worst of them all.

When Liv discovered they didn't know how to locate the Aspis, she seemed devastated. He knew she had no answers on how to do it herself. How could she? He was making sure she was kept in the dark, protecting her against the worst parts of all this. He didn't want her following them to the end. He didn't want her death on his hands. He was carrying too many as it was.

She wanted to help, to save their people. She was good. Too good for him. But he was selfish enough to want her there until it was time to fight.

The worst of his secrets—that he was too scared to tell her— was that they'd already found the Aspis.

Nuo and himself were the only two aware. He was unwilling to share it with the others since they didn't know about his dreams. And he was not willing to share it with Liv because it could break her. The course was set whether she knew it or not.

He wanted her to find peace after all she'd been through. Perhaps it was wrong of him, but a part of him found his own peace with her. With the little time left, he wanted to keep it that way.

She would find the answers in the end, anyway.

It was a matter of time before the Aspis rose. The Ikhor would surely trigger it soon. All the secrets would come springing forth.

Brekt eventually found Nuo amongst the villagers. He'd been

given enough magycris that he was no longer limping—a good sign. Brekt was starting to feel guilty about ignoring Nuo's pain.

He couldn't explain his relief when Nuo crawled from under the cave lizard. He was worried that would be the moment his brother would be lying in blood, cold and blue, just as he'd seen.

Nuo spotted Brekt and inclined his head, likely knowing Brekt wanted to talk without needing to be told. They had been together for so long that it was like they could read each other's minds, knowing instantly what the other felt or would say.

They walked away from the villagers and behind one of the huts. Nuo's shirt was off, showing a number of scars covering his chest, mixing in with the script tattoos down his back. Brekt knew how every scar was made—some were his own doing.

"You look less angry. Did you take it out on someone else or yourself?" Nuo forced a grin, trying to solve the tension with humour.

"A bit of both."

"You were more of an asshole than usual. What happened this time?"

Nuo typically put on a show portraying an open, inviting, well-groomed Guard. No one knew he used words as much as swords. He was often charming, but he could be a lot more pessimistic than he ever let on. Events from his early childhood left different kinds of scars.

"The cave was too much. I'm losing my grip. My focus is slipping."

It was not quite an apology to Nuo, but judging by his face, Nuo understood.

"You know what I am going to say," Nuo folded his arms, "We are the only two who know how much time is left. From what I know of Liv, she won't hate you for enjoying it. I've agreed to keep it from her, but the condition was you forgot about the warnings of the dreams and lived a little. And before you argue that she gets hurt, you know that she will no matter what, so why deny what you both want?"

"She's in the dark, scared. I don't like doing that to her."

"You've tried before to stop things from coming true. It never worked. You'll scare her for sure if you tell her what you've seen. Let it be."

Brekt pushed the hair from his face, "For the first time in my life, there is something good that I want, and I don't know how to do it. I don't know how to be ... good. For her."

Nuo barked a laugh. "You're not good for her. None of this is. But that doesn't seem to be anyone's choice anymore."

"Thanks for the reassurance."

Nuo threw his hands up in the air. "I think you're stupid if you waste your time. Either way, you've already seen her fate. The woman we found was broken. We all saw that. Now? She smiles and laughs, and she's learning to fight for herself. You have good reason to keep things to yourself. Hell, even I've been tormented and insomniac over your dreams. Don't do that to her now. Both of you need this."

Brekt nodded, his attention going between the huts to the river in the distance. The group of women were now pulling Liv into one of their homes. She seemed more relaxed than before. He wondered if she wanted someone to get her out of there.

Nuo snorted from beside him. "You've got it bad, brother. Never seen you like this. She's not what I expected either."

There was a brief, thoughtful look in Nuo's eyes before he wiped it away, hiding himself behind an easy smile.

"Let's start our celebrating. The alcohol here is good. Women are ready to have fun. The men want to do some gambling before the sun sets. I remember the old man, Yor, took me for a lot of money last time we were here."

It would be good for Brekt to get his mind off the woman pulling him underwater. He was drowning in need and, at the same time, choking from self-restraint.

CHAPTER

FIFTY-THREE

Liv

T should have been thinking about everything the Oracle said
—how I would be the end of everything, how I was brought
here for a reason, that I should *know* the reason.

The joke was on her. I didn't know anything about this world
except what the past couple of weeks had shown me, and I wasn't
strong enough to doom anything.

But I wasn't thinking about any of that. I was thinking about
the kiss.

I felt empty when Brekt stopped kissing me. This draw to him
was intense. It was consuming. I was worried I was mistaking this
desire—this pull—for feelings. I was still getting to know Brekt—I
couldn't already be falling for him, could I?

I followed the path back to the village. Brekt had not waited for
me. His strides were too long, and I was soon far behind.

Kazhi stood on the bridge, arms resting on the ledge, looking
toward the waterfall.

I pushed forward, making a path toward her. That's when I felt
the hair on my neck stand, a shiver pulsing through me. I halted
just feet away from her.

She spotted me and turned, leaning on her hip and tilting her head as she leered at me.

The vibration was as the Oracle had described it. I had felt it in the crystals once before. It hummed and disappeared.

"You," I whispered. I tried to remember other moments around Kazhi when I shivered or felt uneasy.

Kazhi's hand slowly went to her belt, landing on the hilt of a long knife—warning and confirmation.

"It would be in your best interest to keep anything you have felt or heard to yourself, Bones," she threatened. "I will also promise to keep my mouth closed to what I've heard."

"That's how you gather secrets—you have magic." My mind raced over the realization. "Why is it a secret?"

"If you try to tell anyone, you'll feel my blade before you utter the words."

I had never considered this woman my friend, but her hostility was surprising, nonetheless. I nodded. I would keep her secrets, but she was going to talk.

"From your face, I'd know she gave you the usual foretelling," she added, "but I also heard what she said. Her visions are images. She interprets them with garishly overdramatic warnings and riddles. I wouldn't let her ramblings get to you."

My shoulders fell, and some of the unease fell away with them. "So, I'm not special then? I won't doom the world?"

"The images were still there." Kazhi removed her hand from the hilt of her knife. "But I would not allow it to lead you on. She told me I would try to kill my closest friends and destroy any hope of saving my people. Only they weren't my friends when I tried to kill them, and other Guards would replace them if I did. Everything is up for interpretation."

"Good." I leaned against the wooden railing. I felt a cool splash of relief after discovering Kazhi's secret. Finally, something was answered.

"I don't know another way to interpret what she saw, but I'm sure there is one." Her stripe-tattooed face shifted into a smirk. At least I had felt better, even if it was brief.

"So, how long have you been collecting my secrets?"

"What do you think? Every second I can. I see she gave you a trinket." Kazhi pointed to my crystal bracelet bound in leather.

"Yeah. Kind of her." I twirled the bracelet between two fingers.

"I'm sure she saw a purpose for it somewhere in your timeline. I wouldn't lose it."

I nodded, wondering what use a bracelet with no magic had.

"Have you ever seen crystals glow?" I continued playing with the crystals, trying to look uninterested in her answer.

"You mean how they grow brighter around you?"

A sudden, overwhelming sense of dread came over me. The Oracle, like the Guards, had warned me to keep my secrets many times. Yet mine had never been safe. Had she told the others?

"Calm down, Bones. You're right to keep it to yourself. I have as well."

"You saw it happen? Or you used magic on me?"

"I saw them faintly when we were training. Your swords. You were getting angry at me, I think, and swore. The glowing caught my eye. I've kept this to myself, unsure at the time what it meant."

"Why didn't you tell me? Do you know what it means now?"

"I have a guess." When she seemed unwilling to share, I grabbed her arm, pleading. Her muscles tensed under my touch, and she yanked her arm from my grasp, grabbing my wrist.

"Crystals hold the *earth's* magic," she said, "The Ikhor stole the *gods'* magic. They are similar but not the same. The earth's magic is pure power. The gods can alter what is around them, sometimes taking from the earth to power themselves. But many have forgotten that there was more magic in this world in the past."

She let go of me, and I rubbed my sore wrist. "Do you mean there were more gods with magic? Or more crystals?"

Her reptilian eyes moved around the village, making sure we were alone. The stripes on her face suited the jungle. Kazhi looked like she was born from the wild with her black tattoos on snow-white skin. Knowing she could somehow use magic made her almost as terrifying as Brekt. Maybe more.

"You saw the drawings in the last cave? The halos over many of the legacies?" Kazhi asked. I nodded, remembering.

"There were more crystals once. Only ever four gods. But over centuries, our people have forgotten the stories of the first children. The children who were born of the gods, who were their direct descendants. They had magic of their own—a faint drop that mimicked the gods' power. They could control elements that catered to their legacy. Imagine a legacy of Night that could control shadows."

"Brekt has elemental magic too?" It made sense.

"Not like the gods' magic, but something close. His is a drop in a vast sea. So insignificant that even he is unaware it is magic and not just a *gift* as he calls it. The halos in that cave showed the first children and their bloodline. Through the ebb and flow of time, the magic faded. A child that is only *blessed* by a god has no magic. Though many would call it pure blood, the blood is not directly that of the gods. The first children remained pure-blood by breeding together, but the magic didn't always stay. There are histories of a great war between magic users and non. It was written the magic users were wiped out. The gods made fewer pure children, blessed by their touch. Until they stopped."

"So elemental magic is watered down in pure-blooded legacies. And the crystal's magic belongs to the earth. Are there any other kinds?" I asked.

She shook her head. "Just the earth and the gods. The pure magic of a god was what the Ikhor stole and corrupted but was unable to control. The crystals hold the earth's magic. It can be extracted and manipulated by us, but only the gods can *wield* it. It can react to other compounds, made into magycris and power weapons, but it can't be used by the legacies. It makes me wonder why it reacts to you."

"There was another set of figures in that cave. They looked

different than the legacies. Could they be my people? From the Lost Lands?"

Surprise flickered over her face. "I hadn't considered that. You may be right."

"So how do you have magic then? Is yours through blood or stolen?"

Her lip curled back. "I did not steal it. That deed was only done by the Ikhor."

The only remaining answer was that Kazhi was a pure-blooded legacy. A descendant of the first children. I knew better than to ask from what god.

"If someone were to find out a person could wield magic, what would happen to them?"

Kazhi watched the jungle, silent. Finally, she said, "Those who seek power destroy power. A magic user would end up dead. If it weren't for our brief history and the task given to you, I would kill you myself for what you have learned."

I could not stop my hands from trembling. Her threat was no lie. Kazhi would kill me.

"How do you know of the knowledge? Nuo didn't know what the halos above the legacies meant. The others don't know of the magic like you."

"I have travelled farther and for far longer than most." Her focus was distant again. Similar to how Brekt had been on the deck of the ship when he admitted his dreams. What had Kazhi been through? Where had she gone to learn such things?

"So, what do you think this has to do with me?"

Her eyes ticked over me as if deciding to continue.

"I told you before that I believed the gods sent you. I believed the light you saw was godly magic. Maybe you've been touched by it to aid you in the search. Maybe the crystals sense that. Perhaps I was mistaken, and there is other magic around. The key will be finding out who wielded that magic and why."

"Do you think *I* could be a first child?"

She laughed, but there was no humour to it. I knew as soon as I asked the question that it was ridiculous. And yet—

"Why else would the crystals glow?" I questioned.

"I am still trying to figure that out. Did you sense any magic or wield any powers in your lost lands?"

"No," I scoffed. "It was a dull, colourless place. I only felt the torment of being there."

"And have you felt anything after coming here?"

I'd felt many things. More alive than ever before. I felt exhilarated at every new touch and flavour. I felt a range of emotions too complicated to explain. And I felt like the world tilted when I was around Brekt.

None of that felt like magic, but the tingling from Kazhi's magic hadn't been obvious either.

"If I did, I get the feeling I would be told to keep it to myself?"

"You're learning, Bones. I've seen enough behind closed doors to know this place will tear you apart for your secrets."

"So, can I trust you?"

"The others do. That should be enough for you. Feel for the truth, stay on the task and follow where the magic takes you. Pay attention to your crystals. Perhaps the bracelet will aid in your search. If you stray, if you disrupt the path set for you, then and only then should you not trust me. Or anyone for that matter."

"What does that mean? What do you know about my path?"

"Only that I can smell destiny and the touch of magic on you. You may be more like the legacies than we all realized."

"You sound like the Oracle now, speaking in riddles."

"Keep an eye on the crystals. Look inside and feel if something else is there. Maybe all the answers you are seeking are within yourself."

Kazhi began to walk away but paused.

"One thing you should consider, Bones, is that to sense magic, one has to be capable of using it themselves."

"But you don't sense magic in me?" I asked.

Her eyes scanned the area before she gave me a scolding look for being so loud.

"I didn't before. Now I wonder if I feel something, but it is faint. However, you felt mine. That means you are capable of some kind of power."

I walked to the other side of the village, toward our shared hut, leaving Kazhi and the thoughts of magic behind. I passed businesses selling clothing and food, and the friendly smiles softened the stiffness in my spine.

They all had obvious signs of Ouras's blessings—animal markings, horns, antlers and sharp teeth. A woman with hair like vines had flowers growing from her shoulders. One woman reminded me of the river running through the village. Her skin shone and sparkled like water. I passed Guardians in black clothes sitting with the locals. They offered me warm greetings.

I was sweating in my long sleeve top. The soft leather pants were sticking. I would have to peel them off when I got a chance to bathe.

I searched for the men, wondering if they were in the hut the villagers had pointed to, but when I reached it, I only found their packs. The inside was large, with a dirt floor, a pit in the centre for a fire and a cooking pot. There were five beds around the walls of the hut, and sheer curtains hung from each to keep the bugs out. Brown and green decor made the place inviting, like a home.

Laughter and voices gathered outside. I turned to see several women my age peering in and waving me out.

They were all chestnut-skinned, like the Oracle. They wore different shades of green and ivory fabric. They, too, had piercings like the Guardians. Even in their cheeks ... were those bones sticking out of them? Rings of metal hung from their lips and ears.

One approached me and lifted her hand to my face.

I pulled back a fraction, "What are you doing?"

"We have not seen such unused skin before, except on a babe. I wanted to see what it felt like."

Her hand came upon my cheek. She reached up and brushed across my brow. Her face was marked with natural stripes, and her eyes were feline—a jungle cat.

Another woman came up and did the same. She had small, soft antlers and tufted ears. Soon I had several pairs of hands on me, and I began to tremble.

A whistle sounded from my side. Nuo and Bastane approached the hut, both topless and hair wet.

"BB, if I had known you ladies were getting to know each other, I would have come sooner." Nuo rubbed his hands together.

"Ass," I muttered. But I was relieved to see his limp gone, and he looked much better after a bath.

Bastane watched the women around me, not hiding his interest.

The woman who had first touched me turned to the men. "We are happy to inspect the Guards as well." She lifted a hand and wiggled her fingers. The rest of them giggled when Nuo blushed and rubbed the back of his neck.

Bastane patted him on the back. "He could use some pampering ladies. He almost got eaten by a cave lizard last night."

A few women gasped and grabbed for Nuo, pulling him away and cooing at him. One girl lingered for Bastane, putting an arm around his waist and pulling him along as well.

The jungle cat lingered, her catlike eyes watching me. "We are having a celebration this eve for the Guards. We will drink and eat and pray for their success. Join us."

She was a beautiful woman. Her hair was cut in a straight line, grazing the bottom of her jaw. It was a dark brown and paired well with her amber eyes. Everything about her emanated warmth. The bone piercings in her cheeks—which looked like dimples—took away none of her beauty.

I was envious of her. Her smile wasn't forced or fake. I thought of the many masks I wore that I still hadn't learned to take off.

She pulled my hand after I nodded. I would go with them. "We will take you to the river to bathe and then dress you. The celebrations begin when the sun starts to set."

I turned back to the road where the men had disappeared and, for a brief moment, was worried that maybe Brekt had gone with some of the women as well. Perhaps I had gone too far with that kiss.

I was led to a pool under the shade of a large tree next to the river. The river was fast-flowing, but along this side of the village, the pools of water were shallow and still.

There were already several women in the pool who were very naked.

The newcomers began to pull off their tops, removing fabrics which covered very little. The one with the bones in her face stopped to help me. "My name is Muha. You look pained. I have a drink that will take the soreness from your bones."

"Thank you. I would like that. And you can call me Liv." I forced a smile while trying not to pale at the nakedness of the women around me. My trembling became shaking—I would be expected to strip as they did, out here in the open.

She introduced some of the other women, but their names grew stranger and more challenging to say. I was soon lost in the faces around me.

Muha passed a thin, light fabric so I could cover myself. I gave her a thankful smile. She continued to radiate warmth as she helped me to peel off my pants. I checked that no one was watching. There were villagers in the distance, but no one paid attention to the pool filled with naked women.

I supposed they were used to it. And, because I had sworn I would not be the woman I used to be, I stopped worrying about someone watching, even if I still held the fabric tight.

"I have never seen such a woman," Muha said. But before I had the chance to be offended, she continued, "I'm sure many men like the rarity of your skin." Her hand came to my arm, pushing me toward the water. "And I think I know which one likes it the most." Her eyebrows went up.

"Who?" There were no men close by.

"The one I saw you kissing by the falls." The girls all giggled at that.

"I think you missed the part where he ended it soon after," I said in a low voice.

"Oh no, I saw that part. But I also saw the swelling in his pants as he stomped away. Maybe he was angry you didn't help him with that as well," she teased.

I followed Muha into the water and sat on a submerged rock. None of them seemed bothered that their breasts were visible above the water. I tried not to stare as they began to pass a bottle around, sharing a drink.

I washed my hands before it reached me. Blood from the Guardian woman still stained my skin and crusted under my nails.

"I saw the swelling, too," another girl said before taking a drink. "It was quite impressive."

"I'm curious about the swelling in the other one's pants. The one with the golden hair."

"I didn't see any swelling there," chimed in another.

"Not yet," she winked.

I was laughing by the time the bottle reached me.

This drink had an earthy taste, like it was made from a root vegetable. But it was strong, and my stomach was empty. It warmed me in the most delicious way.

I passed the drink to the next girl.

"You are not a Guardian, are you?" one of the women asked. She had green eyes outlined by thick, black lashes. Small clovers bloomed from her pale green skin.

"No," I replied, "I am just travelling with the Guards."

"So, have you been with the big one for very long? He seems dangerous. Must be fun to tumble with under the stars."

I tried not the think of tumbling with Brekt under the stars. I had only danced under them, with him as my guard. She was right about one thing, he was dangerous. And angry. And difficult.

"I think she is in heat now," Muha said. They all laughed again.

I made a face, at which they only laughed harder.

They continued to drink and talk of the men I came with, fascinated. Then they moved on to the men in their village and spoke of those who were away trading north of here, hoping they returned soon.

I began to feel like I was floating as I watched them, unable to comprehend that I was a part of this, living this.

My sister and I had never shared this camaraderie. I couldn't imagine these women doing what Rebeka had done, betraying their sisters.

Muha leaned over to me. "I think the drink is taking effect. Save some of your strength for after. We have many more drinks to share with you."

"And the herbs, don't forget!"

"And we should dress her. Let's do her hair with flowers. Make her feel the blessings of Ouras for an eve."

My throat tightened. "Oh. Um, yes, sure. I would like that."

They all stood, splashing as they cheered. Clearly, they were all drunk and ready to celebrate.

CHAPTER
FIFTY-FOUR

I was drunk by the time the sun set. I had tried all the different foods they had pushed on me. They showed me the herbs they smoked, a few laughing harder than before, their eyes becoming glassy and unfocused. I declined to try them myself. Their alcohol was more than enough.

They brought me bits of clothing, and Muha started adding bracelets and necklaces made of leather, bones and gold. Another girl strapped a belt around my waist. Brown fabric hung from it, hardly covering me.

"Maybe a bit longer?" I suggested, and Muha grabbed some more fabric. I was envious of Muha's beauty, with her brown skin showing off her stripes. But I had no desire to feel the stares and deal with the questions about my skin.

They wrapped another piece of the fabric around my back, bringing it around the front and tying it in front of my breasts. It *barely* held me in. They tied one of the necklaces to the fabric so it wouldn't fall.

I sighed, giving up—you could see my whole front and back. There would be no hiding the fact I didn't look like anyone here. Only the alcohol would take credit for why I was brave enough to walk into the village showing so much bare skin.

Muha grabbed my face, frowning. "We can't put any decorations on your face."

"Maybe we can paint it," suggested another while the green-eyed woman started braiding flowers into my hair and tucking leaves and vines into my belt.

But there was something else I wanted them to do, something I was afraid and excited about.

"I did want my ears pierced," I asked, hoping they could help me. "I have earrings I want to put in."

I was glad I was already drunk. One of their husbands put in my earrings. They also found two small snake fangs they put in a second hole beside them. I was now fully uncivilized with bones and crystals in my ears, wearing almost nothing, drunk in a jungle hut with flowers in my hair. What would the Keepers do with this Olivia?

It was enchanting. I'd never felt more alive—terrified, but alive.

They told stories of their families. Their lives seemed simple on the outside but so full when you saw them before you. Would something like that ever be possible for me? I tried not to linger too long on a future that may never exist. Outside, by the river, the girls were making crowns from grasses and leather to wear for tonight. While the women made their crowns, I used sticks and string and made my little creature—my first creation away from my small shack in the Endless Forest. I held it with pride. The girls made faces, unsure what it even was.

The sky was dark when we finally headed for a large area surrounded by homes, where there was a roaring bonfire occupied by villagers dancing. Around the square, people sat on chairs and logs. Conversation, laughter and music filled the air.

The villagers blew into long pipes made of wood. They made the strangest sounds, though I had never heard anyone playing real instruments back home. I was watching them play when Muha grabbed my arm and pointed to my four friends who were sitting together surrounded by villagers.

The four were given large round stumps to sit on, covered in furs and leather. Bastane and Nuo were still topless, their black tattoos visible for everyone to see.

Nuo was drunk, wearing a man's version of the clothing Muha had given me. He had Guardian tattoos of smoke, scales and script covering his entire right leg. He was surrounded by women from the village and the few Guardians I'd seen earlier. They were passing a bottle around between them.

Kazhi sat with women from the village. They leaned close, telling each other secrets. I snorted because she most likely had theirs already. Bastane was being pulled up to dance by the young woman who had mentioned her curiosity about him earlier.

Brekt was sitting alone, arms on his knees, gazing into the fire. I wasn't surprised that he didn't look to be in the mood to celebrate. It was maybe why no one approached him. Shadows danced over his face as he watched the fire. I worried that this time, I had caused some of them.

"Go to your man," Muha said into my ear, "he needs some cheering."

I nodded. Though she was wrong about him being my man— Brekt was as free as the others—she was right that he seemed moody, even for him.

As I walked around the bonfire toward him, his head lifted.

The party might as well have stopped for all I saw of it now. Brekt's eyes widened as he took in my exposed skin. The fabric around my breasts couldn't hide how they moved as I stepped forward. His jaw clenched as he watched. Was he still angry?

I still felt the heat of his kiss, which burned hotter than the bonfire at my side. I thought about how I wanted another. Then I stopped, still several feet away. His head tilted, questioning. I wasn't here to push him. I knew this attraction meant something, but I wanted more. I wanted to see him as I saw Nuo. I wanted to be open and run to him when he was hurt. I wanted to be able to react without hesitation around him.

I needed him to be my friend.

435

I lifted the little creature I had made from sticks and leather, hoping he liked it. I continued walking and stood before him as I passed it over.

A small smile spread across his face when he noticed the crystal earrings hanging from my ears. And if I wasn't mistaken by the glow of the fire, I thought his cheeks flushed with red.

"You've settled in well here," his deep voice hummed.

I balled my fists behind my back—the urge to cover myself was demanding.

"What's this?" he asked, inspecting my creature. He flipped over its long body, trying to figure it out.

"It's the Aspis. Since none of you know how to find it, I thought I would bring it to you."

He stared a little longer. "This is the Aspis?" I was relieved to hear the humour in his voice and to find more than the fire lighting his face. The corner of his mouth tipped up, capturing my attention.

I was breathless when Brekt smiled.

I shrugged to hide how he affected me. "I'm not an artist, but I used to make myself all sorts of creatures back home, so I made this one for you."

I went to sit down beside him. He slid over and moved one of the furs for me to sit on.

"You made things like this?" He still held up the long collection of sticks and string.

"Yes, I spent a lot of time alone, and it would make me happy to see them, knowing they didn't make sense. I gave them names and spoke to them too. It's okay. You can laugh at me."

"The only funny part is the sight of this creature. I'm sorry you were so alone."

"Thanks." I glanced over at him. "I'm not alone anymore, though."

He swallowed, turning away. His hand came up to his hair and pushed it back. Something was different about him tonight, a striking contrast to the waterfalls.

I knew I had to try and reach him, to apologize and say thank you. Which I still had not done. Instead, I kissed him, taking what I wanted.

"I'm sorry," I offered, "I don't know what to say to explain how sorry I am."

"You don't need to apologize, Liv. I shouldn't have reacted the way I did. I lost control over myself."

"You weren't wrong. I was scared—for you and for Nuo—and when I saw how you killed that woman … I saw the man you warned me against. If I had known it wouldn't upset you, I would have embraced you. I want to. And I don't want just the nice version of you."

He surveyed the lines of my face as I spoke, the bonfire reflected in his stare. His sharp features glowed orange in the light. His mouth caught my attention, snaring me.

"Nuo has become a friend," I continued, "With you, it is different. But I want you to be my friend, too, at the very least."

An emotion flickered across his face. "Friendship is not the very least—it is the most important. Even for people—" he paused, searching for the right words. "For people that have more between them. You must be friends. That's where trust begins."

I played with my bracelet, unable to watch him and think at the same time.

"I can't quite explain my feelings in the cave properly. Despite the way it looked, I do trust you. You're the first person I ever told the story of my mother to. The only one I've been comfortable enough to tell. The simple explanation was that I was having my eyes opened further. This is a whole new world. After you killed that woman, even though I trusted you, I worried I didn't understand you. It showed me the divide between us, myself, and everything that exists here. The violent and dangerous people back home were the bad ones. You're even more dangerous than them. It was a reminder we are from very different worlds, and I am not like you."

He laughed, surprising me. A seductive smile lit his face.

"Thank the gods we are not alike. If I had breasts, I'd never get out of bed."

"You know what I mean." I rolled my eyes, thankful he was breaking away from the serious nature of the conversation. "Plus, if you had them, you wouldn't play with yourself."

"Of course I would. I do now."

"Oh my god, I can't believe you just said that!"

He laughed at the face I made—shock and humour mixed as one.

"It's *oh my gods*, Liv. This world is yours now—four gods, remember? I'm having a hard enough time helping you blend in."

He reached around his seat and pulled out a bottle, passing it to me.

"To friendship," he said, and I took a drink.

I passed the bottle back and watched his throat bob as he swallowed. When he finished, he wiped his mouth and sat up straighter.

"In many ways, we are not alike. But in some, I feel like I know you as well as I know myself." He turned toward the fire once more.

"Why do you think that is?" I asked, knowing I was beginning to feel the same with no idea why.

"I told you that I've seen you and have known about you for over a year. You were as present in my dreams as those three were." He nodded to his friends, who mingled with the villagers, oblivious to our conversation. It was at this moment that Kazhi's eyes met mine, and a humming circled my chest. I gave her a look to back off. She may have been checking I wasn't spilling her secret, but some things were still private.

"I knew you well in those dreams," his voice was deep, guttural. "A sign I should have recognized that we would meet in the real world. Even though you are not quite like I dreamt, I feel the same around you now. I struggled, at first, with bringing you along. I gave in for many reasons, but mostly because I wanted to know more about you. I was curious why you appeared so often when I slept."

"Do you have any answers to that yet?"

He claimed not to know how I could wake the Aspis. But the Light brought us together. That had to be important to find the answer to how to wake it.

"I—no. The dreams didn't show you with the Aspis. I'm only glad you're here, beside me tonight, and for however many nights I have left before it wakes."

"I'm glad too."

We both went silent, watching the villagers for a time before Brekt spoke again. "Did the Oracle upset you with something she said?"

"She gave me riddles. Kazhi said I shouldn't put much faith in how she interprets things."

"Kazhi is right. I'm guessing the bracelet is from the Oracle?"

I lifted my wrist, nodding, "You would think if I had a more important task, she would give me a weapon or something. Looks like I'm not meant for anything great—just find a dragon and say, *Wakey, wakey*."

"Wakey, wakey might do the trick." He grinned.

Nuo yelled out from his crowd of women asking who would dance with him. I was grateful to have Brekt's attention directed away from me. The women pulled Nuo forward. They twirled around each other, moving from one partner to the next.

Nuo waved for me to come up. When I shook my head, he made a show of being disappointed but continued.

I enjoyed the silence with Brekt as we watched the dancers and musicians play.

Brekt leaned away from me and grabbed something next to him. A moment later, he had a long hollow reed in his hands and was watching Nuo with an intense focus. He plucked a length of grass, winking at me, and started to chew it.

With his eyes glued to Nuo and a grin forming, he put the reed up to his mouth and shot the chewed-up grass in Nuo's direction.

How Brekt got his target while Nuo was dancing was beyond me. But as I watched, Nuo smacked the side of his neck and looked around, searching for what hit him.

The rumble of laughter from beside me was a sensual caress.

"Is your face feeling any better? It's still quite bruised." Brekt asked, grabbing another blade of grass.

I wondered how often Brekt did this—staying off to the side, being intimidating and unapproachable, all the while secretly playing tricks on Nuo.

"My ears hurt more from being pierced than my face does anymore, and the drink helps." I brought it to my lips again. He watched my mouth as I took another sip.

"What would the people back home think of you now?" he said, repeating my thoughts from before.

"They would kick me out all over again."

"Why weren't you given any help? What about the man you had—or didn't have?" he teased.

"Rebeka found out about us, which was my fault. I was aware I might get in trouble. I didn't know the lengths she would go to, but I knew she would do something. I went to Stephen for help a few days before the soldiers came for me."

I grew quiet, remembering the visit to his home, telling him I was worried and asking for his help.

"He was unable to help you in the end. They still found you," Brekt assumed.

"Not exactly. He shut the door on me. Refused to help at all."

"He didn't offer to hide you? To fight for you?" Brekt's anger was written all over his face, more lethal than when it was directed toward me.

"As I said, he was not my man. It was a passing moment. He gave me some of his time when he was able to hide me as a secret. And then, when it mattered and put him at risk, he shut me out. I didn't expect more from him. I don't expect things from anyone. I grew up knowing you can't always rely on help from others. Too much was at stake for him."

Brekt's face didn't change as he continued to stare. I could tell he was working something out in his mind.

"I wasn't very hurt by it. It wasn't hard to say goodbye to him. I was ready to die if that's what it took to escape the Keepers rather than go to the camps. I was tired of hiding and not living. I was tired of missing out on life and knew it would continue like that forever. So I gave up, calling an end to it all. It wasn't the affair that signed my death—it was the running."

I was thankful I didn't see pity on his face. The fury was still there, but so was something else.

I froze when his hand came up to cup my face. He leaned in. I was so lost in my story I wasn't expecting his lips to find mine again. I didn't move as he held the kiss there for the sweetest moment before pulling away and regarding me once more.

I don't know why I felt moisture on my cheek. It wasn't from sadness or fear.

I think it was from joy.

It was the first time I had been kissed that wasn't for release. He kissed me as if it were an embrace.

He leaned closer to me. "I'm fighting a losing battle with myself, Liv. But I must admit, I like your idea of starting as friends. Though I make no promise that I'll be a good one. I don't want either of us to miss out on any more moments before the end."

"I would like that," I agreed.

And so we sat and watched Nuo make a fool of himself as he danced around the fire.

We stumbled into two wrong huts before we found the right one. Drunk Brekt was a funny thing. He tried to hold on to his serious demeanour while focusing on the stick figure I had made for him. He swore before we left the bonfire that he could see its shape clearly and that I had done an expert job.

We were the first in our group to have made it back. Brekt's hand went to his hair again, playing with it. Pieces were coming loose, and eventually, he gave up and released it. It swung down over his shoulders and back, making him look like a warrior god.

I giggled at the thought.

He pointed to my bed, telling me to get in. I pulled back the netting and fell over the mattress. The bed was heaven. It had feather-stuffed pillows and soft woven sheets.

Brekt went to sit on the edge of his. "Ow," he growled, just as he sat. "My Ass-pis."

"What?" I lost my breath with a laugh.

He shifted and grabbed my now broken stick character out from underneath him. "Damn, I think I broke it," he muttered, examining it. "Hard to tell."

"Might have improved it."

"I'm still keeping it." He attempted to lay flat. He pulled his netting around his bed and lifted his arm behind his head. His hair fanned out around him and over his muscled arms. His eyes were still open, watching the curtain above.

He let loose a relaxed breath and turned to face me, "When Nuo and I were kids, and I woke from my dreams, he would hang upside down from the top bunk and talk to me until I fell back asleep. It was absurd, him hanging like a night bird. I would remind him he was a fish and getting it backwards. I don't think anyone has made me laugh like that. Except now you, Liv. You two are alike. Another thing I didn't expect."

"What did you expect?"

"The person I expected was one-dimensional. She was … spirited." He paused. And I wondered what he meant. "You surprise me all the time. I'm adding humour and creativity to the list now."

"You'd be the first to say that."

He was quiet for long enough that I thought he had fallen asleep. My own eyes had closed, and my thoughts were drifting away.

"If I could meet this Stephen, I would kill him for turning you away. And I wouldn't be quick about it."

I opened my eyes to roam over his hulking figure. He was still lying on his back.

"I wouldn't apologize to you after. My killing nature is all I know. I will show you that I'm not only that. But if others try to hurt you, it's all *they* will know before they die."

"Hopefully, there's not many more." I yawned.

"You're going to live a long life. I'll make sure of it." I could tell he was half asleep, half in the waking world. "I know you were asking for death when we found you. I won't let you have it, Liv."

Despite the calming nature of the drink, my heart raced. It felt like a lifetime ago that I had run for my life and wished for death to end the pain.

"I'm not sorry I didn't listen. I'm only sorry you ever felt that way."

Minutes later, his deep breathing filled the room.

I had a harder time getting to sleep. The events leading up to now since the Light brought me here—the fact that these four had found me, the crystals glowing, Kazhi's magic and the Oracle's riddles—all caused my fears to swirl like a whirlpool, sucking me into its depths. There was a truth I didn't want to admit to myself —one that I wouldn't give a voice to.

But it was there. I felt the answer humming and vibrating, waiting to be acknowledged, waiting for me to go deeper into the pool to face it head-on.

CHAPTER
FIFTY-FIVE

The Guards agreed to rest one more night before leaving. The next afternoon, Nuo led us down a path to a deep pool away from the village, further into the jungle. They spoke little of their duty. This break from being Guards was not only to rest their bodies but to rest their minds.

I wore a cream-coloured, long-sleeved top and loose brown pants that Muha had lent me. They were much lighter than the tight leather. But still, trickles of sweat ran down my back. The sensation made me cringe, like tiny bugs crawling against hot skin.

I walked through rays of sunlight under the thick blanket of leaves. Brightness exploded in my eyes each time I passed through a beam of light. Kazhi was ahead, getting further out of sight. I caught glimpses of her knotted hair through the leaves from moment to moment.

The other three were behind. Nuo and Bastane were lost in the thick green, arguing about who was right about some matter, and Brekt was just behind, offering me warm smiles.

The corner of his mouth would go up when I turned to look at him. Neither of us had forgotten that kiss, and I wanted another. Hopefully, one that wasn't provoked by anger and frustration.

My feelings for him were wild. But wild was irrational and unpredictable—it wasn't my natural state.

As I carefully navigated over roots, I slapped the back of my neck again. I would leave a red mark from all the times I felt an itch at the base of my hairline. I couldn't catch whatever was landing there.

My hair was pulled up, keeping my neck cool, but it left me exposed to whatever continued to pester me.

It happened again, and I smacked my neck. I searched for signs of the pests. I turned to see Brekt looking away.

Suspicious, I faced forward, and without waiting more than a few seconds, I spun back around. He was holding up a long piece of grass, ready to poke the back of my neck.

"You bastard! I thought I was going nuts."

His lips parted in a full smile, forming that damn crease at the side of his mouth. "Took you long enough. Your situational awareness needs improvement, Liv."

His eyes danced with mischief, and he flinched back when I went to swat him.

"Forgive me for not assuming you knew how to be playful." I turned away from him to hide my cheeks turning pink.

His arms swung around me, pulling me hard against his chest and lifting me in the air. His mouth came to my ear, his breath warm against my already warm neck.

"I usually leave the playing for behind closed doors. But with you, I seem unable to help myself."

The heat I felt in my face travelled lower as I wondered what he would be like behind closed doors. When I found my feet again, they paused—his hand slipped around mine. My chest burned with emotion. The warmth of it engulfed me, his skin tanned and rough, a striking contrast against my pale fingers.

Brekt guided me over the large roots. My heart faltered and I lost sight of the jungle. Was this ... was this what falling in love felt like? Teasing, laughter, small moments of kindness?

The kiss had been deep and scorching. It was painful desire

and blissful satisfaction. But this, looking down at his large, calloused hand wrapped around mine as we walked—this was something deeper—a slow swelling in the heart.

Stephen had never made me feel this way.

The swelling dampened as reality sank in. We walked hand in hand, sharing kisses and being playful, all while we headed toward a future that held war and death.

Nuo had warned me—the odds were not good. Brekt was a Guard, and his payment to destiny was almost due. But would that stop me now?

I squeezed his hand, and he turned to me with a sexy-as-hell look. With him, I would soak up every second.

The pool Nuo led us to was not large enough to be a lake but deep enough that you would go under out in the middle. I wanted to run into the water and stay there forever.

Nuo was first to take off his shoes. His bare feet padded on top of a large rock while he removed his top. The script running down his entire back was stark in the daylight. Not an inch was left uncovered.

Pausing only briefly, he jumped right in. He popped up a moment later, saying the water felt great and he couldn't see anything dangerous under the surface.

I removed my boots and ran up to the side of the pool, on the same large rock, close to where Nuo was treading water.

"Can you see underwater?" I asked, eyes wide.

"Of course, BB. As good as I can above." He pointed to his neck. "Wanna have a competition of who can stay under the longest?" He grinned and dove under, disappearing into the deep part of the pool. His second set of lungs must be a blessing when hiding from an enemy.

I scanned the surface for a bubble or a ripple, not paying attention to how quiet it had gone behind me.

I made to turn to see what the others were doing when I was suddenly lifted into the air. A scream escaped me.

Brekt was holding me above the ground, a cocky grin on his face. "You walked into this one, love."

I began to protest right before he threw me in the water. I threw my hands around me, trying to catch myself while falling under.

Cursing him in my head with every bad word I could think of, I swam to the surface. When my head popped above, he was crouching down, waiting for me to appear.

"What if I couldn't swim?" I shouted at him, trying to keep myself afloat. The truth was the water felt refreshing.

"Luckily, we have a Sea-leg as our friend."

I spun around, but Nuo was still nowhere in sight. Brekt was lifting his shirt above his head and throwing it to the side. The distraction cost me. He jumped, landing next to me and causing a wave of water to splash over my head.

My anger did not last long. His playfulness was as refreshing as the pool. I wiped my eyes while my feet kicked below me, wanting to get him back. But he hadn't surfaced yet, either. I spun as I treaded water, searching.

Another scream escaped me as something slid over my foot, and tugged on my toes. Seconds later, Brekt was surfacing.

"Asshole," I muttered.

"You bet." He swam out to the middle.

Nuo finally surfaced, looking pleased. "It's nice to stretch my gills. It's been ages since I've been able to go for a proper swim." He was floating on his back, soaking up the fading sun.

I did the same, turning over to float on the water's surface, watching the world above me.

The wind was blowing, causing a rustling in the leaves. A soft *shhhh* from the jungle rooftop as the world faded to pink and emerald greens. It was the only sound, along with the trickling of water as we swam through it. I felt no vibration of magic. This power was nature, pure and simple.

For the first time in a long while, I thought of home. Not the Keepers or the betrayal, but of my quiet life. I had often stopped to watch the wind in the trees. I'd listen to that same sound to welcome the peace that settled in my soul. It occurred to me that although I was a world away, some things followed you across land and sea—across time.

Thank god—*gods*—it had left the bad stuff behind.

"Did you have water near the north camp?" I asked Nuo, as I glided around the pool, cooling off.

"Not that I could get to easily, or that was pleasant to swim in. Too cold."

"Do many legacies of Sea live close to the water then?" It made sense to me if they could live as easily underwater as above.

"Yes, most do. They band together near the coasts. They tend not to mingle with the other legacies."

"Why is that?"

"Time and culture have made it so. The children of Erabas have always been least liked since their god left without a trace. Mayra is said to be cruel, and as such, her children are as well. However, I haven't met any cruel Sea-legs myself. But when gods are not loved, neither are their legacies."

"So you're admitting you aren't that desirable?" I teased.

He stilled in the water, the ripples around him all but vanishing. He narrowed his eyes. A cruel smile spread across his face as he lowered himself into the water so slowly that I was able to take several breaths until he finally disappeared.

Shit.

My stomach dipped as I turned and swam for the shore as fast as I could. I was not a strong swimmer and knew I would never make it. My feet barely hit the sandy edge when a pair of hands grabbed my ankles, and I shouted, kicking out. I landed in the water, sand and water mixing in my hair.

Nuo popped out of the water and stood, draping weeds over my legs.

"Ew, gross!" I grabbed at the weeds and threw them back at him.

"I like your outfit Liv, though I think it wasn't meant for the water."

I looked down at the cream-coloured clothing that Muha had given me. It stuck to my skin when soaked.

I pushed him back into the water. Bastane and Kazhi were watching us with dull expressions.

"If you guys are done," Kazhi droned, clearly not impressed.

"I'm done." I rang out my hair, the water splashing at my feet.

"Those two will waste as much time as possible to avoid reaching the city," she said, irritated.

I tried ringing out my clothing but decided I might as well stay wet. It would just turn to sweat anyways.

As I went to sit next to Kazhi, a high pitch scream tore through the jungle, reaching us as a fading echo. It had come from the direction of the Oracles village.

Splashing came from behind me as Brekt and Nuo came to shore. Kazhi and Bas were already up and disappearing into the jungle. Two figures flashed past me, and I was left, jarred, near the swimming pool alone.

I gathered my courage and ran after them, scared of what I would find when I reached the village.

I raced toward the yelling.

People were rushing around the village. The evening light turned the figures into shadows passing between huts. Torches were lit like buzzing fireflies weaving between homes. Their shouts were warning others that someone had returned from the nearby village and was gravely hurt.

I followed the crowd collecting in the square, where the bonfire had been the night before.

The Guards stood near the Oracle, who was hovering over a man with her eyes closed, muttering under her breath.

I squeezed through the villagers, who were in tears, grasping desperately at the arms of those holding them tight. The man had been burnt badly, his chestnut skin blackened and seeping.

Kazhi stopped me before I came too close.

Brekt leaned over the man, trying to talk with him, but he could hardly speak. He must have used the last of his energy to get back to the village. Nuo, who I hadn't realized was missing, joined the circle, handing magycris to Brekt. The last of their supply. What did he wish to accomplish? magycris would take time to heal him, and the pain would be unbearable.

The Oracle faced Brekt, who nodded, and he lowered the liquid to the man's mouth.

"We must know what happened," Brekt said softly.

With what little energy he had, the man lowered his head in a nod.

The liquid pooled in his mouth, choking him. His body gave a violent jerk when it slid down the back of his throat, healing enough to help him breathe. But the magycris did nothing for his scorched body.

He coughed, and the sound was incomparable. I put my hand over my mouth to hold back the wave of nausea.

"Fires." The sound that came out of him was made of smoke and churning coals.

Brekt's jaw set, though he kept his face neutral, letting the man take his time to get out what he had to say. It was obvious he'd returned to deliver a warning.

"The village ... gone. Everyone." This caused another wail of pain to pierce the skies. The women whose grief tore through the night were lifted and taken from the circle. My heart lurched as I felt their sorrow. They'd told me their men had gone to that village north of here, trading.

Kazhi grabbed my wrist, lowering my hand from my face. Her eyes held a warning, and I noticed her hand covering my arm. A glow was seeping between her fingers. The crystals were reacting to something. I quickly searched around me, but everyone's eyes were on the man still trying to speak.

"An airship ... then fires. A cloaked figure. Fair hair. Everyone. Everyone." He choked again, coughing through the liquid gathering in his throat.

I couldn't watch anymore, so I focused on my arm. Why were the crystals glowing now? What did it mean?

"Airship. Watch ... for ... cloak." The coughing continued, and the pain in that sound undid me. I couldn't take it. I left the circle of onlookers, facing the fading sun disappearing behind a mountain.

The Ikhor is an evil creature that controls the power of the elements. It will destroy families, burn the earth and cause nothing but destruction until it is taken down.

I searched the skies as moisture gathered on my lashes, blocking my vision.

The Ikhor.

It had only been moments ago I had felt at peace. How quickly it was ripped away.

As the burnt man rasped behind me, trying to force air into his lungs, that little box inside me—the one I kept closed to prevent all the built-up anger from spilling out—pulsed, pushing at me, needing to be let out.

It *hummed*.

My bracelet still glowed.

The last time I saw crystals glow, we were in the cave.

To my right, near the base of the mountain, pathways left the village. Did any of them lead to a cave nearby? I wondered for the second time if the glowing crystals were a clue to waking the Aspis. Was it connected to the caves and the crystals?

I checked if I was being watched, but the others were still huddled around the man. I held my wrist to hide the faint glow still emanating.

I brushed the tears from my eyes.

Fair hair. And a *cloaked figure.* The image tugged at my memory. I had a suspicion.

I blinked away the last tears, looking to the skies for answers to all the secrets in this world. The fading light caused shadows to dance below the tree line. Above them, something moved in the pink sky.

I could have sworn that was the tail end of an airship.

I spun, searching for the Guards. The closest was— "Kazhi," I whispered.

She turned toward me, somehow hearing me over the commotion.

That was strange.

She pushed through the group.

"I just saw an airship disappear behind that mountain." I pointed once she reached me.

She glanced in the direction I pointed. "That would be heading north. Where the village was," she said. "Are you sure?"

I nodded. "Do you think the Ikhor could have a ship?"

Her eyes widened. "Head to our hut. I will grab the boys, and we will meet you there."

CHAPTER

FIFTY-SIX

I t felt wrong hiding the glowing crystals from Brekt and Nuo. But I didn't want to defend myself on another thing I couldn't explain. Brekt's reaction to my being from this world worried me. Kazhi's threat to kill me left me terrified. The other reason was Bastane. He followed the rules of this world, I sensed he would fear what it meant.

If I found the answers, I would tell them, avoiding involving Kazhi and Bas. If the magic users were destroyed in a great war, I didn't want to start one within our small group.

I couldn't connect what made them glow each time. The crystals in my blades glowed in Bellum, then again when I held them while training. The crystals in the caves glowed while the woman attacked me, and now in my bracelet when the man returned from the burnt village.

Could it be related to the Ikhor following us? It was close to us in Bellum, and an airship was following Falizha's ship. I know that's what I saw.

Entire villages were being burnt and we had not found the Aspis yet. The peaceful jungle had put me in a dreamlike bubble, and it burst in a matter of moments.

"We leave first thing," Brekt's voice came from outside. "We don't have time to wait for his healing to find out what he saw."

"We are sure he's not an Aethar misleading us?" Bastane asked. "The burns could be self-inflicted, and he made no mention of Aethars at the village."

"No. Those burns were done to him unwillingly."

The Guards entered the hut, stopping when they saw me pacing.

"Do you think the Ikhor could look like a normal person?" I blurted.

None of them answered, wondering what that had to do with the situation.

"The man, just now, mentioned a cloaked figure with fair hair."

"What are you thinking, Liv?" Nuo asked. "Does this have to do with the airship you saw?"

Kazhi nodded when I eyed her—she had told them what I had seen.

"When we were in Bellum before the Aethars attacked, I saw a man on the street with white hair so light it appeared blue. He didn't resemble any other legacy I've seen so far. Maybe it's a stretch, but he was someone who didn't fit in. He seemed disgusted at what the monk was saying. It's a stretch, but the timing was right."

"You think you saw the Ikhor?" Nuo was trying to be patient. I'm sure I sounded like I was babbling.

"I mean, I guess he wasn't like the painting in the first cave— glowing and everything. But anyways, on the way from Bellum, when on top of Falizha's ship, I swore I saw an airship following us."

Brekt's eyes held mine as he understood where I was going with this.

Nuo chewed his lip, thinking. "It could also have been another ship of Falizha's. She has more than one. But I can't guess who else would have a ship flying around these parts."

"Could the Ikhor be following us? Hunting down the Guards?"

I let the words slip, airing my fears. "What would Falizha gain in coming here?" The glowing crystals aligned with the same events.

"I can't see the gain in it," Bastane added, "The village was small, like the Oracles. If Falizha were here, it would only be to get info on the Ikhor, but there's no way the Guardian City would have heard the news by now."

The Aspis needed to wake and stop this. I needed to remember that was why I was sent here. We needed to go to that library in the city.

Perhaps I hadn't learnt the extent of suffering. But according to the Oracle, I would. And I would see worse following them. They were the Guards, after all. And the Ikhor might be following their trail.

"We need to make plans for our return." Nuo looked at each of us.

"What kind of plans?" I asked.

"We continue with the story of Olivia. She's with me."

I glanced at Brekt for his reaction, but he was focused on Nuo, formulating his own ideas. "They think she's dead," he said in his deep timbre.

"We found her, barely alive. Falizha may try again."

"So why go there at all? Can't we use the library and leave?" Apparently, I was the only one concerned for my safety.

Brekt shifted from one foot to the other. "We need an airship and a crew. Once we have the Aspis and know the location of the Ikhor, we will need fast transportation to follow it into battle."

"Oh." My throat tightened.

"And the reason we've been away so long?" Kazhi asked.

Nuo rubbed his chin. "We say we needed to have tougher training at North Aspis. We were getting too soft at the city."

"It was convenient that we all ran after the botched marriage proposals," she said.

"We don't need to shy away from that. The timing wasn't a coincidence. None of us are afraid to say we didn't want to marry that horrible woman."

"But we need to stay neutral around the Governor." Brekt sat on the edge of a bed, resting his arms on his knees.

"According to Falizha," Kazhi said, "he's put a few nasty people on his committee. All legacies of Day. They're running the whole show now. The city is run by several players that have debts to him. They will do as he says."

"Falizha told you this?" Bastane asked.

"She didn't warn me in the hopes it would help us. She's informing us who is in charge when we get back." Kazhi dodged the question. I doubted Falizha had told her anything.

Bastane frowned, clearly uncomfortable with the news. Was that because he didn't trust them or because they were his people?

"Why didn't you take an airship last time?" I asked.

"The Governor, who controls the money and the ships, didn't see the need. Only now, with the rumours of the Ikhor, will he see it's time for us to make use of one, unlike the few generations of Guards before us." He looked back to Nuo. "If we take advantage of the Governor's help, it's assumed we are also in his debt. More so than we already are."

"Can't claim a debt from the dead," Nuo muttered before realizing he had said it out loud. His expression closed up before he said anything more.

I knew they weren't at the top of the food chain being the Guards—they relied on the Guardian City's resources, which the Governor controlled. It sounded like saving the world had become a political matter.

So they were heading to the city, into the snake pit, unsure which one would bite. They would get what supplies they needed to hunt the Aspis and get out of the city.

The trick would be to persuade the Council to hand it all over.

When we were ready to depart the next morning, the Oracle was waiting outside the hut to bid us farewell.

Each of the Guards had dark circles under their eyes. I was no better off, and the trip to the city would be days of walking.

"We don't need any more fortunes, Oracle," Kazhi warned. "Time is pressing us forward."

"I have a message, not from myself, but from a force so strong that it will not go unheard. I know you return to the City. All paths will meet there."

"Hurry and speak it," Kazhi interrupted.

The Oracle gave Kazhi a withering look, and I wondered about their shared history. Kazhi had earlier shown the Oracle respect but now spoke with familiarity.

I thought the message would be for the Guards, but the Oracle turned to me.

"This energy is an iron will. It surrounds you like the hardest metal and darkest storm. It is a beautiful essence and divine love. It is feminine energy. It will carry itself with you, Liv, into your darkest days. When you feel your heart is being ripped from your chest and your mind is split in two, don't let go. Do not rip away your shield. It will be all that can save you."

The Oracle laid a hand on my shoulder before she turned and walked back toward the village that had gone so quiet after last night's events.

"What do you think that means?" Bastane asked.

It was Brekt's attention that grabbed me.

"I think she was talking of my mother," I trembled.

III

CHAPTER
FIFTY-SEVEN

The Guardian City's towering gates were quiet when we reached the outskirts. The few guards on duty reacted immediately when they saw who stood outside.

It had taken nearly a week of rough travel to reach the city. Every inch of my worn-down, tight black clothing was covered in mud stains.

"These gates, they're made of the same ore as the airships," I said to Nuo as they swung open with a growl. Like a beast waking from a deep sleep.

"These gates and the gates to the southwest are both made from the ore. Parts of the palace as well."

"So the city is old? You said the airships and weapons were ancient, without knowledge of how they came to be."

"This city is very old."

The streets glowed from fire and magic torches. The city hummed with activity even after dark. Music streamed out of taverns, their light spilling onto the stone-covered pathways. It was calm, peaceful, and so very alive.

Guardians were everywhere, packed with muscle and loaded with tattoos.

"Nuo! Bastane!"

461

Shouts came from a small group of men, out for a drink by the smell of them. Of course, everyone within hearing distance turned to see the Guards had returned.

"Guess we won't be making a quiet return," Brekt grumbled behind me.

Two of the Guardians took it upon themselves to escort the Guards to the palace. We were directed immediately to the colossal form of the Aspis's head cut into the mountain. It overshadowed the entire city, its mouth open as if unleashing a considerable roar.

The buildings we passed were the tallest I'd seen. Most were painted red or black, with gold railings on their balconies. I heard waterfalls—many of them—and assumed they came off the high mountains surrounding the city.

"Our rooms are high up there." Nuo pointed to the Aspis's head. "The palace is carved into the mountainside, and the mountains surround the whole city. The palace itself is shaped like the head of the beast. Our suites are located in its horns—two in the first and two in the second. See the balcony there between the horns?" I followed Nuo's outstretched hand as he pointed past the towering head, "The body of the Aspis is carved out of stone and follows the entire perimeter of the city, acting as a wall of protection."

It did look like the body of the beast, taller than all the buildings, making a circle around the city boundary.

We approached a high stone staircase leading to the open mouth of the palace. I couldn't help but think we were walking into a snake's mouth and knowing we'd get bit.

Brekt had hoped for a quiet return, but Falizha herself was waiting for us at the top of the stone stairs. How she had known to expect us, I couldn't guess. She made sure the Guards did not sneak past her.

The surprise on her face was brief but telling—she *had* thought I'd died. She then escorted us with few words, demanding from a woman in a hallway to fetch her father from supper.

The Governor of the Guardian City—Yulen Ravin—Falizha's father, sat slumped in his seat. His large bent form folded the layers of his stomach so that his chair disappeared underneath him. One moment was all it took to make up my mind—the way his eyes scanned the four Guards in front of him, how he didn't bother to sit up as we entered the room—I couldn't imagine there was a thing I would like about him.

"I am glad you have returned to your rightful place, Guards. Tell me, Erebrekt, why such a long absence? Your place is here, is it not? To be at the ready. To defend your people when the time comes. Do you not care for your city of Guardians?"

The Governor appraised Brekt with obvious distaste.

Banners hung from the wall behind the large man. They were white with a painted gold sun—an obvious symbol for the legacies of Day. I thought this was strange, as the city belonged to all Guardians.

The walls were black stone. The back of the Governor's chair was so high in the air that it appeared to be made for a giant.

Falizha stood tall next to her father, looking rather smug. She liked this—next to the seat of power, trying to put the men who had denied her in their place.

"You mistook our absence for disregard," Brekt offered, "We were training in the north, amongst the Guardians we swore to defend. Our teachers there are strict. We agreed unanimously that we needed to be stronger." Brekt paused for the briefest of moments. "I didn't realize the Guards were bound to any place or rules, Governor. I believe our training is most important, and its location is of our choosing."

The tension in the high-ceilinged room grew. The room felt suffocating from the hostility coming from the two golden figures. It was curious since they should all be on the same side.

"Erebrekt of the North, indeed." The Governor's whisper

echoed in the chamber. "Of course, you may go where you wish. It's a shame to hear my trainers in the city are not to your liking. I imagine you enjoyed the long walk in the jungle on your way back to the city. A shame you didn't have your own airship to travel on."

Nuo went rigid beside me. His fists balled behind his back, but it was Bastane who spoke next.

"Governor Ravin, we appreciate any help you may be able to offer from here on forward. As Erebrekt said, we went north for training. He is not wrong—they are merciless up at the north camp. It did us all well to be humbled. I hope you accept our apologies for the delay in returning and offering the city our much-needed aid."

I forced myself not to turn in Bastane's direction. I almost didn't catch the insult in his well-delivered speech. The Governor did need them. I bet he would never admit that to anyone, especially himself.

"Aid *has* been much needed. We could not reach you these past weeks while the city was being swarmed with refugees seeking shelter. I had to explain to them myself that their Guards were not present. I assure you I have taken it upon myself to aid the people in your stead."

"What is this news we missed, Governor?" Bastane asked.

"Had you been more prepared in your training, you would have been here. That you needed so much more after you four were chosen as Guards makes me question if we have the right Guardians for the job. Everyone's future relies on your success in defeating the Ikhor. As it is no secret to you, you would not have been my first choice."

I waited for one of my friends to fire back at the Governor. No wonder they had avoided this place for so long.

"Villages have been burning, and many have perished. Those that have survived have come to the city to seek their Guards and beg them to stop this evil from happening. They want answers. They want to know why the Aspis hasn't woken, why their villages burn while you run around searching caves and hiring whores to follow you."

He sent a pointed look in my direction, scanning me before turning his attention back to the Guards, seemingly satisfied with putting them in their place.

"My daughter tells me that Guard Nuo has brought the woman to my palace. Are our whores not suitable?"

I didn't have to hold myself still—I was so shocked into silence that I couldn't move.

"I would appreciate you not using the term in front of the lady. She is our guest," Brekt warned in a low voice. "I would also like to ask, since we were on your daughter's ship mere days ago, why she had not felt it was her duty to inform the Guards of the Aspis about the refugees swarming the city. Had you not informed your daughter Falizha of the refugees you've been so kind to offer aid?"

The Governor was no longer golden. He was turning as pink as a pig.

"I will remind you that you and your whore are guests in my home. If it slipped my daughter's mind to remind you of your duties, it's because she was doing hers so thoroughly. And you insult her by bringing that woman here after refusing her hand that I so graciously offered."

"Oh, father," Falizha interrupted. "Let Nuo have this woman keep him company. He's already gone through all the women here." A smile formed as her eyes landed on Nuo.

"Not *all* the women, Falizha," Nuo crooned with an equally cold smile.

She bristled, unwilling to continue this argument in front of her father.

"That is enough for tonight," the Governor said, silencing everyone. "You are welcomed back. Nuo, you're ... guest, may stay with you, of course. You four are invited to supper with us tomorrow night. Go and rest. And clean up."

The sudden switch from insults to hospitality was jarring. What games was the Governor playing?

"Father, surely you wouldn't want to be rude and not invite Nuo's woman to dinner?" Falizha's eyes were glued on me.

The Governor nodded while making a face suggesting that he would rather have the Ikhor at his table.

It made my skin crawl to consider dinner with Falizha. I had no intention of being stuck in a room with her ever again. If murder was her first option, what was her second?

We were dismissed and hurried out of the room.

The Guards' suites were situated high up in the horns of the beast. I didn't think my feet could hurt more. Every time they landed on the soft red carpet, a throbbing pain shot up my leg.

I instead focused on the palace around us. The structure was made out of black stone. The furniture and banners were, of course, gold. How had the Governor gotten away with brandishing all the Day decor when so many others lived and trained here?

The Council resided in this palace. Were they *all* legacies of Day?

Brekt dismissed our guide, a young man, gold as the Governor below, at the top of the last set of stairs. We headed down the hall lined with several sets of large double doors.

Kazhi stopped at the first one on our left. She nodded and ducked behind an emerald green door engraved with images of the Aspis roaring. The next was Bastane, who disappeared behind the same green double doors carved with a different version of the Aspis.

The hall continued, and once past Bastane's suite, it opened up with large windows on the left, facing the city. A glass door opened to a broad and spacious balcony—the very one Nuo had pointed out earlier—adorned with comfortable-looking lounge chairs.

Brekt, who walked beside me, caught me eyeing the window. "If I have time, I will show you the city tomorrow."

We reached the third set of doors, where Nuo stopped.

"This is me," he winked over at Brekt. "See you." He waved and snuck inside before we could say anything.

My stomach lurched. I hadn't thought about the rooms. There

were four, and now only one option left for where I would be sleeping.

The hall was suddenly quiet. Which did me a great disservice since that was the moment my heart thumped wildly. I hesitated before I glanced at Brekt, who was watching me with a questioning look.

CHAPTER

FIFTY-EIGHT

"Do you want me to ask Kazhi if you can stay with her?" Brekt's voice was strained.

My building excitement plummeted. I had too quickly assumed we would share a room alone.

My mouth was dry as I studied the last set of doors. I reminded myself what was ahead, what was expected of Brekt. Would I miss this chance?

No way in Hell.

Brekt laughed, the crease appearing on both sides of his mouth. I turned scarlet, realizing I had said that last part out loud.

"Good to know. Though, I think we need to get some rest tonight. If you can contain yourself," he chuckled.

I made a face, struggling to remember how to walk and talk.

The last set of doors showed the Aspis curling around the surface as if flying through the air.

The room was enormous and surprisingly welcoming. It was grand and decorated much like the outside. The walls were black stone. The chairs and carpets were cream-coloured with golden and emerald pillows. An emerald-green divider, carved like a moon and stars, parted the living room from the bedroom. Beside the massive bed, a large set of doors opened to a balcony overlooking the city.

I walked into Brekt's suite and felt out of place.

This room was meant for someone else. Not a lost girl from a miserable forest, sweat-drenched in muddy clothes and smelling like the jungle. It was meant for someone sophisticated, rich and important.

Even Brekt was out of place here. He belonged in the wild too.

A fire was lit to our left, with chairs before it and a small table with a bottle and drinking glasses. The night air travelled through the open doors, blowing the long cream-coloured curtains toward the bed.

The atmosphere was not only welcome—it was seductive.

"Was this your room before?" I asked as he set down his bags and went to pour himself a drink. There were no signs of him in the room.

The light of the fire turned his hair orange and highlighted the muscles in his arms. He poured out an amber-coloured liquid and downed the glass in one shot. He returned to the bottle and poured another.

Was he nervous? I did my best to stifle my amusement. I was relieved I wasn't the only one who felt that way.

He faced me, his eyes roaming, soaking me in. "Yes. I stayed here for a few years. I lived here after I was chosen as a Guard until the Governor tried to pawn his daughter off on me."

"Before you, it belonged to other Guards?"

He nodded, "For many generations. Thousands of years of Guards."

So much history, even in one room. What were the previous Guards like? My best guess included black clothes and tattooed skin.

I wandered the room, inspecting the shelves. "It doesn't look like anyone has stayed here. You didn't leave any belongings behind?"

"I didn't have many belongings to begin with."

"You didn't bring anything from North Aspis? When you first moved here?"

A smile formed as he watched me explore his room. Maybe I was overstepping, but I was curious. I was also disappointed with the lack of belongings. I had hoped for more insight into who this man was. I knew he was loyal to his friends, strong, braver than anyone I had ever met, and he was playful when he allowed himself to be. But I still felt like there could be layers and layers to him that no one ever saw.

"I didn't have anything at North Aspis either. Clothing and weapons were all I brought."

"You didn't have books or keepsakes from your childhood?"

He set down his glass and moved toward his bags. After rummaging around in them, he pulled out something small and walked over to me. On the shelf I was inspecting, Brekt set down a broken collection of sticks and leather—the figure of the Aspis I had made him.

"Now I have officially moved in." He held my stare for a moment, jaw clenching, before returning to the fire and sitting in one of the chairs.

"I don't exactly enjoy reading." He relaxed, leaning back in his chair and interlocking his hands, resting them across his abdomen. "I never had toys growing up or things I collected."

I distracted myself by picking up a small sculpture on a table near the dividing wall, trying to act innocent.

"No keepsakes from old girlfriends?"

I couldn't bring myself to see what was on his face.

"No. No keepsakes."

Frustrated with the lack of information, I watched him over my shoulder this time. "But you did have girlfriends?"

His obsidian eyes were intense, but he was wholly still as he watched me. Standing this far from the fire, I shouldn't feel so hot, but one look from him could warm up the entire suite.

"Describe *girlfriends.*" The deep timbre was as seductive as the room. We hadn't been alone for more than a few moments, and I was already affected.

"Um. I would say a girlfriend is someone you care about. That you—um."

"That you what?"

A shiver went through me. "You know what I mean."

His smile was wolfish, but he saved me any further humiliation by leaning his head back on the chair and turning it toward the fire.

"No, I never had girlfriends."

"Liar," I mumbled as I worked my way into the bedroom, trying not to gaze too long at the large, inviting, and *only* bed in the suite.

"There were never women who were around long enough to care for. So based on your description, I never had one of those."

That stopped me. I eyed Brekt through the green divider.

Had he never taken the time to get to know them? Or had they chosen not to stay long enough? Brekt had a brother in Nuo, but surely there were more people in his life than that?

Not that I had anyone. For me, it wasn't allowed, but for Brekt, it meant that either he or the women *chose* not to.

I lost interest in inspecting his room, which offered little information on the man before me. *Why not just ask him yourself?*

So I did. "Why?" I questioned, walking back to sit across from him.

I would have worried about sitting in the lovely cream colour chair, being as dirty as I was, but if he didn't care, neither did I.

He sat up as I settled in. This room, this conversation—I was adding it to the list of small moments we shared. Like the first time we shared a tent, on the cliff above Bellum, the kiss by the waterfall, or when we sat before the bonfire in the Oracle's village. These moments were intimate. They were ours.

I made a different box inside me, one carved with hearts and stars and every colour of the rainbow. I would stuff all these moments in there so they could never be tainted from those I hid in the other box.

Brekt grabbed a glass, poured me a drink, and flashed me a nervous look while handing it over. He sat back as I took a sip.

"I—I have been with women," he started with a small smile. I rolled my eyes at him, "but I have mentioned before, the way I am around you is not what everyone else sees. Many don't feel comfortable around me. I have a reputation, I guess."

When we were on Falizha's ship, the other Guards were approached, but not him. The same was the case in the small village. Nuo danced, Bastane and Kazhi mingled, but there was a wide berth around Brekt. I had wondered in Bellum if he noticed the reaction those had around him—of course, he did. He was alone most of the time because of it.

The cursed child. Even I was nervous around him in the beginning.

"You do come off as a bit grumpy," I said behind my glass.

His black eyes sharpened on my mouth as I took a sip.

The burn from the liquid slid down my throat and took my mind off the burning I felt lower, if only briefly.

"I must seem boring to you."

I snorted. "I don't think the definition of boring would include a description of you."

An eyebrow of his went up, and I got caught in his full lips as they curved. "If not me, then at least what my life is."

"How would anyone see you as boring? You're a Guard." I made a point to look at every tattoo visible, every muscle showing.

His heated expression dulled, and a surprising amount of seriousness took its place. "Sometimes I feel lifeless."

Lifeless? I held back the urge to reach for him. How did we get to such a deep topic?

"When I talk to you about who I am—when I talk of my past— there's not much to tell you except my history of training or my future with the Aspis. I feel like an imposter. The stories of

Erebrekt of the North—I don't feel any connection to them. All I am are the stories other people have created of me."

Something about that struck me. "I understand feeling like an imposter. I am just figuring out who I am and what kind of person I could be. But I don't see you as that. I see more than the stories, Erebrekt."

It felt strange to have his name on my tongue, but I liked it.

Brekt turned speculative. He didn't judge me for who I used to be.

"I wanted to be this girl I thought my mother would be proud of—a strong woman like her. But after years of fighting against myself, I feel just as much of a coward as when I watched her die. I think she would be ashamed of me. I had always wanted to be a hero, not how I am now."

Shadows move over his skin, though it could have been the fire dancing at our sides.

"What does that look mean?" I asked.

"She would not be ashamed of you, Liv. You are no coward. If being a hero meant you had the skills and the force to win every battle, then we could call Falizha a hero, couldn't we? She has more than any of us as far as ships and weapons go. But I can't say I've ever seen her lift a finger to help another. On the other hand, I've seen you take on the Aethar twice, and one of those times, you were fighting for more than just yourself. In the cave, you fought that woman very bravely. A hero knows the odds aren't in their favour and marches on. That's who you are."

For a moment, I couldn't respond. The world was flipped upside down.

"You think she would be proud?" I fought the tears that threatened to break free while he nodded. "If you can call me a hero, that makes you a saint. You save everyone around you. And your friends love you. They wouldn't if you were lifeless."

"Then maybe you should take your own advice. You wouldn't be with us here if you were just a coward."

"Maybe," I admitted.

Maybe he was right. But I still felt that hollow space inside. I didn't know how to fill it. Perhaps it wasn't hollow. Perhaps it was that box where I hid everything I didn't like, causing a void.

"I was hungry for so long." I ran my thumb over the rim of my glass. "And it feels like there were years of just hunger and quiet. It was an empty existence."

He nodded in agreement. "Yet, you were brought to me somehow. It doesn't feel so empty anymore."

The rest of the room disappeared as I tucked his words safely in my heart.

He held my gaze, unblinking. "With you, I feel things I never thought I would get the chance to."

"I don't want to waste any more of my life, Brekt. You are waking something up inside me."

Something he heard made him look away, but not before I caught the pain that changed his features.

"I don't think we have much time left," he said, "I'm not sure I will find out who I am."

I studied my hands instead of him, trying not to let the emotions well up inside. It was too much, admitting such intimate feelings to him, knowing it would go nowhere.

"Liv." My eyes collided with his, filled with emotion. "I'm not sure sharing a room with you tonight was the best idea." I waited for him to ask me to leave. So, to prepare myself for the disappointment, I poured another drink. "Based on your description, I would say you were the first."

The bottle stopped pouring, and I held my breath.

"You are the first woman I've cared about. You could say that you were my first. Probably my last," he confessed.

I knew I could speak and had a brain to form words, but nothing happened.

"If that's what I could call you," he asked, sitting forward, anticipating my answer.

Because I still didn't know how to move my lips to speak, I only nodded. The same affliction muted him as well. He only nodded once and took another sip from his glass.

We stayed in heated silence, watching each other. How could I label him as *boyfriend*. He was too much for that word. His muscular arms flexed as he reached for the bottle and poured another glass. His massive form, barely fitting the chair, seemed too large and powerful for such a comfortable space and such a silly title.

I wanted to reach out, tell him I had been falling for a long time, but I was scared we were diving head-first into heartache.

Brekt let out a long sigh. "I have no idea how to do this. To have a woman. I can't imagine I'll be very good at it."

Despite the heaviness on my shoulders, a laugh burst out of me. "The only man I ever had shut the door in my face when I needed help. Can't say I have a ton of experience either."

When I thought he would laugh, he only grew more serious. Leaning forward on his knees, he studied his hands. He was silent for a moment, sitting like that.

"Liv, there's something we should talk about."

"That doesn't sound good."

He clasped his hands together and cleared his throat.

"The Aspis will wake soon, and there's something I need to tell you about—"

There was a knock on the door. He dropped his hands and sighed.

The air in the room shifted. Breathing became easier as the conversation broke away, and he rose to grab the door.

Before he could reach it, Nuo walked in.

"Hope you two are decent," he boomed. His hand was up to his face pretending to hide his eyes, but he had his fingers spread wide. In his other arm was a bundle of clothing. "They brought us clothes. I offered to deliver yours, Liv, so they didn't notice you were in Brekt's room, not mine."

"Thanks."

Brekt grabbed the pile from Nuo. Half of it was black, and the other was every bright colour you could think of. Gauzy and lacy bits hung from the side of Brekt's arm. What kind of clothing had they sent for a woman they thought was a lady of the night?

"I'm heading to the library first thing tomorrow. There are a few sections I didn't get to last time. I can think of a few books that might mention speaking, not-really-there, voices."

"Why don't you take Liv with you?" Brekt, looked at me over his shoulder, raising an eyebrow in question.

I nodded, ignoring Nuo's insult, wondering where Brekt would be in the morning.

"Sure thing, BB. I'll grab you when I head down. Sleep well, kids." He left with a wink.

Brekt took the pile of clothing toward the bedroom. I followed.

"Won't someone figure out I am not staying in Nuo's room? Will it cause a problem?"

"It may. But no one would concern themselves about a woman being shared among the Guards." His mouth twitched when I made a face. "But we will keep an eye on you. Don't worry. I will be joining a Council meeting tomorrow morning."

He set the pile of clothes down on the bed, folding his arms over his chest. "I am the group's unofficial leader, so I often attend the meetings on the Guards' behalf. But if you would like, I will give you a tour of the city in the afternoon?"

The thought sent a spark of joy through me. I imagined spending afternoons together was something regular people did.

"For tonight, let's get cleaned up and get a good night's sleep. You are taking the bed. I will sleep on the lounge there."

There was a long cream-coloured chaise opposite the bed.

"That doesn't look too comfortable," I noted, feeling guilty. "I can sleep there. I'm smaller."

"Not a chance. My best ability is that I can sleep wherever I rest my head. I will be fine."

I accepted his offer and stood next to him in front of the pile of clothing on the bed. I would bathe and head to bed early to avoid thinking that nothing was stopping us from jumping into bed together—except for himself.

I grabbed onto a light pink piece and held it up in front of me. It was just strips of fabric with matching slippers beside the pile.

"Ummm—"

Brekt was eyeing the small and nearly see-through piece of fabric, unblinking. He closed his eyes, mouthing a prayer, and ran his hand down his face. "I take it back. I don't think I will sleep at all."

"I can't wear this," I whispered.

"No, you can't. It will be the death of me."

He reached for the black pile and, finding a simple shirt, passed it to me. "Please, for the love of Rem, wear this tonight." His tone was pleading. I couldn't help the laugh that escaped me. He looked tortured.

He stalked away, cursing the Night and mumbling about his self-control being tested. He returned to the liquor glasses and sat down, pouring himself another drink.

I went to the bathing room, a part of me wondering why we were even bothering with self-control anymore.

FIFTY-NINE

I cleaned up in the largest, most luxurious bathing room, tiled with black stone with white veins running through it. The tub sat by a window that looked out over a sparkling city. Miniature figures ambled far below. The steaming water soothed the aches I had from days of walking.

After my long bath, I crawled into the massive bed, wearing the black shirt. Brekt had gone to clean up directly after me. I planned to wait for him, to ask more of the refugees in the city, the possibility of the Ikhor chasing us, and everything in between, but as soon as my head hit the pillow, my eyes grew heavy and sleep took me.

My dreams were vivid, more so than I was used to. The colours were bright, and the images were clear. I began to wonder if I was even dreaming at all.

I was by the fireplace again with Brekt. We both sipped from the same glasses we had held earlier.

He watched me from his chair while I stood in front of the fire, leaning against the warm mantel. I soaked in every inch of him— dark shining hair, dark burning eyes, even darker tattoos—I was helpless. That force between us grew stronger every day.

His eyes devoured my body, stopping for a long time when they reached my chest. His attention roamed over the swells of my breasts. It then lowered to where my desire collected.

I'd never been measured with such a look. Certainly not by Stephen. Brekt's gaze was like worship. He was wholly unguarded in a way I'd never seen.

His hand tightened on the arm of the chair as his body shifted. His demeanour grew hungry. His chest rose and fell, his breathing uneven.

I was wearing the pink gown, and the light of the fire shone through the sheer fabric. Every curve of my body was on display for him. He could see my nipples as they hardened. He saw the curve of my hips.

Somehow, I knew what I wanted and exactly how to ask for it. In this place, there were no barriers, no masks and no future looming over us. Nothing was off-limits.

"I want you to touch me, Brekt," I asked in a husky voice I had never used—so sure of myself, so sure of him, knowing he would give me anything I asked for.

Because he was mine.

"Good. Cause that's exactly what I plan to do. Right where you're standing."

His voice rumbled through me, sending waves of pleasure throughout my body and landing exactly where I wanted him.

He stood, towering over me, and I could do nothing but stare. His hair was down, falling in his face as he moved toward me. The iridescence in his eyes flashed from the firelight, causing a ripple of apprehension. He was feral, gazing at that which he wished to devour.

He reached for the bottom of his shirt, lifting it over his head. I forced my hands to still when I caught sight of his abdomen bunching. I wanted to run my hands along him, to feel the hardness and the warmth of his skin. Somehow I knew I had done just that many times before.

But we hadn't done it before. Were these the desires I'd hidden finally taking form?

He had to tilt his head down, standing toe to toe with me. He reached to grab my chin, lifting my face, so I was looking up into his blazing eyes.

"Tell me again what you want, love. Tell me exactly what you want."

I moaned from what his voice did to my body. "I want you to fuck me."

A tidal wave of pleasure took me, hearing myself say such a thing.

His hands dropped to his pants, unbelting them and sliding them down over his hips. I lost focus on all else when he sprung loose, ready. He was massive and beautiful. I knew exactly how he would feel pushing inside me.

How did I know? This was a dream. And stranger yet, how was I aware I was in a dream?

I stopped caring as his hands held my face. As he leaned in to kiss me, I felt the hard ridge of him against my stomach, the sheer fabric a laughable barrier between us.

I put my fingers up to his mouth and stopped him, enjoying how he stilled, how his eyebrows bunched when I didn't let him lean in any further.

"I want you to kiss me somewhere else first," I smiled up at him.

His returning smile was triumphant. "Tell me where."

Where did I want him to kiss me? Where else was there?

I reached up and ran my fingers through his thick black hair. It was softer than I remembered. My nails scraped the tattoos behind his temples.

I pulled myself up, so my lips were to his ear, pushing my breast against his hard chest. Nothing separated us. My nipples scraped against the fabric of my gown in the most delicious way as I whispered to him.

"I want you to kiss me where I'm most wet for you, Erebrekt. I want you to suck on me until I'm coming on your face."

I would've died from shock—but this wasn't real. I took a shallow breath in disbelief. How did I know to say such a thing?

My knees began to shake. What would Brekt think of me? He'd gone deathly still. Even his chest stopped moving.

I pulled back, wondering if I had gone too far. But I didn't get a chance to see the look on his face.

A low growl came from his chest as his hands bunched the fabric at my sides, pulling it up over my hips. His face was buried in my neck.

His teeth scraped the soft skin below my jawline. "I love hearing my name on your lips. Now, I'm going to make you scream it for me."

My body vibrated, humming like magic, captured by his sensual and raw promise. He left a kiss over the same spot he'd scraped his teeth.

His lips landed on my breast, pulling it into his mouth and running his tongue over the hardened peak. I could feel everything through the thin fabric now wet against me.

His hands held me tight, with the gown still bunched around my waist. He went lower still, getting down on both knees before me, holding my hips and my most intimate part in front of him.

I panicked. What was he going to do? My whole face turned hot as he gazed at me through his lashes.

A crease formed between his eyes. "Is this not what you want, Liv?"

"I don't know. I've never done this before." My voice shook.

He laughed, smiling up at me. "I've done this to you many times. Not in this room, but the location hasn't mattered. You've never been shy about it."

Without knowing what to say, I nodded once, wanting him to continue.

"Hold onto something." He gave me a half-smile right before he leaned forward and ran his tongue along my centre.

It was wicked and dirty. I spasmed, losing balance. I leaned back, and he grabbed my leg to put it over his shoulder. He wrapped his arm around my thigh and held me while his tongue drew slow lines up and down.

I was completely exposed and left speechless because I didn't mind it, not with him.

I grabbed onto his hair, bunching it like he did to my gown.

Seeing him kneeling below me, his tattoos a stark contrast against my inner thigh, him reaching out to taste me, undid any control I had left.

I leaned into him and made a sound deep in my chest. His silky tongue scraped up along my entrance in answer, reaching the spot that ached to be licked harder.

"Oh my god. I didn't know it could feel like that."

He concentrated on that spot, running his tongue up and down in a fast flicking motion, causing my breath to come in quick gasps. The fire blazing at my side was nothing compared to the fire burning within me.

The fireplace grew brighter, the rest of the room thrown into shadow. My bracelet glowed a bright white. Brekt took notice, looking over at my wrist.

The crease was back between his eyes as he saw the fire. But he didn't stop. He was easily distracted by the feast before him.

Brekt held me there, pinned to the wall, entirely at his mercy. He moaned against me—into me. The vibrations touched places his tongue hadn't reached, and I pulled harder, pushing his face closer, moving my hips in pace with his tongue.

It was too much, too intimate, too intense to hold on like this any longer. I didn't understand this burning feeling that was building inside. I would burst if I didn't stop him.

He squeezed my thigh as the other hand let go of the gown and slid down my leg. He made a trail and reached my inner thigh, making his way back up to my entrance.

"Yes," I moaned to the ceiling. "Give me your fingers, Brekt. Give me more."

A growl answered as he slid a finger in, discovering how wet I was.

"You're different tonight, Liv. I like it. I'm hard as a rock down here."

A second finger slid in, and I didn't know how I could take the rest of him if two fingers felt this tight. And when they hit the spot deep in me, as his tongue flicked out, I exploded.

I leaned into him, not caring how hard I was pulling his hair or how heavy I was on his shoulder. I screamed his name as he promised I would, moving my hips along his face and jaw, drawing out my release for as long as possible.

So *this* is what an orgasm felt like.

As I was riding the end of it, I watched him, filled with wonder.

"Oh my god, I've never felt anything like that, Brekt," I moaned.

He peered up at me, seeming confused.

"Wha—"

I jolted awake in a dark room, breathing heavily. My shirt was soaked with sweat. The fire was out, and I was in bed. In a shirt, not a gown.

I sat up, feeling cold and hot at the same time. My body felt a pure, very real relief from an orgasm that should have only been a dream. My legs were sore, like they had been clenched around a face.

Light from the moon pooled into the room and landed on the bed and the chaise where Brekt was lying down.

But he wasn't sleeping.

His eyes were open, wide with shock as he sat up. He was breathing heavily, just like I was. Scanning me, his lips parted.

"Did you—" he started, his voice low and tense.

"I didn't mean to wake you," I said, pulling the covers up, even though I was too warm for them. "I had a dream, that's all."

I would have lost him in the dark if I didn't know he was on that chaise. He went wholly still, disappearing in the shadows so well that I could no longer see him. That drop of magic in a vast sea made him blend in with the dark.

His voice carried out into the room, his words coming slowly.

"Was your dream by the fireplace?"

I couldn't hide my shock. I could die right there. My fingers started to hurt with how hard I was fisting the blanket.

How did he know? Had I been talking in my sleep?

"How—" I began but stopped short when he threw back his covers and swung his legs over the side of the chaise. I pulled the blanket tight, wondering if he planned to join me in the bed.

He grabbed a shirt from a pile on the floor and walked from the bedroom. The door slammed a moment later, making me jump and finally take in a full breath.

I stayed like that for a long time—sitting up in his bed, holding my hand to my chest.

I had dreamt of his tongue. The release couldn't have been real, yet it was echoing through my body.

I looked out toward the balcony into the night. The sky was visible from where I sat. I saw Night's Crown shining over the top of a distant mountain. The constellation Brekt used to guide him when he felt lost. I don't think any constellation could help me find my way out of this.

My breathing evened out as I waited for Brekt to return, so I could ask him what he saw and what had happened.

But he never came back.

CHAPTER

SIXTY

T he sun shone through the window as I paced in the bathing room. The black stone floor was warm against my bare feet where the morning light reached. The wall opposite the window was home to the most oversized mirror this world could manage, meaning I was getting a full view of myself.

I bit on my nails and played with my hair while stealing glances at what I wore. My own clothing was lying in a wet heap beside the deep copper tub, where I tried to wash them by hand. I hoped they would dry by the end of the day so I could wear something more—well, something *more*.

It didn't go unnoticed that I had been in this situation before, pacing in a room after something major shifted my entire life.

Is that what last night's dream was? A major shift?

Yes.

I took in the city outside. The landscape didn't feel new anymore. I'd gotten used to my new world, but what I saw in my dreams last night? I couldn't get my mind away from it.

I didn't know a man could do that with his tongue. Was that what Brekt was like when he let go?

I slapped my cheeks, focusing on the here and now—there was the dinner tonight with the Governor and Falizha. Invisible creatures crept along my skin when I thought of the Governor's daughter.

"Entire towns are burning, and people are fleeing their homes," I told myself. All I could think about was Brekt. I needed to talk to him, but also, part of me never wanted to face him again.

There was a knock on the door, breaking me away from my thoughts.

I shuffled to the main door, the loose fabric of the red gown flowing behind me. The gown was tied around my neck. It came down in two strips of cloth, covering my chest—barely—and collecting at the hips. A gold band was under my breasts, holding the fabric in place, and another around the waist. My back was entirely exposed. The material fanned out in a skirt split down the sides, showing the entire length of my legs.

The fabric itself was beautiful. It moved like a breeze when I walked like I was hardly wearing anything—which, in fact, I wasn't.

I opened the main door slowly, peeking into the hall to find Nuo waiting for me.

He was dressed in an official uniform. The black jacket had two lines of buttons going from the collar to the waist. There were embroidered shoulder marks with black silk trim, and the pants were well-fitted with large, buckled boots up to his knees. He looked like—like a Guard of the Aspis.

His glasses were on, taking away some of the stiff officer's image and adding a touch of bookworm. His hair was combed back, though pieces still fell in his face. His smile lit the hallway when he spotted me.

"I can't go with you today." I didn't let the door open far enough for him to see me.

"Why? You guys still going at it?" His eyebrows rose into the air.

"No. Nothing like that."

"Then what? I have a lot I want to get done today. What's the holdup?"

"I can't leave this room, not in the clothes they gave me."

"Oh. Well, now I have to know." He pushed against the emerald green carvings, opening the door wider.

"No!" I shouted, pushing back against the door. "Nuo, they gave me extremely scandalous outfits."

My strength failed against his. He stepped into the room easily, as though he hadn't even felt me leaning into the door. Eyes going wide, a laugh burst forth as he took in my outfit.

"This was the one that covered the *most*," I cried, hiding my face in my hands. I wanted to tell him it was insulting to laugh, but that was hardly the worst part.

"Where's the dark one?" he asked, "I don't believe for a second nothing happened here last night."

"Nothing did." I dropped my hands. "Wait, did you not see him last night?"

"Not since I brought you these clothes. I thought you and Brekt would have spent the night together?"

"Well, that's not how it ended."

"So, you didn't sleep together?"

"No, not exactly."

My chest hadn't stopped hurting since I realized Brekt wasn't returning after the dream. My head still spun with questions, the biggest being how it was even possible.

"Not exactly? You two drive me nuts. Keep the dress on, Liv. I promise I won't sneak a peek."

"You don't have to sneak. No one does." I fidgeted with the edge of the dress, balling my fist in the fabric to close the gap that exposed the sides of my legs. Nuo's smile grew, and I felt a sting in my palms where my nails dug in.

"We are only going to the library. In the Guardian City, the main occupants are warriors and politicians. Hardly anyone visits there. We will have privacy."

I sighed, hoping that he was right.

I grabbed the matching pair of red silk slippers and let Nuo lead the way, winding down the hallway that was now well-lit with the morning sun. It was surprisingly warm and bright for a hall made of black stone. And thankfully, empty.

If I had worn something like this back home, I would have been picked up immediately and removed from my shack. I felt naked. Exposed. Freed. Bold. Scared. Daring. I was a cluster of emotions so entangled I couldn't hold onto any single feeling at once. It made me a nervous wreck.

I hadn't recognized the woman in the mirror when I changed. My hair was longer and healthier. From my ears hung crystals and bones. My skin had gone from sickly pale to lightly sun-kissed.

But more than that, I looked alive, and for all the fear and uncertainty I felt, I had to be in awe of that.

The power of taking control over my life was potent magic. I wanted more. I wanted it all. I wanted to find Brekt and see if he could really do those things I saw in my dream, and that was not like me at all. I had never been bold or brave. The only familiar feeling was my curiosity, and oh my, was that cranked up a notch.

Nuo led me down several flights of stairs and more black stone halls. We eventually reached a large set of doors open to a cavernous room.

The ceiling was three stories above us. The library could house several homes inside. There were spiral staircases leading up to the higher levels. The left wall was all windows, the sunlight pouring onto seating areas. Velvet green chairs and couches with dark wood desks between them had been arranged under the light.

The sun only reached the seating area, leaving the other side of the room, where all the shelves of millions of books lay, hidden in semi-darkness. Magic-powered torches lit the shelves and staircases, casting a blue hue over the black stone floors and walls.

I followed Nuo to a seating area in the back corner, furthest from the doors, and sat in a giant comfy chair.

"The palace is decorated in a lot of black and green. Are those the colours of another legacy?" I asked.

"Legacies don't have official colours. The Day-legs like to decorate in gold, and Sea-legs like to use blue for the seas. Ouras's children like earthy colours but it's all preference and not tradition. The black and green could have been inspired by Erabas many millennia ago, but I don't know that for sure."

The library was magnificent. I pulled my legs up and tucked my feet underneath me as I stared, open-mouthed, at all the books.

Nuo noticed. "Have you not been in a library before?"

"No, never. I thought I had told you books were forbidden back home. I wasn't even supposed to see one, let alone three stories worth. What are all these books about?"

"Many are histories, stories of the gods, the Aspis and the Ikhor. Those are the ones I have been working my way through."

"And the others?"

"Some are story books, and others are educational, languages, bloodlines and studies of animal species, that kind of thing."

I wanted to know if I could read any books written in the common tongue. I had somehow understood it through the magic that brought me to this world, but I wasn't sure if that extended to words yet.

Nuo was lost in the shelves for a time, pulling books he hadn't yet read and piling them on a rolling cart.

Brekt was supposed to take me out to see the city today. After last night, would he still show up?

I twisted in my chair. Beyond the window, the city spread out below the palace, tucked between several mountains. Waterfalls flowed from them into the rivers running between the buildings and streets. Small bridges and walkways had been built over the water.

The Aspis's stone body, carved into the cliff sides, wrapped around the city's exterior like a wall of protection. It disappeared behind waterfalls only to reappear and continue around the base of the mountains.

The streets were full of Guardians. This city looked like a paradise. One that was overshadowed by a palace full of serpents.

Was there anywhere in the universe that wasn't controlled or plagued with power-hungry people?

Nuo returned, handing me a small book after I requested he find me one. Sure enough, I could read the words—fascinating. The Light, whether it was magic or a real being, had done something to me.

"Are there books on magic?" I asked.

"Magic is mentioned in many of these. What did you want to know?"

Nuo sat at the desk near my large chair. He poured through a pile of books in front of him.

"Nothing in particular." I didn't know how to ask without causing more questions.

He reached into one of his front pockets, pulled out a piece of paper, and unfolded it. It was the paper he pocketed on Falizha's ship before he came to rescue me. He must have found information on the many maps and books piled on that large table in her airship.

After going through several books, he folded the paper again and put it away, slumping in defeat.

"What's on the paper?"

He scanned the room before leaning closer to where I sat, whispering, "There were books on Falizha's ship in an ancient language. I wrote some phrases down to compare to figure out which one it is. I'm coming up short so far."

"What do you suspect the books were about?"

"Not a clue, but if she's interested in them, there must be something important written."

We sat like that for a time, with his nose in one book or another and myself curled up on the plush chair, feet tucked in, reading a romance. It was a silent companionship. One that I cherished more than Nuo realized.

"What else are you looking for?" I asked after he had gone through several books.

"I'm going through the history of the Guards, hoping to find more answers about the Aspis."

"On how to find it?"

"Not exactly."

His honey eyes were contemplative, watching me over the rims of his glasses. A sadness lurked behind the layers that he couldn't hide.

"The Aspis lays dormant in a human body." He waited for my reaction.

"I remember. Do you know where it is, who it's in?"

I tried to pretend the information didn't have an effect. But it cut through me. It scared me.

"History tells us a person holds the beast inside them, and the transformation will occur when it is called forth." Still, his eyes were unblinking, watching me.

The beast inside them. My chest was tight as I tried with all my might not to think what that meant, not to ask the question that had been forming in my subconscious for the past several days. I tried to ignore the images of strange things happening to me when I was around crystals, even in the dream I shared last night.

To sense magic, you had to know how to use it. I could sense Kazhi's. How?

Nuo continued, looking down at the book but not reading it, "What I am searching for is if that person comes back. If the Aspis wins, will it return to the human form?"

If that person comes back. His words sat heavily between us. This burdened him. But if he didn't know who the Aspis was, why would it hurt him to think about what happened to them after?

I was not going to ask because I suspected that Nuo did know who held the Aspis inside them.

"What have you found so far?" I asked quietly.

"All the histories tell us of the battles, how the Ikhor will wake and begin to destroy Arde and the people who live on it. They say the Aspis, once it wakes, is quick to find the Ikhor and destroy it, sending it back to sleep for another Era, saving generations of people and allowing them to repopulate and live in peace. The stories tell of the Guards. Their names are all written down as heroes who guide and protect. They tell of the gods. The Ikhor, once a first child, stole their power to use against them, and the magic is reborn again and again and yet not returned to them. The gods are satisfied with the punishment their children face. Because of the mistake of one, the Ikhor is a reminder of humanity's greed for power, and the Aspis is their humility and redemption."

Nuo let out a sigh, still unfocused on the books in front of him. "But not in any of the stories does it name the person who carried the Aspis within them or if they ever return. They aren't written in history."

Why didn't they name the person? Were they not important? Or did they think it overshadowed the importance of the Aspis?

I walked up to the desk and sat next to Nuo. I pulled one of the books toward me—a book of records.

Picking up the corners of the pages carefully, I looked through several generations of names. Every six hundred to a thousand years, there were a group of Guards whose names were highlighted and marked deceased. The book was huge, and the records went back thousands of years until the pages had names you could hardly make out.

But the Guards who eventually served the Aspis—they all died.

"Couldn't the gods stop all this? Why do they do nothing?" My voice cracked as I fought back tears. Erabas hadn't even stuck around. He just up and disappeared from history.

"If there's a book that tells us what the gods think, I don't believe it is in their children's hands. Rem and Ouras are the only gods that continue to speak to their legacies. Mayra is not seen like the others, and it's rumoured that Erabas is not only gone but deceased. I don't think they would ever explain themselves. They are not like us."

Running my hand across my face, I changed the subject.

"What do they look like?"

Nuo cleared his throat, obviously grateful for the new topic, judging by his voice. "Rem is a golden being, as I'm sure you can guess. It's said he's over ten feet tall, body lithe like a dancer, and voice soft as silk. Ouras is said to have fallen from the branches of the tallest trees in the jungle. He is more fur and teeth than he is one of us. Mayra is a beauty made from the ocean itself. I think I saw her once, swimming near the coast, not far from here. Her hair flows long behind her, as blue as the ocean floor, her eyes are near white, and she can see right through you. But her smile, if you can earn one from her, is more glorious than the brightest day."

He pulled another book closer, thumbing through its pages.

"And Erabas?"

"History has erased him. We know of him only because of the caves and the stories passed on through his people, the few that are left. Some records hinted at a war that went on between the gods. It is believed Erabas was directly responsible for the magic going to the Ikhor, so the others created the Aspis to destroy the evil creature. Erabas was either so ashamed of what he did, he went into hiding, or he was killed."

"Is that what you believe?"

"I think it made it easier for us to have a villain, but I'm not sure what I believe."

The gods reminded me of the cruel members of the Keepers back home—controlling, power-hungry, who wouldn't lift a finger to help those in need even if they were on their knees begging before them.

I went back to the book of names, flipping to the newer entries. I was distracted—the Aspis was lying dormant inside someone. I wish Nuo hadn't reminded me.

I was lost for a time, imagining the past generations of people on this side of the world, until I got to the most recent page, with the newest names written down.

I wasn't prepared for it, how the pain would encase my heart, how much my new friends had already snuck in and made a home there.

Name	Legacy	Status
Erebrekt	*Night*	
Nuo	*Sea*	
Bastane Armel	*Day*	
Kazhi	*Unkown*	

Their names were listed with empty places to mark *deceased*. I was going to lose them.

Nuo must have heard my breathing hitch because he wrapped an arm around my shoulder and leaned his head down on mine.

"Try not to think on it too much."

"Is there no hope?" I choked, trying to keep my voice steady and quiet in the cavernous library.

Nuo shifted, his arm leaving my shoulders and his hand coming up to my face. I turned toward him after a gentle nudge.

"It might be cruel of me, pushing you two together, but I just want him to find some joy before the end. He's known a long time how his end comes. It's a heavy burden. One he has not wanted to put on anyone else. So he's stayed distant his whole life. He never sought joy to hold onto when he would surely lose it. But you are a spark of life for him. He wants it but is afraid to take it."

I didn't bother to wipe the tears from my eyes. I wanted those things, but I would be the one left when they all were gone—unless my new fears were to be believed. Maybe I would meet my end alongside them.

"You'll get hurt, Olivia," he said, startling me as if he read my thoughts, "There's no denying that. But if you gave him your time before death and war come crashing down, I would do everything in my power to repay you in my next life. I'm a little jealous of you two to have found each other before this all goes belly up."

"Belly up?"

"Fish joke, BB."

I cracked a smile, earning one in return.

"And what of your happiness Nuo? Who worries about yours?"

494

"I have never shied away from taking all that is good in this life. I don't carry any regrets with me."

"Have you ever been in love?"

"A woman's love is the only thing I will miss out on. But I had family, not blood family, but one I made. I am happy to go to the end with them."

Footsteps came toward us. Brekt had found us in the library. His eyes were on Nuo's hand under my chin and the tears streaking down my face. Nuo pulled his hand away as Brekt made for the table.

My mouth hung open as time slowed down.

Brekt was dressed like Nuo in an official uniform. He wore all black, which was no different, but this outfit was nothing like his usual. His jacket was high-collared, and two rows of gold buttons ran down the front. There were two gold stripes on the arm of the jacket, around the bicep.

My head swung to Nuo, noticing his was the same, but the details on Brekt stood out so much more.

Brekt walked as if the world around him didn't matter. His stride was full of feral confidence. Gold embroidered cuffs stood out on the jacket, and the front of it opened near the middle, flowing down past his hips. His tall boots reached near his knees, covered with all kinds of straps and buckles. On one leg, he had more straps around his upper thigh, which held several knives.

His hair was pulled back again, showing the shaved sides where his Aspis tattoos ran above his ears and down to the back of his skull.

What caught my attention most was his intense focus on me.

My face heated. I wondered if Nuo embracing me had looked like something else. But when he reached the table, Brekt glanced down at the book in front of me, seeing their names as the last entry.

"Doing some light reading, I take it?" His eyes met mine. I saw everything behind them—sadness, fear, longing, lust. Brekt thought he was lifeless inside—he was anything but. He was more like a volcano, ready to erupt but refusing to do so.

"I tried giving her a romance to read. She wanted to torture herself with boring history instead." Nuo pat me on the back.

"I cry from boredom when reading histories," I joked.

"The council meeting ran late," Brekt said, forgetting the list of names. "They spoke more of the survivors from the villages where the fires have hit. Survivors who've made it here also claim to have seen a cloaked figure burning the towns and an airship in the sky." Brekt nodded at me. So I hadn't been mistaken. "Some claim it was the Aethar. I think the Ikhor has split from the hoard we met in Bellum, covering more ground. I am headed down to the caves to ask some questions, but it sounds to me like we have our Ikhor."

"With all the rooms in the palace, the Council should be ashamed for putting those people down in the cold, damp caves," Nuo muttered, not acknowledging that Brekt had admitted the Ikhor is alive and burning towns.

"Bas was in the meeting at his father's request. He's gone with him now, and Kazhi is wandering the palace," Brekt noted. Which meant Kazhi was gathering helpful information. Would I feel her magic if I travelled the halls?

"Good, we should all meet up tonight before dinner." Nuo pulled more books toward him.

"You not coming down?" Brekt asked.

"I want to stay here."

Brekt turned to me. I wanted to see the caves and the people, so I nodded and stood to join him. I caught Brekt eyeing the outfit I was wearing, and the temperature of the room changed. He swallowed, blinked, and quickly looked away. I forgot I was wearing almost nothing.

I want him to find joy before the end.

I tried pulling the fabric closed again, embarrassed.

"It's not as nice as the pink gown I wore last night," I teased, my face warming after saying it aloud.

Brekt's eyes flashed at my admission to the shared dream.

Although I still had no explanation of how it happened. Perhaps he was going to pretend it didn't.

"Lead the way?" I asked in a quieter voice.

He nodded and began for the main doors.

I looked back, just once, at Nuo sitting in the corner of the library. Light hit the back of his head, casting his shadow over the book before him.

Time was coming for us, faster and faster. The end was in sight. Knowing that I was selfishly finding joy while he stayed behind, searching for how to cheat death, sent guilt crawling through my veins.

But I was familiar with Death. He was a slimy bastard. When you called for him, begging for your end, he didn't show. But when you wanted time to slow down, he would come, smiling, to take it all away.

SIXTY-ONE

We walked quietly through the black halls of the palace. Brekt's presence saturated the air around me. My body hummed with his close proximity.

The regal presentation of his Guards uniform added clean lines to his rough exterior. There was something about the scars and tattoos dressed in a well-cut jacket.

I continued to fidget with my dress, pulling the loose material of the skirt closed. Every step I made had the fabric shifting open, exposing both legs.

Very few people had ever seen me this bare, and one was currently walking next to me—though I still had the desire to flee to prevent him from seeing any more. Once again, I was hiding a blush rising on my cheeks.

"How many villages are living in the caves?" I tried to distract myself.

"Several. They counted over twenty villages burnt like the one north of the Oracle. Many didn't make it here. I'm hoping the survivors will tell us more about the sightings of the Ikhor."

"The Governor didn't ask those things?"

"No. He left it to us. To deal with the aftermath."

"What does the council do then?"

"None see what they actually do. They hide behind the Guards. Our skill on the battlefield and being a symbol of power for the people are tools to them. But for all we are used, we are not included in planning for the Guardians or the city. There's a lot going on with the Aethars—trouble at the borders between our lands and theirs, more than ever before. There's a Guardian camp down that way, South Aspis. They've been fighting them off. The council mentioned that many of the villages burnt were either close to the Aethar borders or Sea-leg villages along the other coast. I don't understand the Ikhor's intent. Those are opposite sides of our continent."

"Do you think it's playing games? It is evil, right?"

"Could be. But something feels off about it."

"Will there be a war with the Aethar?"

"I get the impression the council is preparing for one. They see the fires as an act of war on the Aethars' part, who are supposedly guiding the Ikhor. It was mentioned our airships should be flying, keeping an eye on Aethar activity. They questioned me on what we had seen on our travels here."

"And did they mention helping with these fires instead of just keeping an eye on them?"

"There were more accusations than offers of help. They first wanted to pin the fires on us, the Guards, and our inability to produce the Aspis's whereabouts. They see the number of fires along both borders as a sign that it's a well-planned attack, giving the Council enough reason, in their eyes, to go to war. It will mean invasion." Brekt grew quiet, contemplative, before adding, "I'm worried that ending the Ikhor won't save the people of Arde this time around. That war will quickly follow no matter the outcome."

"What do you mean?"

He peered down at me, his features cast in shadow.

"I think a time is coming when the enemies won't be so easy to see—when they aren't painted on walls or told in stories."

I chewed on my lip, Brekt's fears becoming my own. A future could exist for me here if my lurking fears didn't come true.

My home was said to be destroyed by wars long ago. It could have been what secluded us from the rest of the world. Was it happening all over again?

"Do you think the Ikhor will come here?"

"The number of villages burnt and people displaced from their homes—these attacks seem to be getting closer to us. I assume the Aethars will be called to battle behind it. It would make sense for them to aim for the city. That is what the Guardians need to be ready for, what generations of Guardians and Guards have been preparing for, but it still seems like none of us are ready.

"We will direct the Aspis to the Ikhor. We will help fight and destroy it before it can join with too many followers or become too powerful. We don't even know if its power will grow over time. No history talks about what happens if the Ikhor isn't killed immediately. According to history, the Aspis usually takes it on and ends it quickly. But it hasn't risen yet, even after all the burning."

My stomach sank when I saw an apologetic look in his eyes because it made me wonder. I shoved the worries into that dangerous box inside myself and closed the lid tight before anything bad leaked out. It was nearly overflowing with all I didn't wish to think about.

I had to find out how to wake the Aspis. If I could use magic, perhaps I could make a difference and cut off Death before he found my friends.

"You call the Ikhor an *it*."

"They are not human anymore, Liv. That is one truth that is told with every generation of history—the body possessed is human, but what's left is pure magic stolen from the gods. The soul inside is destroyed by the greed and hunger for power."

A shiver ran down my spine. I tried again to cover some of my exposed skin.

"The records don't keep the name of the Ikhor's host either," I pointed out.

"They are not honoured. It takes a host like the Aethar, with hate in their heart. There are no records of their people."

Brekt shrugged off his jacket and opened it to slip over my shoulders. Underneath, he was wearing a simple black shirt.

"Sorry, I should have noticed earlier you were uncomfortable. We can go back and look for some clothes that will fit you. And cover you some more."

My heart did a little dance as I slipped my arms into the oversized sleeves of his jacket. It was a heavy fabric, weighing me down, but it felt good to be covered. And the familiar thrill of being enveloped in the smell of him, so wild and masculine, calmed my nerves.

"The caves are in the palace?" I asked, realizing we were going further into the mountain rather than leaving.

"They are underneath and run through the mountain the palace is carved into."

Brekt led us deeper, the halls turning pitch black where the magic torches didn't reach. Brekt had all but disappeared. It was awe-inspiring and unsettling how invisible he could become.

We eventually reached a large archway. Torches were lit around it, their light flicking over strange markings carved into the stone.

"They are the ancient language of Night. No one knows how to read them anymore, and books on the language are nonexistent," Brekt explained. "The scripts in the palace hint that it was a warning of some kind about the depths of the caves here."

"I forgot there are languages specific to the gods."

"Those languages they would speak with only their children. Not many speak them anymore. Because these caves never end, there was a warning written here. The first few caves are well used for training, leisure, and just getting away from the city. But the tunnels that lead away from the main caves are endless. Nuo claims that some lead through the mountains and out to the sea."

"So Erabas wanted to warn the people not to get lost?"

"Who knows? It's only a guess."

Brekt was eyeing the characters on the wall.

"Can't you read them? You're a pure-blooded legacy, right?"

He shook his head. "I didn't have anyone to teach me."

I wanted to smack myself because, of course, Brekt had never met his family.

"Do you feel magic?" I asked before thinking. Kazhi had warned me not to.

Brekt looked down the hall before answering me. "Don't ask such questions in public. The use of magic was weeded out generations ago. If anyone can use it now, they would be singled out, used and probably killed for it. People don't like the idea of a power imbalance. And the monks preach it's an insult to the gods. The magic belongs to them. Why would you ask such a thing?"

Was that a no?

"Just something I read in one of the books," I mumbled.

I was surprised at Brekt's answer. I had hoped he was more open to the subject. I wanted to confide in him.

He was already heading down the stairs that descended past the archway, so I also didn't mention to him that I *could* read the characters in the stone. I was scared of what that could mean, and I was scared of what he would say.

Too many things weren't adding up. I could sense Kazhi's magic. The crystals glowed around me. Now I had discovered I could read a forgotten language by a long-dead god.

Too many secrets run this world—yet they are the key to survival.

The Alchemist, the Oracle and Kazhi all warned me to hold onto what I knew. To survive. But my gut twisted, hiding things from Brekt.

The script over the archway was not a warning of the tunnels like Brekt had been told. The characters read, '*To descend here is to embrace all that lies in darkness.*'

But what was in the darkness?

The stone stairwell's ceiling was low enough that Brekt almost had to duck down. The sounds of his boots echoed off the walls while my soft red slippers made none. For once, I was the silent one and not the prowling beast before me.

Our descent took us to the first cavern. We stood high above a dark beach and a large body of water. The stairs continued down along the cave wall with no railing—an easy way to fall to your death.

No light came from the world above—the caves were well underground. But there was a faint glow that made it possible to see. Everything turned a blueish green—the cave ceiling had millions of glowing stars.

"What makes that glow?" I watched my feet as I continued down the long stone steps toward the beach. I held up the loose fabric of the gown, concentrating on simultaneously not falling and peeking above me.

"Those are cave worms. Although it looks somewhat like crystals, they glow like that naturally."

"They're beautiful." I was mesmerized by the sight of them.

"They light up the first few caves but don't seem to like travelling down the tunnels."

"Have you explored the tunnels?" I asked.

"Nuo and I would come down here to train and to avoid everyone else up there. We tried to see how far they went. Turned out to be very far." The iridescence flashed in his eyes. I was growing so used to seeing it, finding comfort when the light caught it.

"And you never got lost?"

"All the time," he laughed.

I smiled, picturing them and wondered how he ever got lost.

We reached the bottom of the stairs, and my feet sunk into black sand. It sparkled under the light of the glow worms.

The cave was enormous, making it impossible to see to the other side where the water flowed. It was wide open, yet tight and suffocating at the same time. The air was strange and magnetic, almost like I felt when too close to Brekt.

He was next to me, brushing my shoulder, and a shiver went through me—the magnetic air could very well be him. It felt stronger here, surrounded and enclosed like this.

We walked along the beach. The figures were hard to see at first, huddled together and speaking in hushed voices.

"Shit," Brekt whispered. "This is bad. There are so many. I need to speak to a few. Ask what they've seen and offer them comfort. Do you mind waiting?"

I shook my head, following him along the beach, pulling the jacket tight in front of me. Brekt approached the crowd of people camped on the edge of the cave against the rigid rock walls. They were set up under the typical cave drawings I'd seen twice before.

Below the symbols of the gods, their children were wrapped in blankets with empty faces, like their whole world had crashed down around them.

I knew that look—empty as the tunnels running off these caves. Grief struck us all down differently. Some grew cold. Some would feel like molten lava, consuming every piece of their heart.

The villagers back home were cold and empty. I tried to make myself into that, to dampen the hate and anger. My box ran out of room for all the emotions that ate away at me. To be cold and empty would have been bliss.

Seeing the children down here struck a chord. I saw myself in them. I smiled at some, all of them Sea-legs, knowing there would be nothing comforting from a stranger's smile, especially one dressed as I was. But they regarded me with no shame or judgment, unlike people would have back home. Perhaps my embarrassment was my own preconceptions.

When Brekt returned to me, his eyes were hardened.

"They all tell the same story. Most did not see how the fires were started. They simply grabbed all they could and ran. They walked here on foot, caring for those that survived who came with them. And mourning the many that didn't."

"How long will they be kept down here? It's damp and dark."

"I don't know why they're being kept down here at all. Something isn't right. As the Council informed me, these are Sea-legs from the coast and villagers from the borders near Aethar lands. But the attacks on Bellum, then the burning of the village in the jungle—it doesn't make sense. It's so random compared to the locations of the others. What is it thinking?"

"The Ikhor?"

He nodded, frowning down at me, his mind far away. "Let's go for a walk. I'll show you some of the tunnels."

SIXTY-TWO

"I thought these tunnels were dangerous to go down," I asked as Brekt led us away from the villagers.

"Not if you're a pure-blooded child of Night." He winked at me. "Plus, we won't be going too far."

"All right, show off. Just don't leave me behind. I have no special abilities or any skills for that matter."

"I would beg to differ," he teased, reaching out for the sleeves of his jacket I was still wearing, rolling them up.

When my hands were accessible, he grabbed onto one and began walking, just like he had in the jungle. My heart warmed. After the awkwardness of the shared dream, I was glad for the feeling.

"How would you know what skills I have?" I peered up at him. He gave me a smile, bending down, his mouth coming to my ear.

"Because last night wasn't the first time you visited me in my dreams."

My mouth went dry. We were talking about this. I thought we would lead up to it, but he went right in for the kill.

We were far from the crowd of people, reaching a bend. Once around it, I found myself under a small entrance to a second cave.

It glowed like the first, though it only had a river running along the centre, not an open lake.

"That's happened before? But I don't remember it."

I knew he had seen me in his dreams. He told me so on the deck of Falizha's airship. But I assumed he saw what was going to happen to me. He had said all the dreams came true.

"Last night was different, but yes, I've seen you in them. Even before I met you. As I said, I've known you for over a year and a half."

He went to push back his hair, and I caught how his hand shook. He was nervous admitting this.

"That was what your dreams were about? I knew you had seen me, but that!" I couldn't even look at him. My chest was rising and falling so fast. What else had we done?

"Don't be embarrassed." He squeezed my hand. "My dreams were the only good I carried with me for a long time."

What he admitted should warm my heart, make me ache for him, but it was impossible to break through what I was actually feeling.

"How can I not be embarrassed? You will have these expectations of me. Which I will never live up to, I might add. I've never done—that."

"But you and Stephen, you were together like that."

"I can now confirm he was not ... adventurous ... with his mouth. What we did together was much more straightforward."

I wanted to bury my face in my hands, but he was still holding onto one. He tugged on it and pulled me to a stop, forcing me to face him. He let go of me and took hold of my arms around the thick fabric of the jacket.

The glow around him softened his features. The desire I found in those obsidian depths had my embarrassment washing away.

The cords between us tightened in my chest. In this space, it was more substantial. I was saturated with its power. My body hummed, like the sound the crystals made, like magic.

"Did you know I was there last night before you woke? Or was that how all the dreams go?" I kept my voice down, trying to hide how it shook.

"I didn't at first. I only suspected things were different when you looked shy. And said *oh my god*." The corner of his mouth curved, "I thought that maybe my dreams were changing because I was getting to know you better. You and your terrible cursing."

"Swearing properly is a hard habit to learn, I guess."

Brekt reached up and grabbed a piece of my hair. He ran it between two fingers and then tucked it behind my ear.

"I am sorry I ran off after."

I didn't trust myself to speak. The softness with which he spoke to me, touched me—I'd never felt so seen, so cherished.

"Did you enjoy the dream?" His expression shuttered, and I almost missed the uncertainty he tried to hide.

I gave him the most incredulous look I could muster.

Uncertainty gave way to pleasure. "I can show you many things I think you will like. I *know* you will like. I've spent many nights learning."

My thighs did a strange thing, tightening, clenching around my desire. It felt delicious.

"But please believe me when I say, having you in real life and seeing how you react to everything, I like it much more than what I've dreamt. It's unexpected. It's exciting. I like not knowing what you'll say or what you'll do. And the way you reacted to my touch last night? It was a gift."

His hand found mine again. "Come on. I want to take you further in. There is a place down here I would like to show you before we leave. We need to get ready for dinner."

I had forgotten about the dinner. Any warmth he had built in me was replaced by cold, nauseating panic.

He lifted his chin toward the other side of the cave, where the river disappeared down a dark tunnel. He pulled me along, slowing when I had to maneuver around rocks and boulders in my soft slippers. Out of the corner of my eye, I watched him move in his Guards uniform. I snorted, and it echoed around us.

I put my hand over my mouth, shocked at how loud it was.

"I was just thinking how ridiculous I am next to you." I tucked my hair behind my ear. "You look so official, and I am dressed like a whore with an oversized jacket."

"Ridiculous is not the word I would use. I can't decide if I like red or pink better."

It took me a moment to realize he was talking about the gown.

"Don't decide yet. There are a few other colours to try on."

He focused ahead with his jaw clenched, making me laugh once more. It felt good to cause such a reaction. I felt powerful.

I tripped over a stone and cursed. The silk slippers offered my feet no protection.

"Those shoes, on the other hand." He stopped, letting go of my hand. "They are near useless. I should pick you up and carry you the rest of the way."

I thought for a moment he was considering doing it.

"I'm fine. I don't want to be *that* girl. Needing to be carried around. What is it you want to show me anyways?"

"It's just a little further. It's through that small tunnel in the next cavern."

We reached the bend, where the water flowed into a short tunnel. The glow from the cave worms faded as we entered the darkness connecting the second cavern to the third. I halted, unable to see the ground. Brekt was a few paces in front of me before he noticed I'd stopped.

"I can't see."

"Of course, you can't." It was a strange sensation, hearing his deep voice without being able to see him there.

I raised a finger I couldn't see and pointed at him. "Don't laugh at me, mister high and mighty. My plain eyes serve me just fine most days."

Brekt snatched up my finger in his large hand and pulled. A moment later, I felt his tongue slide over it as he sucked it into his mouth.

I snatched it away, gasping and losing my breath.

"Sorry, love, I thought you were offering me a piece to taste."

Love. It was not the first time he had called me that.

"If I was offering," I teased, "It wouldn't have been my finger."

A small shriek left me as he did indeed lift me into his arms. His face was so close to mine. His lips pressed close to my ears.

"Perhaps I'll just take all of you."

"For a man who's avoiding having sex with a woman, you sure like to get her going," I muttered while he moved us through the dark.

"If you offer up a part of you, I feel inclined to taste it at the very least. Anywhere else?"

I didn't answer.

"I'll choose next time, then."

This was not the first time he had held me, carrying me through the dark. But it was much more intimate than when he found me in that first cave.

I leaned into him, wrapping an arm around his shoulder, letting his warmth seep into me. The smell of him enveloped me, and I got lost in it.

With him, maybe I didn't mind being *that* girl.

CHAPTER

SIXTY-THREE

"Can you really see everything?" I asked into the pure darkness.

"When you talk, I can see better."

"How does that work? Talking makes you see?"

His chest rumbled against me. "The sound reverberates off of objects. I can then sense where they are. It's a different form of seeing. Night birds do the same. It's how they catch their prey. They make a sound similar to a whistle. I've learnt to make the sound like they do."

"Have you ever hunted for anything like that?" I tried to picture him stalking around at night, whistling, searching for something. It was surprisingly easy to imagine.

"Only to find my way. Maybe I should test it out on you—try and find you in the dark," he whispered in my ear.

I found the idea thrilling, having him hunt for me. It was primal. Sexy.

I squeezed him closer. "I don't think I'd like to be left alone in a cave. Past experience and all."

"Right."

"Maybe outside though ..."

I felt the light touch of his lips against the top of my head.

What was this man doing to me? Although something was tethering us, tightening in my chest, so much of me was being undone. Parts of me were breaking apart and falling away, being replaced with him.

We entered the third cavern. Shallow pools of water flowed off the river, just as black as the lake. The worms in here glowed even brighter. The atmosphere was ethereal, more dreamlike than the fireplace had been.

Brekt was paying attention to the ground, watching where he was stepping, and I greedily enjoyed the shape of his jaw and the muscles along his neck.

The humming in my veins and pulling on the cords grew. My chest squeezed, and my stomach tightened to an alarming degree.

Was it because I was alone with Brekt in a small cave?

He set me down as I glanced around. My bracelet gave off a light glow, and I tucked my arm behind my back. I wasn't the only thing reacting to the cave.

This cavern was round, with stalactites hanging low. Some reached the floor, blocking the view of certain pools.

"There are no cave lizards here, are there?"

"Not that I have seen." Brekt stayed where he was, leaning against a large rock, watching me as I walked along the river's edge and investigated the pools.

"They're cold, the pools of water, making it a refreshing place to come in the hot seasons." His voice bounced around us.

"You've spent time in them?"

Would he have brought anyone down here to the cool waters? When I didn't hear an answer, I checked behind me. But Brekt was not there. Damn him.

I spun in a circle. Nothing.

A shadow moved close to me, one that I had overlooked—a dark spot near the pool of water I was just investigating. I nearly screamed as the shadow took form. Brekt grinned as he wrapped his arms around me, pulling me to him.

"I have spent many days in these pools," he said next to my ear, "but I know what you are thinking, and the answer is no. I've never brought female company down here with me."

"Liar," I said, swatting his arm. "And that was mean. My heart almost stopped. Let me go."

"I think not. I enjoy you in my arms too much."

But he let go, only to lift me again.

"What are you doing? I can walk on my own. Hey—no!"

I sucked in a breath as Brekt walked us into the water.

"You monster, don't you dare put me down now."

"I'll keep you warm."

He let my feet down first. I hissed at the cold water, causing me to hold tight to him as I slid down against his chest. And I continued to hold onto him because he was keeping me warm.

The water came up to my knees, and as my body adjusted to the temperature, I found it wasn't so cold after all. But I didn't let go of him because that felt even better.

"Let's just stay down here for a little while longer," he said in a low voice. I stepped back to see what was on his face and didn't realize the water was deeper behind me.

Losing my grip, I tripped backwards, falling into the pool. I was underwater before I could push myself back up.

When my head was above, I could hear Brekt's booming laugh. I wanted to be angry, but the sound of him laughing, deep and full of genuine humour, was contagious.

"Bastard," I laughed with him.

The waterlogged jacket threatened to pull me back under. He reached out a hand to pull me up but froze as he stared down at me, the smile fading from his face.

"What?"

He swallowed, eyes focused on my chest.

The jacket was open in the front, and the dress, when wet, was utterly see-through. Even in the dark cave, you could see the outlines of my breasts.

His focus shifted, and his eyes met mine. That damn pull was staggering.

I scrambled to get up, moving an arm to cover myself, wondering why I felt embarrassed when I knew he had already seen what was under this dress.

"I've changed my mind, Liv. I don't care if we are late for dinner."

The look he was giving me had turned ravenous.

Dripping water, I moved wet strands of hair stuck to the side of my face. The pull was turning painful. My bones felt tight and strained like I had been training for hours. My breathing hitched and came in short gasps.

"Do you feel that?" I asked, reaching for my chest. His chest was rising and falling just like mine.

His head came down once in a nod, but he didn't make a move.

This need to be near him was pulsating in my veins. What would make it stop? How close must we be for it to diminish?

Brekt reached his hand around the back of my head, running his fingers into my hair. He stepped closer, leaning his head toward me.

His lips were a breath away. So close. His forehead rested against mine.

"Liv," he whispered. A prayer and a plea.

My body sang for him, full of desire. I felt only need—to pull him toward me, embrace him, and absorb everything I could.

I searched his eyes, and what looked back was unexpected. I thought I would find passion, and longing, just as I felt. But I saw pain.

His hand trembled on the back of my head. I knew he was feeling the weight crashing down on us.

His other hand snaked around my waist and pulled me closer. He held me like that, not taking anything, just holding onto something while he went through whatever was in his head.

I let my fingers brush along the scar that ran down the side of his face. The touch tingled at this strange force between us. His eyes closed, and I saw some of the pain in his features lessen.

He let loose a breath, and his arm around me tightened further.

And when I moved my head, his eyes opened a crack. He watched me as I leaned in closer. I had to get up on the tips of my toes, so I could take what I wanted and give what I hoped he needed.

His fingers knotted in my hair, and he pulled me the rest of the way, closing the distance between our mouths.

The moan that escaped me was loud in the hollow, empty cave, guiding him to give me more.

He deepened the kiss, his tongue finding mine. Although just as powerful, this kiss was nothing like the one we shared outside the Oracle's home.

This one wasn't born out of anger or desperation. This one was slow, deliberate and full of a different kind of need. He held me close like I was the most precious thing in the world and kissed me like there wasn't an end coming—like we had a million tomorrows.

He acted as though we could stay here, in this kiss, forever.

The hand at my back moved, finding its way under the jacket and to the bare skin, trailing up along my spine. His calloused hands sent cool waves of pleasure through me.

The silky feel of his tongue against mine erased the memory of every brazen touch I'd had before. I was being remade and reformed with one kiss, one touch.

His kiss showed me what love could feel like. If we had the time.

His hand slid back down, coming to rest just above the swell of my backside. His other hand left my hair and went to join the second, both sliding down over the rounded curves, then further to my thighs and grabbing tight.

I grabbed his shoulders as he lifted me, wrapping my legs around his waist.

He shifted, carrying us away from the pool while I continued exploring his mouth, holding onto him as if everything depended on it. And it wasn't enough. I needed more. I needed all of him.

The pain from the force of the pull was causing an

uncontrollable reaction. My legs wrapped around him tight, clenching and pulling him toward me.

I moaned, low and feral, into his mouth. I found the hardness of him and moved against it with aching need. His arms curled tight around me, moulding us together. He began to move with me, pushing himself into my heat.

It was intoxicating, an addiction I didn't know existed. The need for this was never going to get out of my system, and our time together was running short. I had to take it all now, every drop of him that I could get.

He stopped, and I barely registered that my back was against a rock. He grabbed one of my legs and pulled it down, away from him.

I bit his lip, and he laughed.

"Trust me, Liv. I'm not stopping. No way would I stop now."

I didn't care about words. I ran a hand down his back, over the tight muscles bunching as he held me. I went back to kissing him, letting my leg fall as he asked.

With my back resting against the rock, and the thick jacket protecting my skin, I didn't slip from his grasp.

One of his hands explored my waist, travelling along the soaking fabric, feeling every curve beneath. He quickly found my breast, cupping, exploring and scraping a thumb over the hardened peak, causing my body to squirm with pleasure. The other hand wrapped around my thigh tightened, holding me where he wanted me.

My breast grew cold when his hand slid further down, reaching my leg. He pushed the fabric aside, grazing his knuckles along the soft skin of my inner thigh. I held tight to him, shoving my hands into his hair and pulling him closer as his fingers danced near my entrance. But he lingered there, not going anything further.

I shifted forward against his hand, showing him I wanted more.

"Please," I whispered, breaking the kiss. "Touch me."

"Liv," he breathed, kissing my jaw, kissing my neck.

"Please, Brekt."

"Forgive me for this."

I didn't understand. Why did he sound pained?

But I forgot everything when a finger slid further down and ran across the tight bundle of nerves begging for his touch.

I let out a low moan. Nothing had ever felt this good. I was already so close with just a simple touch, after the need that had built since we entered these caves.

His finger moved, rubbing over the sensitive area, picking up the pace as I squirmed against his hand.

"Please."

His kisses continued to run along my neck. His teeth scraped the soft skin under my ear. His other hand reached the swell of my ass, squeezing it.

He groaned with me when he slid a finger deeper, when he felt how wet I was. He knew how much I wanted this. Wanted him.

"Gods Olivia, you feel amazing. You're every reason, the only reason I would give it all up. Fuck the world—just for this."

His admission undid me. The feel of his finger pushing inside me, and his breath on my neck, the smell of him around me, the taste of him, this magic I felt in my veins that told my body it needed everything he was— I was thrown over the edge, spiralling into a climax that echoed through the caves, maybe through the mountain.

If this is what his finger could do, I couldn't imagine what it would feel like to have the rest of him. But feeling the size of him through his pants, I didn't know how he would fit.

I rode his hand, letting the ecstasy take me as far as it could, while he continued to run kisses down my neck.

When the pulling sensation eased, I rested my head back against the rock behind me. I waited for him to move, to pull my leg back up, to undo his pants, to drown himself in me as I was in him.

But he held me there, shadows moving behind his eyes and across his skin. He was trying to hide from me now?

His forehead rested on mine, and everything that felt like bliss began to sour. Would he not take more? Was he still holding back from me? Still afraid to do this?

I wanted to take over and push him to keep going. But I found my arms resting on his shoulders and holding myself there, wishing away the pain in his eyes.

Nothing about finding my release extinguished the pull or the need. It became a constant drive, bringing us together. I still felt as if I needed to devour everything that was him. But there was a wall between us, one I wished I could tear through. I thought maybe I had been figuring it out, learning about him and how he worked, what he allowed and what he didn't. But the lines were becoming so blurred.

Why allow me pleasure and not take any for himself?

CHAPTER
SIXTY-FOUR

I was wrapped in a towel, staring at the neatly folded outfit on the bed. It was made of spun gold, glittering with jewels and golden beads. A pair of matching slippers sat beside it. I would not be wearing it. I knew who had sent it up.

I searched the room for my clothing and found they were gone, as were the other gowns I had been given, confirming who had sent this dress. Even the one I had discarded before my bath was missing.

"Gold bitch," I muttered, happy to practice my cursing on her. She wanted to make a fool of me.

I lifted the first piece, two triangles of beads and jewels that would cover my breasts and nothing else. They were held together with a maze of straps.

The bottom was a similar beaded and jewelled belt. The very short, sparkling skirt would end at my hips. At least there was sheer panelling continuing down to my feet.

I had three options: don't go to dinner, go to dinner naked, or wear this outfit.

I didn't want to skip the dinner. That would be her win. I was stubborn enough that I didn't want to cower. Being naked wasn't a real option, so I grabbed the clothing and went to the bathing chamber.

Brekt had returned me to the room after the cave, unable to hide his concern. Even as he left me to get ready, he was quiet. His jacket, still soaking, was discarded by the door.

I had little confidence as it was. It didn't help he was unhappy after he touched me.

After cleaning up quickly and not so quickly figuring out how to get the top of the outfit on, I walked back out to the living area. I grabbed the slippers and sat in front of the fireplace, blowing the hair out of my face.

Where were my boots? I raced for the bed, looking under it and finding nothing. I ran to the bathroom. No boots there, either.

They must have been taken with the clothes.

I stared out the window toward the city I had not yet seen. Those boots were the last piece of home I had. With them gone, there was no longer any evidence of my life from before.

I felt something break, a crack in my determination. It was not Stephen and his relation to my boots—it was knowing there was no going back to a time before. As if twenty-five years never existed. I was here for good. If the Oracle was to be believed, I might never see my home again.

After the Aspis woke, I was starting a new life, finding a new path.

A knock on the main door startled me from my thoughts. A young girl, golden as the others in the palace, arrived to announce she was collecting me for dinner.

I peeked past the door, into the empty hall.

"What about the Guards?" I asked. I had never gone out on my own since the attack on Bellum, and now, more so than before, I could find myself in danger.

"The Guards were already escorted down. Master Nuo had me come to collect you, to bring you down as well." Her voice was sweet and innocent. Was I worried this young girl would be a threat?

My shoulders relaxed as I closed the large door behind me. If she thought my outfit was bare, she didn't say. She only led me down the hall to dinner.

It took time to navigate the levels of the palace to the main entrance. I spotted the stairs descending to the Guardian City outside. The girl turned, taking us down another long hall. A set of tall golden doors stood open at the end of it.

Before we reached the doors, a man waiting outside the room stopped us.

"I am to escort you to the room on your right," he said to me.

Without questioning the orders, the young girl bowed and walked away, leaving me with someone new.

"I am to join the dinner," I informed him, pointing to the open doors.

A glow came from fire-lit torches and candles, which sat on a long table in the centre of the dining room. The table was filled with people talking, their voices echoing against the cathedral-like ceiling. At the head of the table, the Governor was speaking to another golden man at his side.

Before I could spot the Guards, the door to my right opened, and a woman stepped out. I stifled a gasp at her appearance.

She was heavily tattooed, which was no different than most in this city, but her tattoos were all black scales covering her entire body. Her eyes were the colour of fresh spring grass with vertical pupils—like a snake.

She wore black clothing, covering just as little as mine did and shaped in the same manner, making me wonder if I was dressed to match.

Her long black fingernails pointed at the man when she spoke, and I noticed her tongue was forked.

"Thank you for bringing her. You may go," she ordered in a rich, husky voice.

He nodded and headed for the main room, disappearing from sight.

The terrifying snake woman scrutinized me. I tried not to stare, so I tucked a strand of hair behind my ears.

"I was informed that Master Nuo's entertainment would join us tonight." Her tone was flat, making it hard to tell what she thought about that.

"May I ask who you are?"

"We are the other entertainment," she said with a humourless smile. "Isn't that obvious?"

She moved from the door and into the room she'd emerged from. I looked to the dining table once more—the voices from the conversation reached me, but I didn't pick up any I knew.

I followed the woman inside, afraid of what I would find.

I was met with several more snake women. The only way I could tell them apart was the length of the night-black hair and the different colours of their snake-like eyes.

Some god's version of dark humour was using me for a laugh— I had claimed that coming to this city was entering a snake pit. Here it was.

Another woman with sky-blue eyes, sitting on the coziest chair I had ever seen, tilted her head toward me.

"You are Olivia? We were told to keep you company until we were called in."

"Yes. Nice to meet you. Nuo told you to keep me company?" I couldn't imagine he would send me in here alone.

She tittered, as did a few of the others.

"I didn't understand why the Guard requested his own entertainment, but maybe I was wrong before about his interests. I didn't think he liked simple and meek."

Another woman, who was in front of a mirror adding gold paint to her cheeks, twisted in her seat. "You also are very bare skinned. I don't see one mark on you. What legacy are you?"

I was not prepared to be on my own in this world. I didn't even have a made-up story to tell.

"I keep that to myself," I said confidently, unaware any bravery had followed me into this room. "I also am not shy and meek. I was only unprepared. I thought I would be going straight to the dinner."

Several girls laughed. The first woman, Green Eyes, spoke again.

"With this table, you will not be given the honour to dine with the Guards. We will be going in when the food has been eaten, and the conversation of politics has started to bore them. The favourite whore of the Guards will not be treated any better than the favourites of the Guardian City."

I was surprised the Guards would let me join dinner yet not sit with them. But of course, they were not responsible for this situation. I wondered if Nuo was still waiting for me to be delivered from my room.

"Is that who you are?" I asked. "I don't mean to offend you. Only this is my first visit to the city."

Her eyes bore into mine. "You are a strange one, I'll admit, but every man has his tastes. I take no offence to who I am, and I speak for the rest, I'm sure. We have chosen to bear the marking of the Aspis. We are his strongest worshippers. Our lives are dedicated to those who aid him, and before the Guards arrived, our customers were the Guardians of this city and its council. Some of us even served the last generation of Guards."

Another woman with black eyes spoke to her companions. "Tonight will be even better now that we have the Guards to entertain. Especially the dark one. I hope to entertain him as long as he wishes."

She looked at me and pursed her lips. "I hope you aren't going to cause issues if Master Nuo wishes to give some of his attention away. It's only fair we all get a shot. We haven't yet been called on when these Guards are here. We are thrilled to serve the Guards who will fight beside our saviour."

I shook my head. "I don't plan to cause any trouble."

She seemed to accept my answer and went back to ignoring me.

"What am I expected to do, exactly?" I asked.

"Who on Arde trained you?" Blue Eyes crinkled her nose.

"No one, I ... took the job on myself."

I was walking into a room full of men and women who thought I was a whore, coming from a place where I wasn't allowed to be alone with a man. This would not end well.

"You will be expected to do as they ask, serve them, sit on their lap, tell them stories, sing for them." Her hand waved in the air. "Whatever they want."

Something horrible took root in the pit of my stomach. This whole thing had been orchestrated to embarrass me.

And I thought the worst part was going to be the dress.

I found a seat near the door and sat uncomfortably, waiting to be called into the main room. Where were Nuo and Brekt? Did they not notice I hadn't arrived?

"You there," the snake woman called, dusting herself with gold paint in front of the mirror, "Come here."

I awkwardly walked over. The woman had painted gold scales along her face and arms, mixed in with her tattooed black scales. She looked me up and down.

"You can't go out there like that. Sit here. I'll do your hair and add a bit of gold dust."

She motioned me to sit. Another woman joined her, and the two started putting my hair into knots and braids, lifting it off my neck and tying it up in an elaborate style. They added a gold chain that sat on the crown of my head and hung down the back of my hair. It jingled when I moved, sounding like little bells.

Like bells you would put on a pet.

Once they had my hair up, which was a strange sight for me to see, they worked on the gold dust. They ran a line down the tops of each arm, ran a band of it around my exposed midsection, and then got to work on my face. It felt like butterfly wings when they dusted it on my eyes.

I hardly recognized myself in the mirror when they were done. But I liked what I saw. The woman before me was beautiful, gold-dusted, with chains in her hair and bones in her ears. She was someone I wouldn't mind learning to live as.

"Thank you," I said, "It's lovely."

One of the women patted my shoulder.

"Now get up. I need the mirror."

I shuffled away and found my seat by the main door again.

A short time later, a man came to inform us we could begin to serve drinks. My heart pounded as I followed the women in, praying that one of the Guards would see me and get me out of this situation.

Instead, I found a gold pair of eyes on me. Falizha smiled at me with pride—she had won in the end. I was now the fool she had dressed me to play.

SIXTY-FIVE

F alizha walked toward me, swaying her hips. With a feline smile on her face, she linked an arm through mine, pulling me to her side.

"So glad I found you. I have a special job for you tonight. I hope Nuo won't mind. I somehow forgot to tell him I was borrowing you."

She pulled me toward the large doors to the low-lit dining hall.

The room was much larger than I had previously thought, with two other long tables full of Guardians. About fifty people sat along the length of the main table, with the Council seated at the head.

I scanned the main table for the Guards and found a familiar large, muscled arm covered in smoke and scales.

Brekt was sitting indolently, holding onto a glass of amber-coloured alcohol while his head rested on his other fist. I couldn't see his face, but he almost appeared to be asleep.

Nuo was still eating, talking to a Council member across the table. The members were easy to pick out in their gold attire, and I was loathe to find I was dressed in their colours. Kazhi and Bas were further down, talking with a golden man who resembled an older version of Bastane. His father, I presumed.

The candles cast a golden hue on the faces around the table. The smooth, black stone wall reflected the room back at me and I watched the snake women moving about. My own reflection was like a golden beacon standing out amongst the black sea of stone.

Falizha tugged my arm, pulling me off to the side of the room, where large pitchers sat on a wooden dresser. She grabbed a full one and passed it to me.

"You can serve us drinks while the other women entertain. The men like to watch how their movements worship the Aspis. Tonight they will worship the Guards. You may have drawn *one* of the Guard's attention, for whatever reason I can't fathom, but with your bare skin on display and no traits from your legacy, you just won't impress the Councilmen at this table. It's best you do the bare minimum tonight and not upset yourself with the disappointment. I'm sure Nuo will pay you to enter his bed another night. I tried getting you dressed for the part, but you're still ... lacking."

Falizha flicked the crystal earrings dangling from my ears and chuckled, seeing them.

"I guess the Guard doesn't pay *that* well."

She twirled and walked away, leaving me gaping after her. I realized too late that I should have dumped the pitcher over her head. That, at least, would announce to the Guards I was here.

I beelined for Brekt and Nuo, when Governor Ravin took notice of me in the room.

"You there. Bring me some more," he said, holding up his cup.

Falizha sat in the seat next to her father, eyes glinting with delight and tapped the top of her cup as well. I imagined myself grabbing her long ponytail and smashing her face against the table.

Every step I took was agony. Who's idea was this, to say that I was just a whore? What good did that do except get Falizha's attention? All to hide the real reason they brought me along.

I stopped and poured Falizha's glass. She was grinning, ignoring that I was even in the room.

The Governor was talking to a man who sat on his other side, and though he was speaking low, I could hear every word.

"We need to fix this situation fast before anyone in the city sees they're down there. It isn't a good image for the palace to have a bunch of homeless riffraff loitering in the caves. We can't very well put them out in shelters in the city. The public will demand why we haven't stopped this. If word got to *him*, I don't think we could talk our way out of that one."

I was pouring the Governor's glass when the man beside him, a tall and thin legacy of Day, whose hair was long down his back and more like honey than gold, nodded in agreement.

"If the people should take notice and ask questions, we can simply blame the Guards for not doing their job. It could work to our advantage, Governor. We could petition for a new set of Guards chosen. If they are not in the running, we could have a better say in the outcome."

My hands shook as I poured. A whistle came from down the table. A woman raised her glass toward me. I left the men, wondering how they could be so careless to talk like that in front of me and why Falizha would let them.

But when I caught the stares of those I passed, I remembered what I wore. They only saw me as *entertainment*. It made me feel sick.

I reached the woman, who sat a few chairs down from the man Nuo was talking to.

From this side of the table, I could see Nuo and Brekt. They both looked as if they wished they could be anywhere else. I finished pouring the drink, eyeing the two, pleading for one of them to see me.

Brekt was still slumped, swirling the liquid in his hand, ignoring the rest of the world.

One of the snake women walked up behind the two and put a hand on each of their shoulders. She ran her hand down their arms and leaned down to whisper.

I inhaled a sharp breath, and my grip on the pitcher tightened.

A feeling I wasn't used to, acidic and hateful, slid down my back. I watched the woman feeling her way along Brekt's arm.

Brekt's eyes rose as if he heard the breath I took. They widened when he realized I stood across from him. Only now did I see a seat next to him—empty. Fucking Falizha.

His glass stopped swirling, and his head raised from his fist. The snake woman misjudged him. Her hand moved from his arm to run down his chest and whisper into his ear.

But Brekt didn't move, didn't indicate that he even noticed she was there. His eyes were on me, and there was *fire* in them.

I lifted the pitcher and walked to the other side of the table.

I passed Kazhi and Bas. Kazhi's black eyes followed me. I knew she was concentrating on the room around her. How many secrets would she pick up in a crowd this big? How many could she hear at a time?

I reached Brekt just as Falizha spoke up.

"Nuo, doesn't your whore look lovely tonight?"

I froze behind Brekt's chair. I had almost made it.

Nuo followed Falizha's raised hand and found me standing there, pitcher raised, frozen. I swallowed as everyone at the table turned to watch me.

Nuo's chair slid back, and he put on one of his masks.

"Yes, she's quite lovely, as always. Come sit with us, have a bite." He gave me an apologetic smile as he patted his lap, and I gritted my teeth. Did he expect me to sit there in front of an entire table of people?

I stepped forward. The snake woman Brekt had ignored grabbed the pitcher from my hands and walked away, sneering.

I was between the chairs when Brekt's slid back. His hands came to my waist and pulled me down, so I landed on *his* lap rather than the one I was headed for.

He must have forgotten the warning to blend in.

"Time to share, Nuo," he announced, and the room paused to watch. It was quiet enough that I could hear the snake women's slippered steps.

Nuo raised his hands in the air. "We have the same taste. What can I say." And he went back to eating.

My heart was fighting its way from my chest. Brekt leaned forward, his mouth coming to my ear, sending a shiver down my back.

"Relax. They want to embarrass us, but we don't care what these people think, and we act as such."

I forced my heart to settle. A plate slid before me on the table. Nuo had arranged some fruit for me to eat. I picked up an orange-coloured slice and popped it into my mouth. A soft sweet, flavour soothed my anger as I chewed.

"I have finally decided. Out of all your gowns, this one is my favourite," Brekt teased.

His hand found my thigh, and his thumb began rubbing against the sheer fabric. I could feel the heat of it, easing the tension I felt, moving it somewhere deeper—somewhere much more pleasing.

"Where do you keep finding these outfits? They get smaller each time."

I blushed while finishing off the fruit in my hand. It surprised me how easily he could make me forget everything I was feeling.

"I'm pretty sure Falizha keeps leaving them for me."

A deep rumble came from his chest, and I could feel it against my back.

"This is the first time I can say I liked the woman."

I turned. Though his smile was easy, what was behind his eyes was anything but. He burned just as I did.

"You must be quite drunk," I said, "To say such a thing."

"Not drunk enough to put up with this dinner. But I'm glad I'm sober enough to see you in this outfit. You're beautiful."

I shied away, embarrassed at the comment. It was the first time he had said those words to me. It was the first time I had ever heard them and felt that way.

His hand found my chin and brought my face back around.

"I'm jealous of every person here that gets to lay eyes on you when you're dressed like this."

"Jealous? Of them?" I glanced around the room. No one was looking in my direction.

"Would you see me differently if I said I wanted to stab all their eyes out?"

"No, I think that perfectly aligns with how I see you," I laughed, and the smile he returned warmed my heart. "Just promise me you'll start with Falizha's."

His arm came around my waist, pulling me tighter so I was flush with his chest. I rested my head against his shoulder as he whispered, "I promise. But only after she's done giving you a full wardrobe."

The dinner continued outside our private bubble. Snakes and venom surrounded us, but for all I cared, they would never sink their teeth in. Today had been perfect—the caves and now this. It should feel inappropriate how I splayed across his lap, but I only felt content.

I should have known one of the snakes would ruin it.

The Governor spoke, grabbing everyone's attention, including, reluctantly, my own.

"I noticed, Erebrekt, you weren't wearing your jacket this evening. Is your attire not to your liking? What else does the Council offer that you turn away."

Brekt didn't move to address Governor Ravin. He continued to lean back in his chair. The arm that was not around my waist lay on the armrest as he tilted his head toward the end of the table.

Falizha was eyeing me suspiciously.

"The jacket is perfectly fine, Governor, only that it got wet."

His arm tightened around me, making me go wild, remembering how it got wet and what happened soon after.

"I would have worn a second jacket, but I was given just the one. I didn't think it mattered all that much. The jacket doesn't make the Guard, Governor."

Ravin glared down the table at him, unblinking. But it was the thin man that spoke next.

"You're absolutely right, Erebrekt. Rising the Aspis is what makes the Guard, which you have yet to do."

Brekt tensed below me. His hand moved from my waist to my hip, holding me in place as he spoke to the thin man.

"Of course, Councillor Filos. But when we do, which will be soon, I don't think the creature will care if my jacket is on or not."

The tone in which Brekt spoke was a borderline insult. I held back my delight when the faces of the gold men and women at the end of the table turned sour.

The Governor's lip curled, and he snapped his fingers toward one of the snake women, pulling her toward him and onto his lap.

She draped herself around his shoulders and began to pet him as he spoke to the Councillor at his side.

Falizha's attention stayed on me, and I returned to my plate, taking Brekt's advice to ignore her.

"We need to get out of this dinner," Brekt said quietly.

Nuo's head tilted in our direction, nodding. And to piss Falizha off further, he poured me a glass and passed me some more food. It shouldn't feel so good to shove it in her face, but it did.

The council members' conversation began to slur, and the Governor's laugh grew louder, drawing more attention to himself than was necessary.

The snake women were all finding laps to sit on, and the lighting dimmed as the atmosphere changed. The other tables full of Guardians were emptying, a few staying to enjoy the snake ladies.

"Nuo, I think it's time you take your whore back to your room and do with her what you will."

I jumped. Falizha stood right behind us, leaning her arm against Brekt's chair. Her smile was for me, and it disappeared as her eyes landed on Brekt's hand that was against my thigh, holding me to him.

"Are you excusing me, Falizha?" Nuo laughed, "I don't believe you hold that power over me."

"Your choice. You know how the party continues from here."

Half of the occupants had emptied the main table. Some had moved to private sitting areas along the wall I hadn't noticed before. The snake women sat in the men's laps, their hands more exploring.

"If you wish to share your whore amongst the group, as I hear they like to do, you may stay. I, myself, am leaving."

A golden arm reached across the table, and Falizha set down a coin in front of me.

"I see the Guards have to share you to keep you paid enough to follow them. I wanted to offer payment in thanks for serving the table."

I would kill her. She was sauntering away, satisfied she'd won tonight, but then stopped. Her body went ramrod straight, as did the others at the table, all focused on the main door.

A bright light shined in from the hall. A very bright light.

Brekt and Nuo, in unison, moved a hand to a weapon. Nuo had a sword on his hip, and Brekt had a knife on his thigh. They watched the door, waiting. The light pouring in from the hall grew brighter by the second.

A humming sounded through the air, and if no one else heard it as I did, they must have felt it. Others winced. Council members who had sat proudly now cowered. The light in the hall reflected against the black walls of the dining room, blinding me.

"Liv, get up now. Go stand with the other women."

Brekt forced me to stand. The snake women ran to the dresser lined with water pitchers. They huddled together, watching the door.

I sensed the threat without understanding. I joined the women. One pulled me in, linking her arm through mine. Her camaraderie was a welcome relief.

Guardians at the table raised a hand to cover their eyes as a being, bathed in golden light, entered the room. It was over ten feet tall, lithe like a dancer and glowing from the magic that hummed from its very core.

Rem, the god of Day, stood at the door, surveying the room.

CHAPTER
SIXTY-SIX

The magic pouring off Rem was numbing. My ears hurt from the vibrations rocking my head, and an intense force pressed down on my chest.

"Do you feel that?" I whispered to the snake woman.

"Feel what?" she hissed. The arm that was linked through mine was shaking in fear.

"Nothing. Should we be worried?" I grit my teeth, fighting back the headache threatening to form.

"Only if he is upset. He may be displeased with the Governor. I've seen him here once before, during a private dinner, unhappy with the Council."

The Guards said the gods were hardly ever seen. Now one was here. The fear was visible as some bowed hastily while others hid behind chairs.

Governor Ravin left his chair to get down on one knee, springing others into action. The woman beside me pulled me down with trembling hands.

I found Kazhi down the table and out of her seat. Several Guardians behind their chairs separated us. She wore a pained look, feeling the effects as I did. We could both sense magic.

"Rise, my children. You honour me," Rem's voice boomed around the room.

Ravin squared his shoulders, standing before the god.

Nuo drew my attention, just out of reach in front of me. He was watching Rem as if confused.

I squinted against the light coming off the god. Rem's short-cropped hair blew in an invisible breeze. His face was so different from his children's, his eyes too wide, and although his iris was as gold as any Day-leg, there were no whites—they were the midnight sky, swirling with constellations.

Nuo turned to me, but I couldn't understand the question in his eyes.

Rem's glow continued to blind me. His movements were hard to track—fluid, quick and inhuman. The humming from his magic pierced my chest, causing my heart to stumble and skip a beat.

"Ravin, I have sensed the Ikhor's return. It has begun to ravage these lands, causing harm to the children of the gods."

His voice echoed off the ceiling, layered as if many men were speaking at once.

My head whipped to Nuo, who was still watching me. He noticed when I understood. He had pieced it together before I had.

Rem—golden light, many voices, carrying the most potent magic in this world. Was Rem the light that stole me from my lands?

Had he been trying to help us all along?

The Governor was babbling, telling Rem how honoured he was, how the Council was doing everything in their power. Rem lifted a hand to stop him.

His symmetrical and terrifyingly beautiful face turned to take in the others who sat at the table past Ravin.

"Ah, the chosen Guards," the many voices said. "Why do you sit here idle?"

Bastane stood from where he had been bowing on the floor, a seat behind Kazhi.

"Your majesty," he said, "It is an honour to meet you. Allow me to introduce myself. I am one of the Guards of the Aspis, your son and loyal servant, Bastane Armel. We have come to the city to receive an airship to aid us in flying with the beast when it wakes. We plan to stay only to gather supplies."

"The world burns, my child. It pains me. The suffering."

Bastane continued to explain to Rem the Guards' plans while I fought to control my reaction to the magic. Was Rem responsible for the magic now living inside me, or was it something else? Why did it react so violently to him?

A hand wrapped around my wrist. My attention snapped to Kazhi's pained face. She had wound through the bowed Guardians to reach me.

"Shut it down, Olivia," she warned, once again grabbing hold of my glowing bracelet. "I can feel you pulsing almost as much as the god. Your damn earrings are glowing too."

She winced and grabbed her head. I found that place inside— my box—carved with the names of the Keepers, the name of my sister who abandoned me. Now, I shoved the magic pulsating inside me down with it all. Only it was past full. It was more difficult than any time before to shut it off. The emotion and the pain were too much.

"Concentrate on something good," Kazhi said in my ear. "Don't let him sense you. I need to leave you here. I need to leave this room. I do not want the god's attention any more than you do."

She snuck away, disappearing behind Guardians and out of sight faster than I could track. I leaned against the wall behind me and focused on what she said. Think of something good.

I thought of Brekt. I thought of all the moments he had shared with me on our journey. I thought of his touch and when he called me *love*. It wasn't an admission, but it was close enough.

I settled the raging storm inside me. The vibrations in the room and Rem's echoing voice no longer affected me as they had moments ago. I focused ahead to find Falizha watching me, her eyes narrowed.

"I wish to see the survivors, Governor," boomed Rem, though

he spoke calmly with raised palms. "I wish to be accompanied by the Guards."

Rem's gaze fixed on Brekt and Nuo, who stood near the table steps away from me. "I have heard of you, Erebrekt of the North. My monks have brought back stories from their travels of your great skills. And Nuo, your brother and fellow Guard." He scanned each, assessing. "It has been an age since the last son of Night stood before me with the honour of calling himself Guard. Your parents must be proud?"

"They are no longer here to see this day," Brekt bowed stiffly.

"Unfortunate. I should have liked to of known more of my late brother's children. Ravin had discussed your betrothal to his daughter, my favoured Falizha."

My chest seized, and not from the magic. Could Rem be an ally if he favoured *her*?

"It is a great honour, do you not think, to be given a union such as this? Come Erebrekt, join Falizha and myself below the city. Let us walk. I would like to offer a blessing to this union. A gods blessing is no small thing. It will guarantee a good match and wash away any doubts you may have had about mixing the bloodlines. Those blessed by me after birth are strong individuals. Falizha is a prize match."

Falizha's face lit with pride. I wanted to wipe the smirk from her face. "Child, take the Guard here to discuss plans for an airship. We must hurry now. Evil things are lurking outside your door. My brethren and I have given you the beast to defeat this evil, but you must aid it. Until the evil of man is no longer a sickness of this world."

Brekt didn't move. It was Nuo who made the mistake of looking over my way, causing the glowing being to shift his head toward me. I stood frozen as his depthless eyes held mine. The god's body followed, turning to face me as his lips slowly lifted into a curious smile. But he did not approach. He did not address me.

Do not speak of where you are from, even if it's the gods asking.

The Oracle's warning had been real. She saw that Rem would be here before me. I bowed my head, hoping with all my might he would not ask. But if I was right, did he not already know?

"Come." Although his gaze remained on me, he lifted his hand to Brekt. "Let us bring peace of mind to the people. Guard Bastane. Join us as well."

Brekt still did not turn my way. He moved away from Nuo, who was left gaping. Falizha, Ravin, Bastane and a few council members followed the god as he moved to leave.

Rem did not look back. He only led the group out the door toward the caves. At the door, Falizha glanced my way as she linked arms with Brekt before passing the threshold.

Only when Rem's vibrant light began to fade did I notice Nuo was before me with his hands on my shoulders.

A scream was stuck in my chest. Why had the Governor not asked Rem to do something to help the people? He could find the Ikhor and take the magic back. But instead, he spoke of unions and blessings.

If Rem brought me here, why was he not helping now?

Nuo put his arm around my shoulder to hold me in place. I had to fight back tears.

Jealousy was a strange thing—it had little to do with common sense and everything to do with unmanageable emotions. I had just seen an actual god, had his thunderous gaze on me, yet all I could think of was his promise to bless a union between Falizha and the man I was falling in love with.

CHAPTER

SIXTY-SEVEN

The palace was a blur as Nuo walked me back to the room, tears streaming endlessly down my face.

Within one dinner, Falizha was able to embarrass me, insult me, pull Brekt away and leave me powerless. Not to mention a *god* just showed up.

"We need to talk, Liv."

Nuo's voice was a crescendo against the soft thudding of our footsteps.

"You saw it too," he said, not waiting for a reply, "Rem fit the description. I think we've found the answer to how you got here."

"I don't think it was him." My voice was hoarse.

"Why? Everything fit. The golden light, the many voices, and only a god would have that kind of magic to bring you here."

Nuo stopped me, pulling on my arm and forcing me to face him. I raised my head, hoping to find comfort in my friend.

"We should go talk to him, B. Ask him. Maybe he can explain how you're to help wake the Aspis and why. Rem could help us solve everything."

"No, Nuo. I don't want him asking me any questions," I lowered my voice to a whisper, "I don't trust him."

Nuo glanced behind me, then to the other side of the hall. He

539

leaned toward me, lowering his voice as well. "Be careful what you say out loud. Especially here. Never speak badly about a god."

"Nuo, the Oracle warned me never to reveal my homeland to a god. She said to hold onto my secrets. Why would she say that if it was a god that brought me here? I think she saw me meeting Rem. Plus, how can you trust anyone that favours Falizha? He has to be nuts."

Nuo forced a hand over my mouth and took another look down the hall.

He was being paranoid. If anything, it was Kazhi listening, and she instructed me as much as the Oracle to keep my secrets.

I pushed his arm away. "I don't care, Nuo. I don't feel like talking to a god or worrying about the Light right now."

"Liv," he began.

"Falizha took my power away from me, Nuo!" I shouted, and he pulled back to watch me.

"I let her walk all over me and humiliate me," I cried, "then she drove the dagger home by taking something I cared about."

I believed Brekt would do nothing, but that wouldn't stop Falizha from trying, and now a god was getting involved. Why would Rem care about such things?

"I want to sit down. I need to think," I said.

Things were spiralling. What the Oracle said was coming true —the appearance of Rem solidified her claims. I had to hide where I was from. I had to hide that I could sense magic.

Then there was the possibility that I would fail and doom the world.

Falizha was curating the dread festering within me. I was losing power—a power I was beginning to sense growing inside me. How did I battle someone like her?

I was stuffing down so much emotion I could hardly acknowledge that something was there, that I was becoming ... more. And thinking I *could* be something more didn't mean I was. Or ever would be.

Nuo led me into his room, a mirrored version of Brekt's. He led me to the fireplace and motioned for me to sit, but I shook my head and began pacing in an attempt to rid myself of the knots forming in my chest.

"He's not going to do anything, B. But you know he had to go with them. We need the supplies, and to deny a god? Suicide. Even if we have never met one, we know that's true. It's not ideal, but it's the situation we are in."

"This whole situation is wrong, Nuo. Rem could force Brekt to marry her. And for what gain? Are you not questioning all this? Why did he come here? For some survivors? Why did he not stop the Ikhor?"

"The Ikhor is our punishment—"

"Oh, stop it," I interrupted. "You're smarter than that. You sound like Bas. You don't need the Council. You four are too powerful to rely on these people. They're horrible. They are exactly what I was running from before I was brought here. How can they be the ones running the Guardians? How can a god, who is good and benevolent, be visiting them for dinners and favouring *her*."

He watched me intently as I moved about the room, trying to control myself and failing. He didn't bother to silence me this time when I was insulting their god. It felt too coincidental that Rem showed up here when we all arrived. The look he had given me ...

I wiped my eyes, fingers coming away gold from the dust painted on my face. The tears wouldn't stop. Ever since the library and the stupid book with the Guards' names dating back thousands of years, this crushing weight was always present.

It was like being in an open field with no trees, no clouds, nothing as far as I could see. I was open game to anything that wanted to fall from the sky and crush me. The future was careening for me, and nothing blocked its way. I just stood there helpless.

I was still the girl who had sat by the river doing nothing while waiting for Death.

"I still think it's worth talking to Rem," Nuo argued, "He is not like the Council. It's known that he is good to the people. He can help us. The Oracle speaks in riddles. Her warnings are from images she can't understand."

"Other things she said are starting to make sense, though."

"Like what? You didn't say what she warned you of."

I stopped, frowning, hoping he saw the apology on my face, "I can't tell you. She told me, warned me, to keep things to myself. After seeing Rem today, I'm inclined to follow those instructions."

"You're keeping secrets?" His expression hardened, his voice going soft.

"She warned me to keep things to myself."

"I'm supposed to be your friend, Liv. Friends don't hide things from each other. That breaks trust."

"I'm scared, Nuo. Keeping to myself helped me survive for long enough."

"You got caught in the end." His tone was frightening. Nuo was showing me a face he often hid. One he'd never levelled me with before.

"I got caught because the person who should have loved me the most betrayed me! And now you are asking me to give away my secrets again! I've learned my lesson, and I'm heeding the Oracle's warning."

"I'm not your enemy, Liv. I'm trying to help."

"I know. I know!" I threw my hands up in the air. "I feel as I did before the Keepers came for me. But I will not go to the god."

I bit my lip, holding myself. He wasn't getting it. My tears were not about finding answers or Rem.

"Falizha paid me, Nuo. Like I was nothing. Like I was below her. I can't stand the feeling of someone trying to control me like that. They were all like that. Everyone always told me what to do and who to be. They tormented me when I was different. I had to hide everything about myself just to *live,* which didn't even work! I was still given to the Keepers."

I left a trail on the carpet. Over and over, I walked the same line across his room. Nuo leaned against the back of a chair, folded his arms and watched me with a concerned expression.

"I thought I was away from it all," I went on, "I thought I was changing. I thought I was stronger, but I'm not. I'm still *her*."

His face changed. He dropped his arms and walked toward me.

"I'm still *her*," I cried and let myself crumple as Nuo wrapped his arms around me, patting my head. "Finding out who brought me here will change *nothing*."

I buried my head in his chest and let my desperation pour out onto my friend.

"He'll be back in no time, don't worry. Things will be— They will get—" But he couldn't tell me things would be all right.

I pulled away from Nuo, and his hands came to my face. Concern was creasing his brow. His thumbs moved along my cheek to remove some of the tears.

The main door opened as he held me, and I turned, my face in Nuo's hands, to find Brekt staring at us. This moment was similar to how we embraced each other in the library. I could see when his eyes flashed that Brekt was thinking the same.

Nuo dropped his hands and cleared his throat.

Brekt took a step into the room, glaring at Nuo. The move was so predatory, so unnatural for how he usually acted around his brother. Nuo's hands went up in defence.

"I'm leaving. You two should talk. She needs to."

"I can see that, but maybe it's not me she's hoping to talk to?" Shadows formed around him as he shifted his attention to me.

The air left my lungs in disbelief.

"Why are you back so early? What of Rem?" Nuo asked carefully.

"I made an excuse to come get you. We need to head back down shortly. Unless you're busy." Brekt's voice was razor sharp.

Nuo shook his head and walked out, passing Brekt, "I'll wait for you above the caves." The door shut quietly behind him.

Brekt had been the one to go off with Falizha, yet I was the one getting this attitude? Not a chance I was putting up with that.

His attention travelled over me, taking in the gold smeared on my arms and face. I knew he noticed the gold on Nuo's shirt as he left. Next, it was the room. He was searching for something.

"What are you looking for?"

"Nothing." His eyes didn't stop wandering.

"I think you're checking to see if I was up to something. Might I remind you that *you're* the one who walked off with Falizha to be blessed together by a god!"

"I didn't walk off with her because I wanted to. I was forced, and I need something she has—the *Guards* need what she has. Perhaps just as you needed something that was in this room and not the one we share?"

"I am in this room because you left me there, embarrassed and humiliated, and it was Nuo who brought me back. You didn't even put up a fight when Rem suggested you marry her. Now you're accusing me of being up to something?"

"Were you?"

"It would be none of your business, would it?" I shouted.

His eyes were unblinking as he stalked toward me.

"Is it not my business, Liv?" he asked, his tone too soft.

"I'm not your woman. I can go where I like."

He halted, taken aback by my statement. His chin lowered, a wolfish smile formed, and the whites of his teeth flashed.

"Are you not?" He took another step toward me. "You let me kiss you like you're my woman. Touch you like you're my woman."

I gave a hollow laugh, and his smile faltered. His head shook, trying to hide the pain that was evident in the hard edge of his glare.

The guilt I felt was brief.

I stepped back, surprised at how quickly he was closing the distance between us, but the wall stopped my retreat.

A soft growl rumbled deep in his throat. I couldn't run. I was in this.

Being backed into a corner fuelled my argument. "I don't belong to you. You think you own me like that, that you can walk in here and check on me?"

"Own you? Don't tell me you believe belonging to someone means you no longer own yourself. I thought better of you."

I flinched, stung by the comment.

"Someone belonging to you," he continued, "means you can have them and own everything that you are with no walls up—you can confide in them, talk to them any way you want. Be with them the way you want. *Fuck* them the way you want because you know just how they like it."

I sucked in a breath. My back was tight against the cool stone wall, and I pressed my hands to it, holding myself together.

He was playing dirty. I prepared to lash back, but he wasn't done.

"Having a woman means I take care of what's mine when she needs it. You don't think I do that for you?"

"So you *do* think I'm yours," I sneered, "I—"

"Yes, I think you're mine!" Delicious heat cut through my anger at the claim. "What does it mean when you tell me all the things you don't tell anyone else? Touch me the way you do? This pull between us?"

I was dizzy from the frantic beating of my heart, watching him prowl closer.

"Is this because I haven't fucked you yet?" He stopped before me. The weight of his large, demanding presence was holding me against the wall. "Don't think I haven't wanted to *every fucking day* since I met you. I see the way you look back at me. I know you want it. I fucking want it too."

His hands came up to my sides, wrapping around me so easily. They were a hot iron band against my bare skin.

"Should I just do it then?" he said in a voice soft as silk and sharp as a blade, "Do you want me to bend you over one of these chairs and make it official? Will that make my claim more real to you?"

I slapped him hard across the face.

Pink stained his cheek, and although he was facing away, breathing heavily, I could tell he hadn't expected that.

Good.

He slowly turned his head, smiling. Only this time, it was lit with something other than anger.

"See? That's my girl, right there. Your walls are completely down around me. I bet you would have never done that back home."

My body was betraying me—I wanted to be angry, I tried to fight him, but the electricity cracking between us took over.

I didn't think before the words left me.

"So why is it you won't fuck me, Brekt?"

I held my bottom lip so he wouldn't see it trembling. He was bringing out the woman with no walls around him, just like he claimed. No, I would never have done or said any of these things back home.

Emotions I couldn't understand twirled behind his eyes.

"I can't— I can't explain it to you." His fingers reached up to touch my chin, but I pushed them away.

"Bullshit. You'd better god-damn-well explain *something*!"

"Because you will die!"

It echoed in the room around us.

"What? What does that mean?" Was he threatening me?

I needed to escape, but when I tried, I was stopped. He pushed a hand against the wall, blocking me in.

"I—I don't know how to say it. I don't ... I can't—" he swallowed, trying to look away again. I'd never seen him with so little control.

But I was done with this.

I pushed his chest. He didn't move an inch. I did it again— slamming both palms against him as hard as I could. We circled back to the jungle again, fighting as we had after the Oracle. Nothing had changed.

"Why does everything, everyone says, make no fucking sense? Ever?!"

"I dreamt of it, Liv," he said, eyes boring into me, trying to make me understand. I could see it from the shadows twisting his features.

Everything in me quieted.

"Dreamt of what?" I asked, scared of the answer—because I was pretty sure I already knew. "Of me dying?"

"Yes." The truth thundered, changing the atmosphere around us. "In the end, you die every time, after every godsdammed fucking dream. And it's not pretty."

"What do you mean in the end?"

The corners of his mouth lifted—masculine triumph with very little warmth.

"In the beginning, we are fucking in every amazing way you could think of. I knew, down in those caves today, what you would sound like moaning before I slid my fingers inside you. It's different every time—where we are and what you ask me to do. I especially enjoyed our dream by the fire."

His hands were at my waist again, fingers digging in tight. It set me on fire in so many different ways. I was burning from anger, blazing from embarrassment. I was ignited by the desire coursing through me at what he admitted.

"The number of times I've come in my sleep to the dreams of the wild fucking. In every position you can think of—" he closed his eyes as if conjuring those images, savouring them.

"So, you dream that you fuck me, then I die?" I said incredulously, not giving away the storm inside me.

His eyes shot open. "It's not only fucking—though I don't complain when it is. Some nights we make love. It's slow, tender, and you feel so fucking soft and warm in my arms. I've seen you in every light, Liv. Heard every sound I could make out of you."

"And yet you can't do it in real life?" I wanted to cry. I wanted to join him in those dreams and know what it felt like to be treated tenderly—to make *love*. How was I jealous of the woman in those dreams when it was me?

"Because after that, you get hurt. Every time. You begin to glow, and that glow becomes a flame. Your screams of pleasure turn to screams of pain as you're set on fire. Every time it ends the same, Liv—you die."

"Oh, now you're just being an idiot."

"Excuse me?"

"You'll stop my death by *not* fucking me?" I seethed. "You're trying to tell me I can be your woman *without* sleeping with you, but I can't live if I *do*. What kind of power do you think you wield? Do you think you control destiny? You think you have the only say here?"

If there was any love or concern in his eyes, it was gone now. He was joining me in burning anger.

"You think this has been easy for me? I've tried to resist you at every turn."

"Hah! Well, it seems easy to me." I turned my head away from him, unable to let him see how it hurt. "You've done your job. Guess I won't die now. How has that worked for other dreams you've had? You stopped those, did you?"

He grabbed my waist and pulled my body flush against him. I could feel how hard he was against my stomach.

I kept my face turned. He pressed into me further, and I swallowed a moan.

"You think I like this? Walking around like this with you around every corner I go? I would have left you at every stop we've made if I wasn't afraid that's where you would die."

Now it all made sense—what Bastane had questioned repeatedly, what I wondered myself—why had they bothered to drag me with them? They knew I didn't know how to find the Aspis or how to wake it. Brekt wanted to make sure he could be there to stop me from dying.

I had begun to think it was because I had a more critical role at the end of this.

"So you bring me along to protect me but won't sleep with me to protect me? This sounds like an endless circle."

He let go of my waist, and the missing heat felt like ice coating my skin. "It won't be forever. Let me figure this out. Let me figure out where this threat is coming from and stop it. Then I'll make love to you in every way that you can imagine."

All of my fight left me. This man—strong, brave and dangerously sexy when he was angry—was more caring and thoughtful than any had been toward me.

"But you forgot, you'll be gone, Brekt. We will never get that chance."

He closed his eyes, and I saw his whole body change as the fight left him, like a mountain towering over me, crumbling in a landslide.

"I care for you, Liv. More than I should after so little time. It's suffocating, the need to have you. But there's something stronger beneath that, and that feeling controls everything. I will not let you die. I will not hear those screams."

He put his forehead against mine, and although he was still, I thought the floor was falling from beneath me.

I had begun to think our attraction was just two lonely people connecting, but it never was—it had been driven by a feeling that he hadn't said out loud.

"Give me time. Nuo's trying to find answers. I will watch over you for as long as I can. I won't let this happen to you."

I wrapped my arms around his waist, leaning into him. His arms came around me, caging me from the world outside. Tears streamed down my face as reality sunk in. Every one of Brekt's dreams had come true.

He had seen me die, engulfed in flames. My suspicions about my role in this future were turning into truths I didn't want to admit.

He was looking for a way to prevent the very thing he was destined to do. I knew what would kill me with flames—the evil the Guards were running toward.

I would face the Ikhor, and then I would die.

CHAPTER

SIXTY-EIGHT

Brekt

"You're in rough shape." Nuo sipped on his drink, his eyebrows in the air.

Brekt set his glass down, savouring the feel of alcohol hitting his veins. They were seated at an unpopular, hole-in-the-wall bar overlooking the city. The sour drink and bland food didn't draw in a crowd, but the view was great, and the lack of customers was even better.

The city lights glowed in the distance. The dingy bar sat at the highest point in the district, so close to one of the city's waterfalls you could feel the mist in the air.

"What do you mean?" Brekt was confused.

"I asked you three times what you thought about Rem's visit, and you didn't hear me once." Nuo took another drink. "I know what's eating you up. I don't understand why you haven't told her yet."

"I'm going to."

"We are leaving the city. You need to tell her before we do."

Brekt's grip tightened on his glass. A nauseating feeling took root in his gut and nothing he did rid him of it. She knew how this would end for her. He had expected her anger but not her dismissal of the truth—as if she wasn't concerned about throwing caution to the wind.

Just to be with him.

She was a gift, one he received too late in his life.

Their visit with Rem had been brief, thankfully. Falizha distracted the god, bragging about the hard work she claimed to have put into helping the survivors. Rem forgot all about his promise to bless them. Bastane had been generous enough to stay on the Guards' behalf, saying he wanted to speak with Falizha anyways, giving Brekt and Nuo an escape.

"I think she suspects something," Nuo continued, talking of Liv.

Brekt found his brother watching him intently, chewing on his lip.

"What makes you say that?"

"She's keeping something from us. She admitted it to me earlier. I think she knows, but she wouldn't say."

"Hmm. Must eat at you that someone is keeping secrets," Brekt said sarcastically. Nuo had trust issues, it was no secret, yet he'd allowed Liv into his life and let her get close.

Brekt hoped Nuo was wrong—he hoped Liv had something else on her mind other than the truth he'd been hiding from her. If she weren't angry at him now, she would be soon.

"She's kept things from me before, for your sake," Nuo added. "This time, it feels like it's something else. She's afraid of me knowing. I don't like that."

Brekt dropped some coin on the table. He wished to walk the streets and experience a few more moments of peace. It was a quick reprieve from the chaos unfolding around them—and it was unfolding. He could feel it. Destiny was vibrating in the air, coming closer.

He walked slowly, wondering if this may be their last night like this, wishing he had Liv here as well. Tonight he didn't let it bother him that Guardians jumped out of his way or stared with curiosity at the most powerful warriors in Veydes.

Tomorrow he would walk with Liv, show her one more place she may never see again. Then the Guards would prepare for the final battle.

The Ikhor was coming, getting closer to the city.

"Falizha said that the newest survivors were from a town closer to the city than the last. I think it's closing in," Brekt warned.

Nuo nodded, watching the people out celebrating the night. "The Ikhor must know the Aspis is in the city. The hour has struck."

Brekt reached out and grabbed Nuo by the arm, halting him.

"I don't know if I properly thanked you for everything you've done over the years. Lately, you've been doing the same for Liv. Thank you for that as well."

Nuo turned away, "I will do it until the end," was all he said.

Neither wished to linger on conversations about the battle against the Ikhor. So they picked up where they left off, strolling down the street in quiet companionship.

Falizha had shown them the airship they would be given and had the numbers ready for the supplies they would need. Everything was in place. They only needed to face the Ikhor and wake the beast to bring about the final battle.

"Kazhi." Nuo stopped walking.

She was running toward them fast enough that Brekt knew something was wrong. When she reached them, she skidded to a halt, and Brekt had to grab her arms to steady her. She shrugged him off, uncomfortable as usual at being touched, and didn't wait to catch her breath.

"Something terrible has happened," she struggled to get out.

"What do you mean?" Brekt demanded.

"Bastane has betrayed us."

CHAPTER
SIXTY-NINE

Liv

I will watch over you for as long as I can. I won't let this happen to you.

When I returned to Brekt's room, there were no butterflies or anticipation. I would be alone in bed tonight. All I felt was hollow loneliness.

I sat before the fire, letting the dancing glow hypnotize me. I knew what I was now. I could feel it lurking beneath. Had the humming always been there? Inside the box where I kept all my unsavoury thoughts and feelings?

I'd believed this world was bringing me to life, that I was gaining my own power—it wasn't me at all.

It was a beast.

Why was my time in this world so short I wouldn't see more than a few cities? Why would I meet someone who sparked life in me and then never get to love them? It would all mean nothing in the end.

The dinner and my confrontation with Brekt had been over so fast that the night was still young. Instead of waiting, stewing in my anxiety, I decided to find Brekt and tell him I knew how to wake the Aspis. I just needed to face the Ikhor.

Rem had been the catalyst for me to accept what I had been feeling inside. What I had suspected lay dormant.

I understood why Brekt could change so quickly and *go dark*. How could you not when you knew horrible truths and kept secrets from everyone around you?

I found my old clothes—returned to the room while I was gone —and dressed mindlessly. I found my boots and felt no emotion toward them being returned. I slipped them on while staring but seeing none of the lush suite.

I left the room, shivering in my cloak though it was not cold, and walked down the hall, unsure if Brekt would still be in the caves. I passed the large windows between the Guards' suites and didn't bother to look outside. I didn't need to enjoy the view. The world was becoming colourless like it once was.

I walked down staircases and through halls, my pace slow and uncaring. If people passed me, I didn't recall.

Once, I wanted to be a hero the way that Brekt was. It was a heavy sadness to be everyone's hope, knowing you would fail. The Oracle warned me of it. Brekt's dreams confirmed it. I would die.

'*To descend here is to accept all that lies in darkness.*'

I stood under the archway going down to the caverns, reading Erabas's language for the children of Night—the cursed ones. The meaning meant nothing to me, yet it felt like I understood it somehow.

Something sparked inside me—a curiosity and a pull to the caves. I welcomed the slight tug after feeling so hollow.

I grabbed a torch from the wall and began my descent. The Governor kept the survivors down there to hide them, yet Rem had known. Nuo had warned me of how the gods could hear us. Had Rem heard Ravin's dirty secrets? Did he know how Ravin thought so little of the people here? Would the god punish the Governor?

The air felt different walking down the steps alone. The hair stood on the back of my neck. When I reached the cavern, everything seemed the same—survivors huddled along the wall, and hushed voices carried throughout the chamber. No glowing light from a god, no sign of the Guards—they must have moved on.

But it was different than before—the cave was smaller, pushing at me, and the air was harder to breathe. Perhaps the god was in another chamber, still affecting me.

A nagging slowed my descent above the dark lake. Perhaps after Brekt's warning, it was not wise to travel alone. But the cords were pulling me tight, driving me forward.

I reached the black sands of the lake and continued toward the pull, drawing me past the huddled people. Tents were now pitched, offering privacy, and food was being passed around. Rem must have scolded the Guardians and the Council about the conditions of the cave.

When I was here before, the pull had been stronger than usual. Brekt had to be deeper in. The pull became tighter still as I entered the second, but he was not there.

My footsteps echoed eerily in the empty cave as I crossed it. The river that passed through made little noise.

My heart lurched—could he be in one of the pools in the third cave? Images of him naked ignited my need. It quickly turned to ice when I pictured another woman there with him.

I found myself hurrying toward the last cavern, eager to see him and lessen the tension building in my chest. With the torch in hand, the dark tunnels were easy to navigate. I entered the third cavern, happy to have reached it without tripping.

Brekt wasn't in the last cavern either.

I rushed toward the river. The green glow from the cave worms and the echoing dampness made it an ethereal nightmare when, before, it had felt like an alluring dream.

Drip drip drip.

The familiar toll made me think of the god of Death.

The pull intensified, buzzing in my chest as I wandered around the pools. Not a humming like magic, but a current demanding I move toward it. I reached the river's end, where the black water floated into a tunnel. I raised the torch to the opening, greeted by nothing but darkness. On the other side of the river, several tunnels opened like dark mouths. The stalactites hung like fangs, ready to devour.

What would Brekt be doing down these tunnels? Was Nuo with him?

The black water moved like liquid night, a bottomless threat. The river was something I wasn't willing to try to swim. It was ghostly the way it moved, and I was afraid to even dip in a toe.

Footsteps sounded alongside the dripping.

I spun so fast that I nearly lost my balance, close to finding out how bottomless the black waters were.

Falizha stood behind me. Two Guardian men stood behind her and another out of sight. All golden, wearing signature black clothes. Each man held a magic torch, lighting the surrounding area in a blueish glow.

"Are you lost, Olivia?"

Her voice reminded me of the screeching birds made at night.

"You remember my name. Didn't think you had the decency in you."

She laughed like we were friends teasing each other. "Forgive me. I have been rude before now. I'm curious, though, what brings you to wander the caves alone? Where are your Guards?"

I paused at her choice of words. *Your Guards.* "They are not my Guards."

She tilted her head to the side, studying me. "You sure about that?"

Drip, Drip, Drip.

Her golden eyes made my skin crawl. A foreboding sensation warned me something was happening I couldn't yet see—that same feeling of standing alone in an open field where anything and everything could go wrong.

"What do you want? If this is just more games, I'll return to my room."

I didn't bother to try. The two men behind her watched my every move.

"I just spent the night thinking, after Brekt and I spent some time alone, about why four Guards—the Guards of the Aspis—are towing along a woman such as yourself. I really don't buy the story of you being a whore. Sorry, but you're not very good at it."

She crossed her arms in triumph as I fumbled for something to say. I could pretend I had no idea where she was going with this, but there was no denying—I wasn't a convincing whore.

"You see, they were meant to find and wake the Aspis. The Ikhor has risen, but the beast has not. I wondered why that is. Could they be stopping it somehow? Preventing the Beast from waking? Maybe because they've been enjoying it too much."

Ghostly fingers ran down my back. What she was saying couldn't be true. They couldn't stop the beast from rising, could they?

"And so I thought to myself," she continued, "Perhaps it's because the Ikhor is too far away. Maybe it needs to be close to the host of the Aspis to wake it."

The host. Did everyone know the beast lay dormant in a human body? Why had I assumed only the Guards knew? Things were going from bad to worse. The sky was now falling on that open field.

"That's a good theory. You should tell it to the Guards," I said, hoping she was just talking to be heard.

She smiled and turned. The two men parted to reveal the last Guardian I hadn't seen.

"Bas," I whispered. My stomach churned.

"First name basis. Must hurt," Falizha laughed.

"I'm sorry, Liv. The others weren't taking action. You saw the caves and how many are getting hurt."

"You went to *her*?" I couldn't believe it. Bastane was standing next to her as if they were friends. I was going to be sick.

"Brekt wasn't very helpful," Falizha added. "Not one for giving up information, that man. So instead, I turned to someone a little closer to me. Someone of my *own* legacy. The Armel family has always been loyal."

I didn't want to feel that hurt again, not after Rebeka. I had kept my secrets from Nuo. And yet it was Bastane who would betray me.

"Bastane was a bit more helpful on the subject, confirming a few suspicions I've had. You appeared a little pained next to the god of Day, like you could feel something responding to his magic. Inside you. I want to ask you one question, Olivia, and I want a thought-out and honest answer from you—why are you with the Guards?"

"They are helping me. I am—I was helping them." I made sure Bastane saw my hurt, quickly turning to anger as I spoke. Why was he even pretending to look sorry?

Not only had he betrayed me, but he'd betrayed the other Guards.

"Bastard."

He clenched his jaw. The box inside me rattled. It couldn't contain the emotions I was pressing down.

I didn't bother with the lie of being a whore, but I would not play along with her current theory. I would hold onto my secrets for as long as I could.

"I made a mistake sending Luli after you in those caves." Falizha walked around Bastane, touching his arm while he just stared at me. "Yes. Don't make that face, sweetie. It was me. But you seemed like a waste and a distraction. You see, this world is too full of watered-out bloodlines like yourself, so weak you can't even distinguish which god favoured you."

Bastane had the good sense to pretend to be disgusted with her. Liar. My grip on the torch tightened while my other hand balled into a fist, nails digging into my palm.

"A gold monk in Bellum was the one who approached me about a bare-skinned girl who claimed to be a child of Erabas," she finished.

Fuck. I'd made mistake after mistake.

That was why the monk's eyes went wide as I followed the Guards to the airship. He was telling Falizha about me, that I was a child of Night. But why?

"I was ready to send someone out to find you so I could deal with you then and there. I could hardly believe it when you boarded my ship with the Guards. But the monk was right. It didn't seem like any god had a claim on you—you didn't look like a child of Night to me. Maybe that means none wanted you. I wouldn't blame them—you are quite plain. If Luli had succeeded, no one would have missed you, Olivia, just like the rest of the bloodline blessed by Erabas. They are all but gone. Not many are left to get rid of."

Bastane took a step away from her. "What do you mean 'to get rid of'?"

"You've been the cause of them disappearing," I blurted. "Have you been murdering them?"

Falizha waved me off and rolled her eyes over at Bastane. She stopped next to one of the other golden men and linked her arm through his.

"Murder. What a harsh word. To answer your question, no. I have never murdered a cursed child." Her eyes sparkled with delight.

Never by her hands. She had others do her dirty work.

"Why?" I asked, knowing I would not get an answer.

"Falizha, what is all this about? What about the Guardian way? We protect the people," Bastane questioned.

She gave him a tiring look. "Erabas and his children are a plague to our world, and you should know that by now, Armel. Everyone does. It's their fault we are in this mess—why the Ikhor comes back every time. The child of Night was the one who stole the magic from the gods, and now we suffer for it."

Something hit me. "Kazhi was never sent to kill Brekt because he was going to be a Guard—it was because he was a legacy of Night."

"Olivia, I would never harm one who will deliver the Aspis to the Ikhor. Or was *supposed* to, anyway. But I do admit to wanting to remove you from the equation. I had thought you were a playful distraction. Now I believe I was so very wrong about you —you aren't just a useless child of Night on my list to dispose of."

Falizha stepped forward, her hands going wide as if to offer me help.

"I know what you are, Liv."

I couldn't retreat without falling into the river. "I don't know what you're talking about, and I need to leave now. Nuo is expecting me back." I lied, trying to move along the edge of the water.

"Nuo wouldn't help me either," Falizha sneered, "Always in a little snit as usual. Won't even hear me out. Bastane is the only one acting true to his station. I'm not here to harm you, Liv. I'm here to do what the Guards have been unable to achieve."

"What's that?" I held the torch tight, but it would be a useless weapon. Why didn't I strap on my swords before I left the room?

Falizha stepped closer. The smile on her face grew into a wicked thing. It was a promise and damnation.

"We are going to hand deliver you to the Ikhor. We will get you close to it, and I will be the one to wake the Aspis."

I stopped breathing. *Wake the Aspis.* The task set out for me that I refused to understand for so long. My building fear slammed home with a crushing force, freeing the suspicion, transforming the fear, and confirming all I dared not think—*I* was the Aspis.

I would wake it *within* me.

Brekt promised he would stop the future. Sorrow hung in Nuo's voice when he told me the host of the Aspis didn't come back after it fought the Ikhor—because they knew. They knew what would happen to me and hid it from me.

"Falizha," Bastane barked. "We discussed taking her to Rem. Not to the Ikhor. I didn't agree to this."

The rattling in my chest fought to be let loose as anger scorched my aching chest.

"We have a duty to our people, Armel, to get this done. Act like a child of Rem, not a Guard. We move. Tonight."

Bastane turned to me, and I spat at his feet. "Don't speak to me."

"Liv, you should've told us you suspected it was you. We could have avoided all this. We could've helped you."

"Help me?" I swung my torch forward, pointing it toward the bastard. The rattling in my chest became a pounding fist. I wanted to take that fist and shove it in his face. "What would you have done differently? You would have taken me to the Ikhor anyways!"

"I wouldn't have done it like this! Not without the others. I don't trust them now. You should've told us. Your actions divided us."

"I was a coward, okay? I don't want to die! You betrayed us *all*."

Bastane flinched. It hit him—he had not only betrayed his fellow Guards but was sentencing me to my death. He knew I would not come back from this. He wouldn't either.

None of that mattered now. What mattered was that the two other men finally moved, grabbing me by the arms.

I kicked at them, fighting to get free.

"Falizha—" Bastane began.

"Enough, Armel. I've received intel of fires several hours south of your family's farm. We fly there tonight."

A wet cloth was pressed against my mouth. What was going on? The cave spun, and Falizha's grin turned sideways. The cave turned sideways with it. Colours began to fade.

"Magycris is a wonderful thing," Falizha's muffled voice was closer to me, though she looked all wrong. "My alchemists in the palace have altered it into a potent drug. Amongst other things."

"What have you done to her?" Bastane sounded closer, too, though I could no longer make out the shape of him.

A wave of darkness crept over my consciousness. My muscles went slack.

Falizha had gained complete control.

And she was going to hand-deliver me to the Ikhor.

CHAPTER
SEVENTY

I woke to my head throbbing and my mouth dry. My hands and feet were tied, and a gag was in my mouth. Why was it so hard to concentrate?

A quiet, dimly lit room spun around me, it's familiar walls made of the rare ore.

The men had loaded me onto the very airship I hoped I would never return to. I was in the storage room where Nuo and I had stolen alcohol from Falizha and her crew.

I wanted to kill her. God—*gods*. It was sickening how often this happened—learning to hate someone so quickly. I hated her like I hated the Keepers.

Loathing crept into me like spiked vines around my heart. The years of built-up rage were struggling against my tenuous hold—it had a target in mind and would shred her to pieces.

I see suffering. I see death and shadows. And hate is in your heart. If you return home, it will mean your failure. If you should fail, look north for the darkness, not south.

Was this what the Oracle had seen? Would I fail because Bastane had betrayed me and separated me from the Guards?

The box I held inside was begging to be opened. I battled to contain it, but the lid shifted. The longer I sat curled in the dark, regaining control over my spinning head, the less of a hold I had on the anger. How could I have been so stupid to go down to the caves alone? I knew what Falizha was capable of, and I knew how little help I was to myself.

Falizha knew where the Ikhor was. I would face it soon. Alone.

Yet, I couldn't feel any part of me being strong enough to change into a black beast—one capable of defeating an evil being.

Falizha would only be placing a helpless girl before the Ikhor. It would probably laugh before it killed me.

No one would have missed you, Olivia, just like the rest of the bloodline blessed by Erabas.

When I left my small shack back home, I was a burden wiped clean from the people there. But here, I had found a place in the world. Two hearts had strings tied to mine. Brekt and Nuo, would they find me? What if I never saw them again? How long would they be alive to miss me?

Maybe the Guards didn't have to die this time. I could *do* something about it. If I was powerful, I could change the outcome.

I rubbed my cheek against my shoulder, attempting to get the gag out of my mouth. It slid down my chin, and I flexed my aching jaw. I struggled with my arms and legs next, trying to work on the fabric around my ankles.

How far could we have gotten in the short time I was unconscious? I had never asked how fast the ship could go. I didn't want to wait to find out.

Weapons and ropes hung from the walls. If I could get to those weapons …

A loud crash sounded from far away. The ship jerked violently, sending me slamming into a crate, swearing. It lurched again, throwing me against the wall. Pain coursed through every inch of my body.

Had the ship crashed?

I shoved my back against the wall, pushing with my feet to stand.

Legs still bound together, I hopped over to the wall of

weapons. Mid hop, the ship shook with a thunderous boom, and the ground moved out from under my feet. I fell against the wall, knocking weapons loose. They rained down, but luckily, none found my skin. A knife was now lying beside me. With it, I frantically worked the ties around my ankles and wrists.

I pocketed the knife and headed for the door.

It crashed open before I reached it.

Falizha stood before me. If she was surprised to see me untied, she didn't show it. She held a sword in front of her, much larger than the small knife I had stolen.

"Wonderful timing, Olivia. I was just coming to collect you. We've arrived." Her voice tolled like a clock striking the hour.

The pounding in my head grew as fear coursed through my body.

She had taken us to the Ikhor.

"Shouldn't you be protecting your crew?" I said, disgusted.

"That's precious. Did you think I would risk losing you? The world outside this ship can burn for all I care. I've worked hard all my life to get as far as I have today."

She flicked her sword, motioning me to move. She was going to herd me off this ship like cattle to the slaughter.

She stood back, letting me walk past her and out the door. Like a coward, I did as she asked—I let her herd me, fighting the urge to deck her in the face.

She held the sword to my back, leading me through the halls to the exit.

"I'm glad you're here to witness this, Olivia, though you won't remember a thing later. I hope you can appreciate the work I've put in for my god and my people."

"So you only care about the legacies of Day?" I asked. "I'm not surprised. You seem like a selfish, gold bitch."

A sharp point of a blade at my back silenced my satisfaction.

"Now, now, no need for name calling." A painful sting rose as she pressed the sword harder. "I care for my people. I follow instructions—collect crystals, horde weapons and ships, eliminate useless bloodlines and make a new world for the Children of Rem. Anyone who gets in the way, I eliminate them as well."

"You're as evil as the Ikhor."

My feet tripped as I struggled to comprehend the horror of my situation. I was walking toward the Ikhor.

"Us Day-legs are the strongest, you know. We have played the biggest roles in history. Aside from when the first child of Night doomed us all," Falizha said.

"Great to know I'll get a history lesson before my death."

"Don't be rude, Olivia. I'm letting you understand why you are here, doing as I say. The strongest families and the toughest bloodlines are Days. Our god cares for us more than the other gods, who are absent and indifferent. Rem is the only one who gives his attention to our world. And it would be a better place if only one legacy existed."

Falizha was planning to get rid of all other legacies. Not just Night, but the children of Mountain and Sea too.

"No more fighting," she went on. "Do you know what that would mean? When the Ikhor rises again, it wouldn't possess a deranged psychopath like the Aethar. With only the golden children left, we would have control of the magic, and we could return it to the gods. Rem and his children will end all this. We will return the kindness he's shown us."

My laugh echoed in the empty hall. "You think you would return the power? *You?* Who thinks she is part of a legacy more deserving? You make me sick, Falizha. You think you are better than others, yet it's you that causes suffering. No, they don't even suffer—they're just murdered." I couldn't believe her. "And your father? This is what he desires? He already has power."

Falizha pushed me onward. "He's not satisfied with running just the Guardians. He aims for the Council to run all of Veydes."

"People won't follow him. They will figure it out. They already don't trust the Council."

"I know," she said, "but when a society crumbles, they look for a leader. They won't care which one stands first."

"And you are the one who will make it crumble," I guessed.

"You have no idea the scope of these plans. This goes so much deeper than you can understand. We are changing the world. This isn't my plan, not even my father's. This goes back to before any of us were born."

"I could care less about your reasons or where the commands are coming from. You're following along with it. Your compliance is to blame. When your god realizes what you're doing, he won't be so kind to you anymore."

I felt her rage simmering behind me. Her sword touched my back, skimming the skin once more.

"Enough. You can't appreciate what I've accomplished. I'll do my job and deliver you to the Ikhor. You won't need to worry if my god will be pleased or not."

The point of the blade pressed into my spine. I winced at the pain.

"The Ikhor is really here?" I forced my voice to harden like steel. A laugh behind me was the only confirmation I got. It was all I needed.

If I fought Falizha now, I would lose—the Aspis wouldn't rise, and no champion would fight the Ikhor. I would be sending my friends to the Ikhor with no beast to aid them.

I never wished to be a saviour. For years, I just wanted to be strong enough to save myself. The thought of being a saviour—it just wasn't in me. No moral virtues came bravely to the surface, taking me to the battlefield. I wished to escape, to save myself. *How* could someone like that be the Aspis?

"I am glad you will die here today, Olivia. You've seen too much now. My father knows I'm weeding out the undesirables. He knows the number of ships and vehicles I've uncovered over the years and coveted away—I could have helped the Guards ten times over. He knows all the moves I've made to lure in the Ikhor and the Aspis. I control how this all plays out. That kind of information will not continue to live on."

"You could have saved all the villages the Ikhor burnt down? You could have brought the people to safety!"

"That the *Ikhor* burnt down?" she sang.

"*You* burnt them all down? Why?"

A cloaked figure with fair hair. It had been Falizha. The villager who had returned to the Oracle burned and barely alive had seen *her*.

"Not all of them. Blessed Day, I couldn't do all that. I timed it with the attacks by the Ikhor. Just a few villages to rid ourselves of useless legacies. They're Sea-legs anyways, not worth the crystals we need to run our ships for more important matters."

Something Brekt had once said rang a bell—*The Council mentioned that many of the villages burnt were either close to the Aethar borders or Sea-leg villages along the other coast. I don't understand the Ikhor's intent. Those are opposite sides of our continent.*

The Sea-leg villages were being set on fire by Falizha.

"Why do you dislike them so much? What have the Sea legacies done to you?"

"They aren't meant to be on land with us. The children of Night were not meant to roam the day. The children of Mountain are tolerable, but they'll have their time when they are no longer wanted."

"But you wanted to marry Brekt," I probed.

"I wanted him dead, not married to me. I would never let a cursed child tarnish my womb," she spat. "I didn't hire the attempts on his life, but I wouldn't have stopped it. And now, I will continue letting the fires spread and focus on more important things."

Something didn't add up. Falizha would love to play hero if it didn't cost her. She would love to brag how she had the most ships, flaunting her power, saving everyone—so why did she burn villages and not pretend she was saving them?

"You don't have enough crystals," I surmised. "You had the ships, but I'm guessing you didn't help because you couldn't run them." Her silence behind me confirmed it. "I imagine if the ships were running, you would have dangled them in the face of the Guards and bragged about how powerful you are. But you didn't want them to know you were only as powerful as the number of crystals in your pocket."

A smile spread across my face. She was riding the control her father wielded and on the assumptions of those she considered below her.

"No need to be a smart ass, Olivia. I'd advise you to keep that filthy mouth of yours closed. You don't need your tongue when you arrive before the Ikhor."

I tried to turn, but she kicked me behind the knees, forcing me to the ground. I landed on my ass, with Falizha above me.

"Why are you hoping so many will die?" I glared at her. "What is the end goal for you? It can't be about your god and having a world of only Day-legs. You won't be alive by the time that goal is achieved."

She grinned. She still held all the power.

"There is so much you don't see that you will never know. Lies run deep in our world."

Too many secrets run this world—they are the key to survival. They are also the reason nothing ever changes. The Alchemist in Bellum tried to warn me. Did he know about what was going on, of the things Falizha was doing?

"You know, I once read in our old texts that the Aspis only ever chose a child of Night for a host. The records are not public and are written in the language of Day. The hosts are never celebrated, but I know the ancient truth. Perhaps it's another reason, over time, everyone chose to hate them. The cursed child started this mess, and none of his ancestors could clean it up. It makes me wonder how you're a child of Night. You display none of the signs the others have."

"Sorry to disappoint."

She lifted her sword again and forced me up, pushing for me to keep going. "The Council hopes to start a war. One that will give them an excuse to unleash on the Aethar. You are helping me with that tonight. Many of the Aethar are here. My scouts warned me of the fires, saying they saw the hooded figure, the real one. They said there were hundreds of Aethar burning the fields, screaming for the Council to show themselves. I might have let slip that the Aspis would be on this particular field tonight and drew the hoard to me."

We approached the hatch. If I could catch her off guard and jump down first, it might give me the seconds I needed to run. I stood over the top of the ladder, readying for my escape, when Falizha shoved me.

I fell into the open air, landing hard in a field with a grunt, eating dirt. I scraped my palms on the short grass and rock, trying to stop my fall. I cursed myself for not seeing that coming.

Tears flooded my eyes, the pain almost too much for my already bruised and battered body. I couldn't take much more— the throbbing from the magic in the cloth, thrown into the airship and forced back out. My energy and power were being leeched from me.

I needed help. I needed strength.

This energy is an iron will. It surrounds you like the hardest metal and darkest storm ... It will carry itself with you, Liv, into your darkest days ... Do not rip away your shield. It will be all that can save you.

The Oracle said this power was always with me.

My mother—she would stay strong. She would get up and fight. I needed to use her strength if it really surrounded me. I needed to force myself to be the hero, if not for the people, then for myself.

The odds were not in my favour, but they weren't zero.

CHAPTER
SEVENTY-ONE

Falizha landed next to me with a thud. She pushed the flat of her boot against my shoulder, shoving me down, pushing my face into the dirt, and laughing.

"Get up," she ordered.

"That's enough, Falizha. We need her strength to wake the beast."

Great. Bastane was here too. I groaned, lifting my head and finally seeing him. He had been waiting under the airship for us.

Night surrounded us, but nothing about it was dark. I went cold inside, despite the heat clawing at my skin. The field was ablaze in a flickering orange glow as embers floated up to the sky above. I was about to face the Ikhor—the screaming that Brekt had seen would soon be soaking through the air like blood.

The heat was suffocating, pressing against my skin, scorching my lungs when I took a breath.

Cries of anger and the clashing of swords rang out from the fields. The battle was half hidden by the haze of heat and flame.

Black figures with tattoos fought against the scarred, burned faces of the Aethars. A killing cry shouted out with each blow that was struck. A song of death was being played.

"The Ikhor is here. It happens tonight," Falizha said to Bastane,

570

who was standing like a statue under the ship, avoiding eye contact with me.

"This isn't how we discussed it. You've brought us to a battle. We could have drawn the evil away from the hoard. Here, there could be massive casualties."

"Ever the purist, Armel. The lives at stake are of no value to us."

"Which lives are you referring to? There are Guardians here, not of your crew. How were the Guards not informed of this battle?"

The mention of the others fanned the rage of his betrayal.

"When they find out what you've done, Bastane, they will make you pay," I seethed. "You think Brekt will let you walk after taking me?"

"He will when I remind him what the goal is." He still avoided me. His golden hair reflected the orange glow of flames. Falizha moved behind me, raising her sword to my back once more.

"I didn't think a pair of tits could distract the cursed Guard," Falizha said. "Men are all the same. Idiots."

"Watch it," Bastane warned. "Remember who you are speaking of. Your station is not above ours."

"Whatever. You're stalling us. My report says the hooded creature walks the field, searching but not engaging in battle. It's the Ikhor. It was the same figure the hoard was following toward Bellum."

Falizha nudged me with one hand while still holding the blade with the other.

"You've seen the Ikhor?" Bastane asked as I stepped forward, away from the hatch. "What else have you kept from the Guards?"

"Anything I didn't trust you with. We are walking the field, and we will let the Ikhor find us. When the beast wakes, and everyone witnesses it was me that brought it forth, I will be given the title of a true Guard. I will help defeat the Ikhor right here on this battlefield."

"And whose name do you intend to erase in the history books?" Bastane growled. "One of my own?"

"I don't care which one. They will all fall tonight. And I will make sure my name is written in their stead. You can stand with me, or with them."

Bastane stopped us, moving in front of me. I cried out when the blade pierced a new area of my back.

"Don't pretend to be offended," I scolded him, "You're to blame for all of this. And here I thought you didn't tolerate monstrous behaviour toward women." I reminded him of the words he'd said to me soon after we had met.

He finally lowered his gaze, meeting mine for the first time since I was captured. He was a good actor, showing me remorse.

"This is the right thing to do," he said as if convincing himself as much as me. "The others forgot what was at stake. You knew from the beginning what this meant to us. You don't think I'm aware I'm going to die right next to you? This isn't about me, or power or glory. This is about my sister, my mother, my brother and his family. All the families that work for our farms. This is about the people who survive *after*. Take a look before you, Liv. This is what others were fighting while you and Brekt were distracted with each other."

I turned away, ashamed.

"What would you expect from such weak blood?" Falizha said.

"If I do become the Aspis, Falizha, I promise you with whatever is left of me; I will turn its power against you. You will not be a Guard. You do not get the honour my friends have. You will not leave this field tonight."

The lid on my box slipped a little more. Falizha's name was now engraved on its side—she would be all it knew.

"Spoken like a true beast, Olivia. You're a much more convincing monster than you are a whore."

She pushed me on. I had no choice but to walk. I shouldered past Bastane, ignoring him as he had me.

The field was a scene out of a nightmare. Aethar and Guardians were everywhere, taking each other to the ground. We moved around each battle, the grass slick with blood. Bastane deflected any Aethar that tried to take our small group on.

The heat of the fires stung my eyes. My skin burned, and sweat gathered at my brow. I was running out of time and had yet to find a way out of this.

The two Day-legs herding me were unhindered, impervious to the flames. It made me hate them all the more. Falizha's golden hair whipped around her by the scorching wind.

I frantically searched the field, hoping we didn't find the Ikhor. But with the intensity of battle and gore before me, I knew it was here. It had to be.

I stumbled around bodies and growing flames. We passed women from Falizha's crew fighting and falling on the battlefield, past the Aethars screaming as they cut down the Guardians.

An Aethar emerged from the flames and ran toward us with a sword held high. Bastane cut them down with one strike of his blade. Nausea clutched my gut, and I turned away from the burning corpse.

"This is your fault," Falizha muttered behind me, "look at the consequences, coward."

I wouldn't, though. The burning Aethar on the ground was there by the Ikhor's doing.

A thunderous shake of the earth knocked all three of us off our feet, and I landed once more on the hard, burnt earth. An explosion ripped the ground open not ten feet away.

Dirt flew through the air, raining down on my back as I ducked. I held my arms over my head, waiting for it to stop.

I swatted away embers burning through my cloak. The sting was unbearable from such tiny pieces. I couldn't imagine what it would feel like to die burning.

I didn't want to die that way.

Another large projectile, engulfed in flames, soared over our heads, colliding with Falizha's ship far behind us. The ship rocked sideways where it hovered and the glowing sails winked out as the magic faded before suddenly glowing again.

Was that the power of the Ikhor?

Bastane was already back on his feet, pulling Falizha up with him. Both Day-legs were distracted, watching the ship being attacked.

My heart kicked up, and I spun to flee.

"*Olivia*!" My name cut through the night, a roar more terrifying than the howling flames.

I spun, looking for the darkness in the burning field.

"Brekt," I cried out. "Brekt!" He was out there.

I glanced back to find Bastane next to Falizha, both going pale. The haze from the flames twisted their forms, distorting what was unfolding. Bastane let go of Falizha. She stumbled back as he lunged for me instead.

"You're in for it now," I shot at him as his grip tightened on my arm.

"I'll deal with him later." Bastane's eyes darted around the field, walking away from the echo of Brekt's voice.

I felt for the pull between us. Somewhere in the night, he was searching for me.

This bond with Brekt—would I feel it when I was the Aspis? Could it be enough to tether me to my human self?

Bastane pulled on my arm, steering me from the smoke and debris. The air around us cleared enough to reveal more bodies were piled up. The battle was escalating.

Falizha reached my side and pointed forward.

"Let's move this way, follow the dead. The Ikhor would leave no one living."

Further we went through the field. Further from where I'd heard Brekt's voice.

My chest burned, and the pain from the pull constricted more than it ever had. I bent over, the force of it leeching my strength.

Bastane let go, moving around in front of me. "Don't make me carry you, Liv."

There was a curse behind us. I spun to face darkness where before there had been fire.

"What—" Falizha began.

The night moved, inky and yet solid. But the blackness was not smoke this time.

A shadow twisted and took form, becoming whole as it shot toward us.

A terrified cry broke free from me as Brekt took shape.

But he wasn't aiming for me.

Brekt cut through the night and slammed into Bastane. One hand wrapped around his neck while the other fisted in his hair. He pulled Bas forward onto his toes, holding him a breath away.

"I could kill you for what you've done."

"Put him down, Erebrekt," Falizha ordered. Her eyes went wide as Nuo came through the night to stop before her.

"If Brekt doesn't kill you for the betrayal, I will," he said to Bastane. His eyes turned black against the flame, and they promised death.

Kazhi appeared next, stopping beside me.

"Are you hurt, Bones?" she asked.

I shook my head. "They didn't get a chance yet."

"You all are making a big mistake." Falizha stepped away from Nuo. "We are here to stop the Ikhor. Bastane told me of the message Olivia received. You all knew the whole time she could have stopped the Ikhor's path of destruction, yet you did nothing."

"We don't make rash decisions. We were figuring it out," Brekt snarled, his eyes never leaving Bastane.

"You'll forgive me once it wakes and we defeat the Ikhor," Falizha said.

"You don't even know how she'll help," Brekt spat.

"I do." Bastane was trying to stay on his feet, choking around Brekt's grip on his neck.

We formed a circle, one facing off with the other, divided. Where was the unified team, ready to face the Ikhor?

That's when I felt it—a vibration in the air. The wind spoke it to me, the call of destiny. The world went silent, only for me to appreciate the scene as it unfolded.

Brekt's attention landed on me, his face changing from burning anger to concern. He felt the change too, or perhaps he felt it within me.

The shift in the air—I was meant to be here. I was meant to be on this field.

I turned from the others. Before me, the field was bare of any conflict—the souls that once belonged to the bodies were already gone. Fires roared on both sides of me, but ahead was a cloud of black rising to the sky, blocking out the stars. Hiding the way forward or the way home.

The tingling sensation crept up my back—we were being watched.

The smoke shifted as a dark cloak materialized, lifting and floating through the night air. The smoke swirled as the figure glided toward us between the flames.

We all waited, watching, holding our breath.

Its movements were slow and deliberate, as if heeding the call. It was holding something, pointing its arm around the field.

The figure was taller than me, almost as tall as Nuo. A long, dark hood was drawn up. Long, flowing hair, so white it shone blue, flew around a face hidden in shadow.

I stepped closer to Kazhi, who had two knives in her hands.

The long hair reminded me of something—*someone*—I had seen before—the beautiful man on the streets of Bellum. The one whose legacy I couldn't pinpoint, who had blue skin with darker markings. He had disappeared down the street right before the Aethar attack.

I was worried I'd seen the Ikhor in Bellum. And I had.

Now the beautiful man stopped fifty feet across the field, far enough away that even Kazhi's blades wouldn't reach him. The heat of the fires cast him into a hazy mirage. His hood turned in our direction. His body followed, facing us.

I could *feel* his eyes find mine. Did he recognize me? Had he been looking for me back then as well?

I was shoved forward, and I cried out as I landed on my knees. A blade pressed against my throat.

"Don't make a move," Falizha warned all of us, including Brekt, who tried to catch me. The blade nicked my neck, and the sting told me she'd drawn blood.

The hooded figure took a step forward and paused, watching.

"Don't try me, Brekt. Or she will die sooner."

Nuo held out an arm, holding Brekt back, whispering something into his ear.

"Try all you like. This is ending now," Falizha yelled.

Bastane coughed and nodded toward the swirling darkness and the Ikhor before it.

The Ikhor's hood shifted to the Guards. He pocketed the object in his hand. Reaching over his shoulder, he pulled forward a bow-shaped weapon, held sideways with one hand, and pointed it directly at me.

The Guards tensed.

"Falizha, stop this. She doesn't know how to wake it," Nuo said.

"I have your beast, Ikhor," Falizha shouted to the beautiful man. "Look upon the face of who will bring you to your death."

Falizha grabbed the back of my head, fisting my hair and holding me still for the Ikhor.

"Hurry it up, Olivia. I don't have all day." She pulled tighter on my hair, making me cry out.

"The beast?" Brekt said. He was so close. Feet away.

I was glad I wouldn't see the disappointment on his face. I should have told him. My heart cracked in two as I waited for my death. Time stood still as the Ikhor aimed his strange weapon higher, likely going for my heart.

How far back did this all go—how much of my destiny was

controlled? Further back from the icy river where I nearly died? Back to when Rebeka betrayed me? My mother's death?

The Ikhor lifted his arm, aiming across the wide space of burning field between us, and took a step forward. But he halted as another figure stepped between us.

"Kazhi," I whispered.

She was looking at the field behind me. "We have more company," she said to the others.

I couldn't turn with Falizha's knife still at my throat. I only heard the scream of Aethar rushing our group and the clashing of swords as they met the other Guards.

"Olivia!" Brekt shouted, fighting back the enemy. "Kazhi, protect her."

"She will be safe," Kazhi promised, "take care of the hoard."

"Move out of the way, Kazhi," Falizha demanded, "I am ending this here. You had your chance and failed."

But Kazhi held her knives and didn't turn away. She focused on me, eyeing Falizha's blade at my throat, calculating.

Something wasn't right. Kazhi wasn't protecting me. She wasn't fighting Falizha. She was facing me, holding her weapons, her back to the enemy.

The fires around me turned ice-cold when I understood how deep the secrets went in this world.

She was not stopping the Ikhor.

Tonight was a night of many betrayals.

My friends fought behind me, trying to protect our group, unaware of how the danger was coming from all sides—even from within.

"You are pointing your weapons in the wrong direction, Guard. The Ikhor is behind you." Falizha raised her knife toward Kazhi and away from my neck.

Kazhi smiled at Falizha, showing her teeth and turned slowly to peer over her shoulder, stepping to the side. Facing the Ikhor but pointing her sword toward me, Kazhi yelled, "Her."

An arrow was released.

I waited for the pain, for the end—and hadn't I been waiting a lifetime? I was ready. I was prepared to meet Death—the cold-hearted son of a bitch.

But nothing happened.

"Oomph."

It was a sound the body makes—the lungs, the muscles, the soul—as it's struck with a killing blow.

The hand in my hair let go, and I spun to find Falizha, eyes wide, gaping down to her stomach. A thick bolt had sunk into her gut. Its tip was feathered and beautifully crafted—a strange thing to note in this situation. It had just missed my head, finding her directly behind me.

She stumbled back. Her hate-filled, gold eyes were filled with a million questions that would never be answered. If I wasn't shocked, I think I might have smiled.

"I don't understand. It should be trying to kill you. You should be transforming now," she said around a mouthful of pain and death. Blood began to pool at the edge of her lips.

I rose to my feet, spinning to find the hooded figure stalking forward again. Brekt and Nuo wouldn't reach me in time, too far in battle.

The Ikhor was closer now. But the transformation wasn't happening. *Something* was telling me this moment was critical—a warning sensation coursed through me, but it wasn't enough to raise the beast.

"Kazhi, you're helping the Ikhor? You brought it here?" I asked.

Kazhi shook her head, reptilian eyes burning with warning.

"That is not the Ikhor. Falizha was mistaken."

CHAPTER

SEVENTY-TWO

S till hooded, face hidden, the beautiful man now stood directly behind Kazhi, tying his weapon across his back. If he was not the Ikhor, then where was it?

Falizha drew a ragged breath from below, clutching her seeping wound and searching for a weapon. No one moved to help her.

Kazhi's scanned the field, watching her brothers disappear in battle, before facing me once more. "You need to go with her now, Bones. She will take you to safety. She will explain everything."

"She? She who?" I asked, confused. I looked down at Falizha, pulling the bolt from her gut with a grunt. "Why am I not going with you? With the other Guards?"

Brekt, Nuo and Bastane had pushed the Aethar back, taking the battle past flames and smoke. I was losing my only allies.

"I have a different mission. One that Falizha is in the way of. It wasn't the Aethar that started these fires. Something else has been plaguing Veydes. It's been leaking past the borders and taking its corruption into Aethar lands too."

"Falizha admitted it was her," I nodded. Falizha let out a wet, strangled cough below us.

"Falizha is a pawn. Now you know you can no longer trust

580

anyone. You must run, Bones. Get out of here. The boys must not see. You must leave."

"I don't understand, Kazhi. What mission?" I asked, then stopped. "How can I not trust Brekt? And Nuo?"

"They don't hold enough power to protect you. Go with her."

Who was she talking of? According to Kazhi, Falizha was a pawn. There was no one else.

"But—"

"It's the safest place for you, away from the Guardians. I know because I have been watching. Listening. Trust me, Liv," Kazhi said, nodding to the hooded figure. Kazhi had said *her*.

Pale hands lifted to the dark hood, uncovering the face of who I thought was the Ikhor—the beautiful man from Bellum. But when the hood was lowered, a female stared back at me.

Blue eyes collided with mine.

She was identical to the beautiful man, with the same dark blue markings covering every inch. Brekt hadn't known of a legacy with skin like this. And now there were two of them.

Something pulled tight around my waist, and my attention moved to Kazhi, who was securing my two swords.

"Trust her. She and her brother have been searching for you. She's followed us since Bellum, tracking your movements. The hoard mistook her movements, thinking *she* was the Ikhor. I found her before the Guardian City, following us in the jungle, and made a plan to bring you to her. I'm sorry Bastane beat me to it. We could have avoided this battle. I have to go now. I am still a Guard until the end of this."

"Then you should be staying with me, Kazhi. Not sending me with a stranger."

The blue woman looked me over as if wondering why I was the one she was stuck with.

"Kazhi," I whispered close to her, "Is she an Aethar?"

Kazhi pulled away from me slowly. She wasn't blinking. Her head went down once in a nod as if apprehensive of my reply.

Kazhi was never apprehensive, and that fact alone told me something here was very wrong.

The blue woman didn't have scars like the Aethar. I was told they all carved themselves up for the Ikhor. The Aethar I had met were vicious and cruel, quite unlike the quiet confidence from the man in Bellum, or this woman before me.

Kazhi wanted me to *follow an Aethar* and leave the Guards.

The ground shook, and another loud explosion sounded from the battle behind us.

"Cursed Night, those Southlanders are going to kill everyone," swore the blue woman. "I told them this is an extraction only." Her voice was soft and buttery, not at all what I expected.

"This is where I leave you, Bones. I need to find my brothers." Kazhi patted me on the shoulder. "Trust the woman." She nodded her head toward the girl.

Trust the woman. The Oracle's message.

Kazhi took off at a run into the flames toward the explosion. The sounds of battle rang out behind me. My friends and allies were all lost to the flames.

At least Falizha was dead. But I was proven wrong when below me, I found nothing but a pool of blood and a discarded bottle. *Magycris.*

"Fuck," I spat. A form limped in the distance toward the airship. The gold bitch was resilient if nothing else.

I clutched the hilt of my sword, facing the blue woman.

"Don't make a move," I warned, pulling my blade free, "I'm not going with you. I am returning to the Guards."

The Aethar had slaughtered Nuo's family. Though she didn't appear like the rest, Kazhi's confirmation was condemnation enough.

The blue woman took a step toward me, and I quickly moved back.

"Kazhi told you to follow me," she said, "I'll take you to safety. You're in danger here, and you know that."

"I'm not following an Aethar," I yelled.

"Why?" Her hands went to her hips. "You've followed one so far."

My grip on my sword tightened. "What Aethar do you think I've followed," I said slowly.

"The one who just saved you, who told me to shoot the golden Day-leg."

The ground was falling out from beneath me—only this time, it wasn't an explosion. My world was spinning out of control with one shocking truth after another.

"Kazhi is an Aethar?"

The woman nodded, looking at me like I was an idiot. "She's one of us. Did she not tell you?"

"No. No! She wants to help the Aspis."

She didn't have the scars. She hated them. She killed them.

"In a sense, yes. She's doing what I've been doing—trying to find a way to separate the Ikhor and the Aspis."

"But the Aspis is going to help the people by killing the Ikhor. We have to help the people."

"We are, trust me."

Trust the woman.

"No, you don't get it," I cried, "I need to stay. The Ikhor—" I searched the field. Nothing but smoke and flame.

"I have been following the patterns, tracking the power signals." She pulled a device out of her coat and tapped it with a finger. "I picked up a huge surge of magic less than a month ago. Knowing it had begun to wake."

That was around the time the Light had found me. I had assumed all wrong. I thought someone had brought me here using magic. I thought Rem, the golden being, was responsible for it.

The Light—it *was* the magic, the magic of the Aspis. It found me and brought me closer to the Ikhor and the Guards.

"I tracked the source of power to Bellum, only for all the Southlanders to show up, making me miss my chance. How they knew to go there, I can't say."

"They said they were following the Ikhor."

"Hmmm. That may have been my fault," she mused. "They got wind I was tracking the magic, wanting to grab it before they did. They've been following my ship ever since. I didn't realize they made it to Bellum until it was too late."

"You were the airship I saw, following Falizha's," I gasped. I had seen one. "The man in Bellum who looked like you, you know him?"

"My brother. We've been working for a while on this plan. The golden Day-legs of Veydes have gotten out of control. They are the reason for my people's suffering. They want to rid the world of every legacy, even some of their own. We worried when you entered the Guardian's ship."

I wanted to believe this woman was lying to me, but everything she was saying was the truth. She knew of what Falizha and the Council were up to.

"Why were you following us?"

"You have the magic. We need to get you out of here. I need you to come with me. My brother is waiting for us."

"The Ikhor is here!" I warned. The rest of the Guardians would be doomed if the Aspis didn't wake.

She turned to me, brows furrowed. What was I saying that was confusing her?

"Come with me," she urged, "I'll explain everything. The Southlanders are uncontrollable. I don't trust being around them. They'll get in the way."

"I'm not going with you." I stepped away.

Sweat was dripping down my back. The woman inched forward, closing the distance between us. "This is the first time in our known history we've been able to track the magic before the beast woke. We have a chance to change the future. We can stop this eternal war, end suffering, and unite our people again."

"After what your people have done?" I screamed. "You're murderers. You kill innocents! You sound like Falizha, wanting the Aspis for yourself."

"Don't be so naive."

"Your continent is a wasteland."

She blew out a frustrated breath. "I will keep you safe while we figure out how to stop the battle. We need you to change the future."

"I can't stop the battle."

"I think you can. That's why we need you in safe hands. The Guardians have been provoking war. They're destructive and controlling."

"They're the ones standing between the Ikhor and the people. How dare you accuse them of being the destructive ones."

"Then you know even less than I assumed." Her lip curled back in a show of disgust.

I shook my head. "I will never betray my friends."

I wouldn't give her more time to argue. I was done waiting on something else to decide my fate.

She tensed, sensing I was about to run.

Do not speak of where you are from, even if it's the gods asking—the Oracle had warned me of Rem, or maybe another god I was yet to meet. *Trust the woman. You will be the end of everything.* Was I dooming the world by ignoring the Oracle's warnings?

The sounds of the distant battle had me losing my resolve. How could I run from Brekt?

I glanced down, hoping to see any change—I inspected my bracelet, but it was void of any signs of magic. The Light was wrong. It picked the wrong girl. Why was the Aspis not waking?

Powerful beings are coming for you. You will try to get in their way. I see death, but I also see hope.

You will be the end of everything.

The woman waited, facing me, leaving her back exposed to a new hoard coming through the smoke behind her. A group, fifty-strong, was charging toward where we stood.

I wouldn't be a hero today, and I wouldn't be a burden. One day, I would have my own power to stand my ground and fight.

I turned and ran. Into the smoke, away from the blue woman.

But any hope I had dissipated. I jumped over a burning pile, holding my breath while the smoke engulfed me. When I landed, I collided with the back of an Aethar.

They had been cutting down the last standing Guardian.

The field had been taken.

And I was now captured.

SEVENTY-THREE

I thrashed and kicked and spat and screamed. But there were too many.

Several Aethar had me by the arms and legs. Even more danced around my captors. They lifted me in the air as if I were a sacrifice to the skies, marching from where I had left the blue woman. They didn't bother removing my swords. They didn't need to—I was helpless.

"We are going to be heroes."

"The Day-leg will pay well for this."

"We have the power in our hands once again. We will rise up. We will conquer this world."

Their mocking cruelty for taking the Aspis chipped away at my hope. I tried pulling a wrist free from the vice-like grip, but it made no difference.

The blue woman was gone. The Guards were lost to me—if they hadn't already fallen.

"Brekt!" I screamed, my throat feeling raw. "Nuo!" Where had everyone gone? I didn't call for Kazhi. I didn't trust she wasn't behind this.

"Look how she calls for the Guards."

"She was fucked so well she was a happy prisoner."

"Did you like being their plaything? You could have been their ruler."

I tried to bite the scarred arm of a woman holding me. She laughed.

"Let's see how she burns first."

They all laughed. The triumphant sound scraped its sharp claws against my soul. They were going to burn the Aspis before it rose.

Above me, I watched the embers fade into dust in the cold dark sky. The last thing I would hear was the screeching sound of blade on blade.

"Set her down. Let her see her captors fall."

My feet hit the ground. The sight before me was the most terrifying of all.

The Aethar had found the four Guards. They stood more than thirty feet away. Kazhi had joined her brothers, and they all held bloody weapons above the bodies of the fallen.

It was Brekt who first noticed who the group of Aethar held.

His face went white with fury, and the iridescence flashed when his eyes scanned the crowd.

Nuo found me soon after. The masks he wore were wiped clean off his face. The true face of my friend, buried under suffering the Aethar had caused his whole life, appeared before me, contorted with rage and a killing promise.

He was more terrifying than the dark child beside him.

I met Kazhi's warning next. She held a hand up, hidden from the other three, as if telling me to stay calm. She scanned the group of Aethar, searching for someone—the blue woman.

Brekt stepped forward, ready to fight through the dozen or more Aethar surrounding me. An Aethar broke from the group with a raised sword, coming down against Brekt's with a crash that resonated in my chest.

I couldn't reach my weapons. I had no powers. I had nothing to offer, and I hated it.

"Blue one!" a woman holding me shouted.

The hooded woman appeared to our left. She halted, standing as a pillar between the two groups facing off. Her gaze darted between Kazhi and me, searching for a way to grab me and leave.

I saw Brekt eyeing the woman, piecing things together. He remembered me asking about the blue-skinned man in Bellum, thinking he was the Ikhor.

The hooded woman grabbed the strange-looking bow from her back, bringing it forward and pointing it at the Guards.

"No!" I screamed, and her eyes flicked toward me before landing on her target again.

A flash of light caught my eye. My bracelet was no longer silent and empty—this time, it was as bright as the moon.

The Ikhor was closing in. The Aethar sacrificing me—it was what Brekt had seen in the dream.

The Aethars began to fan out, making a line. More found their way to us, circling behind me. The hoard was never-ending. Their battle cries reached a crescendo, and my heart pounded along with it. The Guards would lose against so many. They were beaten and bloody. There was only one way we could get out of this.

I had to change.

"Come on," I willed the light in my bracelet. I held my breath, puffed out my chest, and wiggled my body. Nothing worked.

I couldn't find the power of the beast.

Brekt and Nuo raised their swords, Kazhi held her knives, and Bastane pulled his bow tight.

I had no time to brace myself as I was pushed down to my knees for the second time.

"Liv!" Brekt yelled, trying to move forward. But the Aethar tilted their weapons toward me. Others raised their swords toward him.

He was too far. He'd have twenty on him before he could get to me.

"It's okay." I coughed, my throat dry. "This needs to happen."

Tears were streaking down my face. This scene was exactly as Brekt described.

My mother had been on the ground between her attackers. Was this how she felt? Because this wasn't bravery, this was helplessness. This was crippling fear.

A grizzly-looking Aethar stepped in front of me. His face was so torn up that his mouth refused to close on one side. Pale blue eyes stared at me as he tried to smile.

"You've been travelling with the wrong group, pretty girl. The Guards can't keep you anymore. They're heavily outnumbered."

I searched the crowd for the Ikhor, waiting for it.

Brekt's eyes flashed as his eyes scanned the field, knowing his dream was about to unfold. He shook his head, denying the truth. Nuo stepped close to his side, seeing it too.

They lifted their swords in unison. My Guards, they were going to save me.

"Don't waste your time, Guards," the lopsided man spat before me. "She's ours now."

He turned his attention back to me as Brekt and Nuo took down several Aethar. But when one fell, another took their place. Bastane and Kazhi joined the fight, closing the distance but still so far away.

"I saw you in Bellum," the man said above me. "We've been looking for you. The Day-leg is trying to change how things have always been, but I think we will kill her next and keep you for ourselves."

Was he taking orders from Falizha?

"The Ikhor isn't going to win," I spat up at him, "It can kiss my ass if it thinks it will harm the Guards."

"You think to change the nature of the Ikhor?" He frowned. "You think these Guards will be spared? They will die. When you wake, you will do as I ask. Just watch."

Something tingled at the back of my neck, a thought that was eluding me. How would the Aspis be turned against its Guards?

"Where is the Ikhor?" I demanded.

"I'm wondering the same thing. Hurry it up, woman."

If the Ikhor wasn't here, it wouldn't trigger the change.

This Aethar knew he had the Aspis in his hands, yet I could not stop him. They could swarm us, and I was defenceless.

I had been so stupid.

Brekt and Nuo continued to fight. And lose. Bastane and Kazhi were failing at holding the Aethar back. Although the Aethars had difficulty taking them down, the Guards could only fight for so much longer.

You will be the end of everything.

Brekt struck down an Aethar, then faced me. I didn't see his eyes flash. I didn't see heat or affection like I wanted to. I only saw regret.

Then I saw the blade pierce through his chest.

Time slowed down. I could hear the sound of the blade as it sliced through him. I could feel it.

Nuo screamed, taking down the Aethar that had caught Brekt unaware. The Aethar had shoved his sword through Brekt's heart.

Our eyes stayed locked as his brows went up—the only show of pain he let slip.

The box inside me, so full of emotion being held in for years, exploded into a million pieces.

Rage.

Hate.

Longing.

Pain.

Hunger.

Yearning.

Solitude.

Every horrible thought I had stuffed away coursed through me like volcanic poison, breaking free of where I had safely confined it.

I was filled to the brim with the parts of me that had turned rotten. The corrupted pieces of my soul took control.

The world around me transformed, becoming red. The sky was

red. The ground was red. Brekt and Nuo, so far away from me, frozen in time, turned red.

I thought about the old memories I stuffed away in that box. They were red too. But those memories were stained red with blood.

The people around me turned red from *fire*.

CHAPTER
SEVENTY-FOUR

I pulled the flames from the field, controlling them, sending them out around me to burn all that I hated.

I was pain. I was loss.

I was not the hero.

Brekt's dream had finally come true.

My mouth was open in a scream so loud it overpowered the hiss and crackle of the fire I commanded. I no longer heard Brekt's laboured breath or Nuo's cries trying to protect his brother. I couldn't hear Bastane's shouts, what Kazhi screamed back, or anything else from the field beyond.

I heard my screams of pain and the whooshing sounds of the fire blowing in whorls around me. *From* me.

I harnessed the elemental magic of the gods and turned it on the world I hated, the world that created that hate within me.

My screams were not from the burn of the flame—I was screaming from the tug on the cords, pulling me so tight I could feel him there. I could feel the sword in my own chest.

The sound torn from me was nothing compared to the screams of the Aethars as they were caught in my swirling wind of fire.

My flames.

Around me, bodies were falling, charred.

The world was alight as the flame engulfed the Aethars holding me. If I weren't so focused on the vise grip around my heart, my stomach would've rolled at the sight of the hands holding me turning black. I was burning them, and yet they smiled —*they were happy.*

Their charred bodies hit the ground. The man with the crooked smile was already a heap of dust.

We have the power in our hands once again. We will rise up. We will conquer this world.

Let's see how she burns first.

They had known. The blue woman had been searching for the Ikhor's magic. They had all known.

The blue woman, standing between the two groups ten feet before me, barely dodged the flame. Her arm was alight with fire and she fell back, yelling from the pain.

Brekt had never seen me dying. He never saw me as the Aspis waking. He had seen me changing, engulfed in my magic, screaming from the cords between us choking me.

I had become something evil—his enemy.

Nothing is human about them once possessed with its magic ... It's old magic. Over time it has warped and twisted—tainted by the evil minds it possessed.

I had been carrying around the evil, feeding it with the hate and pain I had stuffed away for so long. The Ikhor's magic had been the Light that found me dying by the river. Not a god, not an ally, not someone trying to better the world.

They burn, bury and freeze themselves. They strap themselves to high cliffs to face the brutal winds. They endure it to the point of death to prove they can be strong enough to carry the Ikhor's power. Prove their body won't be ripped apart bearing the burden.

The evil had found a body beside that frozen river. One that had withstood pain to the point of death. It had latched onto all the negative emotions I had never dealt with, too afraid to feel that pain.

When my box was pushing to be opened, it wasn't trying to

force my memories out—it was trying to break free the magic trapped there.

When the magic found me, I must have forced it down, hiding it inside and refusing to accept anything new.

No wonder I never felt like the hero. I never was.

So where was the Aspis?

The Guards all stood as silent warriors, watching me change. The Guards of the Aspis—my new enemies. The ones tasked to kill *me*.

How had Brekt not known? How had he not understood it was my transformation he dreamt of? It had been his warning this whole time.

I raised my palms before me, flipping my hands over. My skin was the same. No physical change.

I met their stares. The Guards. Their faces were contorted in horror, pain and anger.

Brekt held onto his chest, blood pouring through his fingers. He tried and failed to stand straight. Nuo held his shoulders, tears already streaking down his face.

He knew we were losing Brekt.

The fire around me receded. The whirling flames evaporated as I felt a loss so great it rivalled the agony of watching my mother die.

Brekt's pain-filled eyes held mine. I saw regret shining in the black before it was replaced with something darker. What I saw erased any joy left from our memories—distrust.

Brekt, who still stood after being cut through with a blade, took a step back and lifted his other hand. I expected it to reach for the seeping wound in his chest, but he began to cradle his head.

I needed to go to him. My foot landed in the dust of the charred Aethar as I crossed the distance between us.

Brekt's eyes flashed open to pin me in place. Hostility radiated from him, making me pause.

Nuo grabbed his shoulder, spinning his brother toward him.

SARAH L. ROSE

"The transformation is complete," Bastane warned. "The evil has arisen. Brace yourselves."

Why was Nuo not trying to mend the hole in his chest? It was bleeding so profusely that it should be impossible for him to stand.

"Brekt. Brother! Look at me. Look at me!" Nuo cried, panicked.

If they didn't use the magycris, I would. They wouldn't have come without it. My next step slid in ash.

"Don't come any closer, or we will kill you now, Ikhor!" Bastane held his sword high. "Where the fuck is the Aspis. I thought it was her."

"*She's* not the beast, you idiot," Kazhi said.

That's when Nuo's attention finally landed on me. But it was Brekt I was watching, finding shadows swimming under his skin.

"You," Nuo seethed. His face contorted with pain and rage. His voice was not of my friend.

"Nuo? Why aren't you helping Brekt?" My words barely made it across the field.

The blue woman was beside me, leaning down to inspect the burnt corpses. She cradled her arm, the flesh pink and seeping.

If she thought to attack, I could deal with her quickly.

Brekt was going dark, his powers of Night losing control. Swirling and erratic, his skin went from tan to the blackest colour of his tattoos. His shadows were a kaleidoscope—the scales inked into his skin shifted, spreading and growing like they were coming alive.

He'd never changed like this before.

He dragged his eyes up to mine, and I covered my mouth to hold in my alarm. They didn't flash as they usually did.

They were no longer obsidian. They were becoming brighter. Changing.

Nuo's face, his body, his soul *broke* before me. I could almost hear it like the shattering of glass as he watched his friend change.

In my heart—the one that echoed that shattering sound—I knew what was happening.

"It's him?" Bastane gasped. "But how? Did you know?"

596

Bastane grabbed Nuo by the shoulder to demand answers, but Nuo pushed him off.

Brekt moaned from the pain. I could feel that pain slithering inside me, an echo of his own. Skin that would never be tan again, turned. The scales of his tattoos transformed, becoming real. Scales as black as the starless night grew along his arms.

The host of the Aspis was transforming.

SEVENTY-FIVE

B rekt was disappearing before our eyes.

The cords between us pulled so tight it was branding me from the inside. Hot coals were pressed against my spine, pushing me toward him.

"Nuo," I cried out, "Stop this!"

"Liv! How could you have kept this from us?" he spat. "What do you think I can do now?"

"I didn't know!" I pleaded, "I didn't understand."

"How could you not know? He did!" His head whipped back to his brother, who was fighting for control. Blood still poured from his heart while scales formed over parts of his body.

"Brekt, why didn't you tell me," I whispered. How long had he known? How long had it been within him?

"Don't speak to her, Nuo. It's not Liv," Brekt choked out.

Nuo's hate-filled eyes returned to me as he nodded. "Already it's trying to deceive us."

"It *is* me," I pleaded.

Horror gripped me as bits of Brekt's skin flaked away. They became smoke, churning and shredding like the embers of the fire.

The man I was beginning to love was leaving me. He would soon cease to exist. His purpose had been fulfilled, one I had mistaken for mine. The beast destined to return every era became whole.

The Aspis became a real, living thing.

His lips curled back in a snarl. Fangs grew from a mouth now too wide for his face. The eyes that bore into mine, that once held affection, were unrecognizable.

Nuo became a thing of fury. He moved from the Aspis toward me.

"You liar!" He made it several feet before he stopped himself. Still, a world separated us.

"No, Nuo. I didn't know." My body shook.

"You knew! You knew, and you said nothing. He's known for years, so don't lie to me."

He's known for years. It all made sense now.

This is why he was always so haunted by what his dreams showed him—this future. He never saw me dying by the Ikhor's fire. He never saw me as the Aspis. He saw me lighting up, and he saw ...

I've known what was going to happen since I was a child.

He'd had the beast in him for years before the magic found me.

Brekt's eyes shuttered. More skin faded to scales.

He never wanted to touch me, never wanted to have more. Not only did he think I would get hurt, but he couldn't promise me a future. He thought I would die because of him being the Aspis, being near to him. He knew he couldn't be there for me once he changed.

Because the Aspis never returns the human it slumbered in.

Nuo spent countless hours going over old books of history, so he could find an answer, find how to save Brekt.

"Nuo." I wanted to be there with them.

Nuo searched my face.

"Don't you come closer. You don't get to touch him. You're going to kill him. You've already killed him." His voice broke, and my heart did with it. His eyes pierced me like an arrow through the heart. "You will never get to him, Ikhor."

His words rang out around me—a promise from a Guard to his enemy.

"Stop, Nuo," Brekt moaned, hardly able to speak. His hands were blood red, holding his chest. "We knew this was coming. Control yourself, be ready to fight."

"I'm not ready. How could I be ready for this?"

"You have to be."

"Why didn't you tell us?" Bastane said. "We could have helped. We could have figured out who she was."

"How?" Nuo scoffed.

"I saw her react to magic when Rem was in the city. Only I thought she was the Aspis. You should have told us it was him."

Bastane's face twisted. As much as I hated him for his betrayal, I understood his pain. He was losing a brother too.

"And give more reason for the world to cast me out?" Brekt growled, "Another way to be used as a pawn for the Days?"

Bastane quickly abandoned his argument. He knew he would have told the Council, ever loyal to his bloodline.

"I chose to live with the little time I had in peace. It was bad enough I was chosen as a Guard, constantly controlled by the Council." Brekt leaned forward, spitting out blood. The fingers clutching his chest lengthened. Claws curled from his fingertips.

Why hadn't Brekt reacted to the presence of Rem?

Because I held the magic stolen from the gods. The Aspis was a creation they made.

I jumped as someone tugged at my arm.

"We need to go now," the blue woman said. "Once the change completes, the man will no longer be. The beast will come for you."

"No. I have to stay. I can't leave him," I begged her as if she could stop this.

"We must go. They cannot get ahold of you."

"Olivia?" Nuo's voice was filled with malice. There was a question there. He was staring at the blue woman, too far away to attack.

"Nuo, no. It's not what it looks like."

"This whole time. You've been siding with those bastards this whole time!"

"I haven't. I promise."

"Then why are you using the magic of their leader? Why are you standing with them? You've betrayed us. I lost my brother today!" he said through the pain sharpening his words, "This is your fault. You will pay for it."

He was no longer the handsome, carefree man with dimples in his cheeks.

I searched for an ally, panicking. Kazhi watched Brekt in horror. She had not known either.

"Go, Olivia. You won't get far once the beast wakes," Brekt warned.

"Brekt," I cried. He was sending me away. He was no longer protecting me.

"She's not leaving this field. The Ikhor is ours," Nuo said, "The rest of the Aethar too. They've killed everyone I loved. I will hunt down every last one of them tonight."

He lifted a blade from his belt. I remembered how he changed the day the Aethar attacked us on the road. He had a voice like death. Cold, calculating, inhuman.

"You know what I do to Aethar, Liv," he reminded me.

Brekt bent over again, groaning in pain. Pieces of him were chipping away rapidly, he looked more like the beast with every passing second.

Every part of me wanted to run to him, to my friends. I couldn't get the words out. I couldn't think of how to begin explaining myself. I was so afraid.

But if I returned with them, the Council would tear me to pieces.

The fires around me were spreading, and I had no idea how to stop them. I had no idea how I *caused* them.

I was the Ikhor and yet had no idea how to use the magic.

On second thought—

"I'm not possessed," I muttered, facing the blue woman. I should have realized sooner.

She pulled on my arm once more. "Please. I don't want to die here."

"No, you're not hearing me."

I wanted to reach out to Nuo. If he would just listen, he would understand. But things were getting out of my control, and people were in danger not only from the fires but from the growing beast whose eyes were now focused on me.

Did the Aspis know already? Did it sense I was its enemy, the reason it was here?

Brekt's lips were moving, but no sound came out.

Nuo stood next to him, full of horror, as the last pieces of Brekt fell away. The last bit of skin turned to dust, revealing scales beneath. Nuo reached out for the man who was no longer there.

My heart dropped, turning to ashes with the bodies below me.

The last thing to change, the final piece of the puzzle to fall into place, were Brekt's eyes. His iridescence flashed one last time, the fading brown winking out before it turned to yellow—to the eyes of the Aspis.

I see yellow eyes in pain. A broken heart, full of new hatred. Hold your secrets tight. Survive. Do not speak of where you are from, even if it's the gods asking. Trust the woman.

Everything The Oracle said had come true.

Bright citrine eyes with sharp vertical pupils turned to Nuo. Brekt's face changed, growing long and wide. His nose became slits, and his ears drew back, becoming spiralled horns.

Nuo backed away from the black beast that was transforming, growing, expanding, from man to serpent.

It was in pain.

I wept. Did Brekt feel any of that pain, or was he spared the experience of this change?

I stepped forward to Brekt—no, not Brekt, never again Brekt— I stepped toward the Aspis. Its body stretched and curled like a wounded snake. Its chest rose and fell as it tried to catch its breath between hisses and whines.

Its yellow eyes found me one last time, and the field went silent as they communicated something to me.

Something spoke inside my head that sounded an awful lot like the deep timbre of the man tied to my heart. *'Run, Liv.'*

And that's when it collapsed, falling to the ground. A black snake coiled and asleep.

Nuo dropped to fold himself over the growing body of the beast, protecting him, shaking him—but the beast had gone still.

Nuo's head whipped in my direction, to where I stood frozen in horror. His face was broken, pleading.

"Liv, come. Stop this." He held out a desperate, shaking hand—a final lifeline.

His sudden change took me by surprise. His eyes searched mine, frantic. In his pain, did he forget I was now his enemy?

"Nuo, I—" I stumbled back. What was I afraid of? He was my closest friend.

"Liv? Liv, he needs you. We can find a way to stop this."

Nuo was crazed, grabbing the still form of the beast. Clawing at it, praying, searching the field for an answer. Asking *me* for the answer.

"You *must* come with me." The blue woman pulled me again, trying to force me away. "The beast sleeps. We can escape now."

Trust the woman.

I turned to Kazhi, who nodded her head. It was happening too fast.

I shook in disbelief. I was losing everything all over again. I had lost my mother, my sister, and my home. I had made a new family, and now I was losing them too.

I see many futures, the Oracle had said. *But I will not risk swaying you to one path over the other. Your choice must be yours. That will matter one day.*

Was this the choice? To leave my friends and trust the path set before me? I was so concerned about becoming the beast—I hadn't thought I might be the villain.

Was that what I would become?

"Don't be a fool, Nuo." Bastane didn't take his eyes off me but crept closer to Nuo and the beast. "That's not her. Look what she's done. The dust around her."

Kazhi was taking in the black form of the Aspis. "Bastane is right, Nuo. We can't trust her now."

I flinched. Kazhi had felt like my last connection to the Guards. Did she believe I was evil now too?

Nuo waited to see who would answer—his friend or his enemy.

I took a shaking breath, ready to face what I was about to do. He would never forgive me.

"I'm sorry," I said, closing my eyes.

I stepped toward the blue woman.

I would find out how to end this. All of this. But first, I needed to survive. There was no way Nuo could protect me from a continent full of Guardians wanting to end the Ikhor. He couldn't protect me from the Aspis or the Council ready to control it.

Nuo screamed. It was a voice I had never heard from him but one I understood. It was the sound of betrayal. His brother was gone, and his new friend was the reason why.

I kept my eyes closed as his words carved scars into my heart.

"How could you! You side with the Aethar, and we are done. You are dead to me."

"Nuo, I will find a way to fix this."

"You've already been corrupted. The lies began a long time before the evil possessed you. I will find you, Ikhor. I will find you and make you pay!"

I stumbled. Nuo was swimming in the depth of the darkest sea. His hatred had such force it charged the air around us, poisoning it and making it impossible to breathe.

A soft hand tugged me back, and I followed as it pulled me away from the Guards. Away from Nuo and his scorn. Away from the man I was falling in love with, now an unmoving serpent on the ground.

I thought of how far I had come, leaving home and finding adventure in a world away. I thought of how easily that was taken from me. Now, I was going to try to outrun the beast.

But I never would, and I knew it.

I was only minutes born, unsure of my strengths. I was leaving for my own safety but also giving the beast more time to discover its power. I was leaving an Aethar hidden within the Guards, a Day-leg who chose his blood before his morals, and a man who hated me, blind with rage. And they were down one. Brekt was gone.

That box inside of me had shattered. My suffering was transforming into a burning rage. It was boiling inside me.

I had lost everything.

I always lost everything.

No one stayed with me.

No one trusted me.

I had one goal given to me—to wake the Aspis. Now I had.

I had been a fool to think it was me.

I now had answers for the Light, for why I was brought here. The Light had not been sent for good. It had stolen a broken girl from her lands because she was the perfect vessel for evil magic.

It was working. I could feel it wanting to take control.

I wanted to be the hero. I wanted to be like my mother had raised me to be. But she stopped being the one who raised me when she died. My teachers became the Law Keepers, Rebeka, Stephen, Bastane, Kazhi and Nuo—all of them betrayed me and left me to die.

Some became a part of the hunt to make sure I did.

The blue woman pulled me to the edges of the burning fields. I fell into a run with her.

I finally accepted my weaknesses as I ran toward Aethar lands, where I would now hide amongst the enemy.

I would search for answers to questions yet to be asked. About what I was, about how to control it. I would find out where my lands were and how the magic found me there. Something told me it was important I find the truths hidden amongst all the secrets. Gods, monsters, lost lands and magic hidden in pure bloodlines.

I would find the truth, and I would return the magic.

When the smoke cleared and I was able to get a clean breath in my lungs, the relief was overshadowed by screams echoing through the field one last time.

My old friend, who was likely still clutching the beast, never found a way to stop the change.

"You better run as fast as you can, Olivia, because I will follow the beast, and I will be there when it kills you!"

Nuo's promise would haunt me every night for months to come.

I accepted that I failed to be the woman my mother wanted me to be. I couldn't be strong like her.

I would not be the hero for these people—I was now the villain.

But I was not born evil. I was made.

I was the Ikhor—and I was fucking angry.

EPILOGUE

Brekt

His family was divided. Maybe it always had been. Trust and loyalty were often an illusion.

Brekt watched the woman who'd haunted him for too long now, tears streaking down her ash-dusted cheeks, standing with the enemy. *As* his enemy. He had failed her. After everything he had done, every feeling he had fought against, he had failed.

He had been wrong to think it was her death he'd been dreaming of. His dreams had warned him of where the enemy was hiding.

He found her dying in those first caves. If he had left her to die, would he have stopped the Ikhor? Would he have saved his friends? He had persuaded them to bring her along. He believed she was meant to help them. He believed she was meant for him.

The pain in his chest was twofold. Anger and mourning were at war within his heart. It outdid any of the pain in his body while it was being torn apart.

He felt every part of his death. With a sickening horror he'd never known, he watched pieces of himself turn to dust. He felt every inch fade away. He felt the fangs grow in his mouth, the horns grow from his head. He felt his heart fill with blood, but the transformation refused to let it stop beating.

He had this dream since he was a boy, where he walked into the shadows and never came out. The darkness that surrounded him in those dreams had been absolute.

That darkness now stained the edges of his vision. He had never feared the dark. He was its master. He was power incarnate in the hours of Night.

But he feared it now.

His brother was barely holding on beside him. Nuo had never dealt with his pain or prepared himself for when Brekt would change. Nuo was too confident he would find the answers, that he could make the world do his bidding.

Brekt was thankful his brother had stayed with him and held onto his secret. He wished he could make the future better for Nuo. But the time would soon come when his brother turned blue from death. Would Nuo die at the hands of Olivia?

He had failed them all.

What else was he leaving behind that his fellow Guards now had to defend against? The Council, the Ikhor and the killing nature of the Aspis.

Kazhi was watching Liv and the Aethar girl. Brekt had seen the recognition in Kazhi's eyes when the blue woman appeared.

Her black eyes met his, widening. Lies filled this world. Would Kazhi betray the Guards and run after the Ikhor?

She gave the slightest reaction, lips parting. He'd never seen her afraid—she now looked it. But the Aspis would not aim for her. It was being pulled in another direction.

It was killing him—not only the transformation but the godsdamned pull in his chest. Brekt had been naive to believe the force was something good. He had wanted and yet cursed the idea that Liv was *his*. Now she was the enemy.

No, Liv was gone.

Every dream had come true, but not those he'd shared loving her. Why had he not let himself touch her? The memories he would take with him were false. Wherever the soul of Liv had gone, would she take his memories too? She was lost to him either way.

The pull was demanding now. It needed to reach the Ikhor. The Aspis would use it to find her.

She would have the whole Guardian continent come down upon her. No matter how far the Ikhor ran, into Aethar lands or perhaps beyond, to Liv's home, the Guards would never stop. Brekt hurt for her, as much as he felt angry.

It did not matter. Nothing he felt mattered now.

His vision tunnelled. There was no light for him at the end— only black. The Endless Night waited.

Threats and political games seemed so pointless now. It all felt empty. This was the end. His role was done.

He felt his heart stutter, giving one last thunderous beat, then stop.

Brekt could barely see when he lifted his eyes to the woman he loved.

His last thoughts were of her smile, holding a cheap pair of earrings, glowing under the stars.

Then like a wave, the shadow washed over him. He fell to the burning ground, fading off into that final dream.

Acknowledgments

I have many people to thank, but I would like to start off with two women who made this book alongside me—my editors, Sam and Kelsey. When this book was a jumble of ideas and overused words, Sam, you came in like a titan giving me the best advice and crushed it. Draft after draft, you stayed with the story. You replied to my endless emails with so much help and a healthy dose of humour. Your comments made me laugh every time. Halfway through the editing phase, Kelsey walks in and boom—dream team. Your work was so thorough, and you really dove into this world and got to know it as well as I do. Your suggestions for character development and promos are always spot on. It makes me so happy. You girls are geniuses and are an endless amount of help, even when you don't have to be. I will never forget, for the rest of my life, what you have done to get me here.

I would also like to thank the others who helped with reading and fixing it up—Ashley, Emily, Sarah and Belle. The work you put in was invaluable.

Moving on to the very important people in my life who are not part of the book world but play massive supporting roles in mine: Xin, Keven and Emily. You three listened to hours upon hours of me rambling on about my book and gave me excellent advice on the story, the art and even the marketing. Anytime I couldn't come to a decision, one of you was there. And to the rest of my friends and family who all expressed so much interest, even if I will never allow you to read this book (especially my parents, who will never read about Brekt behind that tree), I am grateful.

Thank you to the online community as well. The conversations I've had with fellow authors and book lovers have fuelled my love for books. Shout-out to my book club for their support. You guys rock! How crazy is it to connect with people all over the world and gush about what you love?

And thanks to you, who is reading this. You made my dream come true.

Sarah Rose

www.sarahlrosebooks.com

ABOUT THE AUTHOR

Sarah was born and raised in rural Ontario, Canada, where she loved to explore her backyard in search of magical creatures and talking trees. In her twenties, she spent several years travelling the far reaches of the world. She eventually returned home with an imagination more vivid and overflowing with ideas. Stories began to sprout. Finally, in her early thirties, she began writing those stories down and discovered her real passion. In her spare time, she also enjoys playing music, drawing and practicing martial arts, in which she holds a first-degree black belt.

Curious about what comes next? Sign up for Sarah's newsletter to receive updates. www.sarahlrosebooks.com

Printed in Great Britain
by Amazon